Last Train From Berlin

G·K
Hall
&Co.

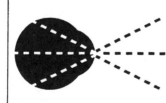

This Large Print Book carries the
Seal of Approval of N.A.V.H.

Last
Train
From
Berlin

W.T.Tyler

G.K. Hall & Co.
Thorndike, Maine

Published in 1994 by arrangement with Henry Holt and Company, Inc.

G.K. Hall Large Print Core Colletction.

The text of this Large Print edition is unabridged.
Other aspects of the book may vary from the original edition.

Set in 16 pt. News Plantin by Ginny Beaulieu.

Printed in the United States on acid-free, high opacity paper. ∞

Library of Congress Cataloging in Publication Data

Tyler, W. T.
    Last train from Berlin / W. T. Tyler.
      p.   cm.
    ISBN 0-8161-7435-0 (alk. paper : lg. print)
    1. Large type books. I. Title.
[PS3570.Y53L3 1994b]
813'.54—dc20   94-7338

Misrepresenting? . . . Sorry, we can't say. The facts are secret, of course, but if you know the secrets, you would know that some persons are misrepresenting the secrets which you cannot know because they are secret. But watch out, fellows, watch out!

— Senator Daniel Patrick Moynihan
The Congressional Record
November 4, 1991

1

A GENTLEMAN IN PLACE

The wind moved to the northwest during the night, blown in by a cold front roaring down from Canada. The temperature had dropped twenty degrees. Young Kevin Corkery shivered, trying to bring himself awake as George Skaff drove down the parkway toward Key Bridge. The passing cars still had their lights on. Below the overcast a dark scud raced across the Potomac where ice had formed along the lee shore and the channel was whipped to an ugly chop. Georgetown was a medieval cathedral town against the sky.

"People walk out all the time," Skaff said. "Get fed up and walk out the door with just the clothes on their back. Half the time they don't know they're doing it, don't know where they're going, who they are." He was a small man with thin gray hair, wearing a gray suit and a gray topcoat.

"The nervous-breakdown types, you mean. I talked to his wife last night. No clothes were miss-

7

ing, just what he was wearing."

The FBI sedan was feverishly warm. Corkery could smell toothpaste. He imagined Skaff belonged to that class of people who get out of bed fully awake, fully dressed, and freshly shaven, briefcase in hand, stepping out to resume their lives at that precise half second when sleep suspended it. Such people never dreamed, never lived in hesitation or in doubt, and never understood those who did. With his small gray head, respectful voice, and coaxing manners, he might have been a tax accountant.

"On the other hand, he could have been called out on something," Skaff said, "working some special Agency operation, and your people wouldn't say a word."

"I don't think so. That's not what they say." Corkery brought a cigarette from his pocket but changed his mind. The FBI sedan was scrupulously clean, smelling of new upholstery.

"It's never what they say. I never listen to what your people say. Right now all Langley's worried about is the press getting hold of it."

"Maybe."

Skaff laughed. "Not maybe, son. I've been at it too long."

A pair of empty tour buses and a service station tow truck rumbled ahead along M Street, deserted on a Sunday morning. Skaff turned off and drove down the steep hill toward the Potomac. On K Street beneath the underpass three patrol cars, a medivac unit, and a white van from the D.C. medical examiner's office were drawn to the curb. A policeman stood in the street, waving an occasional vehicle by. A pair of yellow and black trestles barred access to the rubble of a vacant lot between two buildings; three policemen were searching the vacant lot, heads down. Skaff crossed the potholed street to a blue-and-white police car, Corkery at his heels, still trembling with the cold. His body was behaving as it did during those final moments before an eight-hundred-meter race at the University of Pennsylvania when it no longer mattered whether you won or lost, just that you not make a complete fool of yourself before 1,500 people at Franklin Field. He hadn't seen a dead man for eight years, not since they'd fished a dead Italian out of the drink off the south coast of Sicily. He'd been lost overboard from a water taxi three nights before after drunkenly celebrating a wedding at a seaside restaurant. A garland of sodden, kelp-entangled flowers was still around his neck that bright Mediterranean morning when the boatswain from the USS *Peurifoy* gigged him with a boathook.

A patrolman sat behind the wheel of the patrol car, door closed, monitoring the radio dispatcher as he filled out a report. Corkery didn't hear the first words as he cranked down the window. The corpse had been discovered by an early-morning jogger. His weimaraner had found it and the jogger hailed a cruising police car. They'd expected to find a derelict, dead of exposure, but found the body of a well-dressed man in his fifties.

". . . homicide maybe, they're not sure. No ID

9

on him but they just found something in the empty building over there. Tyrone's checking it out. Could be his." An empty dump truck rumbled overhead, chains and tailgate clanging; static erupted from the radio. Corkery leaned closer. "Caucasian male, gray hair, five eight or nine maybe, a hundred and eighty pounds. That sound like anything?"

"The height's wrong," Corkery said. Skaff didn't turn. A policeman came to the patrol car on the opposite side. "Tyrone's asking where the hell the FBI's at."

"That's me," Skaff said. Corkery followed him across the rubble and over the yellow ribbons closing off the rear of the lot where Tyrone stood with two patrolmen. The medical examiner knelt by a body lying at the base of the brick wall of a partially demolished building.

"Guthrie said you were looking for someone," Tyrone said, his breath billowing out like steam from a locomotive. "We think maybe we got a name now." He looked at Corkery and nodded. Skaff didn't introduce them. His long gaunt face was red with the cold. Beneath the cuffs of blue mackinaw and his gloves, his wrists showed, girdled by cuffs of thermal underwear. The wind whipped up again, roaring between the two buildings.

The corpse lay half covered by a coroner's body cloth, curled in a fetal position, hands at the knees. Corkery squatted down. The face was ashen, the bloodless lips drawn across the teeth in a grimace, as white as the seam of an old surgical scar; clots of blood had dried in the nostrils. The gray hair was thick and coarse. The left cheekbone was discolored; an ugly bruise as large as a hoofprint circled the swollen chin. The wind snatched the cloth free. His shoes were missing. Corkery caught the body cloth and folded it back against the dead man's shoulders. The open eyes stared past him, a chilling look as vast as the winter sea.

"It's not him," he said.

Skaff took off his right glove and reached forward to turn back the jacket lapel. "Frozen."

The medical examiner squatted at the waist of the corpse. His steel-rimmed spectacles had slipped down his nose and his gray hat was pulled down over his pinched ears to keep the wind from taking it. He was heavy in the hips; his blue overcoat had worked itself up about his midriff. "Watch your feet."

"Sorry." Skaff stepped back. "How long?"

"Not sure yet." The medical examiner stood up and moved to the other side of the body.

"Stiff as a post," Tyrone said. "Froze to the ground even."

Corkery held the lowered body cloth as the medical examiner peeled the blood-stiff shirt from the stomach, cracking it like cardboard. Despite the cold he could smell something bloody, raw, and fetid and turned his head. The thick nails and sausage fingers at his knees were those of a man who might have worked with his hands. In the gray eyes, he sensed the dead man's final thought, one

11

of an infinite sorrow and shame.

"Homicide?" he asked. The medical examiner nodded.

"Hard to tell right off," Tyrone said, standing above him. "Get him thawed out first."

"Get him thawed out good enough, maybe he'll tell you himself," a policeman said.

"What do you think, Doc?" Tyrone asked.

The medical examiner closed the bloody shirt and drew the jacket over it. "Knife wound, I'd say. Kidneys. Homicide, probably. Maybe a dump job, killed someplace else. Tossed over from up there." His eyes traveled to the overpass above him where a policeman was searching the coping. "But I doubt it. Nothing tells me he fell very far." He lifted the corpse's right wrist and took a plastic bag from his case.

"You said you had a name," Corkery said.

"Yeah. Ulrich," Tyrone said. "Canadian, it looks like. We found a wallet back there, just inside that window yonder. No money, just a couple of driver's licenses, some credit cards. Looks like the body was stripped, coat and shoes both."

The medical examiner worked a plastic bag over the corpse's right hand.

"Two driver's licenses?" Skaff said.

"Yeah, two. One from Ontario, one from someplace else." Tyrone turned to the policeman holding a manila envelope. "Where was it, where they got all that snow?"

"Quebec."

"Yeah, Quebec. Only this ain't it." Hunching

12

his shoulders, Tyrone shivered and moved his feet. "Hell on tourists, this goddamned town. Every Saturday night." He turned to Skaff, still trembling. "Who'd you say you was looking for?"

"I didn't," Skaff said. "Just someone who wandered off Friday night. What was in his pockets?"

Face numb, Corkery was conscious again of the stinging cold. Tyrone's words seemed carved from it, formed from his thick smoking breath like particles broken out by a steam hammer.

"Nothing much in his pockets, just a tobacco tin and a postcard." Tyrone took the manila envelope from the policeman and handed it to Skaff who put on his bifocals and took out the two driver's licenses.

"You've got two different dates of birth here." Skaff handed the two licenses to Tyrone and removed a small yellow tobacco tin. ERINMORE FLAKE read the inscription on the lid. "British, I think." He opened the tin. A small flat key clung to the bottom of the lid. He held it out. "Did you see this?"

"Yeah, magnetized," Tyrone said. "Maybe a locker key."

Skaff fingered the tobacco. "What is it, Colombian red? That's your generation, isn't it, son?" he said to Corkery without lifting his head. "If it's not crack, coke, or PCP, it's got to be grass, isn't that what folks say these days?" He poked through the tobacco and replaced the lid. "Pipe tobacco, looks like." He drew out the wallet, took off one glove, and sorted through the contents.

13

A slip of paper fluttered to the ground; Corkery retrieved it before the wind caught it. It was a French five-franc note, torn irregularly in two. The tear bisected the serial numbers and the *Banque de France* legend. "What do you make of this?" Skaff said.

"I didn't see it," Tyrone said. "What is it?"

"A French bank note, torn in two. Odd. What do you think?" He passed it to Corkery. "Seen anything like it recently?" He brought out the postcard, glanced at it, and turned it over. The postcard was a view of the Washington Monument, unaddressed. "Could be a tourist. Maybe our lab should take a look at this stuff."

"I thought you said he wasn't the fellow," Tyrone said. "You birds can't make up your minds, can you?" He shivered and stamped his feet again. "Goddamn duck weather, better out in a blind somewheres. You ready to take him in?" he called to the medical examiner. "My ass is freezing."

"Just about." Two orderlies had joined him with a stretcher on which lay a folded blue blanket. "I'm freezing too."

Tyrone looked at the stooping, turnip-shaped figure. "I don't wonder, Doc. You got more to freeze. You know what they say down in the country. Butter spreads but lard's hard. Don't bend over too far, we'll never get you stood up again."

"How long could a body lie here and no one see it?" Corkery asked, moving aside as they lifted the corpse to the stretcher. The medical examiner stood up, red-faced and winded, his glasses

14

misted. "Hard to say."

"All weekend, maybe," Tyrone said. "They're demolating that building over yonder, so if he was here Friday, some of the workmen would have seen him sure enough."

"It had some rags throwed over it," one policeman said.

Corkery turned. "What kind of rags?"

"Just old rags."

"Wipers' rags," Tyrone said, "junkman's rags, old folks' rags, like what you see rambling down the streets these days pushing an A and P cart ahead of it. You hardly don't know what it is, neither, old folks, young folks, grandma, grandpa, black or white, you can't tell. They all look the same. Cold don't know the difference neither." He moved toward the gutted brick building and stopped outside the sashless window where a few dirty rags lay. "Covered him with those right there." Corkery bent down. "I wouldn't root around, son. Get you a quick case of the herpes." Tyrone stepped through the window.

Corkery followed him, then Skaff. "So someone took his coat and shoes afterward," Corkery said. "Then covered him, is that what you're saying?"

"That's what I figure. He wasn't wearing a topcoat. Same fellow must have took his shoes. Wouldn't look like a fellow would come all the way down from Canada to see the sights barefoot, would it, George? Not unless he was an Eskimo. Better have your lab check that out too."

The broken concrete floor inside was littered

15

with jackhammer rubble; a battered gray compressor stood just inside the door. In the far corner were scattered a few cardboard mats, smashed produce crates, sardine tins, and the ashes of a recent fire. The corner stank of urine and excrement.

"A kind of neighborhood hostel, you could say," Tyrone said, his voice loud out of the wind. "Real friendly-like."

"Someone found him, already dead," Corkery said.

"I'd say so. Stripped off his coat and shoes. Probably before he was froze up."

"Sure about that, are you?" Skaff said.

"Goddamn right. You ever try to skin a pair of pants off a froze-up dead man?"

"Never had to try. How come you'd know about that?"

"Korea," Tyrone said. "Coming back from Chosen in '50, forty degrees below zero. When I got to Hŭngnam, I was wearing five pairs of britches. Don't ask me where I got them neither. Seventeen years old, scared dumb, didn't know, didn't care."

They went back out into the cold. A cream-and-blue van from a Washington television station was drawn up on the street next to the patrol car. Two men huddled at the window talking to the driver and another policeman; one carried a shoulder camera. The medical examiner's van and the medivac unit were gone. "Maybe someone's called in, reported him missing," Tyrone said. "We'll get out a missing persons." A patrolman left the group on K Street and came back across the windswept lot toward them. The TV film crew wanted to talk to someone.

"Nothing to say," Tyrone told him. "Not me anyway, not now." He looked at his watch. "Let George talk to him." He winked at Corkery. "Anyway, I got to get along home."

"Still got wife problems, have you?" Skaff said.

Tyrone smiled, a long appreciative smile that took everyone in. "All night long. You ever hear the one about the naked jogger?"

The wind roared in again. Corkery looked skyward, the world familiar once more — a Pennsylvania morning under the December scud off the mountains; snow weather, deer weather, holiday weather, Corkery standing at the oil drum outside the highway department equipment sheds where he worked during his high school summers, back from the University of Pennsylvania for Christmas break, listening to Abe Runyon, Orville Crawford, and Charley Fargo talk about dogs, deer, grouse, quail, women, the Steelers, engineering division incompetence, poor supervision, and rotten maintenance. Their familiar landscape, like Tyrone's, never changed, thank God.

They stopped for coffee at a café on M Street and drove back across Key Bridge. The wind had died down and the overcast was low over the Virginia hills and the gorge of the Potomac as they climbed the parkway. Remembering something Dudley's wife had told him the previous afternoon, Corkery was leafing through his pocket notebook.

"She told me she couldn't find his diary. She wasn't sure what that meant."

"Odd, one of your people keeping a diary."

"More of a journal, she said."

"What's the difference?"

"I don't know. More intellectual, I suppose. Thoughts and ideas maybe."

"Would you call him an intellectual?" Skaff asked.

"Dudley? I don't know. Not after thirty years in harness, I suppose. Who is?" The missing Agency officer was three years removed from the clandestine service and planned to retire that winter, a decision he'd been quick to share with any number of colleagues he'd seen in the corridors at Langley that autumn. He'd also made the same decision five times during the past three years, but each time postponed it, which made him a bit of a bore. "Would you?"

"Call him an intellectual? Never met one myself," Skaff said dryly. "Not in my business."

"Confusing." Corkery slipped the notebook in his pocket.

"Sometimes you'd rather be confused. That's what I tell my new people. Better than thinking you already have the answers."

"Think so?"

"Like being scared. Being scared helps, keeps you on your toes. End up seven hundred miles off in the middle of the Baltic if you're not, tanks bingo, crew in the drink."

"You were air force?"

"Used to be. SAC — B-47s. Navigator."

"I'll be damned."

"That's what I used to say every time I woke up. What the hell am I doing way up here? Those aren't Grandma's bedsheets hanging on the line down there, it's the Arctic Circle. So sometimes being confused helps, keeps you on the right azimuth. Not air force, were you?"

"No, navy. I wonder who the poor bastard is." Overhead a jet thundered unseen through the murk, following the river toward National Airport.

"Ulrich? Tourist, probably, someone just in town, maybe got lost. Probably nothing. Another weekend homicide." They passed through the gate. May through September the surrounding woods were a forest of Robin Hood green, but now the trees were bare except for the oaks; copper leaves hung from the limbs like rotting fruit. The parking lots were nearly empty. Through the trees the flanks of the huge building were as dull as chalk cliffs. Skaff stopped at the main entrance.

"I'll let you know what Tyrone turns up," he said. "Call me if you get anything. I'll be home after twelve."

In the second-floor suite, Adrian Shaw's door was half open. Bent over his desk and writing furiously, he didn't lift his head as Corkery looked in. At his elbow was a clutter of memos and telegrams. With him was Elinor Wynn, the special projects officer, bringing him the overnight NSA communications intercepts from the D-staff. He

19

supposed they were putting together a cable for Abbott, the Division chief. He was in London that week, leaving Shaw at the helm. Seeing Corkery, Elinor came quickly across the carpet, her auburn hair bobbing under her dark blue beret.

"We're awfully busy right now. It's one of those days. No interruptions, sorry."

"What's he decided to do about Vitale's memo?" Carl Vitale from the Security Division had talked to Louise Dudley at her apartment on Saturday afternoon. The meeting had annoyed Shaw, who mistrusted the FBI, Security, and Vitale in particular, a short, olive-skinned ex-FBI agent with a Queens, New York, accent. He'd sent Corkery out to console Louise Dudley and put a better face on Langley's manners. Shaw may have been right; with his sleek dark hair, Roman nose, and racetrack clothes, Vitale reminded Corkery of a pool hall hustler and bookie he knew in Philadelphia during his college days.

"Vitale? What about?"

"Frank Dudley."

"Oh, that. I'm sure that's the *least* of his worries right now, dear boy." She closed the door.

He went back the inner corridor to his office, a small windowless cubicle with beige partition walls, a green metal desk, and a single safe next to the bookcase. Under the prickly Shaw, he spent most of his time waiting there in solitary, waiting for Shaw's door to open, for conferences from which he'd been excluded to conclude, for cables he hadn't seen but only heard about to arrive in his daily reading folder. Shaw's door was usually shut, like Julian Abbott's, whose habits Shaw imitated. What Abbott accomplished by strength of will, intellect, and reputation, Shaw achieved in slyer ways; slight, gray-haired, and in his late fifties, he was as secretive as a shrew. Corkery's hqs apprenticeship under Shaw had been spent in familiarizing himself with methods and procedures, running useless name checks, writing useless case summaries, and occasionally helping draft a mission directive to stations in the field. Only once had he helped identify hard target priorities for stations or deep cover operatives in the field, and then in Italy, where he had served. Apart from that, he was left pretty much in the dark. The office routine was largely administrative, by the numbers, the old navy way. There were times those first months when a few words from Shaw or Abbott drawn from their own institutional memories, would have saved him hours of scut work. They were never offered.

During his posting from Rome he had known neither man, although when he returned to Langley for reassignment he'd been told Abbott had asked for him. He didn't know why. He found him coldly forbidding during their first meeting. Shaw's secretiveness seemed to him merely feline, like Elinor Wynn's, but Abbott's as obscure as Job's, like his intimidating silences, made of some darker stuff. They hadn't exchanged more than a dozen words since.

On the wall next to his desk hung a map of

the Mediterranean, his only attempt to brighten up his monastic cell. In a bottom desk drawer were pictures he'd brought with him from his navy days; he'd intended to have them framed but wouldn't now. There were photographs of Lt. K. C. Corkery, USN, slumped in the CIC chair of the missile frigate USS *Peurifoy* as it prowled the Mediterranean, of Corkery receiving some pointless little Middle East Task Force citation from Admiral Yeaston in the thick slanting sunlight at Bahrain, his blond hair bleached white, of Lt. K. C. Corkery in dress whites looking up from a water taxi at Piraeus with two congressmen from the House Armed Services Committee aboard, both in seersucker suits, both a head shorter, on their way to lunch with the captain, Corkery sent as equerry instead of Lt. Commander Knox because the captain, in his own words, wasn't sure Knox wouldn't step on his dick again as he had with two visiting senators when he'd spilled the beans about the potheads in the gunnery division and the Black Muslims with the Apache headbands down in engineering. They seemed better days now.

Someone from the Soviet Bloc Division in a coat and tie stuck his head in the door, looking for Elinor Wynn. Corkery said she was with Shaw. He studied his notes, found what was troubling him, reviewed Dudley's 201 personnel file from central registry, and left his office. Shaw's door was still closed. He continued on through the deserted halls to a far stairwell and climbed to the third floor. Dudley's office was at the end of the

22

building in a depressing little cubicle overlooking a gloomy inner air well. It was even gloomier that morning as he prowled about. He searched Dudley's desk calendar and his telephone book, didn't find the name he was looking for, and went through the desk drawers and the single barlock metal cabinet in the corner. In the folder in the second drawer were copies of his recent correspondence, all answering letters from the public asking for declassification of Agency documents under the Freedom of Information Act. The other drawers were empty. There was no classified file, no pictures on the wall or desk, no framed diplomatic parchment or award citations, no books in the bookcase, and no personal mementos, unlike the office on the other side of the partition whose occupant had hung African raffia mats on the wall, a few diplomatic commissions, a 1965 diploma from the National War College, and a walnut-and-silver plaque from the Athens, Greece, Lions Club. Whoever he was, he was obviously happy in semi-retirement. Dudley's office, by contrast, was an abandoned station on the road to nowhere. That was a falling off too, as puzzling as his personnel file.

He was a Harvard man, recruited for the Operations Directorate after postwar service in Berlin with the U.S. Army. His early career was impressive, or so Corkery thought. He'd been a special assistant to the Deputy Director for Operations, was twice a deputy division chief at hqs, chief of operations in Vienna and Berlin, and chief of station in Oslo and Copenhagen. His file carried the designator *Sov Bloc Red*, which meant he was known to the Russians, unlike Corkery, who was one of Langley's budless saplings, *Sov Bloc Green*, unknown and unidentified even after three years in Rome. But Dudley's file perplexed him: an auspicious start, two prosperous decades, and then an abrupt falling off, a sudden vacuum ending here in this airless little tomb a few steps from a freight elevator. Some kind of bureaucratic lesson there? Corkery didn't know. The file gave no clues.

"I suspect all his talk of retirement was the only arrow left in his quiver," a drawling office director from the European Division told him. Corkery had found him at his desk, come in to read the overnight cables on a Saturday morning. His name was Spencer, a willowy man with sweeping gray hair wearing a double-breasted English pinstripe. A little long in the tooth for an office director and overdressed for a Saturday morning, Corkery had thought, both warnings he wasn't a man to be trusted. "A way of reminding others he was still very much alive," Spencer had added maliciously. He remembered the elevator doors closing on Dudley on a busy Monday morning a few weeks earlier as he told the European Division chief of his retirement decision. The Division chief was late for a meeting upstairs; Dudley was blocking the elevator door. It was an hour when those not at a meeting or on their way to one had no existence at all so far as the senior ranks at Langley were concerned, and such, Corkery gathered, was Fran-

24

cis Eliot Dudley's disgrace.

In his hand was a Styrofoam coffee cup with a plastic lid. Folded over his arm was his beige Burberry with the plaid lining showing. Under it was the *New York Times*. His shoulders were erect and as he spoke he lifted himself to his full height, six foot two or so, an unconscious habit among shorter men that didn't go unnoticed. He delivered his news with his usual peremptory authority, even though the subject was trifling, which made him sound like a fool. With his ruddy handsome face and his thinning chestnut hair, he didn't look like a fool nor did he look obsolete, not from the photographs Corkery had seen. Except for an additional fifteen pounds he looked very much like he had when he'd left Harvard and been recruited in one of those drab old temporary buildings near the Lincoln Memorial, long since torn down.

A few listening from nearby as they waited for their elevators would probably have pitied him, Corkery imagined. Someone told him later that in an age of satellite sensors, infrared scanners, modems, and integrated databases, he had the look of an old cavalry officer whose polo mount had been mechanized and his command transferred to the motor pool but who maintained the old tally-ho fiction down to the whipcord trousers and the horse country shoes. He had arrived late that morning, as he arrived late every morning, and was on his way to the secluded little office in Public Affairs hidden away at the end of a seldom-traveled corridor next to a freight elevator, the final station on that long retreat from the operational frontier. There he shared a secretary with two other Agency elders who, like him, had time to fuss over their luncheon schedules, compete for their lone secretary's affection to get their typing done, disappear for long periods in the library or cafeteria, and arrive late or leave early for some undisclosed assignation.

Corkery saw it all in his mind's eye, even the annoyance on the Division chief's face. Senior officials at Langley had too few minutes in the day to be delayed in the halls by those with nothing on their minds except personal misfortune. If they were in the corridors at all they were moving briskly toward an elevator or a conference room, not to be intercepted except by those sent with a summons of greater urgency. The corridor nomads, of whom Dudley was one, convoked one another regularly on their way to and from the cafeteria with word of another kind: an upcoming trip to the hospital for long-postponed prostate surgery, the death of a dog or an old colleague, storm damage to the house in the country not covered by an insurance rider. The fact that Dudley was so frequently in the halls and his news so depressingly personal was evidence enough retirement was long overdue.

Shaw insisted Corkery was mistaken. Dudley's career wasn't at all impressive; he'd been misled by Dudley's curriculum vitae. They'd argued late Saturday afternoon at the walnut conference table in Shaw's office. One of the Old Boy Brotherhood,

Shaw had said contemptuously. His early assignments reflected his seventh-floor connections, not his ability; his recent assignments spoke for themselves.

"A minor slot in Congressional Relations which proved a failure," he'd said scornfully, reading from Dudley's personnel file. "The inspector general's office for eight months, also a failure." Since then he'd been working in some obscure little shop in Public Affairs. "Senior reviewing officer, whatever that means. I doubt it means very much."

"I meant before that —"

"Before that, he benefited from his connections, not his ability." It was Phil Chambers who brought Dudley to Berlin as one of his deputies after he'd blotted his copybook in Vienna. His wife had died, admittedly a factor in his subsequent decline —

"His first wife died later," Corkery recalled, reaching for the file.

Shaw had refused to yield it. "The date of her death is of no significance whatsoever." He'd gone off afterward to study Mongolian in England at the University of Leeds. A sabbatical, pure and simple, arranged by Phil Chambers and a few other sympathetic souls on high; Roger Cornelius was responsible for his assignments to Oslo and Copenhagen over the objections of the European Division. The names meant nothing to Corkery, who'd listened as Shaw spoke of an earlier decade when his own career had evidently faltered. Dudley had maneuvered for chief of station in Vienna

27

but his last patron had retired and the post went to someone else. Those his own age who hadn't enjoyed his early success had no regrets as they passed him by — Dudley, the class coxswain and lightweight, lifted on the shoulders of his elders. The indecisiveness known to his subordinates but concealed from his seniors by that ramrod stiff back and those preposterously squared shoulders was now evident to everyone. Slow in decision and impossible in execution, he'd talked instead of the old days; a kind of bureaucratic tortoise, Shaw said, the first to draw in at the least sign of trouble, the last to emerge, maddingly refusing to sign off on a cable or a staff study until everyone else had signed off first. The busiest offices soon found ways to ignore him. Personnel had recognized the signs and responded with assignments appropriate to his collapse. His file spoke for itself. Dudley had seen his day, someone who'd peaked early but lingered too long, prolonging a career that long ago had reached a dead end.

Corkery wasn't convinced. He took Dudley's desk calendar and his telephone book and went back downstairs to his office. Like Shaw, Vitale thought there was little to Dudley's disappearance. "Some kind of family problem," he'd said on Saturday as he dropped off his memo. "That comes through loud and clear, even though she was trying to soft-pedal it. Something happens that gets them both upset, he walks out Friday night, she calls us the next morning. That usually means a domestic blowup of some kind." He thought Frank

Dudley would be back on his feet by midafternoon, home again by evening.

His memo concluded with a few observations on the domestic aspects of the case: Dudley's nights out alone on the town, his depression, possibly a drinking problem, a certain tension in the household caused by the retirement question. He thought they might have had an argument Friday night and suspected Louise Dudley had seized the opportunity to bring her husband's erratic behavior to official attention. He recalled the case of a senior officer whose erotic private life had been ignored by his superiors until his vengeful wife's repeated telephone calls to the weekend duty officer had forced the issue. He had been summoned to early retirement.

The memo was useless, made worse by Vitale's FBI-acquired writing style. Corkery disagreed with his conclusions but had none of his own. Down the hall Shaw's door was still shut; Elinor Wynn's raincoat was still lying across Miss Fogarty's desk.

During his first month in the division Elinor had been one of the few appealing faces in an otherwise unwelcome assignment. With her constant bustle and her insolent green eyes, she'd intrigued him, but more recently he'd found her moody and unpredictable, the telltale signs of an incipient spinsterhood. She'd invited him twice for dinner. He was told she did that with most of the new officers. He'd taken her out to Wolftrap to a Gordon Lightfoot concert. They got stalled in traffic coming home; she'd confessed she'd been bored to tears. Her second dinner invitation was more intimate — he was the only guest — but the clam chowder tasted like soapsuds and the casserole like cat food. She had four cats. After dinner they walked over to a concert at Lisner Auditorium and listened to a cellist and violinist playing Bartók on an empty stage. There were twenty-three people in the audience. Corkery decided she was eccentrically New England, a cultural light-year away from small-town western Pennsylvanians like himself. He hadn't yet reciprocated her second dinner invitation and doubted he would.

Impatient, he telephoned Louise Dudley. "Me again, Kevin Corkery, sorry. Nothing new, just a few more questions if you don't mind. Could I stop by?"

"Not at all. To tell you the truth, I rather expected you."

An officer on the German desk called and wanted to clear a cable about the Erika Kissling case. "Who's Erika Kissling?" A secretary on the West German counterintelligence staff in Cologne, detained three days earlier on suspicion of espionage. Corkery said he'd have to talk to Shaw or Elinor Wynn. "Typical," the desk officer said, and slammed down the phone. The counterintelligence staff often had that effect on other divisions.

At one o'clock he cleared his desk and locked his safe. Shaw had gone upstairs. He scribbled a note reminding him to look at Vitale's memo and ask for a redraft. He left it on his secretary's desk.

Outside the parking lots were empty. The wind had come up. Flat iron clouds sped southeast; patches of sunshine were spreading across the heights of Georgetown. He drove his secondhand Mustang down the river, sorry he'd left his Alfa Romeo at home. Silver gray, shark snouted and dolphin sleek, the Alfa was the only pleasure he had these days. He'd bought it during the last month of his posting to Rome from a navy commander in Naples, transferred to Diego Garcia in the Indian Ocean. The poor guy had been brokenhearted, the Italian mistress he'd had to leave behind, but there were compensations. He was refitting for a tropical mode. In his Naples BOQ were scuba tanks, spear guns, and a wet suit, still in cellophane. In the trunk of the Alfa were chamois cloths and sponges, a ski rack, and a spare fuel pump for those long weekend treks to the Italian Alps. It was a European model, factory pure, no U.S. emission controls, no tracheotomy whistling away power; a 2000cc engine, overhead cams, Pirelli tires, a six-speaker Blaupunkt stereo, and leather seats, small enough compensation for two years in the Langley fog factory.

Joggers were staggering along the paths in Rock Creek Park. A few cyclists wobbled along the verges, husband-and-wife teams in orange jackets. A shiny new blue Toyota drew alongside. He studied the blond behind the wheel, yielded to her new owner's pride, and let her pass. SUGR BABE read her Virginia license plate. The old Mustang was sluggish and didn't accelerate well. He

31

couldn't catch up. Three girls were tossing a Frisbee in a roadside picnic park. He slowed to have a look but the engine misfired and blew a rocket out the exhaust. Bad timing. They ignored him. Except for the wind it was a day for raking leaves and tidying up lawns, mulching the azalea beds, and watching NFL football until dusk, trying to forget tomorrow was Monday. Tomorrow, the same car, the same long mushy beltway drive to Langley from his rented rambler in Bethesda; outdragged by vans and old pickups, whiplashed by overloaded diesels, trashed by overpaid beltway executives with cellular phones in their Mercedeses and BMWs, already on the horn to their brokers. He hated Washington weekends.

The Dudley apartment was on the fifth floor of an ivy-covered Tudor apartment house out on Connecticut Avenue beyond the zoo. The dim foyer with its leaded glass windows, orange sconces, and faded wall tapestries carried the memories of an earlier Washington, of trolley car commuters, corner pharmacies with marble counters and no security grills, no drugs, no crack, no SWAT teams. Black-tie evenings at Constitution Hall would have seated the entire Washington bureaucracy. The old elevator with its iron gate and bright brass smelled cleanly of metal polish. An elderly woman leaning on a cane and smelling sweetly of heather accompanied him as far as the third floor. She was wearing an orange wig and studiously ignored him; not bad manners, he decided, just chemotherapy.

Louise Dudley opened the door. She was a tall gray-eyed woman a dozen or so years younger than her husband, wearing a beige cardigan, a woolen plaid skirt, and brown walking shoes.

"Sorry. Me again. I hate to bother you on Sunday."

"Not at all. Come in." Her gracious calmness the previous day had surprised him as much as her appearance. Her light-brown hair was long in front and along the sides but short at the back of her neck, fastened to the side with a brown barrette, a youthful touch. "No new developments, you said." She led him down the long hall to the living room.

"Not yet. It was something you mentioned yesterday about a phone call."

"A phone call? Sit down, please. I'm really hopeless at this sort of thing. What phone call?"

"Thursday night, I think." He moved to the pale blue couch, notebook in hand. "That's right. Thursday night."

She didn't recall at first, watching him silently from the wing-backed chair as she searched her memory. Then she nodded. "Now I remember. Yes, Thursday night."

"Could you tell about it, everything you can remember? I sort of skipped over it yesterday."

A little before eight on Thursday night she had picked up her husband's coffee cup from the lamp table in the study and stooped to retrieve the scattered sections of the *Washington Post* from the carpet next to the armchair. Her husband was in the

33

rear bedroom, typing an addition to his résumé on his old Underwood typewriter. She moved to the television set, which he had left on, but before she reached it, the telephone rang. She crossed to the desk and answered. An abrupt foreign voice had asked for Frank Dudley. She'd asked who it was. A hesitation, then a tinny echo, the gabble of distant voices, the click of heels on a pavement, a distant horn honking. She thought he might be calling from an airline terminal. German, she decided, European certainly. Abruptly the background noises ceased, as if he'd pressed something over the mouthpiece. He said he was an old friend.

A man in a hurry, she concluded, a man caught between planes. She went to fetch her husband and met him in the hall near the kitchen door, come to refill his whiskey glass. She was afraid he would ask her to say he wasn't in, something he'd done frequently of late, always to her embarrassment, but he didn't. He took the call in the study as she watched from the doorway.

He answered curtly, his usual tone when unsure of his caller. Strangers were quickly intimidated, the effect he intended. He didn't seem to know who his caller was. "Who? I'm sorry, I can't hear you. Whom did you say?"

He listened silently, his frown deepening, his eyes on the television screen. She came in to turn it off and he turned his back, facing the bookcases. She went back to the kitchen. A few minutes later he returned to his bedroom but reappeared shortly in the kitchen doorway in a coat and tie. "I've

34

been summoned. Someone I haven't seen in years. He just got in and leaves in the morning. I said I'd have a drink with him. I really couldn't turn him down."

An unexpected phone call, a mysterious summons, the regimen he'd once thrived on. She'd followed him down the hall, suggesting he ask his visitor out there. He said he didn't have a car. She said he could get a taxi.

"He doesn't know Washington and doesn't trust taxis, not at night." He could pick him up; he said that meant two trips. She asked where they were going to meet. "At his hotel, just down Connecticut."

"Where was he calling from?"

"His hotel room. He was still unpacking, sounded exhausted, poor chap. I won't be long. It's just so damned inconvenient, that's all." He didn't look unhappy but seemed invigorated. He frowned as he opened the closet door, found his Irish hat and thorn-handled umbrella. "It's not raining," she reminded him.

He returned the umbrella to the closet. "It's just a bloody nuisance, that's all. The poor chap needs a bit of counsel."

He might have been an unemployed actor, summoned for a reading. The gestures were transparent by now but still he persisted, playing out a role that had long lost its credibility. She recognized the tone and now identified the gestures. But why the claim the call had come from a hotel room? His voice was rich, generous, and forgiving, not the voice of their long solitary evenings together. "I hope you won't make any plans for the weekend," she'd said. "We are going to the country, aren't we?"

His eyes closed in an instant of pain. He hated submissiveness.

"I'm sorry," she said. He was never deliberately unkind, never, and that was the cruelest part.

"Certainly we're going to the country. Why shouldn't we? And we'll have a rattling good time."

He gave her a reassuring smile, a peck on the cheek, and marched out the door. She went to bed at eleven and lay sleepless in her bedroom, waiting for the sounds of his return. She didn't hear his footsteps until after one o'clock.

Corkery said, "Did he mention his meeting the next morning?"

She shook her head. "No, not a word."

"And that was the last time you saw him, on Friday morning." She nodded. "So Thursday night he said it was an old friend but he didn't mention a name?"

"No, but he probably knew the name would mean nothing to me."

"Did he ever mention the name Ulrich to you?"

"Ulrich?" She frowned. "Ulrich? I don't believe so. Why? Is it important?"

"It might be. So you had no idea who he was or where he came from, just that he was a foreigner and didn't know Washington. German or European, you said."

"I thought so, yes."

"Out of breath, you said."

"Yes, as if he'd just run up a flight of stairs."

"Not excited, just out of breath."

She gave Corkery a small smile. "That's drawing a very fine line, isn't it? I'd say not excited, no."

"You thought he was phoning from an outside phone, a public phone."

"I'm sure of it."

"That struck you as strange at the time?"

"Yes, I thought so. But I'm sure the explanation was probably a simple one. He once got quite a few calls from old friends passing through, although not recently. I thought it odd but then I put it out of my mind. I didn't really relate it, not in the slightest." She smiled again. "I was quite right yesterday, wasn't I?"

"Right?" The gray eyes were so direct, so clear he doubted they could conceal anything from anyone.

"You do enjoy mysteries, don't you?"

"Pretty much. And you don't remember ever hearing the name Ulrich."

"No, but we could look through his correspondence if you think it important. I'd intended to anyway." She led him back down the hall to the antique cherry desk in the paneled study. Beyond the window the sun splashed through the trees.

"Did Vitale look at his papers?"

"No, he didn't seem interested." She opened a drawer and brought out a thick file folder held together by a metal clip. "He wasn't very well organized in keeping things. Copies of his letters. I hadn't realized there were so many. Ulrich, you say?" She set them aside, opened the second drawer, and removed a thick letter file. "More letters." She took a manila envelope from the bottom drawer, opened the flap, and withdrew the photographs. Some were official, some not, taken at diplomatic receptions, at cocktail parties, at picnics, during winter or summer holidays, many identified by the notation and date on the back: Oslo, Copenhagen, Berlin, Munich, Southern France.

"It's the way he once was, she said, sorting through them. Her fingers were long and slim, the nails unpolished. "Much too sad now."

"He had a remarkable career."

"He did, didn't he? I often told him that, that he had nothing to regret. Here he is with Jessica, my stepdaughter." She handed him a photograph taken outside a stone farmhouse in partial ruin. At Dudley's shoulder stood a dark-haired girl in blue jeans looking up at her father. A gnarled old cypress tree overhung the stone wall behind them; beneath were a sandpile and a mortar box. The front of a Volkswagen minibus was visible in a rear shed. From the dry scrub Corkery guessed the photograph had been taken along the Mediterranean littoral. On the back was a faint penciled notation: "Eric P's — 1st Day."

"The picture doesn't do her justice. She's very much like her mother, so I'm told, very lovely. Very talented, too. She's a painter. She's here in

Washington now, she came last Thursday. I talked to her yesterday morning, just after I called Langley. I didn't remember she was here when I called."

"Here in Washington?"

"Yes. It completely slipped my mind. I felt terribly embarrassed. It occurred to me afterward he might have stayed the night with her, but he hadn't, fortunately. I don't mean fortunately. I mean it might have been unfortunate, my calling Langley when he might have been at Jessica's all the time. He wouldn't have forgiven me. But he wasn't there, of course —" She looked away in dismay toward the opposite wall. After a moment she nodded toward the single oil painting hanging in a gold frame. "That's one of hers. Les Baux in Provence, one she did a few years ago. She didn't much like my having it framed. She denies so much of her early work but Frank loved it. So do I."

Corkery got up to look at it, wondering if her story was as simple as the one she was trying to tell. He doubted it was, but her mysteries were personal, matters few could lay hands on. "It's very nice. Why would she deny something like this?"

"I wish I knew. She's very headstrong."

He went back to the desk. "He planned to retire this winter. Did he know what he was going to do?"

"Not yet, no. I think he was a little worried about the future."

"A little down at times?"

"At times, yes."

"Depression, you think?"

She was slow to reply. The sound of moving traffic was faint on the avenue below. "I suppose a little, but not depressed so much as uneasy, a little on edge. But I wasn't worried in that way, that he'd do something rash, something —" She faltered, unable to find the word, and brought out another set of photographs. "I don't know where those were taken. They look quite happy, don't they, father and daughter. She must have been on holiday from her boarding school in England. She was terribly unhappy there. She refused to adjust, but that's Jessica. She always had a will of her own. I'm afraid I don't know those people." She held out a photo of a group of men sitting around a table in a German bistro. "Drinking partners, I imagine."

"Looks like it. This one here must be Oslo. He skied?"

"Cross country a little but not for years. He loved to ice-skate. He was on the hockey team at St. Paul's. Do you ski?"

"Some but not much these days."

"No? Where's your home, Mr. Corkery? I don't quite detect an accent."

He mentioned the name of a small town in western Pennsylvania. To his surprise, she knew it. "That's lovely country, quite lovely. I prefer the mountains myself and that's where we found our country place, not quite in the mountains but nearby. In Maryland. That's Bavaria, I believe."

Corkery paused over a yellowing enlargement taken of a group of men in front of a stone fireplace. Next to Frank Dudley was a familiar face. "That's Julian Abbott, isn't it?"

"Is it?" She took the photograph, studied it, and nodded. "Yes, I think it is. He and Julian were close at one time. Not so much recently." The phone rang and she moved to answer it. Corkery heard her mention storm damage and broken limbs. "Our neighbor in Maryland, Colonel Davenport," she said as she returned to the desk. "We were supposed to spend the weekend there. There was a storm last week and I called to ask him to drive by and see if everything was all right. I think that's about all here." She returned the envelopes to the desk drawers and led him back the long hall. "We keep a few trunks and footlockers in the basement storage room, old army footlockers from years ago. I doubt they're of much interest but you'll probably want to look through them. He does his typing in his bedroom. He's a terrible typist but that doesn't discourage him." Through one door was the kitchen and through another a smaller hall lined with built-in cabinets. His was the first bedroom, a large masculine room with a sand-colored pile rug and sand-colored drapes. The walls were hung with old maps and whaling and nautical prints. An antique cannonball bed sat between the two windows. On the wall above the dresser were two very old U.S. Navy commissions, one signed by Theodore Roosevelt. "That's his father's. He spent some time in Antarctica. I believe he knew Admiral Byrd. One of Frank's great-grandfathers was a New England whaler. He's very proud of that." A small oak desk stood in the alcove. On the typing leaf was an old Underwood typewriter covered with an oilcloth cover. Next to it was a three-drawer oak cabinet with a globe atop it.

"We both work back here." She sat down and opened the first drawer. "I have my own study in the guest room on the other side of the bath." Inside were bundles of canceled checks and government travel vouchers. "Do these interest you?" Corkery brought a chair near and looked through them. In the second drawer was an envelope filled with European bank notes and a tobacco tin heavy with foreign coins. "He certainly lost money on these, didn't he?" She brought out an English pound note.

"Probably. I have the same problem, getting caught at airports with a pocketful of foreign coins. Have you thought of anything else since yesterday?"

"Not really." She opened the bottom drawer and took out a file folder. "I certainly made a botch of it yesterday, didn't I?"

He looked up. "With me? How?"

"No, you were very kind. With Mr. Vitale. I had the feeling he thought Frank and I had quarreled. I knew what he was thinking. I felt terribly helpless. I didn't quite know what to say. We certainly hadn't quarreled." She searched through the file folder. "We never argued. I know that sounds like a cliché but it's true. He hated confrontations and bent over backward to avoid them. In that way he was poorly equipped for what was expected of him."

"Poorly equipped in what way?"

"I suppose he lacked ruthlessness, for one thing. But that's what a wife would say, isn't it? Jessica, who in most ways is very unlike her father, said once he was the kindest person she'd ever known. We were arguing about something and I was a little short with her. I said yes he was, much too kind — he's been supporting her for years. But that was wrong of me. Probably one can never be too kind. In Frank's case there was a constant struggle between his career responsibilities and his sense of fairness and decency."

"That's sometimes the case."

"In Frank it was often drawn out in an agonizing way. Do you hunt? Frank used to, but not anymore." She showed him two country-road maps of rural Maryland. "Not far from our farm." She brought out another folder, opened it, and handed it to him. "This is his retirement file."

Corkery searched through it. "How did you feel about his retirement? Was it something you talked about?"

"Occasionally, yes. I was for it, definitely. I'd been hoping he'd do it for years, encouraging him every way I could. I felt he'd given all he had to give, that the time had come to move on to other things."

"How long had he been considering it?"

"For three or four years. He first mentioned it when he was working for Julian Abbott. They had a disagreement about something. It was a terrible time for him. He told me he was going to leave."

Corkery looked up. "He worked with Abbott? Where?"

"Here in Washington. You didn't know?"

"No. It's not in his personnel file."

"No? Probably because he didn't stay very long, just a few months. Everything changed after that. During the last few years or so, he had less responsibility, less authority, less involvement in other people's lives. He was terribly bored."

A clock ticked from the bedside table. From down the hall came the chimes of a grandfather clock, tolling the hour. She heard it, lifted her head, and got up. "Would you like a cup of tea? I think I would."

He put the file aside and took another folder from the drawer. Inside were letters dating back several years. Attached to the back of the folder by a paper clip was an airmail envelope, addressed to Frank Dudley through the embassy in Bonn. The paper clip had rusted, leaving a small stain on the foreign stamp. Inside were a few odd newspaper clippings. One was from a Frankfurt newspaper reporting the death of a German bank executive in a highway accident near Munich. The second was the obituary of a British Foreign Ministry official clipped from *The Times* of London. The third was a Xeroxed copy of a *New York Times* wire service item from Tass. In the margin was an emphatic question mark.

Moscow, Oct. 18 (TASS). The Military Collegium of the Supreme Court of the USSR has tried A. A. Andreyev on a charge of high treason. It was established during the trial that Andreyev had been recruited by a foreign intelligence service and collected state and military secrets for transmission to a foreign intelligence service. The criminal was punished according to law.

"I see you've found something," she said as she returned. "I've put the kettle on. It'll just be a minute. What is it?"

"I'm not sure. It was clipped to the back of this folder." He handed her the Tass item.

She nodded. "Yes, I once wondered about that too."

"You've seen it before?"

"Several times. I found it in the pocket of one of his jackets I was sending to the cleaners. He must have been carrying it around for weeks. I left it on his dresser, where he lets things accumulate. Then I saw it again later, some unlikely place. A book or a magazine, used as a bookmark."

"Does the name Andreyev mean anything to you?"

"No, nothing. Do you think it might mean something?"

"I don't know. It's just odd."

"It certainly seemed to obsess him, didn't it? That's the teakettle. Come along. We deserve a little rest."

In the kitchen, she poured out the tea and opened a tin of Danish butter cookies. "If you still enjoy mysteries so, that tells me something," she said. They sat at the cherry table in the alcove. "I doubt you've been very long with the Agency. Am I right?"

"Not long. Five years."

"That's not long at all."

"So everyone tells me. Since we talked yesterday, have you thought of anything else, anything unusual, anything out of the ordinary recently?"

"Unusual?"

"Incidents you couldn't explain. Dinners missed, late-night appointments, out-of-town trips you couldn't account for?"

"No, not really."

"There's one other thing. It's a little awkward but it's been on my mind."

"Please, ask anything you like."

"Someone suggested a nervous or mental breakdown. I wanted to ask your reaction to that."

"It's all so bizarre I wouldn't rule out any possibility right now, even that."

"So it did occur to you."

She nodded. "I think it did, yes."

♣ ♣ ♣

The sudden Sunday evening deluge had moved on, but a few raindrops were still suspended on the sunporch windows at the rear of the old federal house in Georgetown. Two drinks had arrived by dumbwaiter from the kitchen below, appearing mysteriously behind the white-paneled door that Phil Chambers had just opened, enormously pleased with his creaky contraption whose muscle power had been supplied by an invisible arm below. His guest, who had asked for a vodka-lime, had been impressed, not merely with Chambers's sleight of hand but Chambers himself. He was Frank Dudley's former chief in Berlin and Vienna; nine years retired, he lived a reclusive life in his Georgetown house, working on a book. He was in his early seventies, short and stocky, with a shock of white hair and quick blue eyes. His shapeless gray flannels had fallen low about his hips; the gray sweatshirt under a gray cardigan was sprigged with leaf crumbs. He had mistaken Corkery, wet haired and wet shoed, for the paperboy, even though it was Sunday night and Corkery had telephoned ten minutes earlier.

"Don't be an idiot," a woman's voice had boomed up the stairs from the English basement where she'd been silently monitoring her husband's front door manners, waiting for the inevitable faux pas. "Since when did the paper man start collecting on Sunday night?"

So Chambers had apologized, all the more so

when Corkery had identified himself. He brought him a towel to dry his head and invited him to the rear sunporch for a drink, saying he'd been moping about the house all afternoon after a quarrel with a mysterious manuscript. He was grateful for company.

"So what's this about Frank Dudley? Walked off you say? When?"

Friday night. He'd gone from Langley to a diplomatic reception at the Norwegian embassy and no one had seen him since. Chambers didn't seem alarmed. "A bit strange but nothing to get upset about. I wouldn't worry too much, not yet at any rate. Very deliberate, Frank is." A banging from below carried him out of his rattan chair and back to the dumbwaiter, whose door had yawned open. He closed it. "She has me on rations, why the dumbwaiter is here. Can't be running up and down stairs every half hour, can we? She's keeper of the keys. Doctor's orders." He sat down again. "Frank had a reason for everything he ever did. Had his own code, not like a lot of them out there, wouldn't let anything violate it. What the Prussians call *Pflichtgefuhl.* Moral stubbornness, that stiff-necked sense of duty that always seemed to get them into trouble. Why they were such marvelous soldiers."

"Louise Dudley said he came to see you a few times recently."

"About his retirement, yes. The retirement crisis. He once thought he had a few years left, but that's usual, isn't it? He'd changed his mind.

You know Louise?"

"Just since yesterday." She'd once worked for the Agency, Chambers said, a foreign exchange analyst in the intelligence directorate, where she'd once briefed a middle-aged widower on certain peculiar Russian hard-currency transfers through Swiss banks. Dudley had found her quiet manners and old-fashioned rectitude as fascinating as her expertise. They were married a year later. Following the marriage, she'd left the CIA, worked for a time with the International Monetary Fund, then the Washington office of a New York consulting firm. There were no children. Jessica was the only child by his first wife, Tricia, a beautiful woman, intelligent, lively, extravagant, but incredibly complicated. "Used to give marvelous parties. She could do anything — ride, ski, shoot — a magnificent snap shot, the best I've ever seen. Incredible woman, a humdinger, as we used to say. Before your time, I suppose. One of those women you never forget." Louise Dudley was the reverse, never a beauty in her youth, a woman who'd flowered too late for the first dance and might have missed the ball if it hadn't been for Frank Dudley. Serene, reserved, and withdrawn, she was more a companion for middle age, a woman who'd helped restore her husband's self-esteem after the emotional devastation of the first marriage; respect rather than love seemed the passionless bond between them. They rarely entertained at home and seldom went out. Dudley's occasional appearances on the embassy cocktail circuit were bachelor affairs; the Danish, Norwegian, and FRG embassies kept his name on their national day list; no one on the staffs quite remembered why.

"But who's to say?" Chambers stirred uncomfortably in his chair. "She's different from Tricia, that's all. Remarkable too in her quiet way. She's been a great help to him."

"You called it a 'retirement crisis.' "

"So I did. I don't think he'd reconciled himself to the fact his day was over. That's why he came to me, I suppose, hoping I'd tell him it wasn't. I couldn't. Like the man who should have been talking to his priest but was babbling to his bartender instead. He was depressed, no doubt about it. But there was something else too, something else bothering him, something he couldn't get his hands on. I don't know what it was. I had this feeling, that's all. But that gets tricky, doesn't it — mental states."

"Mental breakdowns, you mean."

"I wouldn't say breakdown, no. Half the people I know are walking the edge one way or another. My barber thinks the trotting races are fixed, my dentist believes in UFOs. The neighbor to the north plays the flute, baroque, Sundays all day long. Works for the SEC. Jogging's quieter. Saw a woman this morning along the C and O canal carrying a papoose on her back. The White House has a resident astrologer." He said this without smiling. "So I wouldn't speculate on his mental condition, his or anyone else's. I'm too old. That's one thing I learned. Official secrets are always trivial compared to private ones."

"When did you last talk to him?"

"Last week. Monday or Tuesday. He brought me his curriculum vitae, the what-do-you-call-it for the business world out there —"

"Résumé?"

"Résumé, that's it. So it was all down there, everything he'd done. Russian he didn't claim, French and German he did. His German wasn't bad. Tricia's was better. He was with the U.S. Army in Berlin, 1946–47. Then the Mongolian. He doesn't speak it, never did, but he put it down. Very literal-minded, Frank is. Takes everything so bloody seriously. I told him it was silly, he wasn't applying for an Oxford fellowship or the roost over at Georgetown where all those morbid old intelligence buzzards end up, squabbling over the last bones of the carcass, fighting a war that ended years ago. The Cold War. Not a Soviet specialist, are you?"

"No, sir."

"Didn't think so. Don't have the look. *Pas trop de zèle*, Talleyrand used to tell young diplomats like you. That's been our problem for over thirty years. Anyway, I told him it was a different world out there. They don't care about some little in-house medal you've won for keeping your nose clean. How's your drink?"

"Fine."

"Good. Frank didn't understand that. He'd been too long inside the system, doesn't really understand it's only a game, that the scrip they hand out is redeemable only out there in their Never-Never Land. Like Oz, you see. Washington, too. The people in the street don't give a damn. Don't take it too seriously, the farce side of it. Most of it seems to be farce these days, beginning in the White House. Not a Reagan man, are you? How old are you?"

"Thirty-three."

"Thirty-three! My God." He laughed. "Thirty-three looking for fifty-nine. That's the eternal problem, isn't it? Your generation trying to understand ours, you youngsters trying to solve what we couldn't, put together the wreckage we left behind. We did, too, made a bloody mess of it."

Corkery heard the rattle of pans from the kitchen below. Water dripped from a gutter to his rear. "So he wasn't really ready for retirement," he said after a minute.

"Not really but that's not unusual. Most people aren't. I wasn't. After so many years in any executive bureaucracy, something happens. It's true of Chase Manhattan, true of politicians up on the Hill. I remember what Khrushchev once said, that a kind of death comes to politicians before they die. He'd been thrown out, retired, now they were giving him a little medal, something he could take to the grave with him. He died eight years later, forgotten except for his family and a few friends. He hadn't existed for almost a decade, not in any sense he understood. Tried to commit suicide at one point. We didn't read about it but it's true.

So that's what happens. After a time, people define themselves only in relationship to the system. When this is taken away, nothing replaces it. They die in a way, as if it were a matter of moral identity, which it isn't, of course. Just rubbish. Bureaucratic systems have no moral center, not the Hapsburgs', not ours, not theirs." Chambers seemed to lose breath for a moment. He got up and moved to the fireplace, searching the mantel for something.

"Power, you mean."

"No, not just power. No Washington politician or bureaucrat has any real power. What they have is privilege, the illusion of power. In time they mistake one for the other. I had it, Frank had it, you have it. You've been overseas?" He didn't find what he was searching for and sat down again.

Corkery nodded. "I was in Rome."

"Well, there you are. Everything done for you, everything arranged — cars, air tickets, medicals, schools for the kids, the PX, the liquor ration, the house, the furnishings, the servants. You see the same symptoms in elderly tourists traveling abroad, a kind of creeping infantilism that gets worse as the cruise gets longer. Gallop aboard like honeymooners, get taken off in a wheelchair. What about twenty-five, thirty years in harness? Well, look at Nixon. Watergate would never have happened if he'd walked to work like Harry Truman. Completely out of touch. Can Henry Kissinger drive a car? I asked myself that during the oil crisis in '74, waiting in the gas lines while the stretch limousines roared past. But that's not what we're talking about."

He remembered Dudley telling him he'd had lunch at the Metropolitan Club with Stuart Phillips, formerly chief of the European Division and now executive director of the new Atlantic Fund. He'd offered encouragement but no position; he needed fund-raisers, not staff. He'd also talked to Alan Whitmore, now of Whitmore and Kyle, a public relations firm representing a few Middle East sheikdoms. He'd had no luck there either. Chambers frowned, remembering something. "There was someone else he was going to look up. I can't remember who it was but he mentioned the name to me when we last talked. Who in the hell was it?"

"He was looking for a job? I had the feeling he was well fixed financially."

Chambers thought so. Tricia had left him fairly well off old New England money, but in trust. He was still troubled. "Who in the hell was it we talked about? Something odd about it, come to think of it." He got up from his chair, crossed to the dumbwaiter and shouted down the shaft. "Who was it Frank and I talked about last Tuesday?" He waited. "Dudley! Frank Dudley. Who was it I said Frank asked about?"

Corkery couldn't hear the reply. "No, that wasn't it." Chambers shut the door and returned to his chair. "Her memory's worse than mine but she won't admit it." He brought a cigar humidor from the table to his right, removed a cigar, sniffed it suspiciously, and put it back. "It'll come to me. What else?"

"I had the impression Dudley's last few assignments were something of a comedown."

"Pretty much. Congressional Relations, Public Affairs. Mucking the Augean stables. *Pis allez,* I told him. They're buggering you, time to get out, no regrets."

Raindrops rattled the windows again, blown from the overhanging trees by a sudden gust of wind. A police siren screamed through the streets. "How would you explain it, I mean the way his career fell off?"

"Hard to say. His age, for one thing. One of the last of the old guard. Wrong place, wrong time. There was a lot of gossip, none of it worth repeating. Some thought he'd lost his nerve, that he pussyfooted too much. That's rubbish too. You have to pussyfoot sometimes to find your way through the mine fields. That's what the bureaucracy is all about. People survive by rising to the same level of pussyfooting, all mediocrities."

"It goes with ambition, I suppose."

Chambers laughed. "You're too young to know that. That's a truth for your old age." A voice had lifted from the dumbwaiter shaft but Chambers ignored it. "There are dozens of reasons why someone might go off for a long weekend, go off in solitude that way, all of them personal. Christ knows I felt like it often enough. Who do you work for in CI, whose shop?"

"I've been working for Adrian Shaw."

Chambers made a sour face. "Abbott's monk, we used to call him. Don't get trapped out there, the way Shaw is. Abbott thinks he'll outlive us all. Maybe he will. In London, is he? Julian needs to get away, get away and stay away. He's pickled himself out there, all that dead air. An intellectual fossil. Like an iron lung, his office used to be. My wife says the air in his house in McLean is twenty years old. Don't stay, not if you can avoid it."

"I'm not there by choice."

"Good. Make the best of it, then get out, see the world, don't join the cause."

The voice again lifted from the dumbwaiter. Chambers got to his feet, carrying his empty glass, and picked up Corkery's, despite his protest.

"Relax. It's probably still raining out. We'll have one more drop. Where did you go to school?" He crossed to the dumbwaiter and tugged at the rope but the glasses remained in place. He leaned forward. "Never mind the horse is blind," he shouted down the shaft, "load the cart!"

A moment later the tray began to descend.

Among Dudley's acquaintances Corkery spoke with at Langley Monday morning, few were surprised, none was shocked, but then none supposed he might do something rash, not in the slightest. Langley was his club; he had no other. They were more concerned about the embarrassment he

56

might bring the Agency should word leak out. A few joked about that too. One remembered the case of Colonel Hespeth, an old OSS officer and later DDO's war-horse from the '50s who'd slipped away from his daughter's custody at the house on Q Street and had been found the following morning on the Potomac Club boat landing in bathrobe and carpet slippers, his fine white hair blowing in the wind, asking the keeper of sculls about the boat train to Warnemünde on the Baltic.

Corkery had been slow to see the point. His fingers raced backward through the pages of his tattered notebook: "Hespeth? Who the hell's Hespeth?" Someone he missed? "Retired, you say?"

"Oh, yes. Fifteen years now, I suppose. Like Dudley — in a manner of speaking."

No one of consequence, just another ghost from the past, a few wisps of fog still prowling the ramparts.

A middle-aged officer who'd worked with Dudley in Oslo puffed on his pipe and said he wouldn't be surprised if Dudley hadn't checked himself in at some private sanitorium, like Harvey Winshaw after Tehran, or taken sanctuary with old friends in the Vermont mountains, *vix medicatrix naturae*, as he'd done after a similar personal crisis twenty-five years earlier when he'd taken refuge in England after his wife's death. But he was wrong about that. Corkery had found the death report in central registry. Tricia Dudley was still very much alive when Dudley began his study at the

University of Leeds. She died alone at the Pied Bull Hotel in Kent in the English countryside: "death by misadventure," the coroner's report read. He wasn't sure what that meant either. Phil Chambers had identified the body.

A middle-aged doctor in the medical division told him he doubted Dudley had suffered a mental breakdown, but who could say? Compulsive wandering accompanied by amnesia often occurred among epileptics, called poriomania, "the wandering mania," by some neurologists, fugue by others, but Dudley wasn't an epileptic and had no history of wandering about in a trancelike state. Dudley's preretirement physical showed no abnormalities. His EEG hadn't hinted at any seizures in the temporal lobes where such disorders betrayed themselves.

"Fugue, you say?" Corkery said. "Like Colonel Hespeth, you mean. The fife-and-drum he was marching to?"

"Who?"

"Never mind. Thanks. I may be back."

Dudley's indecision about retirement wasn't the only thing that annoyed his associates. One of Dudley's colleagues in Public Affairs told Corkery the missing man had a habit of delaying the weekly staff meeting while he discussed the significance of the morning headlines, the latest cabinet shake-ups in Bonn or Paris, the new coalition in the Italian parliament, or the latest *Pravda* comment on the anarchy in Warsaw. It was as if he was still very much au courant and they weren't — true enough, since he seemed to know more than they did, his chief in Public Affairs in particular, a Reagan political appointee brought over from the Hill, and all of it very interesting, no doubt, but none of it relevant to their drudgery as stall muckers in the Augean stables of Public Affairs, as Chambers had said.

So there seemed to be little to the Dudley case as Langley knew it by Monday afternoon. The feeling was that Dudley would be found and brought back in a few days, dazed but contrite; retirement would be speeded up, medical leave compassionately arranged until the final day, the fait accompli subconsciously brought off by that anguished side to Dudley's nature that had finally humiliated the proud professional into hiding, unable to face up to his obsolescence. No one was alarmed about the security aspects of the case, no one so concerned he might assign Dudley a darker, more suspicious or treasonable motive; such wasn't his nature. Langley was his club as everyone said, he had no other. This was the final indignity, Corkery realized, the ultimate irony: Frank Dudley a failure even in failure.

No one, that is, except the seventh floor. But with Abbott still in London and an overburdened Shaw at the helm, communication between the seventh and second floors had been intermittent during the weekend, to say the least.

The detached brick house, recently renovated, sat at the bottom of New Hampshire Avenue in a neighborhood of new garden apartments, small new hotels, and federal and Victorian houses. The Kennedy Center and Watergate were a few blocks away. The bricks had been repointed, the brick walk was newly laid. A copper-roofed bay window and front steps had been added. Azaleas, rhododendrons, and Japanese holly, recently mulched, shivered in the cold wind.

The young woman who answered the door was slim, dark haired, and out of breath, wearing an odd mixture of harlequin clothing that suggested she'd been changing when he rang. Her face surprised him, one of those rare, lovely faces so perfect in its symmetry he was taken aback for a minute. A limp woolen herringbone jacket with the shoulder pads removed hung from her slight shoulders; below were gray knickers, dark blue hose, and black pumps. She'd just returned from shopping, looking for endive — unsuccessfully, as it turned out. Yes, she was Jessica Dudley. Who was he? The man who'd telephoned her an hour earlier? She invited him in. Strips of fiber paper lay on the newly refinished floor. The large front room was unfurnished, the bare white walls newly replastered. It was a gallery, she said, or soon would be, an art gallery belonging to her friend Margot. The living quarters were upstairs.

"It was supposed to open last month but the builders got terribly behind. Now she's planning for a January opening. I hope she makes it. She had a gallery over near Dupont Circle but lost her lease. It's the best thing that could have happened. I mean, the neighborhood there's so utterly down in the mouth. The Willis Gallery. You've heard of it, I'm sure."

He hadn't but said nothing as she led him into a second large room smelling of fresh paint, plaster, and floor lacquer, empty too except for two stainless steel chairs with black leather seats and a black leather ottoman on a strip of white carpet in the corner near the bay window. "This room is perfect for interrogations by the way, all blacks and whites, but the fumes give me a terrible headache. It's poly-something-or-other, probably carcinogenic. Please. Sit down. You came to talk about Daddy."

She sank down on the ottoman but immediately got up. "I'm looking for an ashtray." She disappeared through the door and returned with an ashtray, the herringbone jacket removed, wearing a long-sleeved blue woolen underwear shirt and red suspenders. She put the ashtray on the ottoman. Still standing, she gathered her dark hair from her neck and repinned it, elbows raised. "The wind's awful today, isn't it? Do you smoke? My cigarettes are upstairs. You don't look like a smoker."

Corkery brought out a package and gave her a cigarette. She sat down, inspected the filter and brand name, and sat forward to let him light it. Her face continued to intrigue him, a face whose perfection never ceased to astonish, that gave pleasure just by being near. "Corkery. That's an odd name. Should I know it?"

"I don't think so."

"Good. It's a relief not being expected to know everyone. I'm constantly being introduced to people I seem to be expected to know. You're with the Agency, you said on the phone. What did you want to talk about? Daddy?"

"Your father, yes. When you last saw him, what you talked about."

"Let's see. What day is today?"

"Monday."

"Oh, God, it is, isn't it? Has it been four days already? I'm still in another time zone. I got in from Paris last Thursday and we had lunch on Friday, I think it was. Yes, Friday. We had a so-so lunch, the food I mean, and a nice chat. We talked until two-thirty or so. He was fine. I have to tell you all this is unnecessary. There's a perfectly reasonable explanation for his going wherever he's gone. He's entitled to a little privacy from time to time, even though she might be upset. You've talked to her?"

"His wife, you mean."

"Louise. She's the most insecure woman I've ever met in my life. She's hopeless. She's the one who began all this, didn't she? Telephoning his office to say he hadn't come home, which is absurd. She's utterly vacant at times. Economists can be so quick in some ways and so dull in others. If they were really as clever as they pretend, we'd all be millionaires, wouldn't we? When she told me over the phone, I couldn't believe she could be so gauche. You're not from a diplomatic or

Agency family, are you?"

"No. Why?"

"If you were, you'd understand. But you've lived overseas, haven't you? Where did you go to school?"

"Penn."

"Where abroad?"

"Rome. Listen, Miss Dudley —"

"I love Rome but not Romans so much. The men, I mean. Even the street sweepers think they're Marcello Mastroianni. Whenever I get exhausted with the French, which doesn't happen very often, I go to Rome and get myself cured, *subito*. I usually don't last more than two days. Would you like a drink? Tea, coffee, a Bloody Mary?" She got up. "I think I would. Do you know Paris? Why don't you come with me? I hate talking through doors. It's right in here. What would you prefer? A Bloody Mary. I think that's what I want."

She opened a cupboard in the bright new kitchen, standing on her tiptoes, and brought down two glasses. "Georgetown is awful these days, isn't it? I wish the goddamn teenagers would stay in the suburbs or their high school gyms or wherever." She brought out the ice and turned back to the counter. "Margot and I were there Saturday night. I felt antiquated, like I'd lost my youth. My basic fear is that I'll wake up at forty and discover I have no talent. That absolutely paralyzes me. Doesn't it you? What's your talent, by the way? Don't answer. It's better not to know. I'll

63

find out in time. People with utterly no talent are always telling me about theirs. That's our age, isn't it, mediocrities talking as if they had talent. If they did, they'd talk it to death. Do you ever watch TV talk shows? Genius doesn't talk at all. Painters are supposed to be nonverbal. I'm not. That may be a clue. I hope not. I've never been to a shrink either. The vodka is in the cabinet to the right of the fridge. Oh, Christ, that's the phone. Stand perfectly still and maybe it'll go away."

She stood in place, unmoving, and so did Corkery, holding the bottle of vodka. The phone kept ringing. "It's not the doorbell," he said finally. "It may be for me."

"Would you mind answering? I met the world's most boring people at a cocktail Sunday night, people I hadn't seen in ages, and Margot was dumb enough to give them her number." He gave her the vodka and crossed to the ivory wall phone inside the door. "Just tell them I've gone to New York. No, Boston. I have an aunt in Boston. You're Margot's cousin from Evanston, just visiting. Would you mind? I'll just mix the drinks and pretend I'm not listening." She caught his arm. "And don't let them bully you, which is what happened to Margot."

Corkery answered. A voice with a prep school drawl asked for Jessica Dudley. Corkery told him she wasn't in. After a short exchange, the caller hung up.

"You did that beautifully." She handed him a Bloody Mary. "Who was it?"

"Someone named *Winston*."

"Winston? Oh, God, Winston. Winston McIntosh. Poor soul. He wasn't the one I expected. It doesn't matter. People are always out when he calls. He expects it. His father used to be one of you, by the way. He was with Daddy in Berlin, but Winston's definitely Washington law firm now, *tout à fait*. We were brats together overseas. Why don't we sit in here?" She sat down at the kitchen table but immediately got up again. "Let me get my cigarettes."

She disappeared up the rear staircase. When she returned she was wearing a white cable-knit sweater. "Now we can talk. I'm sure everything will be all right. Daddy simply isn't a person who'd walk out, never, not without telling me. He never does anything without a purpose, never —"

"His wife is worried that he might have had an accident," Corkery said. "That hasn't occurred to you?"

Not in the slightest. She had utter confidence in him. His work was often unpredictable but she'd grown up with it, unlike Louise, who knew nothing of overseas life. "But we're not overseas," Corkery reminded her. She ignored him. She'd loved growing up abroad, although she'd quite despised her English boarding school. She'd also gone to school in Rome and Geneva. She adored coming home for the Christmas holidays, in Oslo, Copenhagen, but Berlin especially. She was young then; Berlin was mysterious. She and Winston played pretend games on the trams and the S-bahn.

65

"I was very much an overseas brat, I suppose. I could never adjust to life here. How about you? You're well adjusted, I suppose. You look well adjusted. I never adjusted here, not really. It's all very sad. Most of my friends are gone now, married, scattered." She sighed. "Except for poor Winston. You know Winston, I'm sure. Everyone has a Winston in her address book. He's the kind who has to call everyone up at six o'clock on Saturday night to find out where the party is. If you have to call everyone up at six o'clock, the party's over, isn't it? I suppose that's why I don't live in the States. If I did, I'd know I was a failure."

"One thing I wanted to ask —"

"I'm talking too much, aren't I? I am. Don't be so polite. The same thing happened after my first exhibit in Paris. People said afterward I shouldn't give interviews. I really shouldn't. I ramble on too much. That's always a disadvantage, they say. In my case I don't think it matters, so much of what I say I don't really believe anyway. It's like trying on clothes, isn't it? Ideas, I mean. If something fits, you may wear it for a while but not permanently. Eventually, out it goes, fashionable or not, like last year's shoes. Don't you think so?"

"Ideas? Probably."

"It kept me in hot water in school, trying on ideas, I mean. In school, especially in England, where everyone had this idea she was being intellectually fitted for life, like a truss or a wooden leg. Maybe some of them were. I mean, Camus

66

was marvelous in his day, so was Eldridge Cleaver and radical chic, but who wants to be a Black Panther for life, certainly not Patty Hearst. That was my generation. Yours too, I suppose." She sighed again. "Do you find that, I mean a sense of not belonging anywhere?"

"I did after I left the navy. Not so much anymore. Listen, Miss Dudley —"

"I think it happens to diplomats' children, Agency children. Not so much military children, who were little bastards to begin with, but who wouldn't be, raised in a military stockade."

Corkery laughed. She gazed at him innocently.

"I'm perfectly serious."

"I know you are. It's the way you said it. Did your father tell you whether he had any plans for the weekend?"

"He said he'd be busy, that's all. I asked him to come to dinner Saturday night and he said he'd be busy, so I let it drop."

"His wife said they were going to the country for the weekend, the place out in Maryland."

She groaned. "Is that what she said? It's so desolate, like Outer Mongolia. He's not so keen on going out there, whatever she says. Buying it was her idea originally —"

"Where did you meet for lunch?" They met at the Cosmos Club. It was terribly warm and she was still groggy from jet lag. She would have preferred someplace else, it was so sexist. She hated men's clubs, but it was his treat and she was practically broke. They talked a little about his retirement, where he would go and what he would do. She didn't want him hanging around Washington. She wanted him to retire to France. While visiting friends, she'd found a villa in the south of France, one he might like. It was very much like the secluded farmhouse on the Spanish coast where they spent their holidays when she was a child. She'd gotten some photographs from the French agent and wanted to talk to him about it. It was near Entrecasteaux, fifty kilometers north of St. Tropez.

"That's beautiful country," Corkery said.

She seemed surprised. "You know it?"

"Not well, but I know it. I saw a weekend road race near there when I was in the navy. At Draguignan to the east. I also saw your painting of Les Baux. I liked it very much."

She made an unpleasant face. "That was done ages ago, very unoriginal, very derivative." A different tone had come into her voice. "Now I'm between styles, which means I'm not painting at all. But I don't want to talk about that."

"At lunch, he didn't say anything about where he was going for the weekend, just that he'd be busy. Did he have anything with him or in the car, an overnight bag, a briefcase?"

"Just an attaché case, crammed full, as usual."

"He opened it?"

She hesitated. "At the table, yes. Why?"

"That's what I'm asking. Why did he open it?"

Again she was slow to reply. "To write me a check. I might as well admit it. He opened it to

68

take out his checkbook. I was just about flat broke and wanted to borrow some money. That was another reason I'm here, why I came back from Paris. I've found an apartment in Paris I want to buy and need 600,000 francs. You won't breathe a word of this to Louise, will you? I'm supposed to be this fantastic success and I don't have two thousand dollars in the bank. I thought if I talked to him, maybe I could convince him."

"So you did. He wrote you a check."

"For a six-month option, that's all. He said we needed to talk about it some more." She sat back, shoulders slumping. "Selfish of me, wasn't it?"

"Was the check drawn on a Washington bank?"

"No, not Washington. A bank in Boston, the one that handles Mama's trust. Margot deposited it for me Saturday at her bank."

"What color was the attaché case?"

"What color? Brown, the same color it's always been. Why?"

"He has several attaché cases then."

"Not that I know of."

"The briefcase I found in his apartment on Saturday was black leather, the same one he carried to the office every morning."

"What difference does that make?"

"I don't know what difference it makes. That's what I'm trying to find out."

"It probably doesn't make any difference at all." The house was silent as she emptied her glass. "I think it's very nice of you taking such an interest in Daddy, even if it's all so unnecessary. Daddy is terribly dependable. If he had to go someplace over the weekend, it was just temporary, something he couldn't avoid. If I were worried I certainly wouldn't be sitting here like this." Conscious of Corkery's silence, she glanced at her watch and quickly got up. "My God, we've been talking for hours. I really have to get dressed now."

At the front door, Corkery said, "If you can think of anything, anything at all, just give me a call. I'll check back with you in a few days, keep you informed."

"Thanks, I will. But remember, *entre nous,* okay?"

She was looking beyond him at the street. Someone was getting out of a blue BMW at the curb. He heard her angry whisper, "Oh, Christ, it's Winston." The door closed softly and she was gone.

He drove down 23rd Street and onto the parkway, unable to make up his mind. He'd known young women like Jessica Dudley; in many ways she was like the daughter of the Deputy Chief of Mission in Rome he'd dated during his years there, at thirty-four still her parents' darling, not yet housebroken, and thoroughly screwed up. At one time or another she'd studied art history, medieval printmaking, marine archeology, industrial design, and city planning. At the time Corkery dated her she was working as a script girl for a bisexual Italian producer of film documentaries who'd become her father-confessor. Like Jessica Dudley she was the daughter of a certain class of Americans whom God, privilege, and the imperial dollar had sent overseas during an age that had all but vanished and would never come again. She'd attended boarding schools in Switzerland, France, and Italy with the sons of equally privileged English, French, Italians, Iranians, and Saudis; spoke French, Italian, and Spanish better than her parents; knew the night life, the plays, films, and artists better; knew the mountains and beaches better; was beautiful, bright, oververbalized, and dreamily creative with a sophistication that came easily and would last a lifetime, even when it had nothing more to say. She enjoyed her parents' privileges as if they were her own: the villas and apartments, the servants, chauffeurs, and diplomatic passports, the embassy car sent to the airport, the guest house at the beach or in the mountains. By fifteen she'd learned to talk like an adult, drink like an adult, be introduced at cocktail parties and formal dinners as if she were an adult, plan her holidays with her friends in Rome, Paris, or Geneva who were adults; but now she was thirty-four, a child no more, and lost somewhere in between. The party was over.

Apart from what Jessica had told him about a brown briefcase filled with official papers, what she'd given him was pretty thin stuff: a few adolescent confessions, some scatterbrained finishing school chatter, and a few throwaway lines, none very important. She wasn't worried her father might have had an accident, never mind no one had heard from him for three days, never mind either her mother's body had been found at the

Pied Bull Hotel in the English countryside after a two-day disappearance. Why had she bothered? A little flaky? Maybe that was what she'd intended. He wondered if she'd been putting him on.

A telephone message from Skaff was waiting on his desk at Langley. Dudley's station wagon had been found that afternoon in a parking lot at Dulles, parked since Friday. He called Skaff but he was out. He made two phone calls to Langley numbers he'd found in Dudley's desktop appointment book, but both men had left for the day. A little before seven he left his office and wandered down the corridor to Shaw's suite. His door was still closed. Miss Fogarty didn't look up from her keyboard. "He's meeting with someone from upstairs." Fortyish, reddish haired, and implacable, she disapproved of junior officers in general and Corkery in particular. In heavy traffic on the parkway one rainy morning approaching the CIA turnoff he'd cut in front of an old Ford Falcon with a rusting CD emblem. He hadn't known she was at the wheel. She'd slammed on the brakes, her $50 Thermos had rolled from the front seat and smashed to the floor, its glass liner breaking. She hadn't forgiven him.

He strolled out the door and down to the washroom. The half-lit corridors had the look of a museum after closing hours. The silence had begun to infiltrate the halls and ascend the stairwells; empty elevators arrived mysteriously at deserted stations, summoned by those already departed, filled with the smells of hand lotion and cigarette

72

smoke. The voices of the green-smocked cleanup crews echoed from the utility rooms. When he returned to the suite, Elinor Wynn's rust-colored raincoat was lying across the chair outside Shaw's office. The door was still closed. He went back down the inner corridor and stood in the doorway talking to Ernest Percival, who was frowning over his computer screen, working on a last-minute cable for Paris. A walk-in, a Romanian apparently, part of an airbus purchasing delegation. Max Underwood, the Latin American expert, was gone from his office next door. A powerfully built man sat waiting in the chair near the desk, a briefcase on his lap. His reddish-gray hair was so closely cut Corkery thought he might be military, someone from the Agency's Special Operations Group or maybe a military type from DIA, the Joint Chiefs, or the Navy Yard, bringing Max some new imagery from the satellite watch group. The shoulders bulged in the tight blue suit like sand in burlap; in his lapel was the Vietnam service bar. The man smiled and stood up. "Don't think we've met. Earl Huggins. I'm new aboard." A hard cold hand gripped Corkery's, as thickly hided as one of his grandfather's Christmas hams. The smile was that of a man for whom nothing was spontaneous; he might have been cracking walnuts with his teeth.

Corkery turned back to his own office. Elinor Wynn hurried by. He caught up with her just outside her office door. "What's Shaw got going?"

"Don't you know? He's made a total mess of it as far as I'm concerned." She slung her coat over the chair in front of her desk, pulled off her beret angrily, and took a notepad from her leather dispatch case.

"Mess of what?"

"Everything, dear boy. They're furious upstairs. They didn't get the memo about Frank Dudley until this morning after staff meeting."

"What difference does that make?"

"All the difference. As it happens, Dudley had a four o'clock appointment on the seventh floor on Friday afternoon. It was canceled at the last minute and postponed until this week. Now they're furious because no one saw Shaw's memo reporting him missing until this morning."

"Who was the appointment with?"

"The number two. Very hush-hush it seems. No one was told about it." She rolled a piece of paper into the carriage and began to type. "Sorry, but I have to get something out."

"What did Dudley want to talk about?"

"That's the mystery. You know how we all adore mysteries. No one seems to know except the principals, who aren't talking. Something internal, a few in-house skeletons, I suspect. With Dudley in limbo these past years, what else could it be? Julian will be livid, of course. Something happens under our very noses and we're the last to know."

"You know we found his car."

"We? *We?* And what else have we been doing all afternoon?"

"Okay, the FBI. Someone told me Dudley used

to work here in CI. Do you know anything about that?"

"Please! I have to get this out. To add insult to injury, we now have this dreadful Huggins creature prowling about."

Corkery turned in the doorway. "Who is he?"

"Someone who finds people."

"What kind of people?"

"Riffraff, what else? Ugly people." She banged angrily on a few keys and looked at her notepad. "Would you please go away."

Corkery found Shaw's door half open and Shaw alone in his office, which still smelled of his departed visitor's cigar smoke. Since Shaw didn't permit staff to smoke in his office, his visitor was probably down from the seventh floor.

"I was about to call you," he said wearily, rising from his chair to walk around his desk and sink down in one of the brown leather armchairs in front. "The seventh floor is a little agitated. They didn't get Vitale's memo until this morning."

"So Elinor said. What was Dudley's appointment about?"

"No one seems to know. If they do, they're not willing to say. I've just got their memo. Protesting his retirement, I suppose, although they believe otherwise. Someone evidently made a call on Dudley's behalf, called the deputy and asked that he see him. One of Dudley's well-connected friends in the retirement community, they recall. Dudley always had a cavalier way of using people. There's some confusion as to who it was. Phil

Chambers may know. I've put in a call to him. The only thing the seventh floor is willing to tell us is that Dudley wanted to discuss a subject of the utmost sensitivity, quote unquote." He gazed disagreeably at the paper in his hand. "The appointment was originally scheduled for Friday afternoon but at the last minute had to be postponed. It was to be rescheduled this week. Now, of course, Dudley's gone. The appointment wasn't listed on the seventh-floor schedule. Dudley insisted it not be." He paused, lifting his eyes. "That's an admirable touch, isn't it? Also patently transparent. If someone about to be forcibly retired wishes an audience on high, what better way to tempt their curiosity —"

"He wasn't forcibly retired."

"Let's not disagree. Perhaps he wasn't but we don't really know, do we? Retirements are as inevitable as the tides, but in some cases even more so. The secretary reported that when Dudley arrived Friday afternoon, he had a package in his briefcase. A package?" He turned to the second page. "Here it is. The package was a manila envelope — I'd hardly call that a package, but then secretaries are merely paid to type, aren't they? It contained quite a few documents. Xeroxed, apparently. While Dudley waited, he sorted through them. He seemed agitated, he seemed tense. Does she mean nervous? Every time someone happened by he returned the papers to his envelope. *Happened by*? How in God's name do you happen by in the director's suite? Returned them ostentatiously, it seems — my word, not hers. She continues to insist on nervous. Yes, there it is, nervously, quote unquote. The feminine touch. Evidently she was sympathetic. She asked if he would like coffee or tea. He declined. Women always found Dudley sympathetic. She assumed the documents in the package dealt with the subject he'd come to discuss. Pure speculation on her part."

"She didn't see them."

"She saw them. You mean did she examine them. No." He gave Corkery the smile of a man who thrived on small victories. He often played the same fussy game in reviewing Corkery's drafts, batting his words back at him like shuttlecocks, his final volley an overhead smash delivered with the full weight of an abridged *Oxford English Dictionary* he kept within reach behind his desk, splintering Corkery's verbs and adverbs into their constituent Latin molecules.

"She claims she saw the security classifications. Top Secret Umbra, among others. It would be, wouldn't it? At four fifty-five she told Dudley the appointment had to be postponed and she'd inform him when it was to be rescheduled. He left. At five thirty-five she called downstairs to tell him it would be rescheduled this week. Dudley had gone. No one has seen him since."

Shaw let the memo drop to his lap and drew a handkerchief from his pocket.

"What color was his briefcase?"

Shaw gazed at him over his handkerchief. "What

color? Who in God's name knows what color? Who could possibly care?"

"Was it brown or black?"

"I haven't the slightest idea. Nor do I know what color his tie, his shirt, or his shoes. Nor do I —"

"The briefcase I found in his apartment was black, the same one he carried to his office every day. On Friday afternoon he was carrying a brown dispatch case filled with official documents. That's missing too. He didn't take a suitcase with him that night, no clothes except what was on his back, just a briefcase filled with official papers."

Shaw bent to search through the pages. He paused, traced a paragraph with his finger, and nodded. "Brown. It was brown, she says. I don't know why she would have noticed —"

"The feminine touch."

Shaw looked up for a long perilous moment but decided to let it pass. "Unfortunately, they link the two on the seventh floor, the appointment followed by his disappearance. Now the FBI has found his car. His passport is missing. He was supposed to turn in his official passport after a trip to London last spring but didn't. It's all suspiciously intriguing, isn't it, but then Dudley always had a bit of the theater in him. God knows what will happen when the press gets hold of it." He looked at Corkery accusingly. "You haven't had any inquiries from the press, have you?"

"No, sir. None —"

"Good." He picked up the memo and studied

it silently for a minute. "Possibly we could have handled it differently and avoided all this. That's what Abbott will say. Not that the results would have been any different, not in the slightest. But misplacing a memo for forty-eight hours, that's absolutely disgraceful. Security thought we were handling it, but I distinctly remember telling Vitale to send his memo upstairs, that it was more a Security than a CI matter. We agreed about that, remember?"

"Oh, hell, yes. Absolutely."

Corkery didn't remember at all, of course. What he remembered was that Shaw had been undecided about Vitale's memo as late as Monday morning, when he'd again raised it with him, but he was enjoying rare privileges that evening and sharing Shaw's intimacy was one of them. It was twenty after seven. The windows were dark. At this hour Shaw would normally be in Abbott's office, Jay Fellows, the number two deputy also there; the inner sanctum, the *Sanctum Sanctorum*, the three of them discussing Moscow, Vienna, or East Berlin, updating Leningrad's RMD, or the hard targets for some Soviet Foreign Ministry asset just returned from Algiers or Damascus. For a moment, he imagined he'd penetrated the citadel, but at that moment the door opened and Elinor Wynn came bustling in. She glanced at him angrily as she marched to Shaw's side and handed him a draft cable. He looked at it over Shaw's shoulder, a presumption Shaw didn't notice as he tracked the sentences down the page with his pencil. It was an immediate circular instruction to the field describing Dudley's disappearance. He made no corrections and offered no suggestions, accepting the draft as it was, all of which told Corkery how crushing the defeat he'd suffered that day.

"I suppose this will do," he said, rising to limp toward the door. He suffered from sciatica, most noticeable after he'd been too long in his chair or was feeling sorry for himself.

Elinor Wynn glanced at him contemptuously from behind and then at Corkery. "I cleared it for you, since you seem to be action officer on this mess. Pro forma, anyway. I left a copy on your desk."

"Thanks, honey. I'll do my best."

Outside Shaw paused at his secretary's desk and asked her to phone upstairs and tell them they were on their way. Phil Chambers was on the phone. Shaw took the call at her desk, asked a few questions, and nodded in silence, watching the clock on the far wall. He put the phone down and moved on. Chambers had made no telephone call to the seventh floor on Dudley's behalf and didn't know who did. At the door Shaw turned, discovered the memo in his hand, and thrust it at Corkery. "Put this back on my desk, will you?"

"What is it?" Elinor asked, still angry.

"The memo from upstairs the special assistant brought down. You have a copy. Shall we?"

They went out the door.

As he returned to Shaw's office, Corkery looked at the paragraphs Shaw had quoted. Attached to the memo was the seventh-floor secretary's statement but beneath it was a note typed out on Elinor's typewriter with its small pica:

Subject: The Dudley Disappearance

At 12:30 during yr absence over lunch I spoke to Julian in London on the green phone. He is concerned about the Erika Kissling case but doesn't intend to fly to Bonn. He is very upset about the 7th floor's interest in the Dudley imbroglio which he believes designed to embarrass him and CI in particular. He asks that we
— identify whom Dudley has been in contact with in the intel community, retired or otherwise, and why;
— determine if he has had any recent discussions on the Hill, with congressional staffers in particular;
— identify whom he has been in touch with abroad — cables, phone calls, etc. — availing ourselves of NSA Elint Material to that end, i.e., a Special Watch;
— keep Security Div and FBI intrusion to an absolute and pro forma minimum;
— assemble examples of Dudley's recent irregularities or aberrations, i.e., has he sought medical help?

Corkery looked up to discover Miss Fogarty watching him suspiciously from the doorway. He dropped the memo on Dudley's desk and left. Pure CI surrealism, he decided: none of it made any sense.

The blustery wind jarred the Mustang and whistled through the seams in the canvas top as Corkery crawled forward through the morning traffic along Massachusetts Avenue near Dupont Circle. At corners pedestrians with wind-lashed overcoats and hands at their hat brims waited for the lights to change, backs to the wind. He turned in an alley on P Street and parked in a loading zone behind the hotel, ignoring the sign. Skaff was waiting on the loading dock, standing motionless in the wind, his hands in the pockets of his gray topcoat. His black Plymouth stood next to a police car at the end of the dock. A hotel foreman in a brown smock shouted at Corkery from the back of a refrigerator truck and moved to the top of the steps. "You can't park there."

"Who the hell says? It's a bust. Where's the freight elevator?"

"Over there. You kidding me?"

"He's with me," Skaff said mildly, moving forward from the doorway. "We won't be long."

The room was on the third floor. A linen cart sat on a strip of blue carpet outside the door. Inspector Tyrone was inside talking to a plainclothesman and a district policeman. He turned as they came in and nodded to Skaff and then Corkery.

"Just talking about you, George. Found something." He crossed the room, lifted a briefcase from the dresser, and put it on one of the two double beds. The other bed was still unmade. "His name's Ulrich, all right, one name is, anyway. That's how he registered downstairs. Left his room Friday. No one's seen him since. Was supposed to check out yesterday."

"Canadian?" Skaff looked at the suitcase opened on the bed. There was an odor in the room Corkery couldn't identify.

"Canadian. Some of him was anyway." Tyrone sat down on the bed and opened the briefcase. "Remember the key in the tobacco tin, the magnetized one? Fits this briefcase here." He emptied the contents on the bed. There were three sets of specifications for development projects in Iraq, Pakistan, and Indonesia, a paperback tourist guide to Montreal, and a manila envelope containing two stamp albums and an airline ticket. Corkery picked up a gray-jacketed set of specifications, issued by the International Bank for Development in Washington for a microwave network in Iraq, scheduled for tender in sixty days. The other two projects were for communications facilities to be bid in February. Skaff opened the stamp books. "Engineer, stamp dealer, or what?" Corkery picked up the airline ticket, an Air Canada flight from Dulles to Montreal.

"That's not all," Tyrone said. "What was it you said the other morning, that it must be dope or pot?" He got up and beckoned to the young de-

83

tective who was leaning against the door, arms folded. "Caruthers here worked narcotics last year, third district over in Shaw. Show them, why don't you." The detective moved to the bed, took a penknife from his pocket, turned the briefcase with the handle facing him, and pulled away the inner lining. Working from the inside, he unfastened the two screws that held the leather handle in place. "One case he worked was two Latin American brothers," Tyrone said. "Had them a used-car lot over in Arlington, Mercedes mostly, running them secondhand up from Florida. Did a lot of cruising in D.C., Shaw District. Come to find out one brother took him a lot of vacations. Traveled light all the way to Bermuda for a Saturday night in the sun. Carried a briefcase like this here. Toted eighty pounds easy, coke in, cash out. Caught him over at BWI airport, carrying six hundred grand on him, wasn't it?"

"Four hundred," Caruthers said. The two screws removed, he inserted a knife blade in the upper lining. After a few seconds' probing, he tripped the spring and lifted away the false bottom.

"Neat as pie," Tyrone said. "If it wasn't coke, it was green stuff, isn't that what you said?" He removed the two passports from the false bottom and handed them to Skaff. "Seems like he was worried about his passports, hiding them like that. Must have been a check kiter. Two names, same face."

One was a Canadian passport issued in Ottawa

two years earlier to a Hans David Kruger; the second was a West German passport issued in Bonn to Otto D. Rauchfuss.

"I thought you said his name was Ulrich," Skaff said.

"That's the name registered downstairs, the name on the two driver's licenses. We didn't find any passport on him, nothing in his suitcase either."

"So which is he?" Skaff said, holding up the two passports and looking from one photograph to the other. "Ulrich, Kruger, or Rauchfuss?"

"The same man, that's all I know. The body out there in the morgue no one's claimed."

Corkery said, "The airline ticket's in Ulrich's name." Skaff took the ticket and passed him the two passports. In the Canadian passport, Kruger's face was mustached and the dark hair was cut short, the face somber, rather dull, eyes glazed against the strobe lights, as if whatever life quickened the muscles of the face had sounded from its surface the moment the shutter had clicked the way a trout left the surface of a pool when the first twig broke. In the German passport Otto Rauchfuss's hair wasn't gray but dark brown, also longer. He was smiling, a gap-toothed smile, the eyes whimsical under the shaggy brows, as if he'd just shared a joke with the photographer.

"They're all of the same man," Corkery said. "But I think this photograph in the German passport is the most recent. Otto Rauchfuss."

"How come?"

85

"The Canadian passport photo is of a younger man."

"You think so?" Skaff wasn't sure.

"Carrying some money with him too, I'd say," Tyrone said, lifting a few $100-bill money wrappers from the bed cover. "Any of all this got to do with the man you're looking for?"

"Not sure yet," Skaff said. "What's that smell?"

"The bathroom, I think," Corkery said. Skaff followed him through the door. The astringent smell was most noticeable over the washbasin; on the drain was a residue of yellow liquid and a dried scum of lather, hair, and a black pepper of stubble particles.

"Do you know what the smell is?" Corkery asked. Tyrone had noticed it too. Skaff said he would get a lab crew in. "Another thing. The maid hasn't been in since Friday. That's odd."

"Friday morning he gave the cleanup maid twenty dollars and told her not to bother. You still haven't told me who you're looking for."

"I put the name in this morning," Skaff said. "His name's Frank Dudley. I don't think there's any connection but I don't know. No one's seen him since last Friday afternoon."

The phone rang and Caruthers took it. Corkery looked in the closet where a single suit hung, a dark-gray wool suit with a vest. Hanging under it was a white shirt, recently worn, and a wrinkled maroon tie. The inside label in the jacket was from a Swiss clothier with outlets in Bern and Geneva. The pockets were empty. The shirt was French, like the shirts in the suitcase on the bed.

A desk clerk arrived from downstairs, a small, dapper Latin American, dark skinned, dark haired, and impeccably groomed but in agony, convinced he'd been summoned to be asked about his immigration status. He had been on duty the Thursday afternoon Ulrich registered. The scented white handkerchief never left his hand, first at his forehead, then at his neck and temples, then back to his forehead. He immediately showed Tyrone his green card. Tyrone told him his green card didn't interest him. Finally assured he wasn't being questioned about his immigration status or that of his wife, nephews, maids, cooks, bottle washers, and scullery help downstairs, he tried to be helpful but wasn't. The Canadian passport photograph Tyrone showed him meant nothing; the West German passport confused him even more. Tyrone sent him away. From the cashier's office they learned Ulrich had made no phone calls from the hotel, had ordered no room service, no drinks from the bar, and taken no meals there.

"I'll get a lab crew in, run a name check," Skaff said as they went down in the elevator. "Then talk to the Canadians and West Germans here, find out about the passports. You'd better stay out of it for the time being. Langley too. We don't want to jump the gun, get the press all heated up." He offered Corkery a stick of gum.

"No thanks. Thursday night Dudley got a phone call. That was the night Ulrich checked in here. Louise Dudley took the call, a stranger calling from downtown. She thought he was German." They left the elevator and went down a service corridor. Two hotel electricians in white coveralls stood aside to let them pass. Corkery pushed through the metal-clad swinging doors to the loading dock. "Dudley said the telephone call came from a hotel room. She thought it came from a phone booth. All Dudley said was he was a stranger who didn't know Washington and didn't trust taxis. He drove to meet him. He didn't mention it the next morning."

Skaff frowned and put on his queer little gray hat with a red feather in the band. "German?"

"German. Dudley disappears the next day. Saturday morning she reports him missing; Sunday morning we find a body, lying there maybe since Friday night. Ulrich, Kruger, Rauchfuss, whoever. Add it all up. Maybe he's why Dudley disappeared."

"You think so?" Skaff frowned, lips pursed, shoulders hunched against the wind. "Vitale didn't mention any telephone call, not in the memo I saw. You sure?"

"I'm sure. Who's Vitale? Some night some GSO paint crew is going to repaint his office door and he won't be able to find that either."

"You told your people about this?"

"Not yet. I want to run a couple of tracers first. Think about it. Let me know what you get from the name checks and lab report. Jesus Christ! Hey! Hey, wait!"

A black policeman wearing an orange-and-white

traffic vest was leaning over the windshield of Corkery's Mustang, clamping a pink ticket under the wiper. Skaff watched from the loading dock as Corkery jogged across the loading zone. The loading dock supervisor was watching too. The two stood arguing and after a few minutes the policeman removed the ticket, laughed, gave a wave of his gloved hand, and went on down the alley, shaking his head. Skaff was impressed. Corkery was a quick study all right. Maybe too quick. He wondered what Langley's young apprentice had told him.

2

PROWLING THE RUINS

The caravelle climbed from Heathrow and veered toward the channel. Head turned, he watched the crater of light from London burn through the autumn twilight until the glow dimmed and he could no longer find it at all. Departures filled him with sadness, but not this one; he had spent two days at a faded little hotel in Lambeth, trying to appear inconspicuous. As he leaned forward to look down, the earth's weight moved massively against him and he sank back. His body felt terribly heavy. The shriek of the engines subsided as the turbines throbbed toward cruising speed and a crescent of moon lifted over the port wing. Through a break in the clouds he saw the long hairline wrinkles on the moonlit channel below. A few yellow lights drifted here and there, fishing boats and trawlers out from the coast. Searching the darkness above the dusk-entangled earth, he discovered a night filled with stars. Against the galaxies the plane had

90

no motion at all, a sudden stillness he found reassuring, and he was again grateful for the miracle of who he was, for the mystery that was taking place: a continent to be explored, a new beginning after all these years.

"Paris?" the French stewardess asked.

"Paris." He turned toward her with a tourist's guilty smile and asked for a whiskey. An attractive young woman, she smelled of saffron. The seats next to him were empty. The cabin lights glowing through the darkness reminded him of another flight, another time. A child was sleeping on the seat across the aisle, sprawled like a rag doll under a pale blue blanket. In the seat pouch in front of him were copies of the *Financial Times* and an airmail edition of *The Economist*. A businessman's flight from Paris to London that afternoon, he supposed. He reached forward to lift *The Economist* from the pouch, glanced at the index, and opened to the middle pages. A massacre in El Salvador; a coup in Ghana; a bomb in a Frankfurt bistro. Unable to concentrate, he replaced the magazine and sat back. In transit he preferred silence and self-absorption. Passing high over the earth at six hundred knots was quite enough. What was one to make of the disorders far below, the ugly irrationalities of men in crisis? At 27,000 feet, these were only surface vibrations, like the rattle of crockery from the galley behind him. The French had a name for it he recalled, but he couldn't remember the idiom. Too long on the shelf, he supposed.

It was chilly in Paris. A light rain was falling, drifting in shafts as white as snow in the headlights of the bus ferrying passengers across the tarmac toward the fog lights of the terminal. Passport control was crowded. Emigrés in winter woolens were queued at the windows. Beyond the glass exit doors a mob of relatives and friends waited, crowding the passageway. French customs officials kept the queues in order. In front of him an old man and woman carrying an oilskin portmanteau looked about with bewilderment. The younger couples smiled bravely; their round-faced children looked about in bewilderment at the drenching lights of the terminal, at the soundless tears and joy of their relatives waiting beyond the glass doors, at the shriek of turbines from the darkness outside where red, blue, and yellow parabolas described the ascent and fall of aircraft, swearing the windows like thrown flares. He wasn't sure of the emigrés' nationality. Not Russian; Romanians possibly.

"Juden," said the French passport clerk as he opened his U.S. passport. He stamped it with the entrance cachet without looking up. "Juden," he repeated.

German? Why German? he wondered, returning the passport to his attaché case. At the glass doors he remembered there would be no car waiting, no escort officer from the Paris station, no confidential briefcases to bother about. He was alone. Brought back to earth, his weight returned by the pavement under his feet, he found a taxi, still euphoric, forgetting to ask the fare.

The small hotel off Rue des Saints-Pères on the Left Bank wasn't as he remembered. Dim and musty, it smelled of old bed linen. The foyer chairs were shabby, like the Persian runners whose motif had sunk into obscurity. In a dark corner a soundless black-and-white television set was turned on. Facing it were three empty velveteen armchairs with soiled antimacassars. On the fourth a white cat lay sleeping. On the rug below were a pair of felt slippers and a discarded magazine. The small bar and restaurant was closed. Four damp-haired Swedish schoolteachers stood at the reception desk where an Algerian clerk was rearranging their rooms to bring them closer together. His room, like theirs, was on the third floor. His only luggage was his brown attaché case. The rest had been delayed in transit but would arrive tomorrow, he told the desk clerk, who took no notice. He asked about messages; a businessman would always ask about messages. The desk clerk searched the few envelopes under his blotter and shrugged. No messages.

Leaning forward, he asked him to look again.

"Schofield," he repeated politely, spelling his name. Again the desk clerk searched through the envelopes. Not a friendly face, this Algerian's, but rather coarse, like a Penobscot Indian. He prided himself on his ability to inspire confidence. It may have been his appearance, something in his bearing that invited trust, someone you might ask to watch a piece of luggage in a terminal ticket line, as a

Scottish woman had done at Heathrow, someone to hold a place in a theater queue, to placate an embittered secretary, to resolve an acrimonious interdepartmental quarrel. It wasn't that he was cheerfully avuncular; he was too tall, too slim, someone who stood apart from the crowd, someone dependable, or so he saw himself: someone to inspire loyalty.

There were no messages. He boarded the small cage lift on the landing and ascended to the third floor. Under the lamp at the small desk inside, he counted out the French franc notes he'd brought with him and discovered he was woefully short. He would have liked to walk about a bit, perhaps stroll along the Seine, but he had left his umbrella behind and had no change of clothes. Tomorrow would be a long day, perhaps another departure, another flight, but not in wet shoes and a damp suit. He sat at the desk, writing in his journal as the rain splashed against the gabled dormer. He sat for almost an hour and filled five pages. His own prose often gave him pleasure, although others found it gnomic. He was rather like an actor, writing his own parts. Curious, forgotten details had returned: he recalled the East German watchtower radar that could pick up movements up to 8,000 yards and wondered if this was still so. If something went amok, one could go south toward Witzenhausen on the border between Saxony and Hesse. Did the West Germans still have their Bundegrenzschultze flotilla on the Baltic? But this assumed Andreyev was in East Germany. He thought it unlikely. If in East Germany, he was most certainly in prison.

Startled by a sudden sound in the narrow street below, he lifted his head, forgetting where he was. Not Berlin, no. A hotel in Chelsea, in Barcelona? At the Hotel Astoria? Which Astoria? He saw the franc notes lying under the cone of lamplight, the ticket envelopes, the packet of English cigarettes. He was in Paris but no longer a tourist. Still anxious, he waited for another sound to follow. The telephone; he has been waiting for the telephone to ring. He disliked telephones. Should he call now or wait until morning? Otto's flight was scheduled to arrive at eight-twenty GMT. Wait until morning? Yes, morning would be better. Very tricky, all of it, but then beginnings always were. They'd always lived with the improbable but over time the improbable took on substance, gathered weight and body, accumulated bone and flesh: meetings would be convened, task forces assembled, technicians assigned. In 1954 who would have dreamed of the technological miracle of the KH-11 reconnaissance satellite that would evolve from their search for a crude platform in space? How many of these impossible initiatives bore his own initials there in the bottom left-hand corner when he'd been in the DCI's office and had helped staff them out?

He put his attaché case on the bed and sat alongside, putting his documents in order. A very substantial body of evidence, no doubt about it. He locked them away and slid the attaché case beneath the bed. He washed in the bathroom, drank a glass of water, and stood at the window smoking a cigarette, listening to the murmur of Swedish voices next door as the schoolteachers planned their morning excursion.

He remembered the French expression then, the idiom he'd been searching for on the plane: *"l'histoire événementielle,"* the history of surface vibrations. That had been the history of their times, the history he'd been most sensitive to as others went their blind, destructive way.

He had to sleep in his underwear, which he disliked. Despite his exhaustion, he slept badly, a sure sign. Dawn came and he stirred from bed, pulled on his Burberry, and padded to the window. He couldn't read his wristwatch. The numbers had long ago lost their luminosity in the leeching offices at Langley. The night was absolute in the street below, but after a moment's concentration he detected a paler fog prowling the distant street corner. Dawn was coming, he thought gratefully, searching his pockets for a cigarette. His flannel bathrobe at home had neither body nor shape. On the lapels were a burr of muffin cinders, a few golden marmalade smears; in the pockets were rough-cut tobacco crumbs, brittle aspirin fragments from a March bout with influenza in Washington, a few wooden matches left from the Christmas fire the previous December. These pockets were cold to his hands. It wasn't his bathrobe at all. He was awake now. He turned on the lamp and discovered it was two-thirty, a terrible hour, the hour you woke to your own demons, terrified and alone. He returned to bed.

At seven he got up, still exhausted, shaved, dressed, and went downstairs to order breakfast. The smell of coffee and toasting buns hung in the stairwell. Two Swedish schoolteachers sat in the tiny dining room across the foyer from the front desk, drinking coffee and sharing a green-jacketed Michelin guide. The Algerian desk clerk had been replaced by a middle-aged Frenchman who told him room service wasn't available. He had no choice but to take his breakfast in the low-ceilinged dining room. The tables were crowded together, allowing little passage between chairs. It was much too bright. Unaccustomed to eating breakfast with strangers, he was uncomfortable. He'd brought no newspaper, no magazine, no guidebook. He drank his coffee, ate half of his croissant, and escaped upstairs. The two Swedish schoolteachers, now joined by a third, looked after him curiously. So did the plump African woman from Mali who was bringing him more marmalade and coffee. A curious man, they decided, intent on being disagreeable.

A fine rain hung in the streets and obscured the rooftops. The damnable rain. He walked purposefully, shoulders back, tall and erect in his raincoat, although he had no immediate destination. The streets were coming to life. Crossing a busy boulevard along Rue du Bac, he caught sight of himself approaching a Banque de Lyon window — the tall stalking stride, the crushed hat, the familiar Burberry. What would they think? He remembered Forster from the Paris station. He'd had drinks with him in his flat on Rue du Bac during his last trip to Paris from Langley. Was the station still renting the flat? What would they think, seeing him there in full daylight, a forlorn tourist lost between planes? Washington was impossible, he'd told Otto. Paris too? Glancing up, he found he was moving toward the Quai d'Orsay and turned away. Why had he remembered Forster, that foolish man? Glanville was station chief now, Glanville with his flaxen hair and his pale Nordic eyes. He saw them in their bright offices, heard the rustle of shared secrets, smelled the ink of the teletype machines, the solvent of the duplicate copies. Coffee was nearby. Glanville's secretary would be reviewing his appointment book. In Rome, London, Berlin, and Bonn, the same ritual: the overnight cables would be assembled, the station officers would be at their desks in their little vaulted rooms, reading each other's mail like wicked schoolboys back from the weekend, snickering over their seductions.

At a telephone booth in the rear of a tobacco shop, he dialed Otto Rauchfuss's office number. There was no answer. He hung up and dialed again. Still no answer. Too early, he told himself. In a men's shop that had just opened he bought an ugly gray felt hat and a cheap plastic raincoat of the sort George Tobey once wore — George Tobey, that impossible man. An hour later he returned to his hotel.

"I was expecting a call about my lost luggage." He spelled his name for the desk clerk. There were no telephone messages. "I'd like to extend my stay," he added. He'd booked in for three days.

"Pas possible."

"It's really not possible," a man named Jensen from personnel had told him. "You've had your day. Sooner or later the time comes for all of us. It's time now, time to move along." A plump balding man in a wash-and-wear suit, he smelled of liquid soap from a Langley washroom dispenser. He was part of the new breed, a colorless little man with an accounting degree recruited from some prairie college. He remembered him as a young administrative assistant helping with travel vouchers.

"Why isn't it possible?"

Impossible because the hotel was booked up. He was prepared to argue but heard two English voices approaching from the lift. Parked on the narrow street outside was a dark green Land Rover with yellow UK plates. Secretly inquisitive, the British, a society riddled by eavesdroppers and informers. The costs of an ossified class structure, Phil Chambers had told him in Berlin, where in addition to everything else they'd had to deal with the malice of the British station.

He walked some more that day, along the Seine and up through Les Halles. Grayness everywhere, in the overcast sky, on the pavement, in the damp streets. He avoided Rue de Rivoli, where he might be too conspicuous. Again he telephoned Otto

Rauchfuss but again there was no answer. He felt a moment of panic. Had he made a mistake? He found himself scouting for hotels.

In the early afternoon he bought an *International Herald Tribune* and searched its pages in a nearby restaurant. The floor was wet; only a few tables were occupied. He found nothing of interest in the paper; the news from the continent only reminded him of his own desolate isolation. What retirement would be like, he supposed, looking out at the gray street. Phil Chambers was little more than a ghost now, prowling his Georgetown house, pretending fulfillment in the imaginary companionship of his imaginary book. He'd seen through his pretense, knew his secret misery as well as Eva Chambers did. The price they all would pay sooner or later. How would one escape that? The rain began to fall more heavily, chasing pedestrians to cover. He sat at his table and watched.

In midafternoon he ventured across the Place de la Concorde and continued west. On a narrow street north of Rue Saint Honoré he passed a small cinema. The display board showed scenes from an old French movie, one he vaguely remembered from thirty years earlier. Tired of wandering, he bought a ticket and went in. The theater held only a few afternoon customers and had the close, unwholesome smell of a vagabonds' doss house. He sat alone in an empty row, puzzling over the rural colloquialisms of a remote French village. Brittany, it seemed. Fatigue and anxiety had weakened him and now sleep claimed him. He awoke unsure of where he was. On the screen Ginger Rogers and Fred Astaire were dancing cheek to cheek. He sat up and looked about. A trick of memory? No, he was in Paris, watching a French-edited review of the American musical comedy. Top-hatted dancers in black stockings and silver-sequined tights descended a long spiral ramp from a towering black marble ziggurat erected against the shimmering zodiac of a Hollywood sound stage. The camera lifted, the dancers multiplied, thousands it seemed, moving down the ramp to the music of Irving Berlin. He remembered the cinema on Rheinstrasse in Berlin where he and Nina von Winterfeldt escaped the cold. Very much like this one, that theater; as warm as a winter fireside. Some day when the past was disinterred, this little scrap of celluloid, like a Babylonian ziggurat, would survive as nothing else, the papyrus and cuneiform of a civilization that had once flourished so extravagantly between the two oceans.

As he stood outside in the rain, recovering his directions, a stranger in a strange city, his depression returned. Dark shapes moved by, strange faces, wrapped in their own thoughts. A film noir cityscape, Berlin again during the brutal winter of 1946–47, the coldest in human memory, a city in rubble, a city no longer, Germany a nation no more. He sometimes escaped its desolation on Sundays to ice-skate alone at the edge of the Grunewald, imagining for an hour or so he was in the New Hampshire or Massachusetts hills, as he had that Sunday afternoon. Returning, he'd seen a slight figure in woolen trousers and a knitted cap lurking near his G-5 jeep. Under the seat on the driver's side he'd left two bottles of a '42 Moselle Captain Shrader had given him that noon at the Wannsee Hotel. A German boy, a thief: he called out, the thief fled, carrying the heavy bundle, and foundered in the drifts. The cap fell off, the bundle of faggots broke open, and her blond hair tumbled free. She lay at his feet in the snow, a frightened ghost of a German girl come to forage for firewood in the Grunewald, her face summoning memories of toboggan winters in Massachusetts, of adolescent summers along the shore. How incredible it had all been! How miraculous! He'd driven her to his flat in Schöneberg, filled a basket with coal, and drove her to that great block of bombed-out apartment buildings on Reinerstrasse where she lived with her grandmother, the two of them the only survivors of the proud von Winterfeldt family from the feudal estates of East Prussia. Alone, dressed as a boy — protection against the rape and violence of the *Plunderfreiheit* — walking along the horse-drawn farm cart, she'd brought her grandmother safely across snowbound East and West Prussia, through Pomerania to the Oder River and on to Berlin in the winter of 1945.

He stood in the dark Paris street more than forty years later, remembering a face he'd never forgotten. He felt the coldness of the Berlin streets, the cold wind down the long stairwell on Reinerstrasse, saw her waiting for him in the late-afternoon dusk in the fifth-floor flat, sitting at the window with a book on her knee, the reproduction of Dürer's *The Apostles* on the wall behind her. Nina von Winterfeldt, a gentle Catholic girl from Protestant Prussia, a Prussian princess among Berlin commoners. "Not only German but Catholic as well," his father had written. "Marry her? *'Das ist doch Blodsinn!'* Have you lost your mind?"

Lifted weightless on the memory of the past, he had wandered onto Rue Saint Honoré. What was he doing? He was looking for a telephone. He crossed the street to a brightly lit row of shops and found a phone outside a pharmacy.

"I'm going to call Otto, for God's sake," Tricia would say in despair. "If your people can't manage to get Jessica on the Pan Am flight to Frankfurt, Otto can!"

If anyone could manage it, Otto could — Otto, who'd found medicine for Nina's grandmother, sulfa, English whiskey, a tin of tea, Otto with his nimble ways and his shrewd smile, Otto who could always coax hope from despair, a few flames from the ashes.

There was no answer, just ugly silence. The phone continued to ring. He saw the phone, the dark silhouettes of his closed office, the empty chair, the empty desk outlined against the twilight at the window. He had come all this way, all this distance, and stood outside a pharmacy shop in a strange city to hear a telephone ring in a deserted room. *Otto,* he pleaded silently, *Otto, for God's sake, where are you?*

Thirty minutes later he stood looking blindly

at the American embassy from three hundred yards away. Cars were streaming by, homeward bound, their lights on. He stood on the wet pavement like a man betrayed, his ugly hat dripping rain. At that moment he felt a sense of absolute loss. Four telephone calls, each unanswered. Another awful mistake. Youth, even middle age, could escape its folly, outlive its mistakes, as he had once. For a man in the final twilight of a failed career there was nothing beyond, no escape, nothing except nullity or madness. *Die Stunde Null,* Nina had called it: Zero Hour, that moment, that precise instant when a man, a family, a city, a nation, a civilization, a present and a past, ceased to exist. Even without youth, we still cherish love, still search for it, as she had, sitting in the cold light of the fifth-floor window, everything denied, reading her little books as she waited for him. Who was left here in this city of strangers? *Otto! For God's sake! There's no time!* Except for another return to his ugly little hotel room, he had absolutely no idea what he would do next, like Nina and her grandmother, huddled in the ruins of a civilization in the old woman's house in Charlottenberg at *Die Stunde Null;* the Wilhelmplatz, the Adlon Hotel, all tombs; the Tiergarten a smoking forest of splintered stumps, and above them all the roar of their nothingness, like the roar of the winter sea off Cape Ann. He had no imagination to comprehend it then, none to comprehend it now, and this was its terror.

♣ ♣ ♣

Louise Dudley left Corkery alone in the apartment that afternoon with her spare keys and instructions for the dishwasher repairman if he called. He spent the first hour at the antique desk in the study, reading Frank Dudley's correspondence. Some letters were dated eight or nine years earlier, carbon copies on tissue to old friends and classmates, to colleagues retired in Vermont, Florida, France, and Italy. They weren't helpful. No Ulrich, Kruger, or Rauchfuss. None commented on his personal life. He couldn't imagine why he'd kept them. They were badly typed, filled with strikeovers and patched with ink insertions, even on the carbons.

If Dudley's letters did little to flesh out his mental picture, the bedroom closet gave the missing man style and a recognizable aroma: tweedy, a touch of gentlemanly spice, the tang of old leather. He never threw his shoes away. On the closet floor he found twelve pairs. He was a tall man, six foot two or so. He favored tailor-made suits from a Boston clothier; flannels, the odd tweed jacket, but never in the office, seersucker jackets in summer, heavy-soled shoes with thick welts, foulard and regimental ties. There were several dozen of both.

The framed photographs on the bedroom wall above the dresser were forty-year-old photographs of athletic teams from St. Paul's and Harvard, yellow with age. He'd played tennis and hockey. Lying on the bedside table was a work by a German

105

scholar on the Spanish Inquisition and a tattered collection of Conrad's essays, evidently his recent bedtime reading. On a single scrap of paper marking a page in the latter were written the words: "Like the courts of the Spanish Inquisition, they were men possessed by the demon of an insane idea." On the same table were a half-dozen books held upright by a pair of mounted scrimshaw bookends. The Book of Common Prayer and a tattered family Bible dated 1889 were both dusty. A collection of essays by C. S. Lewis and an English edition of T. S. Eliot's *Four Quartets* showed more frequent use. The T. S. Eliot was without a dustcover; the gold title on the spine had disappeared from frequent handling. A few passages were underlined. It had been purchased in a London bookstore. Next to it was another thin volume of verse, *Lord Weary's Castle*, by Robert Lowell. "From Tricia, Christmas, 1949" read the inscription. Liked verse, did he? Numerous passages were underlined. A few quatrains for what ails us? Not quite enough either. In the drawer below he found a bottle of sleeping tablets and two empty brown vials of Valium.

The few hats on the closet shelf had seldom been worn. One was missing, Louise told him — an Irish tweed hat. At the back of his typing desk were a pipe rack, a half-dozen pipes, and a canister of rough-cut European burley with a withered slice of dry apple atop it. He hadn't realized Dudley was a smoker. Louise had said he kept a journal, but kept it where? The top drawer was littered with pipe cleaners, government-issue ballpoint pens, pencil stubs, hotel book matches, and two plastic swizzle sticks from a cocktail lounge on Capitol Hill, Au Plaisir. Stuffed in the second drawer was a manila envelope marked "stocks and bonds." Inside were nineteenth-century deeds to Massachusetts and Connecticut real estate and sixty-five pages of family genealogy, some typed, some written in a faint squirrelly hand in a metallic ink you couldn't buy anymore, tracing out Dudley's New England squirarchy. His forebears had fought the Indians in King Philip's War in 1675. One paragraph, circled in pencil, identified a pair of dining-room oil portraits, circa 1730, or so the margin notation read. The notation had been made recently. Why?

He didn't remember the paintings and went to find them. The dining room was across the hall from the living room and in front of the kitchen. The walls were pale green and paneled in white below the chair rail. The small fireplace of green Italian marble was identical to the one in the living room. A crystal chandelier hung above the cherry dining table. In the center was a vase filled with bittersweet. A few green plants stood on white cast-iron pedestals in front of the bay window, spilling their green leaves to the sill below. Over the cherry sideboard he found the pair of ancestral portraits described in the desk papers. Very heavy, too. He lifted them down and examined the pine backs. They were old and smelled of centuries of dust, but the hanging wires were new and so were the brads holding the backs in place. A small gold and black sticker, also new, identified a Georgetown frame shop. Recently cleaned? He returned them to the wall. Above the fireplace was an oil painting of a New York river valley on a brilliant summer day. Two similar paintings hung in the hall. Someone evidently collected nineteenth-century Hudson River paintings.

So much for genealogy. The man still eluded him, despite the silver-framed picture in the bedroom, retouched for finish at the expense of character, like most studio portraits. The assorted photos Louise Dudley had shown him on Sunday offered the random look, a backward glance, the face in partial profile, but rarely the full figure. The man who sat hunched over his old Underwood, pecking out letters to friends, carefully correcting the flimsy before he filed it away, who was he? He liked documents, didn't he, liked the smell and feel of them, liked fussing over them. Why? He didn't hunt anymore, didn't fly-fish in Maine or New Brunswick, didn't play tennis, didn't ice-skate, once his passion, belonged to no clubs, just accumulated all this useless paper, kept with the neurotic compulsion of an archivist. Why? A man whose life was slipping away?

"Something occurred to me driving in," Shaw said that morning as they met briefly outside his office door. It was said in the mildest of tones; his eyes were on the open cable file in his hand as he spoke, as if it were a matter of minor significance. "You might inquire as to whether Dudley has been seeing any doctors recently — covertly, I mean." Psychiatrist was what the old fox meant. Louise Dudley had told him no, not to her knowledge.

He returned to the study and went through the photographs again, separating them in time and place — Berlin, Oslo, Copenhagen, London, Washington, the ruined farmhouse on the Mediterranean coast where the Dudley family had once spent their summer holidays. The photographs told him nothing. He returned them and stood up, looking about the study to see if he had missed anything. He remembered he hadn't realized Dudley smoked either. It hadn't even occurred to him. Why? Because all he knew were the written records, words on pages which all smelled the same, all abstractions. He didn't know the living, breathing man, only his official facsimile brought from the archives. The little things, he reminded himself; always the little things. The room was silent, the sunshine bright outside, splashing through the trees as it had on Sunday. On a shelf in the center of the bookcases was a display of statuary: a Phoenician terra-cotta, a bronze figurine, eroded by the sea, a few Greek coins bought in Turkey and mounted under glass. On the opposite wall was Jessica's painting of Les Baux. Yet something was missing. He didn't know what it was until he stood in the center of the study, holding Louise's key ring, turning to look at the books, the bookshelves, the desk, the pictures. Then he knew. There was nothing of Louise Dudley in the room, not on the walls or shelves or in the drawers.

Her own study was in the guest room on the other side of the bath. There were two bookcases, a table holding an IBM computer and monitor, a desk and a second table, stacked neatly with documents. Lying in full view was a gray-jacketed feasibility study for an IBRD project for Turkey. Her bedroom was at the end of the hall. He entered it now, very quietly. It was a white room with a white dresser with a white skirt, a white bed, a white carpet and white drapes. Her fragrance was palpable, pursuing him like a reproach, those gray eyes, so clear, so direct, he could never imagine her concealing anything, now hinting at mysteries he would never understand. He looked at the pictures on the wall and then the two framed pictures on the dressing table. One was a sepia portrait of a middle-aged couple sitting on a wicker sofa on a wide summer porch. A silver lake lay in the background between dark, corrugated hills. The gray-haired man had a kind face, wore a mustache, white trousers, and a gray coat. On his knee was a straw hat. The gray-haired woman bore a resemblance to Louise. He supposed the picture was of her parents. The second photograph was of the same man but now older, his eyes dimmer; his hair and mustache were white. He sat in an office at an old-fashioned rolltop desk. Corkery turned the photograph over and found on the brown sealing paper the name of an Elmira, New York, photography studio. Probably her father. He stood for a minute at the dressing table but then turned and went out.

In the basement storage room he found the army footlockers Louise had told him about. They lay in the rear corner behind an antique Victorian dresser and an oak bookcase. A pile of book cartons sat on top. Inside one he found an old trout creel and a canvas pouch filled with fly rod reels, a pair of ice skates, felt-soled waders, a half-dozen watermarked German and French conversational texts from the Foreign Service Institute dated years earlier, and a few spools for an old tape recorder. In a carton at the bottom were three manila envelopes. One held a few European postcards, unsent, a handful of European road maps, and a musty, water-stained *Pocket Guide to Germany* issued in 1945 by the War Department Morale Service Division.

On the inside cover Dudley had printed his name in a boyish hand: Frank Dudley, G-5 staff, Berlin District Hqs., US Mil Govt. 1946. The text was annotated in the same handwriting. The word *syphilis* was boldly underlined. In the margin he'd written "*Eintrett streng verboten!* — Entrance Strictly Forbidden!" A young man's joke? How old would Dudley have been then — eighteen, nineteen? Probably. He'd left Harvard to enlist and returned after his discharge. On the unprinted pages inside the back cover he had made a number of entries at different times, some in pencil, some in pen:

Nina Grafin von Winterfeldt, Apt 63. Charlotte Stolper, 560 Augustplatz, Apt 41. Fraulein Walter, 115 Richterstrasse. Margarethe and Erika Goltz, Bendlerstrasse. Botho Jagger. Franz Hopf. Married DP. Ask UNRRA? Meet Nina, 7:30. Cafe Wein. Tomorrow ask Dr. Mayhugh about getting some Sulfa. Get Gold Flake, NAAFI. 1500 Marks. Otto Kippensammler. Fix radio. Ask for receipt.

Otto Kippensammler? Odd name.

He put the pocket guide aside. In the corner of the locker was a metal ammo box. Inside were dozens of color transparencies taken during the Dudleys' summer vacations in Europe, faded and washed out, some scrawled with mold blossoms. At the bottom was an oilskin pouch, very dry and brittle. Inside were two thick spiral notebooks bound together with cord. The first entry was dated Cambridge, Mass., 1945, but after fifteen pages, the chronology was broken. A half-dozen pages were torn out. The diary resumed in December 1946: "Berlin, AC/S, G-5, BDH."

Assigned as an aide to the assistant chief of staff, G-5. Dudley shared a flat in Berlin's Schöneberg with two other young American GIs working as clerk-typists in the U.S. deputy commandant's office. Bitterly cold in Berlin that December, the coldest winter in European history. The temperature hovered well below freezing; the Spree was frozen over and so were the Elbe and the Rhine. A British coal train was looted by a German mob outside Munich, or so Ralph Frazier told him over lunch at the British Club. He attended a formal dress ball in the great, gilded baroque halls of the Kammergericht, the Allied Control building, where he bumped into Kyle Pinckney, a Harvard classmate, down from Frankfurt for the week. They reminisced at the window and watched the snowflakes floating down, as large as goose feathers. In the snowy courtyard below, French, Russian, British, and U.S. troops paraded back and forth: Something out of Tolstoy, Kyle said. He got terribly plastered on champagne punch and neglected to bring the jeep battery inside. Two days before Christmas he gave a small party at his flat. He ice-skated on a finger of the Wannersee out beyond the Olympic Stadium. Returning to his jeep one bitterly cold afternoon, he'd seen an emaciated woman thrashing about in the snow. He'd thought she'd caught a hare in a trap and was skinning the bloody carcass *en place,* but no, the poor creature had just given birth. Incredible the scenes one came upon in the streets: the *Tageblatt,* the daily list of those dead of hunger and cold, had increased 20 percent in less than a week. Over lunch Major Dawson told him after gas service had been restored the previous winter, the Berlin suicide rate had increased by almost 50 percent. Incredible when you thought about it. By the first week of January, the temperature dropped to five degrees below zero. Astonishing bargains could be found among the antique shops that had sprung up along the K-Damm. Outside one he'd bought a set of an-

113

cestral silver salvers from an old woman who'd lost all the teeth in her upper jaw. Young Otto Kippensammler had followed him about all that afternoon at the Black Market near the Bahnhof Zoo in the British zone, trying to flog an elegant Persian miniature wrapped in a piece of dirty tablecloth.

Otto Kippensammler again? What happened to the foundling born in the snow? He flipped back through the pages. Had he missed something, a few pages torn out? Had Dudley brought a midwife, a doctor, wrapped it in GI swaddling, taken it to the manger in the BDH motor pool? Christmas, wasn't it? No, he hadn't missed anything. More bargains along the K-Damm, more dining at the Embassy Club, more champagne punch, more ice-skating.

It was while ice-skating that he first met "her." He'd thought at first she was pilfering his jeep. Thieves were everywhere, alone or in bands, like the Lehrter Barnhof gang, made up of German war orphans, ferocious Russian deserters, and other miserably displaced nationalities. But no, she wasn't a thief but foraging for firewood. *"Her"?* The word was underlined. Corkery flipped back through the pages but couldn't identify *"her."* He had drinks at the White Horse restaurant on the K-Damm with Tom Merlin (Hasty Pudding), now a fledgling *Time* correspondent based in London. After dinner they dropped in the Roxy, a terribly seedy second-floor nightclub. The young German girl they invited to share their table asked for Coca-

Cola and sipped from her glass as if it were vintage wine. Tom thought this terribly funny; Dudley was embarrassed and saddened by it all. Tom took her home. The poor girl was barely eighteen. He'd witnessed such suffering he wondered if his months in Berlin had begun to make a difference, had made him wiser, had separated him even more from his peers, from family and friends. Did any of them understand? He felt terribly lonely. Two days later he dropped in to see *"her,"* again unidentified, taking along a crate of coal sequestered from the motor pool, a tin of coffee, and canned goods. Sixteen frozen corpses had been found in the boxcar of the coal train come from Hamburg the previous day. Arriving at her floor with the sack of coal, the coffee, and canned goods left with Corporal Jimson in the jeep below, he was uneasy, afraid his gift might be misunderstood. The dreadful state of the German economy made even the simplest humanitarian gesture difficult; Berlin women called their Allied soldier-lovers their "protectors." He decided he couldn't offer the coffee or tinned goods — too vulgar — only the coal. She was pleased to see him, her surprise as genuine as her gratitude, no misunderstanding there, or so he hoped. She invited him in. Her grandmother, a tiny fine-boned woman, brought Meissen cups from the cupboard and they had tea à la Anglais, as the old woman said. She spoke beautiful English. Her father had been in the diplomatic service before retiring to the family estate in East Prussia. He had served in Washington and traveled in the

American West. What year was that? Eighteen seventy, she recalled. He was astonished. His uneasiness forgotten, they talked for an hour. The family house in Charlottenberg was still in rubble, still roped off, entrance forbidden although occupied by a few rubble rats. All this time Corporal Jimson was left waiting in the cold street below. The grandmother invited him to call again as Nina stood shyly by. What pleasure an hour of civilized conversation had given him! At the jeep again he changed his mind and climbed the long staircase with the tin of coffee and the canned goods. He didn't wait to be thanked, merely put the box inside the door after Nina opened it. Corporal Jimson misunderstood. "She musta been some piece," he said. He was from Odessa, Texas.

So that was her name, Nina.

He called on Nina two afternoons later. Her grandmother asked him to dinner the following Saturday night, Nina being too shy herself, or so her grandmother said. They dined by candlelight in a bare room warmed by a coal fire, bundled in sweaters. On the table was all that remained of the Nymphenburg china service brought from East Prussia in the winter of 1945, wrapped and hidden in the snow-wet straw of the horse-drawn farm cart that carried the two of them on that great migration of human misery that stretched from Königsberg along the Frische Nehrung across the Vistula to Danzig and on through Pomerania to the ferries of the Oder River. Millions of refugees had fled to safety from the barbarous Russians — most terribly of all, the Mongols. *Die Flucht,* she called it, the great February flight of wagons, horses, sleds, drays, horse carriages, the sick, wounded, and dying, children, Italian and French prisoners of war, Ukrainians, and Poles, all trudging the 250 miles of snowbound roads and marshes, reversing the migration of her family six hundred years earlier to the barbarous East Prussian frontier. She had been ill some of the way, convinced she wouldn't survive, lying on a goose-feather mattress on a wooden bedstead under a canvas shelter while Nina, her granddaughter, wearing the boots, blouse, and cap of one of their Ukrainian field hands, walked next to the farm horse. She melted snow each morning for water, dug potatoes in the fields to add to the provisions brought with them, and ransacked fresh straw for the wagon and oats for the horse, this lovely young girl who later foraged alone for firewood in the Grunewald. All this yet she was too shy to invite him for dinner. The Russian planes came from time to time; they didn't talk about that, or the bodies they'd seen drifting down the Oder.

More visits, more civilized conversation.

Five weeks later Dudley had called at the U.S. Consulate, opened the previous year, and spoke to a vice-consul about Nina. His purpose wasn't clear. An immigrant visa? The following paragraph had been inked out.

Odd journal. The Berlin entries continued for eighty pages. The last entry was dated Cambridge 1948. Corkery looked at his watch and knew he didn't have time. Reluctantly he returned the two notebooks to the oilskin pouch and replaced the box in the footlocker. But then he changed his mind and slipped the pouch in his jacket pocket. The second footlocker was behind the first atop a pine blanket chest. Inside were bundles of winter clothing and blankets wrapped in dry cleaners' cellophane, smelling of moth balls. He lifted the bundles aside, groped about, felt cold metal, and pulled out a folded blanket. As he brought out the snub-nosed Colt .32 revolver, a thick manila envelope hidden beneath the folds slipped to the floor. The revolver was new and had never been fired. The chamber was empty. A new revolver and no cartridges? Odd. He emptied the locker but found nothing more. The envelope that had fallen to the floor was labeled in red Magic Marker: MAINTENANCE AND INSTRUCTION MANUALS — MARYLAND FARM. Inside were repair and parts brochures for a jet pump, a chain saw, and a lawn mower. Bound to them by a paper clip was a Xeroxed document that didn't belong there at all. It was from the Directorate of Operations at Langley:

INTELLIGENCE INFORMATION REPORT

WARNING NOTICE

INTELLIGENCE SOURCES AND METHODS
INVOLVED

SECRET   CONTROL: DCI 4/98351

1. ENCLOSED AS PAGES 2-23 IS AN UNEDITED ENGLISH-LANGUAGE DOCUMENT WRITTEN BY SUBJECT DESCRIBING HIS EARLY LIFE AND AN ATTEMPT BY UNKNOWN SOVIET INTELLIGENCE AGENTS TO RECRUIT HIM DURING A RECENT VISIT TO MONTREAL, CANADA. SUBJECT'S RELIABILITY IS UNESTABLISHED.

My name is Alexei Alexovich Andreyev, so I will use that name, although names are irrelevant and I'm not even sure that is my true name. My purpose here is not to name names but to tell my story as honestly as possible, sparing no one, including myself. Naturally I hope the reader would have a good opinion of me, but on that score we'll let the cards fall where they may.

I was born in a small village near Dubrovo in the USSR in 1933 or 1934, the year being uncertain because my parents, both teachers at Dubrovo, weren't married at the time, although sharing the same roof. I thus began life with a certain ambiguity about my birth. After their marriage, they moved to nearby Twer, where the marriage date was set back and my birth date advanced in the interest of respectability, Twer being more respectable than Dubrovo. All of this is without permanent significance, since my parents died of typhoid two years later. I was bundled up and carried back to the village where I was born in the arms of the old woman in whose house my parents had lived, who had attended my mother at my birth and my parents in their final illness, and whom the officials at Twer mistakenly thought a relative, an error the old woman made no attempt to correct. Except for the unfailing kindness of the old woman and her crippled, halfwitted daughter who showed me nothing but love and devotion, I have only a vague recollection of those early years. I remember the old woman, her small house, the muddy roads, the sunflowers in the rear garden, the cobbler's bench outside the kitchen door where in the summer her daughter sat, the sun on her hands and face, but nothing of my parents. I think this gave me a certain advantage in life. I was free to invent myself, so to speak.

When I was six or seven, the old woman died and the crippled daughter was placed in an institution. I was sent to Moscow to live with my mother's older brother. His name was Mikhail Rudyev, a minor official in the Ministry for the Construction of Power Stations. I went to Moscow alone by train. I recall the rattling coach, the smell of strange metal, smoke, and damp woolens, the glasses of sweet hot tea, and the endless landscape passing by my window. I recall none of my fellow passengers. I don't remember who bought the ticket or put me on the train. Strapped to my oilskin valise was my most prized possession, a copy of *The Soviet Atlas of the World, 1929 Revised Edition*, which had been left among my father's books.

How many memories that tattered, water-stained volume recalls, how many deceptions as well. Twer or Dubrovo, the village where I was born, is now 30 kilometers west of where it was during my childhood. Lake Lagoda has been similarly relocated. The coastline of the Gulf of Finland has also been altered. These are but a few examples. There are many more.

One way or another every imperial capital ultimately betrays itself, imagining that nothing can escape its imperial edict, whether the motion of the planets, the drift of the stars, or the geography of the earth. This was as true of Athens, Rome, and Constantinople as it is now of Moscow. The cartographers of the Chief Administration of Geodesy and Cartography in Moscow, directly responsible to the Council of Ministers of the USSR, are the most recent navigators aboard this ship of fools. The 1967 edition of the *Great Soviet Atlas of the World* whose falsifications I have just cited is a case in point. How can one abide a system that, among its crimes, would perjure your childhood memories? History is one thing: every age rewrites the past. But the systematic denial of the contours of the earth, maps that lie? How can one —

Andreyev's narrative was abruptly broken off at this point. Eleven pages were missing. The document resumed in a city Corkery thought was Montreal:

Boris and I left the hotel and walked up to Mount Royal Avenue where we strolled for a time, past the art galleries, past the museum, past the tall apartment buildings. The wind was cold, dusk was falling, and the windows were brightly lit. I was depressed by the shop windows, the expensive furniture, the women's gowns, the silks and furs, the soft lights of the apartments high overhead, the doormen in imperial blue uniform under the blue canopies. I was depressed the same way I'd been depressed by Fifth Avenue in New York the first time I'd walked there on a pleasant spring evening when the light was beginning to fade, a stranger passing unnoticed among expensive shops, limousines, and beautiful women.

For foreigners in general and Russians like myself in particular, there is something very inarticulate about New York, America too, for that matter.

I discovered this that spring evening in New

York because I was just beginning to feel like an American with my American English. As when you have a new pair of shoes and want to walk about in them, to rediscover your feet, as it were, I wanted to express myself with someone in my American English, preferably a beautiful young woman who might find my accent quaint and me intriguing. I could do this now because I was not simply free to do so, a man who had rediscovered himself, reclaimed his freedom, able to speak his mind, as I am doing in this letter, but because I had come to America and spoke American English.

But there I was on Fifth Avenue in New York passing all those bright shop windows with their expensive jewelry, furs, silks, and antique furniture. As my spring stroll lengthened I began to realize that to truly express yourself in America is to be able to buy a few of these very fine expensive things. But this requires a great deal of money, especially on Fifth Avenue in Manhattan. So although my English was better than the elflike little diamond cutter and his wife who joined me uninvited at my table in the Automat near Columbus Circle that day, speaking Yiddish, expressing yourself in America isn't a matter of knowing the language but a matter of money. So that is what I meant about America being inarticulate. It is not so much to people that Americans talk but to things, and the words they use are money.

A simple Russian like myself, on the other

hand, appreciates words for their own sake. He must, of course, since he has nothing in his pockets. If in America money talks, as they say, in the USSR the ruble is deaf and dumb; but in Russia words have more weight and substance than coins and in ways few Americans understand.

For example, you'll find that men in prison, or women too, keep their daily accounts in another way, counting their possessions not in coins but in their heads, by which I mean in memory, which is nothing more or less than keeping and maintaining their sanity. Sanity is a personal possession as unique to each individual as his nose and ears. No one may claim it, not institutes, not political parties, not propaganda ministries, not doctors, not ecclesiastics, not historians. Sanity belongs to each individual alone and regardless of how insane the world in which he lives is as recognizable to him as his fingernails, his thumbs, his hands, his toes, even his shirt buttons, all of which the universe has connected to him and to him alone. A man is the soul of sanity in the privacy of his mind, body, and soul, although he may appear quite different in a crowd when all the ugly little passions in his head fly off to join the other ugly little passions swarming about him to be multiplied a millionfold in some collective lunacy, like angry bees swarming in a hollow tree. In this way a crowd is an idiot, the collective swarm of all that is worst in us. We have to look no further than Hitler's *Sportsplast* or the Council of Ministers of the USSR to recognize this. But when each man returns home, he is again at one with himself as he enters his little flat, sees his room, his furniture, his sleeping children, his Bible, his almsbox, his masonry or carpentry tools, his shirt buttons, his crooked thumbs and friendly fingernails, all these seemingly insignificant details joined to him by the universe which declare an identity uniquely his own, however insignificant. So in this way he is again made whole, a contented husband and a contented father.

But in a prison cell — and many nations these days are prison cells — he has no personal possessions and no freedom. His hands are ugly, his fingers those of a stranger, his thumbnails those of a corpse. He has nothing except what he possesses in memory, in the deepest recesses of his mind and spirit. So the daily inventory of a man in prison begins and ends in memory, in words and words alone that at their most intense discover themselves in poetry. So it isn't unusual to find that men and women shut away in prison with nothing in their pockets are forced to live completely within themselves, to count the currency in their heads and hearts, so to speak. In this way they show remarkable mnemonic gifts, particularly in remembering or creating poetry.

The Russian people, being so poor in their more extravagant possessions that in America count as freedom, have always been gifted in poetry. Poetry is the currency of the rich in spirit even if poor in possessions. For Americans, however, who have known neither tyrants nor dungeons, it is more their possessions than their memories that declare who they are.

So this is what I learned that first spring evening as I strolled down Fifth Avenue in my new American suit. By the time I reached my ugly little hotel near Columbus Circle, I was no longer pleased with my new suit, my hotel room, or my American English. I began to quarrel with myself in Russian, which shows you how miserable I'd become. Even if I spoke American English as richly as Walter Cronkite, whom I'd been listening to every night since my arrival to help with my diction, I would still be a deaf mute as far as most Americans were concerned. I had no words, no money, to talk to all the fine expensive things around me.

I didn't tell Boris all this, of course. I said very little as we strolled down Mount Royal Avenue. His suit was European. He didn't have the manners of a Russian diplomat but he did have a certain moral crudeness that, even more than the accent, convinced me he was a Russian of a certain type.

What he had to say to me that evening was simple enough. I had been in exile for many years — those were his exact words, *exile* — but had little to show for it. I could expect no less than five nor more than eighteen years' im-

prisonment given the fact that I was a condemned man under article 64a, condemned by
the Military College of —

The document broke off here. The remaining
pages were missing.

Corkery refolded the pages, put them in an envelope together with the two spiral notebooks and
the Handbook for Germany, remembered Louise
Dudley's smile at the door, and felt like a thief.
First the Tass item carried about obsessively by
Dudley, reporting his trial and execution, and now
this. Why? Who was Andreyev?

A dying winter sun waxed the high brick wall
at the rear of the garden in Georgetown. Eva
Chambers, her white hair fiery with points of gold,
led Corkery down the rear steps and pointed to
the gnomelike figure on a far bench under an old
maple tree whose trunk was knotted and gnarled
with old amputations. "He always picks the coldest
day of the year. Don't get up!" she shouted. "Your
second childhood has come to join you!"

Chambers looked up blankly as she marched
back inside. A leaf rake and two bushel baskets
sat on the brick walk nearby, filled with ivy and
boxwood clippings, a few green walnut hulls, and
a clump of shriveled turnips. He looked up expectantly as Corkery joined him. "He's back, you
found him."

"No, sir. Not yet."

The light in his eyes faded. "Too bad. This is

my garden." His eyes moved away, inviting Corkery to inspect it, traveling from the flower and vegetable beds in front of the far brick wall to the rose garden beneath the high windows of the sunporch. "It doesn't look large but it's enough. Gets me out of breath. Like a mule with one lung, she tells me. Do you have a garden?"

"No, but I wish I did," Corkery lied. "Shaw tells me the same thing. I don't have the time." He thought garden tools the leg irons of the middle-aged Washington galley crews, shackled all summer long to rakes, hoes, and fertilizer bags. His rear yard in Bethesda looked like a Brazilian rain forest well into August when his neighbors began to complain over the tops of their beetle-infested rosebushes. Tennis was his game, quick, slashing, and brutal. The tennis club was only fifteen minutes away. There his victories on the court weren't so much triumphs of talent but determination. Lanky, graceless, and stubborn, he was a tireless retriever.

Chambers lifted himself heavily from the bench. "Make time. You'll learn more in a garden in one planting season than you will an office lifetime." He moved stiffly toward the house. "Not back yet, eh? Odd."

"I think so too. There's a lot to his career I don't understand."

"It's your youth. There's a lot to all of us none of us understand. The heart has mysteries no one knows." They went into the house. On the enclosed sunporch the light was fading. A pale copper

128

autumn sun dusted the leaves of the jade plants, the African violets, and the Royal Worcester plates in the antique cabinet. Chambers didn't turn on the lamps. He groped his way to the rattan chair and sank down.

"I keep asking myself what went wrong," Corkery said. "Louise Dudley told me he once worked for Julian Abbott over at Langley but didn't stay long. Do you know anything about that?"

"Why would it matter now? What is it? You want to find Dudley, find him for yourself or make a reputation?"

"No, not a reputation. It's the mystery."

Chambers laughed with pleasure. "Good. We forget, don't we? It is a mystery, an old-fashioned whodunit, and a damnable one at that. For me too. Have you talked to Abbott?"

The question was so abrupt Corkery had no chance to reply.

"Let's be honest. You probably don't like Abbott, do you? Not everyone does. At your age, I wouldn't have either. He was a man I worked with, not a man I admired."

"He's not back from London yet."

Chambers was silent, watching the light dissolve against the far windows. "George Tobey," he said finally.

"Sorry?"

"George Tobey. Worked for me in Berlin. Retired now. That was the name I was trying to remember the other night. Came back to me this afternoon when I was outside in the garden. Frank had been up to see him, drove all the way to Delaware to talk to him. A bit odd, too. I've never been to his farm but Frank talked about his place, his woodworking shop out in the barn, his duck hunting. Said he wouldn't mind living the same kind of life but couldn't afford to. Tricia was partly to blame. She had very expensive habits. George Tobey is different, not Frank's type at all. That's what surprised me. Grew up in a Pennsylvania coal town, went to Pitt on a football scholarship. The family was Ukrainian and they changed the name." He turned aside to light the table lamp and open the drawer. "Do you duck hunt?"

"I don't much get the chance anymore."

"A loon, do you know what that is? Not a duck, not really, but it looks like a duck. Goes underwater, then bobs up fifty yards away. Then he's gone again. You never know where he's going to pop up. He's not a duck, just a bloody nuisance."

Chambers removed a pad from the drawer, tore off the top page, and leaned forward to hand it to Corkery. On it were Tobey's address and telephone number in southern Delaware. "Call him, tell him you spoke to me. He worked for Abbott over at Langley for a time. I think he was there when Dudley was but I'm not sure. I don't know why Dudley left. A little abrupt, everyone thought, but who knows? Gossip and envy are like termites. Once in the house they're the devil to get out. Institutions are much the same way. I hope this doesn't annoy you. It annoys my daughters."

"No, sir." It was near the dinner hour. Corkery

130

could hear the sounds of pots and pans rattling in the kitchen below. The aroma of simmering vegetables mixed with the dry heat of the front hall as Chambers led him toward the door. He could smell turnips cooking. "Thanks again. I'll keep you informed. One last question if you don't mind."

"Not at all."

"Do you remember a Russian named Andreyev, Alexei Andreyev?"

"Could be. Why?" His voice was different. In the twilight of the hall Corkery couldn't see his face.

"I found the name among Dudley's papers, the Tass report of an espionage trial in Moscow. Shot apparently. I have the feeling he was once in the U.S. I think Dudley must have known him."

"Do you have it with you?"

"No, but I'll bring it next time. Thanks again."

Chambers closed the door and peered to the side to see if the porch light was on. He sometimes forgot in the thick dusk of the shortening winter days. He turned and groped his way down the stairs and through the dim back hall to return to the garden and the clutter he'd left on the walk.

"Digging yourself in deeper, aren't you?" She stood in the kitchen door, holding the top of a double boiler. "What did you tell him this time?"

His mind went blank. "To take up gardening."

She laughed. "You're an old fraud, you are. You never did, not until it was too late. Why would a young man like that take up gardening? I thought

131

your book was the only thing that mattered these days."

"In a way it is."

The laugh came again, rich and merciless. "You can fool others, you can't fool me. Gardening now, is it? Two weeks' worth, when everything's dead in the ground. It's turnips we're having, my turnips, not yours." She held the pan toward him. "Lovely, aren't they? Next year I suppose you'll be giving harpsichord lessons."

Darkness had fallen when Corkery returned to Langley. The access road was patched with drifting smoke from a leaf fire. The solitary guard post with its pods of light reminded him of a deserted midnight port, Pearl Harbor or Subic Bay; the lights and masts of the building gleaming through the trees might have been those of an armada lying at anchor. He'd forgotten the time. It was six-fifty when he reached the second-floor suite. Miss Fogarty sat at her desk, her brightly rouged morning face as wilted as the flowers in the vase on her desk. Another secretary sat typing nearby. Both looked up as he sauntered in, eyes pursuing him reproachfully as he moved toward the inner corridor.

"Something wrong?"

Miss Fogarty looked at the wall clock. "He's been asking for you all afternoon. You'd better tell him you're back."

The door was half open. Shaw, busily scribbling on a yellow legal pad, lifted his head, immediately stood up, and told him to shut the door. "Why didn't you tell me?" he shouted. "Why didn't you tell me about this man Kruger?"

"Kruger? Who the hell's Kruger?"

"Kruger, Otto Rauchfuss, Ulrich, whoever he is! The body they found Sunday morning!"

"Oh, yeah. Sorry. What about him?"

"I'm asking you why you didn't tell me!"

"Tell you what? You were tied up with Elinor. Skaff was going to send me his lab report so I could finish my memo —"

"Finish your memo! There's a phone, a door!" He flung out his arm, pointing to it. "You should have told me, told me immediately!"

"I tried to, I intended to —"

"Intended to? What in God's name does that mean?" He banged his chair back and stepped from behind his desk. "Someone from the FBI phoned me, asking me what we'd learned! I had absolutely no idea what he was talking about. Then I got a call from upstairs, asking what we were doing. I had absolutely no idea!"

"Sorry. Maybe I should have." Corkery had never seen Shaw so angry. The door softly opened and shut; someone circled behind him.

"Sorry isn't good enough! Where in the name of heaven have you been?"

"Working on the Dudley case, talking to a few people —"

Jay Fellows, the number two deputy, moved into Corkery's view toward Shaw's desk, reading a folder tagged with a red priority marker. He wore a woolen sack suit, gum-soled European shoes, and a fussy little Edwardian beard, cinnamon colored and neatly trimmed. A fluent Russian speaker, he'd spent most of the past decade in the field. At hqs he handled only the most sensitive cases, those whose details even Shaw wasn't privy to.

Corkery had never dealt with him and knew little about him except that he had a lovely wife with silver-tipped hair who drove a silver-gray BMW and sometimes picked him up at the front entrance. She had long legs and nice thighs. From the lazy way she undressed herself getting out of the car he had the impression she didn't mind showing them. Her husband was too preoccupied to notice, poring over some monograph or a folded newspaper as he opened the door. Maybe that was her problem. Corkery thought the beard made him look like one of the Romanoffs' lost cousins, waiting for the restoration. Elinor Wynn said he was hopelessly conservative; his maternal grandmother was a Russian aristocrat who'd fled to Berlin in the twenties; the children had a French governess. Seeing him there in Shaw's office, he knew he was in trouble. Shaw continued to shout: "Doing what, please tell me!"

"I just did. The Dudley case. I dropped by to talk to Phil Chambers."

"A body with two false passports is found and you're pestering Phil Chambers! I want your memo and I want it tonight!"

"I have the FBI report," Fellows said without lifting his head. "I think it will do."

"I nevertheless want his report."

"Could I see the FBI report?" Corkery said. "It might help speed things up."

"When you've finished yours!" Shaw cried. "Go write it! *Now!*"

OD to swabbie in an hour. Phil Chambers had been helpful; Shaw had chewed his ass. The memo took fifty minutes. The secretary he shared had gone home. He had to type it himself on her word processor, but the keys were different. It didn't read well. Two paragraphs were gibberish, something screwed up in the software. His mind was elsewhere: Why was Jay Fellows there? Why was he interested in the FBI report? Why was Shaw so spastic? What he was doing was dumb, just DOD stupid. They had the FBI report. Why did they need his?

They didn't. It was just by the numbers, the old navy way. Gunny Shaw, his summer camp DI: "Gimme fifty, Corkery! On the goddamn deck now! Don't smart-talk me, mister! Make it deuces, double up, asshole rising! Now!"

That was the old navy way too; make plebes of us all. He tore up the first printout, went back to his word processor, and began again. His small office smelled of someone's hair oil. Who'd been prowling about? Corkery's barbershop, that's what it smelled like. What would the deckhands on the USS *Peurifoy* say if they saw him now, Lt. Kip Corkery, intel officer, pecking out his laundry list on a million-dollar mainframe computer. Also film officer: "Hey, Lt. Corkery, sir! Can you get us two Clint Eastwoods for five Daffy Ducks? Hey, what do you say, sir?" They were taking on fresh vegetables off Crete.

He returned to his secretary's desk, draft in hand. Don't forget the sir. Lt. Kip Corkery, the Cartoon Kid, now the Office Weenie, that's what they'd remember. How do you exit this goddamn mess, not blank out the message center, zap the NSC, dim the White House press room lights, blow Reagan's TelePrompTer memory, lose every cipher in the inventory?

Then he was finished. Fifty minutes but too late. Down the hall Shaw's office door was closed and locked. Miss Fogarty's desk was clear, her chair empty, the morning flowers dumped in the wastebasket. Both had gone home. Elinor Wynn had also left. He remembered she'd been dodging him for two days. She wouldn't have helped: Abbott's sweetheart, as sly as a parlor cat in keeping their secrets. He moved on. Admirals' country here. The *Sanctum Sanctorum* was deserted, only a single doorway lit in that secret vaulted office behind Abbott's. The overhead lights were off, the desk softly illuminated by a green-globed library lamp. Jay Fellows sat reading, leaning back in his chair, reading and waiting, like a diplomat scholar in residence at the Foreign Affairs Council in New York, waiting for his limousine to take him to Lincoln Center. What else was he waiting for? A phone call? A cable? A summons from the D-staff, maybe a satellite intercept from Andropov's Zil limousine hot line?

Corkery knocked respectfully at the casement and waited.

Jay Fellows finally looked up.

"I've finished my memo." He ventured in, seven steps, no farther, the way young naval aides-de-camp were taught. "Shaw's gone home. I thought maybe you'd want a copy."

"Thanks, I'll look at it."

"I made two copies. Actually, I made three. It's not too complete, I mean, like the FBI report."

"I expect not. Just drop it in the box."

He stepped forward to put the report in the in box on the corner of the desk, careful not to touch anything. On the blotter nearby were three thick folders with red and yellow priority tags. On the desk and table were four phones, two black and two green.

"There's one thing I mentioned but didn't go into." He was conscious without looking at it of the open book on Fellows's knee. "I mean, the stuff in the washbasin at the hotel room, the oily stuff. Skaff was going to get a lab crew in." He would have given a day's pay to know what he was reading.

"He did." Fellows didn't lift his head. "It was a solvent for hair dye. Much ado about nothing."

Corkery retreated backward across the room, eyes to the front, nothing seen, nothing heard. He banged his head against the open door and moved smartly out, no salute necessary. Lt. Kip Corkery, fetching Admiral Yeaston his morning coffee and a copy of *Neptune's Locker*, the daily press rag.

Back in his office, he slammed his safe drawers closed, twirled the dial, signed the log, and turned the red cardboard tag over to CLOSED. On the floor to the side he found a confidential cable from Oslo that had slipped from his in box. He crumpled it angrily, then smoothed it out. Maybe he would toss it in the well under Miss Fogarty's desk, let the old battle-ax take the rap. Then he saw his initials in the upper right-hand corner and stuffed it in his pocket. Kid stuff. The halls were deserted, the elevator empty. He rode down alone.

That was just peachy, wasn't it? Shaw blows a head gasket and makes him write a report no one is going to read and then takes off like a big bird for the TV suburbs. Then Fellows, decent old chap, looks up from his Turgenev to tell him it was much ado about nothing. He crossed the deserted parking lot toward his forlorn secondhand Mustang alone in the rear with its rusting rocker panels and tattered top. Another screwup. Someone had tried to rip off his Alfa's six-speaker Blaupunkt stereo, right here in the goddamned CIA parking lot. He should have dropped a line to Jack Anderson, maybe Evans and Novak.

What he thrived on was spontaneity, what he got on the second floor was suspicion and mistrust. Shaw was worried about Abbott coming back, finding out he'd screwed up with Vitale's report. That was why he'd been so crabby — find himself out in the cold, like Frank Dudley.

Why had Abbott sacked Dudley in CI? What had they quarreled about?

138

No one survived Abbott's mistrust; those who provoked it were fired outright, not moved elsewhere, the way Dudley had been. Even his apostles couldn't always fathom his neuroses; some of the faithful, like Shaw, had long given up, but their faith survived, as had Elinor Wynn's: they dreamed Abbott's dream, gritty old Cold War one-reelers in black and white, Pathé News from 1947 to 1951.

"Don't be too hard on him," she told him in her limp Radcliffe drawl that first month when she'd been feeling him up. Like Corkery, she'd been a scholarship student. Her father taught Romance languages at Deerfield Academy in Massachusetts. She'd been very intellectual during those first conversations, the grad school whiz kid, sharing her seminar notes. He thought she came on a little strong. She had attractive hands but short ragged fingernails, her right hand, not her left, whose nails were shaped and lacquered but unpolished. She was ambidextrous, maybe a schizoid. She also had an occasional run in her stockings. He wondered what her bathroom clothesline looked like. She was also ten pounds overweight but he liked her eyes, a woman's eyes, a cool jade sometimes, then hazel, then blue, he didn't know. They changed like the sea. Not knowing was what he liked.

"I often disagree with him about the same things," she told him at one of their luncheon confessionals. "In some ways Julian has the mind of a shrew, very minute, very microscopic, always

139

fixed on the detail at hand. That's his strength. With him, it's never the big things, always the little ones. His mind is an accumulation of those millions of little mosaics we walk over and never see. That's how he made his reputation. If you take him away from that and ask him about the larger picture, the macropolitical world, he's sometimes been wrong. He was wrong about the Sino-Soviet split, about Eurocommunism, about Harold Wilson and Willy Brandt. He was wrong because in terms of their contemporaries, both men were larger than life; they defied categorization. I think he's failed there because his mind is less accustomed to working in that dimension. History in the larger sense often gets away from him, like it does most of us. I mean, have you reread Burckhardt recently? Anarchy frightens him, the way it did him and does most foreign policy intellectuals. Kissinger's in the same tradition."

She was blowing smoke, the way grad school sophists did; smart but stupid. She was saying Julian Abbott liked his facts small and dead, like an entomologist, but anarchy wasn't what she meant either. Had he read the Italian deviationists? she asked; did he know Fraschi?

"Not recently. I don't go much for Fellini either. What's this guy's latest flick?"

"Don't be so cynical. Julian finds it hard to cope with passion, whether with people or ideas. He's also sentimental. Don't be too hard on him. He needs people like us. You'll understand. I know you will."

Sure, but she'd said she liked music too. Two scarecrow fiddlers scratching out Bartók on an empty stage. He'd heard better harmonics from a highrise elevator console, dinging off the floors. Why should he trust her? It was the enigmatic Abbott who chose him or so she said, something about the work he'd done in Rome with the Italian Pastrego against the Red Brigades. He'd admired his drafting, his persistence, his common sense. But neither Abbott nor Shaw had mentioned it and never would, she said. "Just be patient and one day it will all come, the way it did for me. I mean, once they trust you, that trust is absolute."

He took no consolation from that. She'd worked for Abbott for nine years.

He was an odd-looking bird, tall and cadaverous, with a high forehead, thin gray hair as fine as silk, a long aristocratic nose, and ice blue eyes. Slightly cockeyed too, which gave him a sad, mournful look. He favored dark suits with a faint chalk stripe, always a vest, and English-made shoes that had the luster of old calfskin pickled in port. He seemed to Corkery as remote from contemporary Washington as some medieval scholar at Georgetown, as weak-eyed as a Vatican bat as he flapped his way about campus. Elinor cautioned against casual judgment; he had an unerring eye and a deadly wit, she claimed, able to pierce the disguises of others at a single glance from behind those curiously tinted spectacles. Corkery wondered if they'd pierced hers.

Abbott had grown up in the Balkans. His father

141

had been a professor at the American college in Sofia and at Robert College in Istanbul. He was educated by private tutors and studied in Geneva and at Harvard. His Balkan experience led to his assignment in OSS and his interest in Soviet studies. He'd since become one of the resident deans of the CIA school of determinism. Nothing the Russians did was without purpose; even their errors had a sinister intent: if a Soviet intelligence effort failed, it did so by design; if a penetration agent was exposed, he was being sacrificed to one more highly placed; if an Agency officer screwed up, his intent was treasonable. This made him a bit paranoiac, some thought, although they'd indulged his eccentricities for years, the darker side of that hypochondria that was responsible for the elaborate dehumidifier and air-filtering devices in his office that casual visitors, like Corkery, the naïf, mistook for tropical fish tanks.

"The guy lives in a cork-lined room," he'd told Elinor after his eight-minute introductory visit. What he meant was that he had no more spontaneity than *Pravda* or those seventy-five-year-old Politburo cadavers pickled in Marxist brine wheeled out every May Day for their annual airing atop the Kremlin wall. That being the case, no one survived his mistrust.

So why had Dudley?

He didn't know, didn't care, wouldn't hang around long enough to find out. Even the smell of the second-floor suite every morning brought on the same paralysis, numbing his better self —

the same grumpy greetings, the same secret faces, the same claustrophobic silences. A new life for himself after the navy, he'd thought, but after five years he was still half in, half out.

His mind elsewhere, he left the parkway too fast and braked hard coming down the ramp. The driver of the Mercedes behind him leaned angrily on his horn and maneuvered to pass. Corkery flipped his wheel and blocked his way.

"Screw you too, Commodore."

That was the old navy way, playing chicken with Soviet shadow ships in the Med. He slowed to slip a cassette into the stereo deck, taped from one of the records he'd lugged around the Med during his navy days.

On the beltway the gray Mercedes shot past on the inside lane. He flicked on his high beams and saw an angry hand waving, index finger raised. The blond head seated alongside turned to look back in triumph, her eyes owl-bright in his glare. He flicked his dimmer switch a few times and cranked down the window.

"Be cool, Mama! This is where it's at!"

The Mercedes sped on.

More kid stuff. Disgusted, he cranked up the window and turned up the volume. Driving back and forth to Langley, he moved in another slip-stream: Corkery, the Stereo Roadie, grooving down the beltway to Neil Young, Lightfoot, Crosby, Stills and Nash, and Jerry Garcia, eyes peeled for passing singles in their chirpy little Datsuns and Toyotas. Corkery, the Eternal Adolescent, Elinor would have said, like Admiral Yeaston, commander of the Middle East Fleet at Bahrain, who told him one evening after too many gin slings there was too much of the boy in him for much of a future as a navy line officer. Yeasty was Annapolis; Corkery wasn't. That was a joke too. The U.S. Navy was the biggest flotilla of floating frat houses in the world. But the admiral was right. Sooner or later he'd bag it and move on, out of Abbott's Cold War trenches and on into the twenty-first century. Maybe he'd go to California, take a few classes at Berkeley, look up some old shipmates in Silicon Valley, get out on the cutting edge. If nothing else, there were all those wide open spaces during the drive west in his Alfa.

"We're institutional orphans," Elinor had said when she'd seen the Naples Navy sticker on the rear bumper. "Both of us. You in the NROTC, then the navy, me a grad school foundling."

Her eyes had measured his as she sipped her Chinese tea in the quiet McLean restaurant of her choosing where they'd gone for lunch — a $32.50 rip-off. Were they green or hazel?

"What's wrong? You don't agree?"

"Nothing. I was just thinking."

He was thinking about her incipient spinsterhood, the years ahead when the light down on her arms began to darken as it climbed her cheeks and upper lip, like Miss Fogarty's, whose freshly powdered morning face was a mime's mask, her scent so repellently sweet it reminded him of a

144

hospital sickroom, another of the penalties of a spinster's weary middle age. He knew she was serious. Green, he decided, but the Chinese teapot was green and so were the placemats. She'd eluded him again, offering no more, but he'd wondered about the remark during his long solitary drives. He couldn't make up his mind, but what could you think about in the stereo slipstream, Neil Young and the Band scattering your thoughts like roadside litter, like Grace Slick was doing now.

He was home. He left the Mustang on the street. Leaves were thick against the front steps of the thirty-year-old brick rambler but less so than that morning. Two days of breakfast and dinner dishes were piled in the kitchen sink. He found a silver-throated German pilsner in the refrigerator, poured it in a plastic thermal cup, and took it into the bathroom, where he showered and shaved. He dressed, turned on the Mexican sombrero lamp in the front hall — abandoned by his ex-roommate after she'd moved out in a snit, taking the rest of her furniture with her — and left by the back door. The driveway leaves, ankle deep a week ago, had been scattered by the strong autumn westerlies and now sat securely in his neighbors' plastic leaf bags. Strong winds make busy neighbors. He roared out of the garage, scattering a few more to their newly mulched azalea beds, and headed back to Washington in the Alfa Romeo.

The brick house was in a quiet Capitol Hill neighborhood five blocks from the Library of Con-

145

gress, painted a dull brown with rough-hewn limestone sills, cut-glass windows in the massive front door, and a hideous turret on the southeast corner. Corkery thought it looked ugly enough to be abandoned. An iron fence enclosed a small neglected yard overgrown with ivy and unpruned lilac and hydrangea bushes that obscured the bay windows, shuttered from the inside and protected by iron security grills. Parked in the areaway north of the front steps was a maroon Volvo station wagon. In the rear was a small garden reached by a brick walk along the side. In the center of the garden between a mulberry and maple tree was an arbor, and in front of it a small flagstone patio about which were arranged a few weathered redwood chairs that remained there all winter. Behind the kitchen was an enclosed porch.

Stocky and dark haired, she lived alone with her cats, drove the same Volvo year after year, wore the same winter and spring coats, left her house at the same hour each morning and returned late each evening. Known to her neighbors at a distance, except for her sameness there was nothing memorable about her. The fact that she kept such long hours and lived alone with her cats was evidence enough there was little to her life worth inquiring about. Some said she did translations.

Corkery rang the front bell a little after nine. The front rooms were dark but her Volvo was parked in the areaway and he saw the light reflected from the kitchen against the wall of the neighboring house. The front light came on and he heard the deadbolt being shot back. Elinor peered at him through the crack.

"What on earth are you doing here?"

"Have you got a minute?"

"I'm getting ready for bed."

"I'll just take a minute."

"At this hour? Have you been drinking?"

"No. A couple of beers, maybe. Why?" The cold wind blew across the porch, rattling the dead ivy that partially obscured the side wall. She slipped the chain and opened the heavy door. A quilted bathrobe was across her arm. "You certainly have been drinking. I smell something." She led him into the dark living room and turned on a dim table lamp. The house had the same musty smell he remembered from his two earlier visits, the first on a rainy night when he hadn't been able to find a parking space and had arrived late to join the other guests, all friends from Langley, all older, all intelligence scholars, all eccentrics in their own way. Candles seemed to be everywhere; he'd thought there had been a power failure. Grown accustomed to the darkness, he realized they weren't candles at all but undersized bulbs in ghostly Victorian shades. "Elinor's Fortress," someone had called it. He'd seen none of the guests since. Apparitions, they'd seemed, ghosts from the covert world, a kind of Capitol Hill Table Tapping Society.

She was about to run her bathwater upstairs. "You smell like a brewery. Can I get you something? Coffee maybe?"

"Nothing thanks. I won't stay long. I wanted to ask you something."

"What about? Office business?"

"Yeah. Frank Dudley."

"At this hour? Don't tell me someone's involved me in his silly little affair."

"Nothing like that. I heard Dudley worked for Abbott in CI and they had some kind of disagreement."

"Disagreement? Sit down. And take off your coat, for God's sake. Don't be so dramatic." She took his overcoat and flung it across a Victorian chair. "Dudley's had problems with practically everyone the past few years. Who singled this one out?"

"Why hasn't anyone told me Dudley worked for Abbott?"

"Oh, God. Here we go again." She sank down on the loveseat near the cast-iron fireplace. "That was ages ago. Are we going to start dragging all that rubbish out of the closet? Why should anyone have mentioned it? It certainly had nothing to do with his walking out." Her voice was as disagreeable as it was with the office secretaries.

"Why wasn't his CI assignment in his personnel file?"

She pulled a cushion from the end of the loveseat and moved it behind the small of her back. "I heard it was some kind of gentlemen's agreement. They had a misunderstanding and Frank agreed to transfer out of CI and Julian wouldn't write a fitness report. Why all this now? Why tonight?"

"What was the disagreement about?"

"I don't know."

"If you had to guess."

"Frank's performance, I suppose. He was so stuffy. He had his own code, totally one-dimensional. He wouldn't let anything violate it. Oh, for God's sake, I don't know what it was. Don't ask." Uncomfortable in her position, she got up and found another satin pillow in the chair opposite. "He was just a tiresome bore, he took himself so seriously."

"You mean he wasn't the good soldier everyone else is."

"Don't be dull. That's always the way with Julian, I told you that. Loyalty comes first. You have to believe in him absolutely." She lifted her feet to a stool, her skirt falling way, showing her thighs. She was often careless that way, how she sat or slouched, as if her body weren't of the slightest interest to her or anyone else, and she defied anyone to suggest it was.

"But you don't remember what the disagreement was about?"

"Not precisely, no."

"That's odd. You and Special Projects always know. You're Abbott's eyes and ears."

She looked at him suspiciously. "Not in this case."

"What was Special Projects doing at the time?"

She was slow in answering. "A lot of things. Different things."

"Who were you under then? Abbott or the senior deputy?"

149

"We drifted. Abbott kept us apart."

"Like now, his own operational unit?"

"Something like that, dear, yes."

"I can find out easily enough." The rumor was Elinor had been involved in a domestic black bag operation targeted against an Eastern European embassy in Washington. The FBI had gotten wind of it; the attorney general had complained to the Carter White House.

Her eyes met his defiantly. "Do then, by all means."

"The FBI's interested in the Dudley case. Washington's their turf, not Abbott's. They've got an itch."

"Oh, God." She laughed contemptuously. "You are desperate, aren't you? Like Frank Dudley, that pathetic has-been, that Don Quixote. The FBI doesn't frighten me and you certainly don't either."

"What do you mean, Don Quixote?"

"Just that. Nothing."

It crossed his mind she'd meant something else. "You tell me they had a disagreement but Dudley wasn't sacked, just moved on. A gentlemen's agreement. Why?"

"Julian's a kind man too. People forget that."

"What was the trade-off?"

"What trade-off?"

"If Dudley screwed up, Abbott could have sacked him on the spot. But he wasn't sacked, Abbott let him walk. What did Abbott get out of it? There had to be a trade-off."

"I don't have any idea."

"Think about it. Maybe Abbott screwed up as much as Dudley, maybe a covert operation the seventh floor and the FBI wouldn't forgive, something that had them both in hot water. Maybe a black bag operation here in Washington. Both would keep their mouths shut, a gentlemen's agreement." He was watching her face but saw nothing except mistrust. "Maybe that's what Dudley's appointment on the seventh floor was about last Friday. He was retiring and decided to spill the beans."

"Goodness, what a shrewd little detective mind you have." She leaned forward to bring a leather cigarette case from the table. "I was wrong to encourage you early on, I thought you had bigger worlds to conquer, dear. Certainly not this nonsense."

"Don't kid me. You work on all the newcomers, part of Abbott's unofficial screening board."

She had lit the cigarette but now withdrew it in an angry squall of smoke. "That's a contemptible lie and you know it!" She puffed at the cigarette again and got up to fling it in the ash-filled grate. "It's ugly, what you're doing!"

"Who headed Special Projects when Dudley left?"

She moved back to the table, picked up the leather cigarette box, and dumped the stale cigarettes in the brass scuttle. "Albert Colwin. He died last year."

"When did you take over?"

"As a matter of fact in '76 but I had nothing to do with all this, and if I ever hear you try to involve me in any way, I'll go straight to Julian. I should anyway."

He sat back. *With all this? With all what?* Still active, was it, still a conspiracy, still a cover-up, all of them still involved. "There must have been a trade-off. It wouldn't make sense otherwise."

"It's the witching hour and you're imagining things, dear. You've also been drinking. Give me a cigarette and then go home to your warm little room cozy."

He got up and held out a cigarette from the package. "What room cozy?" She took the pack, removed three, and put two in the leather case.

"Like a tea cozy, except life-size. Your house-mate, obviously. Vinyl plastic."

"What makes you think I have a housemate?"

"Eager-beaver little ensigns like you always have a housemate. I even know what she looks like. Blond, probably, very cuddly. She wears nighties that don't quite cover her buns. Dumb as toast, probably." She laughed. "Vinyl plastic, like your seat covers. She's probably just like that cute little nurse at GW Hospital that woke me up at three o'clock every morning last year to give me a pain-killer and ask If I wanted to go potty." She laughed again. "Anyway someone told me you had a house-mate."

"Who told you?"

"It doesn't matter. My sources. That was really a vicious thing you said. I don't bat my eyes at all the new officers and I certainly don't ask them to dinner to meet my friends the way you did." He lit her cigarette and sat down again. She was still watching him. "Well?"

"Well what?"

"Is that what you think or are you going to apologize? If you don't you can get out of my house."

"I apologize, sorry."

"How sorry?"

"Sorry I brought it up, sorry I hurt your feelings. You don't make it any easier. You're pretty remote sometimes, pretty moody."

"You didn't hurt my feelings and my moods aren't your problem, dear. And while we're speaking so intimately, you're not much to brag about yourself, Ichabod. Worry about your own problems, don't get yourself embroiled in Dudley's nonsense, in something that happened years ago. You're going to make a mess of it, make a mess of your reputation and everyone else's. You realize that, don't you?" She drew her knees onto the sofa, pulling her skirt over them. "Julian admires your work, that's why he asked for you. Your mental energy as much as your drafting. I told you that. Both very much impressed him."

"Oh, sure. Yeah. Shaw chops up everything I write. I give him sirloin and it ends up Hamburger Helper. So don't give me that. He just crucified me back in the office."

"What about?"

"The body they found."

She laughed. "Don't worry about that, dear.

They just got caught with their pants down, FBI-wise. You know how we all adore the FBI. Don't take it too personally."

"How the hell do they expect me to take it?"

"My, we are feeling sorry for ourselves, aren't we? If you're so desperately unhappy, why don't you go back overseas?"

"I'm trying."

"You at least have that. You're lucky. I stay, year after witching year. Julian prefers stability, meaning people like me. Loyalty, dependability, the responsibility that goes with it. Did it ever occur to you that this mess, this tizzy you and everyone else seem to be in, is exactly what Frank Dudley intended?"

"A couple of times, yeah. So what's he trying to do?"

"A preretirement crisis, I suppose. Forgotten men often crave attention and he's very much forgotten. Probably trying to attract sympathy from the seventh floor. They're all such idiots up there these days he may succeed. That would be a pity. We have too much corridor deadwood as it is." She got up. "We're both being very silly. You've succeeded in waking me up and totally wrecking my tub time. You've also upset me. I need something to settle me down. You can stay here and feel sorry for yourself or you can join me."

He followed her, moving through shadows smelling of dust, airlessness, and old books, of threadbare rugs that smelled of cats. Coming into the yellow brightness of the kitchen with its worn lino, grease-spotted range, and shabby cabinets, it occurred to him she lived a miserable life.

"What would you like? I think I have some beer."

"Beer's fine. Tell me, what do you think of Frank Dudley? Just speaking personally now, not officially."

She opened the refrigerator and handed him a bottle. "He was interesting at first but didn't impress me. Do you want a glass?"

"No, thanks. Didn't impress like the rest of us, is that it?"

Her eyes coolly took him in. "Men are all the same. It never occurs to you, none of you. You see only what you want to see." She stooped to open a cabinet, took out a bottle of brandy, and poured a few fingers into a snifter. "Sorry." She handed him a bottle opener. "It's so simple and everyone tries to make it complicated, the way you're doing. It isn't complicated at all and neither is Frank. He's what most men think they are but aren't, try to pretend to be, but can't. He never tried to fool anyone. It wasn't his nature. He was just what he was, nothing more, nothing less." She raised her glass. "Cheers."

"Cheers." Corkery drank and watched her swallow, her eyes closed. "Was what?" The top two buttons of her blouse were unfastened and the pink lacework of her brassiere was visible against her pale chest.

"What finally made him so tiresome. We don't have many like that, but he was completely genuine, a very kind, very gentle man." She took another swallow. "In a word, a gentleman. The complete, virtuous, old-fashioned gentleman."

He waited but she had nothing more to say. "That's all?"

"That's all. Don't look so shocked. *Exit Omnes.* The play's over. Disappointing, isn't it? You look for the answer your whole life and when you finally find it, that's all there is — another dismal bore. But that's exactly what he was, never anything else. The forgotten gentleman with his pathetic chivalry, his code of honor, all those traditions you're born to on Beacon Street and all the abstractions as well — honor, devotion, loyalty, love, religion, responsibility. All those values he thought everyone believed in but didn't, just words. He always did what a gentleman did because that's what he was. *Sensitive* is the word we use, *civilized* is what we mean. Women saw him this way: the forgotten American gentleman. An extinct species. Most of them are stuffed away in a closet these days, writing literary essays. Men saw him differently, which is sad. For the completely masculine American man, he was a fool, obviously. That or a closet queen. Also sad. A Greek among Roman circuses, and I'm not just talking about Langley. So that's what it comes down to, the proper gentleman who always did what proper gentlemen do, not quite religion, not quite faith, not quite anything but there it is. How do you explain it? I don't know." Her voice had grown distant. Her hand was at her hair. "But there you

156

are, darling, one-dimensional. He wasn't my type. Yours either. I've said too much."

She sipped again from her glass, shutting her eyes, as if his expression annoyed her.

"That's interesting."

She smiled falsely. "I thought you'd appreciate it."

"You said you looked for him your entire life but then he was just another bore. He didn't try to come on with you, did he?"

Her face was suddenly cold. "Don't be ridiculous. That's exactly what I'd expect from you. I don't know why I bother. I've told you all I intend to tell you. Now finish your drink and please go."

"You see?" He followed her back the dark hall. "I say something and you get touchy. It's always this way."

"I'm not touchy, I'm disappointed. I try to tell you something difficult, something personal, and the only thing you can ask is whether he got me into bed. That's degrading. It demeans both of us." She handed him his coat.

"I didn't ask if he'd gotten you into the sack, I asked if he tried. There's a difference."

"If you're a man, I suppose there is. Now just go, please. I'm very tired."

"But not for a woman, is that it?" He liked looking at her face. Her expressions always intrigued him, even when she was being bitchy. "I suppose you're right. Sorry."

"I usually am."

"Can I finish my beer?"

"Please do."

Awkwardly he emptied the bottle, wishing she wouldn't watch, but she did. "I don't have a house-mate anymore. She left."

"Did she now." She didn't seem surprised.

"She worked on the Hill. She went back to San Diego to work in her congressman's office there. I met her at Wolftrap, on the lawn there. The cheap seats, remember?"

"I remember."

"She went for the Doobie Brothers. I didn't. Mexican food too. I'm from Pennsylvania, by the way. Western Pennsylvania, the high shoe country, not the Main Line. We don't go much for tamales and Mexican refried beans, not for breakfast, anyway. My friends call me Kip."

"So you told me."

They'd been through the same routine before but this night nothing was working. "Thanks for letting me in. I value your judgment, I really do."

Silently she took back the beer bottle.

"One last question. Who's Alexei Andreyev?"

"You are sly, aren't you." She turned away to the door and slipped back the bolt. Answer enough, he supposed.

"Nothing personal. Just a habit." He pulled on his coat. "You say Dudley had his own code, no one else's. Was that why he screwed up — forget about Abbott — why he didn't make it to the top? Differences with the executive bureaucracy?"

Her face was still turned away. "In principle,

158

yes. He was the perfect staff aide. Nice young gentlemen usually are, especially tall, polite young gentlemen out of Harvard. Staff aides don't have to think, just arrange." Her voice was tired. "When he reached the point where he had some operational responsibility, he couldn't cope. Being a gentleman wasn't enough. You have to be a bit of a bastard too, like you and me — and don't argue, Kevin, please, I'm too exhausted. He wasn't a bastard, not in any way. In the clandestine service where a lot doesn't get reported, that wasn't too conspicuous, not when others were willing to ignore it or cover for you. The perfect gentleman, the perfect front man. So they kept him on, let him host the cocktail parties and dinners, bow to the ladies, light the cigarettes, decant the port, and keep everyone entertained while they were upstairs buggering the *chef du cabinet*. Sad but true."

He moved across the threshold. "Problems of conscience, problems of execution, what?"

She shivered at the door, shoulders hunched as the night wind stirred her dark hair, uncovering the thin shell of her ears, giving her a different look. "You really ought to learn to listen more carefully. It might just lighten your very considerable intellectual load."

He turned. "You call that an intellectual load?" He laughed. "Christ, Elinor, the only thing you've been telling me is that he's got a silver spoon stuck up his —"

She slammed the door.

Everything but the "dear boy" he remembered, finding his way down the dark steps. A definite improvement but not much. But Ichabod had been the unkindest cut of all.

3

TIME IS MEMORY

He had crossed the Seine and was walking parallel to Rue des Francs-Bourgeois, or so he hoped. It had drizzled that morning but at noon the sun had come out, drying the pavements, though a few puddles remained. As he climbed away from the Seine the wind grew gusty and the sky darkened again. It could be a patch of low-flying clouds; in Paris you never knew. The sidewalk was narrow and twisting, like the cobblestoned street. He didn't move into it because of the small cars and trucks that came rumbling without warning around the tight little curves. Everything had gone wrong that might go wrong; being struck down in the Marais by some homicidal Frenchman in his clattering little Renault didn't seem beyond the realm of possibility. Suspended in a vacuum, like a train waiting in a station, he had felt himself slipping backward, but this afternoon his edge had returned. He was very much in the hunt again.

161

The previous day the French press had reported a sixty-hour slowdown by European air traffic controllers to protest wages and working conditions. Most international flights had been delayed, many canceled. A little after ten that morning he had telephoned Otto Rauchfuss's Paris office from a public phone outside the Invalides métro entrance and for the first time someone had answered; a woman's voice, brief and abrupt. Otto had been delayed; he was expected the following afternoon. She asked for his name and number. He said he would call later and hung up. Otto was probably among the inconvenienced transatlantic passengers.

The narrow street he entered lay in deeper shadow, as dim as winter twilight; along it were small shops, small groceries, fetid little bars, and an occasional butcher shop. Algerians congregated in the tiny bars and tobacco shops. If someone left a doorway as he was passing, he had to step into the street to permit passage. Dark unfamiliar places were what he disliked most about foreign travel; passing an afternoon in the purest crystal light high above the clouds and then descending into murk and shadow, a wet tarmac unspooling, the sinister silhouette of a strange terminal, a strange car, a subversive little hotel on some dark narrow street, your foolish bag there on the bed, the leather still cold from the cargo hold. That part of traveling always troubled him; not the anxieties so much, not the depression, not something psychological at all. At the end of a long, long journey, one would hope life had something more

162

to offer than a cold suitcase waiting on a cold ugly bed.

He had changed hotels. The entrance was a few quick steps from Boulevard St.-Germain. It had no dining room, no bar, and no ground floor. The desk was in a tiny foyer up a steep flight of dark steps from the street, stairs without carpeting or rubber matting. Except for the glass plate near the door and the ugly black sign twenty feet higher, unlit at night and dwarfed by the electric signs of the restaurant on one side and the appliance store on the other, few would have known the hotel was there. It had no lift; the stairs that climbed from the desk were dimly lit by dusty glass globes high on each landing. His room was on the fourth floor. It was gloomy, a little damp. Autumn already seemed like winter. He'd bought a brown sweater to wear in the evening. The faucets dripped and there was no radio, but to his surprise when he pushed open the drapes in the dormer window he could see the Seine through the cleft in the buildings to the rear. Stone steps to the west of the hotel led to a cobbled alleyway that wound to the Seine.

Curious how active memory was when time was idle. He might have filled a book those past few days. All kinds of detail came filtering down, like the sea at fifty fathoms, the slow, silent rain of memory. He remembered those early trips with Tricia to Venice and Trieste, Trieste dark and raw in the winter mist, Venice smelling of sewage; gray-eyed Nina with her book, looking out over

163

a gray Berlin sky as she waited for his jeep in the street below. Miraculous how they'd shared their lives, she seventeen, he nineteen, both orphans of glorious summers and winters past, his in the Massachusetts hills and on the shore, hers from that belle époque on the family estate twenty kilometers southwest of Königsberg in East Prussia, both huddled at the edge of existence in the dead-end rubble of Berlin. How brief it had been. Each morning she went to the Catholic church in Nicolskoi to light a taper and pray for her missing brother, lost from von Kleist's First Panzer Army in the Caucasus in 1942. In the spring of 1947, the Russians held a million German prisoners of war. Three times she'd journeyed to the Gruenfeld camp near Frankfurt-on-the-Oder in the Soviet Zone, where groups of prisoners were periodically returned, ragged, emaciated, and diseased, the walking dead. Three times she'd returned alone, heartsick at the suffering she'd seen and the memory of the brother who hadn't returned. Each time he tried to console her, taking her to dinner, bringing flowers when he could find them, the Michaelmas daisies she loved that once grew in the back garden of the house in Charlottenberg when she was a child. She'd received a letter from the Borovichi camp in the Leningrad region but had heard nothing since. Nina and her grandmother were all that remained.

The street emptied into a small square where the shadows dissolved and the sky lightened again. To the west down an intersecting street, he saw a patch of blue sky. The clouds were moving in that direction and so should he. Or should he? He approached the building on the corner to read the street sign and moved off to the north toward a métro entrance.

He couldn't go back, not yet. To return to what? The way back led through the same damp, dark little rooms, past the sinister silhouettes of unfamiliar terminals, a flight crowded with noisy tourists, the turmoil at Kennedy, the sullen queues at La Guardia, the claustrophobic seats, the long cab ride out to Connecticut, the elevator smelling of brass polish, the sterile sameness of the apartment, the vacuum of his office at Langley. A kind of madness in that. Tricia had hated Washington. She wanted to live in Maine, paint, wear sabots, garden, sail, and make love in front of the winter fire built from the sea wrack.

Return to that? With Abbott still in residence, who would listen? Because the Cold War simplified so much, unreflective men thrived on its barbarous simplicities; Langley was still in their grip. When so much could be explained by so little, truth so simplified, virtue so easily identifiable, evil so politically explicit, those who knew little about history, communism, Russia, poverty, hopelessness, and despair had no difficulty explaining the conspiracies arrayed against them. Men like Abbott would triumph while men of decency, wisdom, and humanity annulled themselves; action or its illusion triumphed, always under the pretense of decisiveness: "Be thought strong," Washington's decrepit wise men whispered, "otherwise we will be thought weak."

The Cold War was a symbol of their times. Like Vietnam, as Phil Chambers said, "that lurid blaze," as Joseph Conrad wrote of the French Revolution, "in which the insufficiency of minds and administrative systems stood exposed with pitiless vividness." It was Washington's war, Washington's civil servants who buckled on the swords and trumpeted the victories as the small towns silently buried their dead. It ended as a national disgrace. How could so many wise men be so wrong? Time would give the answer but too late. Like Abbott, like the courts of the Spanish Inquisition to which he belonged, they were men possessed by the demon of an insane idea.

Why else would his seventh-floor appointment on Friday have been canceled? Abbott was responsible. Now it was up to him. Ahead of him was a playground where children were playing. They were wearing skullcaps. Jewish, he supposed. A few hundred yards beyond was a corner restaurant with a glass-enclosed terrace in front. He would have liked to have a drink but three men sat at a table outside, despite the cold. He continued on to the métro and rode out to the flea market, where he wandered among the secondhand clothes booths where the Africans and Algerians shopped. He bought a pair of dark trousers a waiter might wear, still smelling of the clothing bales, dull black shoes to match, cracked at the seams, a thin gray overcoat, and a blue beret. His purchases jumbled in a five-franc plastic shopping bag except for the beret, which he put on, he took the bus back to the Marais. The beret made him feel odd. Strange how oppressive a different identity was, even for a few days. Few mastered it. For most the pseudonyms at the embassy switchboard or the cable cryptonyms were as lightly assumed and as easily surrendered as a black-tie party mask picked up from a silver salver at the front door and left there afterward. They never lived the role. For those who did under deep cover it was far different. He remembered Eric Prosser sitting with Tricia and him and a German couple from Pullach in a Munich nightclub, watching a French mime assume the faces of a lifetime: childhood, adolescence, happiness, sorrow, anger, and old age. The final face wouldn't pull off a hideous grin that crushed the life within. Everyone at the table was laughing except Eric Prosser. His face was an agony. How long has he been there now, twenty-five years?

He couldn't have done what Eric had done, never. Only certain men could. The most successful were men with no identity of their own, men with neither pride nor self-respect, like the poor wretches brought out of the displaced persons camps. What was their identity? Who were they? No one knew. Civilization was crushed in them, like the concentration camp victims: *Volksschaedling,* Otto called them in his broad Berlin dialect, disgraces to the German people. For him, an American and a New Englander, even learning a foreign language was difficult. Something in him wouldn't yield, wouldn't surrender his native tongue for the mindless mimicry of a tutor's German or Russian. Different cultures, different values; barbarians, some of them.

He left the bus in the Marais and wandered about for an hour like a tourist on pilgrimage, searching out churches, secluded parks, and restaurants. He doubted Otto's office would be secure. The staff was probably French, like the woman who answered the phone. By accident he found the route he'd followed earlier that afternoon and passed the small playground and the restaurant with the glassed-in terrace. He drank a glass of beer inside and made a few entries in his notebook, a pocket-size Paris guidebook open on the table in front of him. The beret returned to his shopping bag, he resumed his wandering through the gathering dusk back across the Seine.

That night in his fourth-floor hotel room he put his documents in order to simplify Otto's search for Andreyev among his network of Russian friends in the Soviet emigré community in Berlin, among royalists, aristocrats, old Bolsheviks, right-wing Ukrainian nationalists, scholars, journalists, and God knows who else. He remembered a bitter winter day before the Berlin Wall. Otto had led him to the restaurant in the old Hotel Kempinski in East Berlin to meet an antique dealer. He'd been surprised to see a number of elderly gentlemen with neatly trimmed beards, all Russian emigrés, all come to take their afternoon coffee.

168

Tricia had been searching for a Russian icon for her aunt for Christmas. Otto had dealt with old Russian emigrés in his earlier days when he was flogging antiques among the shop owners of the Kurfürstendamm. That afternoon he introduced him to a seventy-year-old Russian with a spade beard who brought out an age-darkened icon wrapped in a scrap of altar cloth. He couldn't see its details in the gloom of the restaurant, but Otto had vouched for its authenticity. What was the idiom he used when running an urgent errand for Tricia? *"Es geht um die Wurst"* — "The sausage is at stake," that was it. A price was agreed to and Otto delivered the icon three days later, wrapped in the same scrap of altar cloth. A Boston museum appraiser told Tricia's aunt it was worth a fortune. That was Otto for you.

He awoke before the light was in the streets, bathed, shaved, and dressed, impatient to get on with it. The clothes he'd purchased the previous afternoon were still in the plastic shopping bag. He spread the documents on the bed and studied them again, returned them to his briefcase, locked it, and put it in the bottom drawer of the dresser, wrapped in his brown sweater. He had coffee and rolls at a restaurant five blocks to the south. A little after nine he called Otto Rauchfuss's number. A man answered, speaking French with a German accent. Otto hadn't arrived but had been expecting his call. He was anxious to see him.

"Otto gave you my name?" he asked.

The voice hesitated. "No, only that a friend

would call. Do you have this address? Can you come this afternoon?"

"I'd prefer to meet elsewhere." He fumbled for his pocket notebook, found the street in the Marais and the name of the café. Now he chose the hour, not for today but tomorrow. He repeated it a second time and hung up.

The Portuguese cleaning woman was tidying up his room when he returned. A small Frenchman stood just outside, talking to her through the door as he buttoned his cuffs. An official-looking serge jacket with brass buttons was over one arm. He nodded to the Frenchman as he passed. A minor government official on assignment from the provinces, he guessed, recognizing the dark serge jacket and the thin stripe on the trousers. He had the feeling they were talking about him. He would have to move again, he decided after the door closed. He brought his attaché case from the dresser and inspected it. Nothing had been disturbed. He wondered what had made them suspicious. There was nothing of him in the room, nothing left behind, not the slightest shred of an identity. It was the little things that gave you away. Perhaps it was the way he was dressed, the Burberry, the welted shoes. He didn't quite know what to do about either; he was excessively fond of both.

Otto Rauchfuss's West German passport was au-

170

thentic but the identity of the holder of the Canadian passport was in doubt. The Ministry of External Affairs in Ottawa had issued a passport to one Hans David Kruger eleven years earlier. A German prisoner of war held in a Canadian camp in Manitoba in 1944–45, Kruger had returned to Canada as a landed immigrant in 1951 and settled in Toronto. In the late '60s he'd applied for a passport to visit his sister in Dresden, East Germany. His passport had been periodically renewed in Ottawa or at Canadian embassies abroad, but issued to whom? Hans David Kruger, it turned out, had never returned to a permanent address in Canada, at least none that was known. The fingerprints of the unclaimed body in the D.C. morgue weren't Kruger's but Otto Rauchfuss's, who had traveled from Berlin to Montreal and on to Washington on Kruger's passport.

The West German authorities in Bonn had been searching for Rauchfuss for questioning. He would have been detained had he attempted to leave the Federal Republic, his passport withdrawn; Bonn was bewildered when the West German embassy reported his corpse in the D.C. morgue at 19th and Massachusetts. No relatives were listed on his most recent passport application except a sister, living in Karl Marxstadt, East Germany. There was something odd about that too; the Otto Rauchfuss known to the British, French, and U.S. authorities in Berlin since 1945 had no living relatives. All had perished in a firestorm in Neukölln in Berlin in 1943. Young Otto was a street orphan who'd fended for himself in the Berlin rubble, much too successfully, as it turned out.

"Otto Rauchfuss, yes, a Berliner with a very dubious past, to say the least." Shaw lifted his head from a telegram to peer at the notes on his legal pad. "A low-level intelligence peddler. We've had a burn notice out on the man for years, warning our people away. What he was doing here last weekend no one seems to know."

"No one's told me anything about Rauchfuss," Corkery said. "I haven't seen any cables either."

"Sit down. Is Skaff your primary FBI contact on the Dudley case?"

"George is, right. I talk to him every day. Just five minutes ago as a matter of fact. Why?"

"Would you say he's been cooperative?" Shaw got up and limped to his second safe in the corner, his back to Corkery, hiding the dial as he fiddled with the combination. Corkery thought he looked ridiculous, a toothless old dog trying to bury a worthless bone.

"Very cooperative. Why?"

Shaw brought out a green folder and returned to his desk. "I got the Rauchfuss file this morning. I've marked your name here for distribution. See." He pointed to a white circulation slip. "You would have been next on distribution."

Corkery couldn't read his name from across the desk. "I can't see it."

"Well, it's here, I can assure you." Shaw turned a page in the folder and read it silently. "At one time he had a few small businesses in Berlin," he began, "shipping and transfer, a car rental company, a travel agency. Owned a small transient hotel at one time, also did some packing and shipping for the Berlin base, on contract, packing and household shipments."

"U.S. government?"

"Evidently. Apparently he began as a warehouse clerk for the U.S. Army in Schöneberg in the late forties, an AMG depot. Let's see — yes. In the forties. He left, rather he was dismissed for suspected theft of truck parts, but the CID didn't press the case for lack of evidence. He started his own garage, then a transport company. The Brits had some suspicion about his involvement in a car theft ring as early as 1946. Odd. The lad could hardly drive. Then there were a few black market operations with some commissary NCOs, sulfa drugs, penicillin, but nothing was ever proven and this came out much later. A very ambitious little man, it seems."

"That's ancient history. The black market kept Berlin alive in those days, Germany too. What's he been doing recently?"

"The same sort of thing. Very shady business."

"Shady business. My, my."

"Are we being sly?" Shaw didn't look up. "Shady business is shady business. At present Otto Rauchfuss is a partner in two import-export firms, Klemenz Technik and AG Electronik. Computers, it seems, computers and computer software. They do business with the East German ministries. He's also a principal partner in an odd little Swiss company in Bern. Interbahn AG. Has offices in Berlin and Frankfurt. The official Swiss trade registry claims it specializes in the sale and production of communications equipment. Production? In Switzerland? How facile the Swiss are. What do the Swiss produce except clocks, bank accounts, and Swiss cheese?"

"Ski snow." Corkery sank deeper into his cushioned chair.

Shaw pretended not to hear. "Otto Rauchfuss, yes. A man of dubious practices and even more dubious connections. His postwar black market activities attracted the notice of the East German intelligence services. According to one British source, he was recruited in Potsdam in 1949. Does that improve upon *shady?* But that's ancient history now, as you say. A low-grade intelligence peddler, no doubt about that. What's more relevant is that his Swiss company is in serious difficulty. The Bern firm is under indictment in federal court in New York. It was involved with some Brooklyn firm, illegally trading U.S. electronic components through Bern and Vienna to the Soviet bloc. Otto Rauchfuss is named, so is his partner, a German named Vogel, another *Grossschieber* from the black market days. Do you know what *Grossschieber* is?"

"Candy man, I think, someone who deals in sweet stuff. Maybe a black market gangster."

Shaw looked up. "I didn't know you had German."

"A little."

"Really. From where?"

"University, then the navy. I was going to Bonn on the Naval Attaché's staff but was sent to the Middle East fleet at Bahrain instead. What about Vogel?"

"Klaus Herman Vogel. A Saxon. He has ties to East German intelligence, to Stasi, no doubt about that. Did some ugly work for them in Berlin and Bonn some years back, very ugly: blackmail, sexual entrapment, among others. Now he and Rauchfuss are both under federal indictment in New York."

"Is that why the West Germans were looking for Rauchfuss, for extradition to the U.S.?"

"That's not clear." Shaw sorted among the cables. "Vogel's Frankfurt office manager was arrested a few days ago at Frankfurt International Airport by the German Border Patrol. The Hesse state prosecutor's office claims he'd falsified export applications for certain electronic components. Rauchfuss and Vogel are on the same watch list." Shaw closed the file. "You say George Skaff has been cooperative."

"Very cooperative."

"It would be useful to know what conclusions the FBI seems to be drawing about the Rauchfuss case, something they haven't shared with us. Did the Justice Department and the FBI quietly bring Rauchfuss here to offer evidence in connection with the U.S. indictment? Or did they bring him here for other reasons?"

"Not that I know of —"

"I was not asking, I was posing the question.

Who knew he was here? The federal attorney's office in New York, Justice, the FBI? These are answers they don't seem to be sharing with us. I want you to talk to George Skaff —"

"Easy," Corkery said, getting up. "Can I use your phone —"

"Not here. Sit down. I want you to go talk to George Skaff in confidence and learn as discreetly as possible what conclusions the FBI has drawn about Rauchfuss. You're not to say that I, Adrian Shaw, asked about the case, nor that Langley had expressed the slightest interest in Otto Rauchfuss. Do you understand?" His eyes lingered benignly on Corkery's face as he explained these points of protocol, as if hypocrisy were an operational asset that didn't go unappreciated. Corkery felt Julian Abbott's invisible hand from the office fifty feet away. He had returned the previous evening.

"That doesn't make any sense," he said.

"Do I detect a lack of enthusiasm?"

"Yeah. A lot. It doesn't make sense. What's the point?"

"What's the point?" Shaw leaned forward over his desk, trying to pierce Corkery's unhappy gaze. "I should think the point perfectly obvious. In this way we'll know the FBI's conclusions without seeming to have any interest in knowing. Isn't that always the point, to know precisely and in all detail what those whose interests aren't identical with our own don't intend us to know or would deny us —"

"This is Washington, Adrian, not Berlin or Moscow. You're talking about the FBI."

"Of course it's Washington. Does that change anything? Value depends upon who gets a piece of information first, doesn't it, whether in Washington or anyplace else. Its very substance depends upon who gets it first. Surely you know that by now. If you know nothing of counterintelligence operations, you certainly know something of the stock market."

"Why don't you pick up the phone and ask?"

"Why don't they tell us?"

"Ask them."

"We intend to but in our own way —"

"Right now, I mean. Did Rauchfuss know Frank Dudley?"

Taken by surprise, Shaw hesitated. His eyes moved away as he opened the file and closed it again. "I don't know. No one seems to know."

It occurred to Corkery that he was lying. "Has anyone looked into it?"

"We've asked, we're asking now —"

"I haven't seen any cables."

"Haven't you? I thought you had."

"Look, am I action officer on this or not?"

"Certainly. Has anyone suggested otherwise? That's why I called you. Go talk to Skaff."

As action officer Corkery was also given the responsibility — "tasked," in Shaw's crisp instructions — of drafting a daily status report to be on his desk no later than four o'clock each afternoon for forwarding to the seventh floor, all clearances complete, from Security, FBI liaison, Domestic

Contact, and those Langley geographical divisions that might have received a Dudley sighting from their field stations; Foxrun sightings, they were called, under Frank Dudley's cable traffic codeword.

A few Foxrun cables were on his desk when he returned from Shaw's office. London had reported a Dudley sighting in a taxi queue outside Heathrow. Someone lunching with a Foreign Office first secretary at White's thought he'd seen him hurrying into a Humber at the curb outside driven by a blond woman of indeterminate age. An immediate cable from Oslo reported Dudley at the Osttbanestasjonen train station in the company of a Norwegian security official, carrying a nylon bag and a tennis racket and hurrying toward a waiting car. The Norwegian official, known to Dudley during his Oslo tour, was contacted; after some perplexity and with some embarrassment, he'd admitted that he was indeed at the train station that morning, and was accompanying someone of Dudley's height and figure, but the man wasn't Frank Dudley. He was a minor Norwegian diplomat who'd been discreetly summoned home from post because of irregularities in his financial accounts. A cable from Paris was intriguing. Waiting for a traffic light on Boulevard Montparnasse near the La Coupole restaurant, an officer from the Paris station who knew Dudley thought he saw him standing just off the curb, arm lifted, attempting to flag down a taxi. He was sufficiently struck by the resemblance to turn his car around in the next block. By the time he returned, Dudley had vanished. He drove on, pursuing three taxis ahead of him, but lost two in the traffic. The third was carrying a pair of American tourists who'd obviously wined and dined at La Coupole.

Even the Latin American division had reported a few sightings. One was on a busy sidewalk café on Avenida de la Paz in Tegucigalpa, Honduras. Twenty-four hours later another Tegucigalpa sighting was reported, this one in the lobby of a luxury hotel favored by American businessmen and the American military. A third, less definite, took place on the road outside Aguacate. Dudley, dressed in dusty suntans, had been seen arguing with a local taxi driver. It didn't seem to matter that Dudley didn't speak Spanish, had never served in Latin America, and had never shown the slightest interest in Latin American affairs.

The fact that Dudley sightings occurred in geographic clusters, like UFO sightings, made Corkery uneasy. He wondered if anyone had ever given serious study to the phenomenon. Incestuous inbreeding from a few paranoiac ideas was characteristic of Julian Abbott's counterintelligence staff, if not the Cold War, but to infect other geographic bureaus, an entire bureaucracy, or all of official Washington with the same insanity was something he'd never considered. Maybe it was worth a congressional investigation. But how? Congress was part of the problem.

Drafting the daily status report had become his daily burden, leaving him with less time to pursue his own leads. Elinor Wynn drafted a separate daily status report based on telephone, commercial telegraphic, and diplomatic cable intercepts obtained by D-staff from the National Security Agency's codebreakers and electronic eavesdroppers at Fort Meade, but her daily report went separately to Shaw. Corkery never saw it. He complained about this, arguing that as action officer the material was essential. Shaw took his point. Thereafter at ten minutes to four Elinor would march into his office and drop her report on his desk. "Satisfied?" she would say, and stalk out.

It was always typed on a single half page and always contained the same two words: "D-staff negative."

Skaff was at his desk in a corner office with pale green walls, rummaging through four different stacks of papers. On one wall was a degree from Capital University in Columbus, Ohio. At his elbow was a ceramic coffee cup with the name G. T. Skaff glazed in letters so jagged the name seemed a threat, but on this bright morning he seemed no more ominous than usual, just his usual colorlessly efficient self wearing a white shirt and a figureless red rayon tie. An FBI agent had wandered in. Skaff introduced him as Fred Rittenhouse. He sat on the arm of a chair in front of the desk, smoking a cigarette and looking moodily toward the window where the sun lay as bright as paint on the street.

The autopsy had concluded Otto Rauchfuss died

on Friday night. "Punctured spleen and kidneys," Skaff said, handing him the report. "Internal bleeding. Homicide. Beaten up, stabbed with a serrated knife. Tyrone thinks it started out as robbery and then someone got rough. All of a sudden it's a homicide. These foreign tourists don't know."

"What do you expect?" Rittenhouse said morosely. "They're foreigners, they're in Washington, the nation's capital."

Corkery looked up at him curiously. "Any suspects?"

"Black guy. Late Friday night he was in a liquor store up at the top of the hill on M Street, plenty of cash. A couple of hours earlier he'd been hustling pocket change out on the sidewalk, dead broke. Used to be a scaler, a cut man for a Georgetown fish market. Same kind of knife. They found a stocking mask in the lot near the old warehouse."

"Tyrone have a name?"

"Guy like that don't have a name. Black male in his thirties, six foot one or two. Heavyset. Stoned, like all of them." Drawn by a siren in the street, Rittenhouse wandered to the window and depressed a metal slat to look out. The late-morning brightness took on a milky glare through the streaked glass. The siren faded away and Rittenhouse turned toward the door. "Let me know if you need anything, George. Nice meeting you, Corkery." He wandered out gloomily, leaving the door open.

"What's his problem?" Corkery said.

"Fred? Bad case of D.C. depression. The morn-

181

ing body count. Got here a month ago from Portland, Oregon." He opened a desk drawer and searched through it.

"I talked to Shaw this morning. He told me Otto Rauchfuss is under indictment in New York."

"Federal indictment, yeah. Did some business with a Brooklyn company, trading U.S. electronic parts to the Soviets. Integrated circuits, stuff for making microprocessors. Otto Rauchfuss's one of the partners. The other's Vogel, a nasty piece of work. Funny Rauchfuss turning up here." He didn't look up. "Who papered him?"

"The passport? I don't know. Has the Justice Department asked for Rauchfuss's extradition?"

"No, nothing. Not even thinking about it."

"Then maybe the East Germans papered him. An operation of some kind, maybe in Canada, maybe here. Maybe a bagman, maybe a drop, maybe a meeting with someone. You remember the French bank note we found, the one torn in two?"

"Think so? Yeah, I remember. A piece of trade craft, you think?" Skaff's gray head was hidden behind the desk as he bent to retrieve something he'd dropped. "Wouldn't be your people brought him over, would it? Working on something?"

Corkery laughed. "Christ, no. Shaw's asking the same questions you are. He's blundering around in the dark. If the Agency papered him, I wouldn't be here."

Skaff's head popped up again. "Just thinking out loud."

"If the Justice Department didn't know Rauchfuss was here and we didn't either, then maybe he came on his own, maybe to cut a deal with someone, maybe with Justice, maybe with us."

Skaff banged a drawer shut and opened another. "That'd make sense. Maybe he knew some of your people from Berlin, the guys at Dahlem, the U.S. mission, the Agency base there. Decided to look someone up, make a deal. We drop the federal indictment, pump his basement for him, find out how this high-tech bootlegging operation works in the GDR, who else is behind it."

"Frank Dudley was in Berlin. He got the telephone call Thursday night."

"Could be. Where the hell did I put it?" Skaff was still rummaging through the drawer. The phone rang. He ignored it.

"Maybe another way. Maybe Rauchfuss had something on Dudley; they met, had an argument, Dudley got scared and took off."

Skaff picked up the ringing phone: "Call me later." He hung up. "Other way? What other way? Walk me through it."

"Maybe the East German Haupt-Ableilung owned Dudley. Maybe they had for years. I don't think so but it's a possibility. They find out he's retiring, don't like it, and send Rauchfuss over. They had an argument, maybe a fight. Dudley got scared and left town."

"Blackmail? Could be but I doubt it. People like Dudley don't chitchat holding a fish scaler's knife.

Not with his pedigree. Where the hell did it go?"

"I doubt it too. Just another stray cat. None of it adds up. What are you looking for?"

Skaff stood up and leaned over to search his correspondence box. "Something you got me started on. Here it is." He withdrew a document from the bottom and handed it to Corkery. It was a Xeroxed copy of an Army CIC field report from Munich years earlier, covered by a red and white FBI classified sheet. "Andreyev, the Moscow trial you found in Dudley's papers. Well, that's him, Major Alexei Andreyev, or so he said. He interested a lot of people. No one ever figured him out, not our people, not yours."

Corkery took the file. "I'll be damned. You know the case?"

"Not at the time, but you got me interested. Pretty weird, all of it. First Dudley, then the East Germans, now Andreyev. Gets your blood moving, like the old days. There's more downstairs. That's yours for starters. Hungry? Let's go to lunch."

They left the office. "All this?" Corkery said, flipping through the pages. "CIC? This goes back fifteen years. How the hell do you people ever keep it all straight?"

"We don't, that's what it's all about. No beginning, no end, no artillery, no bomb runs, no foxholes." Skaff pressed the elevator button and pulled on his coat. "Take a few prisoners, get a few walk-ins, drunks, most of them, walking stiffs, dead-enders, like this Andreyev, but that's about it. What they used to call the Cold War. Before

184

your time, most of it. It's been going on since the Crusades."

In Hesse along the West German border, darkness had come early that autumn afternoon. Two NCOs from the U.S. 2nd Armored Cavalry squatted in their border observation hut to peer through the rain toward the East German village beyond the frontier. Their radar had picked up movement a thousand yards beyond. The corporal fixed the greenish glow of his Starscope on an abandoned farm road interdicted by the wire fence along the border where a crossing had been unsuccessfully attempted the previous afternoon. A truck had tried to run the barricade but had rolled over, bringing down a section of the fence. The two occupants were pinned in the cab. The Vopo motorized patrol in pursuit had taken both into custody. One had to be dragged to the Vopo personnel carrier. Both were farm laborers who'd stolen a truck.

That morning a crane moved the truck off the barricade and section of downed fence. The break had been patched with wire but the heavier mesh hadn't been replaced.

As the American corporal watched through his Starscope, a Russian-built jeep stopped on the road near the repaired wire. Two men got out, leaving the jeep lights on. During the past week an East German army mapping detail with two Russian advisors had been seen along the road with transits and sight-rods, remapping the salient in the border. The Russian jeep with its lights on had the same markings as the jeep seen near the mapping detail.

In the light of the headbeams, one man cut quickly through the temporary wire, moved on as the other followed, limping badly, and cut through the heavy fence to the west. The two followed the ditch along the abandoned road and disappeared into the woods. The American corporal moved his Starscope to the East German observation post and saw no movement outside. The lights of the two vehicles parked below the East German watchtower hadn't come on. Five minutes later the two border crossers reappeared, climbing the hill toward the wooden hut. The Russian jeep was still at the barricade, its lights dimmer. A few minutes later the three Americans inside the hut heard drunken voices as the defectors tramped up the wet hillside through the rain.

They brought them inside. In the darkened hut they couldn't make out their faces or their uniforms but could smell the alcohol and the rank animal smell of wet woolen uniforms. An East German major and his NCO driver had fled from the GDR, or so it was first believed. The NCO driver was carrying a bottle of Polish vodka in his coat pocket; the uniform under the major's damp woolen coat wasn't East German but Russian, a discovery made in a well-lit office at the 2nd Armored Cavalry's hqs where they were driven. The Soviet jeep remained on the interdicted road, its lights growing dimmer. Not until seven the following morning was it found by an East German patrol.

"Some people got a little suspicious about that, the Russian jeep standing there all night," Skaff said as they returned from lunch. Corkery followed him down an empty stairwell. Skaff's words volleyed off the walls like voices from a racquetball court. "He won't come clean right away either. He finally says he's Russian but not an officer, just an NCO fed up with barracks life, but he's still lying. They find out when the Germans at Pullach get an intercept from an East German military channel about a missing Russian on a mapping detail, an officer named Andreyev. That's who he turns out to be, Major Alexei Andreyev."

Skaff opened a door to a large, brightly lit basement room filled with rows of green and gray filing cabinets. File searchers sat on castered stools at open file drawers. Corkery followed him down a middle aisle. "He's debriefed in Frankfurt and they bring him over. Your people don't think much of him, although they don't say why. The Pentagon thinks he's the real McCoy. They find a place for him, helping edit technical manuals on Soviet armor and armored tactics, but that's not what Andreyev wants."

"What's he want?"

"A job over at the Agency, working with the Intelligence Directorate, doing what he does best, but your people won't touch him. They wouldn't tell anyone why. One thing did turn up. Word got out they gave him a polygraph at Pullach and he flunked. DIA thought your technicians had screwed up and wanted your people to flutter him again but your guys refused. So what do you figure? They didn't trust him. Whether it was the polygraph or something else, they didn't trust him."

"And they never told anyone why?"

"Not a word, like he didn't exist. Anyway, Defense found a place for him and Andreyev was pretty hot stuff for a while. He testifies at hearings up on the Hill for the Pentagon about the Soviet threat, the Warsaw Pact, all the missile rattling going on at the time — shake, rattle, and roll, that whole goddamn circus DOD puts on at budget time. Andreyev fits right in. Lectures at the National War College, gets invited to armored maneuvers down at Fort Bragg, the whole dog-and-pony show. But pretty soon Vietnam's getting worse, Johnson's out, and it's the new Nixon crowd and a whole new ball game. Now it's Kissinger, China, and détente. Europe and NATO aren't much making the headlines anymore, the Pentagon's got its head stuck up its ass in Vietnam, and what Andreyev has to say doesn't count for much. They pull his plug. DOD dumps him. He's pretty well pumped dry anyway. He drops out of sight. Hi, sweetie. Ken Obie in?"

Skaff stopped at a secretary's desk at the far end of the room. Behind her through a glass-partitioned wall a man in shirt sleeves was at his desk talking on the phone. "Tell him we're here."

He led Corkery through the door into an office

opposite, empty except for an oak table and four chairs. A green blackboard hung on the wall opposite the partition and near it an empty tripod. Whatever had been written on the board had been erased. The brown glass government ashtrays were filled with cigarette butts.

"So Andreyev drops out of sight but he's still around. Remember Mickey Mantle, how he turns up working at some bush league golf club up in New Jersey? Joe Louis, what was he? A bouncer out in Vegas? Andreyev's like that. He drifts here and there, gets his U.S. citizenship, starts his own business, goes bust, starts another. He likes women, is footloose, doesn't care, is in and out, like a lot of people in this town, big news for a time but now a small-time loser who can't make it anymore. He winds up with a two-bit translation office over on East Capitol Street, doing contract work for a few federal agencies and the Library of Congress. So everybody's forgotten about him. Then a few funny things happen."

"When was this?"

"Seventy-six, I think it was. One night Andreyev spots a face he thinks maybe he knows in a little bar over on Pennsylvania near his office. The guy's sitting in a corner in front all by himself when Andreyev comes in. It's dark, he can't see him too well, but he has this feeling. When he leaves, the guy's still there, giving him the fish eye. Two weeks later, the same thing. He's up on the Hill, dropping off some translation he'd done for a House subcommittee staff. There's a

Defense budget hearing down the hall, the place is crowded, journalists, TV cameramen, purple suiters from the Joint Chiefs, DOD spear-carriers, and he has a hard time getting through. He sees the same guy, standing in the crowd. Something clicks and Andreyev remembers: the guy's a Russian, someone he knew from the old GRU days in Moscow. He knows he's right when the guy follows him and says something to him in Russian. Andreyev loses him on the stairs but it worries him. He looks up his old FBI housemother and tells him about the two incidents."

"The FBI had a watch on Andreyev?" Somewhere behind Corkery a hot-air blower came on.

"We did for a long time but we'd dropped it by then. His old housemother was Carl Rawson. He's retired now, down in Alabama. Grows catfish. But there's something funny about the way Andreyev reported it. He waits maybe two or three weeks before he gets in touch with Rawson. When he does, he can't come up with a name."

"A coincidence or did he think maybe this Russian was sent to contact him?"

"He doesn't know but thinks that's a possibility. So do we. First thing we want to know is who this guy is. Is he local, someone from the Soviet embassy, or someone they sent in, maybe down from the UN? Or maybe an illegal, but that wouldn't make any sense. Too risky. We need a name. Andreyev can't give us one. Maybe he doesn't know. He remembers this guy from Moscow all right, we can't shake him on that, but all he remembers is his face. So we get some photographs together of the Soviet mission people and have Andreyev look at them, an evening slide show. Nothing. Zero. There are a couple of Soviets we think might be our man, two or three that spend a lot of time on the Hill nosing around. Two were just posted to Washington out of the GRU Second Directorate in Moscow. The GRU was Andreyev's service in Moscow, so that would fit. One was running illegals in the U.S. and Latin America, or so the Agency said, and that would fit too. I don't remember his name. It's in the file. Worked out of the Soviet fisheries office over on Decatur Street. But we don't get anything. Andreyev passes over our suspects without batting an eye. While we're getting more mug shots together of the Soviet UN crowd up in New York, we tell Andreyev to play along if the guy approaches him again, this Comrade X whoever he is, to act interested. Right away you people over at Langley put the kibosh on that. No dice. You don't tell us why. Just no dice. Funny, right?"

Skaff glanced through the glass door, got up, and disappeared into the adjacent office. He stood talking with the man at the desk gave him a requisition slip, and returned. "They'll get the files for us. Where was I?"

"The FBI wants to use Andreyev but Langley says no dice."

Skaff glanced at his watch, took out a cigarette, and sat down. "Right, no dice. They stonewalled at first, but then a week later they laid it out for us over at Langley. Someone in CI, your shop. Rukowsi, Rudowski, something like that. One of Abbott's deputies. Turns out you people have this Soviet defector out of Paris. A KGB type, high level. Takes a goddamn fire brigade to pump this guy's tanks. It turns out he knows all about Andreyev or claims he does. He tells your people Andreyev defected in East Germany under GRU control. Had a few hard target priorities. Missile-site preparation in the continental U.S. was number one. Bomar missiles was another, Bomars and Hawkeyes maybe. Anyway, he says Andreyev worked under GRU control, supported by some illegal here in the U.S., a third country national, but then after a few years he got restless and slipped the leash. Then when things weren't working out for him after he left the Pentagon, he got homesick. This KGB defector told your people Andreyev had sent a letter to his ex-wife in Moscow, telling her he was fed up and ready to come home. He tells us the GRU Center back in Moscow was thinking about contacting Andreyev and putting him back to work, a Sov asset in place. After that, a one-way ticket home." Skaff smiled and finally lit the cigarette he'd been fiddling with. "That puts a whole new patch on Grandpa's overalls, doesn't it?"

"So maybe this guy Andreyev spotted in the bar and up on the Hill was sent to contact him."

"Looked like it. But then a few people working the Sov circus here began to backtrack. They remembered how Andreyev didn't report the two

192

incidents with this Comrade X until two or three weeks later. After what the KGB defector told your people, they figured maybe this Comrade X had already made contact with Andreyev and the two got a little worried, thought maybe someone had spotted them together. So they came up with the idea of Andreyev telling the FBI. That made sense too, only we never found out. Next thing we know Andreyev takes a trip to Europe — Vienna, I think it was. Bingo. He disappears. Takes a powder. The last anyone saw of him he was getting on a planc in Frankfurt."

"Disappeared?"

"Disappeared, flew the coop." A woman with a leather driving glove on one hand came in with a wire basket holding a few green and manila file folders. Skaff signed the log she gave him and she went out. " 'Barnswallow,' that's the code name." He shuffled through the files. "Here it is. One last thing. A couple of weeks after Andreyev takes a powder, a half-dozen diplomats over at the Soviet mission get called home. I mean quick, called out in their nightshirts, hustled out to Dulles and bang, they're gone. Some sort of shakedown is going on, something big, but we never hear, not a peep. We figure they were looking for someone. Whether they found him or not, we don't know." He opened the files and spread them on the table. "Take your time and leave them with the secretary outside when you're finished. If you need anything more, I'll be upstairs. I've got a three o'clock meeting."

The first report in the file was the CIC file from Munich he'd read at lunch. The file didn't include the CIA debriefing at Frankfurt or any other CIA document, notably the Andreyev letter, a fragment of which he'd found in the Dudley basement storage locker. There were periodic assessments by Andreyev's FBI control officer, reports of debriefings, FBI routine surveillance, and a memo by the FBI officer who'd attended the CIA briefing at Langley reporting that Andreyev was a dispatched GRU agent. The name of the Soviet KGB defector wasn't given; his cryptonym was AE/Crevice. There were a dozen reports by FBI agents after Andreyev's disappearance and interviews with staffers on the Hill, the Library of Congress, and the National Science Foundation, where Andreyev had done some translation work. They remembered him as a pleasant man, a little unkempt, a man who cared little about appearances, whose suits and shirts were uncared for. Brilliant in some ways, his Washington contacts reported, puzzling in others, a man who drank a lot and had few close friends. There was a single picture, taken for his DOD identification card. The face was round, with a badgerlike fullness to the jowls; the dark hair was thick and uncut. He was smiling.

When Corkery returned the four file folders to the secretary outside, his questions were still unanswered. Upstairs, Skaff had left for a meeting. He went out into the blustery November cold and walked up Constitution toward the State Department and the Bluebird shuttle to Langley. Whoever he was and whatever Dudley's obsession, Major Alexei Andreyev was little more than another Washington abstraction.

Melvin Sterner, a Soviet analyst in the Intelligence Directorate, couldn't recall why his name was jotted down in Dudley's desk diary. It was late in the afternoon when Corkery found him, bent over a yellow legal pad in a book-lined crypt smelling of aromatic pipe tobacco. A few books and monographs were at his elbow.

"Your name was written down three times in four days, as a matter of fact," Corkery said. "Just a note, reminding him to call you about something."

"Call me? That's odd. When?"

"Last October."

"Can't think of what it might have been." He was in his fifties, round-faced and beginning to bald. He wore a pair of red suspenders over a blue oxford cloth shirt. "Where was he working?"

"In Public Affairs."

He frowned, pushed his chair back, and opened his middle desk drawer. "I don't have much contact over there." He fussed about among his papers. "Is it important?" Soviet analysts resisted intrusion on their turf, like fussy medieval historians shut up in contemplative gown and slippers within their high-walled palatine gardens, resisting the barbarian nomads who swept down from the clandestine services outside the walls, looking for booty.

"I'm not sure. You knew Frank Dudley?"

He nodded sourly. "I knew him but not well."

A bloody nuisance, was he? Join the club. "Did you see him much when he worked in CI?"

"No, not much. Abbott runs a closed shop. October, you say?" He frowned over a spiral appointment book he'd withdrawn.

"The first week in October."

Two men were passing along the inner corridor, murmuring over a typed draft. On the windowsill near Corkery's chair was a stack of Russian newspapers, their pages bleached yellow by the sun. "Come to think of it, there was something. Our monthly serial listing, I think." He closed the drawer and got up, moving to the bookcase, where he took a mimeographed list from the top shelf and searched its pages. "That's right, our subscription list. We put out a monthly list of articles on the Soviet Union, articles of general interest to Soviet specialists. Last September we revised the list and weeded a few names. Dudley's was one we dropped. He wanted his name retained. He wanted some back issues, the ones he'd missed." Sterner returned to his desk and sat down. "That was it, I remember now. He called me."

"He tried to keep up with the literature?"

"I suppose so, but you can't really, there's so much published. I don't think he read Russian, didn't speak it either, but that doesn't matter. The titles are in English. If there's a demand for some article not in English, we'll have it translated. It's

196

a full-time profession, just keeping up with the articles, to say nothing of the translations. Some translations are done here, others are contracted out."

"Do you remember what subjects interested Dudley?"

He picked up his pipe and searched for his tobacco pouch. "Articles of general interest, I suppose. My impression was his interest in Soviet studies didn't go very deep." From down the hall came the sounds of safes slamming closed.

"He didn't mention what he was looking for?"

"No, just that he was missing a few back issues, September or October, I think. I told him we'd taken his name off our list but we'd reinstate it." He lit his pipe. "Not much help, I'm afraid. Where is Dudley these days?"

"On medical leave," Corkery said. "Thanks."

Burton Womack, another name from Dudley's desk diary, was less forthcoming. He found him in a brightly lit room off a remote basement corridor in a distant wing of the building he'd seldom visited, a large room lined with bar-lock cabinets and gray safes. Five men sat at separate desks, heads bent over stacks of documents, like readers in the silence of a library reading room. The office reviewed confidential documents for sanitization and release to the public under the Freedom of Information Act. Dudley had worked with Womack and others on the staff during his assignment to Public Affairs.

Womack was Dudley's generation but a southerner. Tall and rawboned with a tired face, tired eyes, a tobacco-dark voice, a wash-and-wear short-sleeved shirt and a shoelace tie, he smelled of failure. His office received few visitors; there were no chairs in front of his desk; he had no secretary. He stood as they talked, asking Corkery where he'd served, how long he'd been aboard, what he did in CI. It was an old ploy, the fox romping with the hounds, and Corkery let him play it out. Public Affairs received most FOI requests, sent them to Womack's shop, which located the files, sanitized them, and tried to clear them with the originating offices, which refused. It was a can of worms. He didn't recall the cases Dudley had shown any interest in.

"Your shop's the worst," Womack said. "CI has always had its own rules. Nothing gets by Abbott, nothing his people have ever touched. They've got a rule of thumb up there. If you think it'll go public, shred it, dump it, bury it. Nothing gets past, ever. Zilch. FBI or State opens up a case CI was working, fuck 'em. They'll deep-six it, burn it, shred it, you name it. They don't put anything down on paper these days. Who cares? Me, I'm treading water till Monrovia."

"Did Dudley ever work a CI case for someone named Andreyev, Alexei Andreyev?" Shaw had insisted CI had no file for Major Alexei Andreyev. The registry archives were also blank.

Womack gave a harsh laugh and picked up his coat from the back of the chair. "You're working for those guys and you come to ask me that? Come on, let's get serious. What'd they do, send you down here to nose around, see if their flanks are covered? I never heard the name. Neither has anybody else. Sorry, I gotta close up."

So Burton Womack had worked a few CI cases for release to the public, had crossed swords with Abbott or Shaw, maybe about the Andreyev file, and had gotten scalped. Now he was on his way to Monrovia, which seemed about right; Monrovia was the pits.

He went back upstairs. On his desk were a half-dozen cables reporting Foxrun sightings, all to be incorporated in his daily status report. One reported Frank Dudley had been seen at the Pickwick Club in Belize, having lunch with a bearded Cuban expatriate, a known drug dealer and gunrunner. Two others reported sightings in Honduras. Another was from Nicosia, Cyprus. Suntanned and bearded, Dudley was seen standing in the cockpit of a forty-five-foot sailboat of unknown registry, quaffing gin slings with two young bikini-clad lovelies, Greek or Lebanese, the source couldn't be sure. The sailboat had left port the following day. Off to Cloud-Cuckoo-Land no doubt.

He sank despondently in his chair and sifted through the cables, a spot trader in the intelligence commodities market, all of them worthless. The phone rang. It was Miss Fogarty, reminding him his daily status report for the seventh floor was thirty minutes late. Shaw was waiting. "Jesus Christ. Give me a few more min-

199

utes for God's sake."

"A problem, perchance?" Elinor asked from the door. She strolled in, delicately holding her D-staff report between thumb and forefinger. She paused, waved it seductively over his desk a few times, gave it a final flourish, and let it drift free. "That's for the other night," she said, turned, and went out.

4

AN OLD
SONG-AND-DANCE
MAN

Guidebook under his arm, he strolled through the
Marais toward Rue des Francs-Bourgeois, found
the dark little street meandering away toward the
northwest and followed it, passed through the
small square and continued on, hunched in his
threadbare coat, his ugly gray hat pulled low on
his forehead. He stopped as he recognized the intersection and the playground where the Jewish
children had been playing. It was deserted. A chilly
afternoon wind pushed broken clouds from the
west; fallen leaves rattled across the gravel. They
were inside now, in their classrooms until six, he
remembered, pausing to reflect upon the brick
school building through the bare trees. They would
be watching through the high windows as the long
sad afternoon faded into dusk. He smelled chalk
dust, winter woolens, the brine of the hockey rink

at St. Paul's, and remembered the heartbreak of a winter afternoon denied. He recalled a scrap of schoolboy Wordsworth that so often came to him while ice-skating: "When we have given our bodies to the wind."

Carried back again, the current always moving him backward into the past. Why the past? What was he searching for?

The small restaurant with its enclosed glass terrace was thirty meters up the street. The building opposite supplied any number of windows for a static surveillance post. A poor choice? But this cold afternoon the tables had been withdrawn from the front pavement. He would sit inside the enclosed terrace, at the window, if possible. It was possible. The front tables were empty. He was five minutes early and sat at the third table to the right of the door, facing the street, his coat still on. The terrace was chilly. A few midafternoon customers sat at the covered tables inside the restaurant to his rear, where the light was brighter. A white-jacketed waiter came out the glass door and wiped the green metal table. *"Un pression,"* he said, ordering a glass of draft beer. The waiter returned inside and he unbuttoned his coat, took off his gray scarf, and pushed it into his right-hand pocket so that the end trailed away. He kept his gray hat on. He took a packet of cigarettes from his pocket, removed one, and left the pack atop the folded newspaper on the table.

He kept his eyes on the street as he smoked and drank his glass of beer. The wall of a church just west of the deep apron of pavement obstructed his view in that direction. Across the street was a dry-cleaning shop, to the east the intersection where cars passed slowly and infrequently. It was a quiet neighborhood. Two elderly couples moved by, bundled against the cold. One was trailing a collapsible grocery cart. A young woman wearing a gray sweater over her white smock crossed the street from the dry-cleaning shop, entered the restaurant, and left with two espressos. Ten minutes later two men appeared from the direction of the church. They stood on the curb for a moment, talking, then moved into the street. Both wore hats and overcoats. One took a tape measure from his pocket as they returned to the sidewalk and squatted down over a metal plate. One rose, paced off a half-dozen steps toward the front of the restaurant, looked uncertainly at the pavement at his feet, shook his head, and rejoined his companion. They consulted for a few minutes, squatted down again, and measured the distance from the metal plate to the curb. A cream-colored taxi came slowly into the intersection and stopped as the driver turned to his passenger in the backseat. He watched, waiting for the passenger to get out. The two men had entered the enclosed terrace. They went to the glass door, looked in, but didn't enter. He ignored them, looking at the taxi instead. The figure remained in the backseat as the taxi turned east. The two men left. Gas men, he decided as they disappeared in front of the church. His fingers were shriveled with the cold.

Fifteen minutes passed. No one entered except a small dwarf Frenchman with a limp, an oversized shoe, and an incredibly large head. He paused at a table just outside the glass door and hoisted himself into a chair from which his feet dangled. A club foot, Dudley noticed. The Frenchman's voice was very loud. He insulted the waiter, who laughed as he wiped his table, insulted the bartender through the open door, who laughed as well. An unfortunate man but a happy man, Dudley thought as he listened, a man sitting at his accustomed place in his accustomed bar. The waiter brought him a second glass. The dwarf's raillery continued. A Punch-and-Judy figure, he decided. The jokes grew tiresome. After bringing the Frenchman a third glass, the waiter closed the glass door. The dwarf continued to talk to himself. They were alone on the terrace, separated by a single table. The man was a damnable drunk. Dudley avoided his eyes, gazing out through the window instead.

Possibly his choice had been too ingenious. Perhaps Otto's colleague hadn't been able to follow the directions he'd given over the phone, lost in the labyrinth of little streets and cul-de-sacs. Otto had never chosen his office help for its cleverness; he preferred men not too inquisitive, not too imaginative, not too bright. "Dull men make the best bookkeepers," he'd once told Tricia, a sly smile pinching the corners of his eyes. Ten minutes later Dudley rose, paid his bill, and left. He had waited too long.

Disappointed, he was in retreat again, back into

the past, following a narrow pavement on a narrow street that would lead nowhere. He made his way down a twisting street where the afternoon sun was hidden. He crossed a bridge, head still down, and thought he was on the Left Bank. Turning a corner, he saw the Seine below. He was on Isle St. Louis.

Another impasse, another delay. It was all utterly improbable. He had done all he could. He'd been attending a sick cousin in rural Massachusetts, he'd say after his return; Langley would understand. He would retire, work at something, leave his desk at six o'clock, like the French children in the school, out into the winter twilight, his life spent, drift on inconsequentially toward its conclusion, his madness complete.

To rejuvenate himself that night he took a taxi out to Montparnasse and entered a large festive restaurant for the third time since his arrival, a restaurant he'd known in better days. It was crowded, as always; he had no reservations and had to wait. He was escorted alone to a center table with red leather seats. He had oysters and a bottle of Chablis. The oysters required his careful attention, the laughter consoled him, the wine made him light-headed: he shared the conversation of strangers. He regretted leaving but the queue had grown. He hurried with his coffee and stood up, summoning the waiter to signal the vacancy. Two middle-aged women briskly took possession of his table, removed their gloves, and sat down, not looking at him. He pulled on his coat, crossed the street, and hailed a taxi. Reaching Boulevard St.-Germain, liberated by the oysters, the wine, and the company of strangers, he discovered he wasn't ready to return to his ugly little hotel room. The stars were out and he walked along the Seine where he could see the heavens better. Incredibly complicated, the constellations. Too complicated to think about; one could only wonder. His life too, his situation, all incredibly complicated. Even as a child his life had been absurdly odd, terribly lonely, other lives ridiculously simple, abundant in love and affection. His father a naval officer who preferred sea duty and Antarctica to family life; his mother a neurasthenic invalid with a passion for theosophy. He strolled past the dark Tuileries, thinking of Tricia and the Maine coast, of Jessica and the Paris apartment she was so fond of, of the old stone villa in the south near Entrecasteaux whose photographs she'd brought him. Probably it reminded her of Eric Prosser's Spanish farmhouse on the coast below Barcelona where they had spent so many summers. It was late. He felt better. The traffic had vanished now.

Reluctantly he entered the dark doorway and climbed the steps through the smell of mop water and moldering wood. He supposed he should search out Jessica's flat. He'd written down the address. In his room on the fourth floor, he recovered his attaché case from the dresser drawer wrapped in the brown sweater, and sat down on the bed.

Something was amiss. Had he left it like this?

The hasp of his silk-lined writing case was open. The papers beneath weren't in order. The curriculum vitae he'd prepared with Phil Chambers's help was in the wrong envelope; the pages from Andreyev's long letter to the Agency had been returned in random order. He spread the documents on the bed. Someone had gone through his attaché case, had read his curriculum vitae, the Xeroxed copy of Alexei Andreyev's long letter to the Agency, the Chernishevsky article, and the documents he'd prepared for presentation on the seventh floor. Missing from the inner pocket was the plastic case for traveler's checks with the dozen twenty-dollar bills tucked inside. Someone in Paris had pillaged among papers that gave his name and every position he'd held these past thirty years, every detail of his life, all that was most privileged and confidential. The vulgarity of the theft shocked him, the ugliness of the hotel room frightened him: evil hands plundering the silk-lined leather writing case Tricia had given him twenty years ago. He felt unclean, debased, sullied. Still angry, he resolved to find more secure accommodations the next morning.

Thirty feet away on the same floor a short, thickset man sat on his bed, fully dressed and still wearing his gray hat. His gray overcoat lay over a nearby chair. He'd registered at the downstairs desk two hours earlier. A small stainless steel portable console sat on the table next to the bed. With one ringer he pressed the plastic button microphone into his right ear, cupping his ear with his short thick fingers. He listened abstractly, his gray eyes fixed off in the middle distance. He heard the creak of bedsprings, the sigh of a mattress, and the rustle of bedcovers. He continued to listen for ten minutes, his head turned now as he watched the tiny intensity meter on the console as it fluttered like the beating of a tiny heart with the noiseless vibrations in the room thirty feet away where the two listening devices were hidden.

Satisfied, he removed a small transmitting device from his briefcase and signaled the black Renault waiting below in the street: two quick pulses, then two more. The car slowly drove away. He took off his hat, removed his shoes, withdrew a magazine and newspaper from the briefcase, put them at his side, lifted his feet, and settled back. It would be a long night, broken only by the steady rhythm of Dudley's breathing. On the badly printed cover of the Danish magazine a thin blond woman, naked except for black hose, was holding a plaited black whip. He studied the photograph, turned a few pages, and dropped it aside. The German newspaper was from Frankfurt. On the second page was a dispatch from Bonn. A woman named Erika Kissling had attempted suicide in a West German prison. He folded the newspaper twice, ignoring the Bonn dispatch, and turned to the European soccer scores.

George Tobey lived across Chesapeake Bay in

a rural area toward the ocean southeast of Milford, Delaware. Corkery missed the turnoff in the fading winter light and stopped at a small crossroads service station to call Tobey again. In the warm little office a radio on the shelf was playing country and western to three empty chairs; the concrete floor smelled as if it had been mopped down with crankcase oil. He heard a banjo, a bass, and Emmylou Harris's guitar-string voice. Through the open door to the garage bay a mechanic was banging a truck tire from a rim. He could barely hear Tobey.

His farm was three miles to the south along a patched asphalt road without a centerline. There was no mailbox, just a single red reflector on a locust gatepost at the entrance. The white frame house was set well back from the road on an embankment. A black Ford F-300 pickup truck was parked in the gravel drive. The porch light was on but the house was dark. Waiting in the darkness, Corkery could smell the brine of fresh manure.

The shadow filling the doorway had no face but softly spoke his name and led him back the dark hall to the kitchen where he said he'd been cleaning up. "Frank not back yet? That's not like him, not like him at all." He was a large man with heavy shoulders and thick graying hair; the deep-set eyes took in Corkery with a nod and didn't linger. He wore an old jacket with blue woolen arms, the kind worn by amateur athletic teams. A few pine curls clung to the sleeves. He had a woodworking shop in the rear shed and had just come in to clean up and feed the dogs. His wife was away. The sink was filled with dishes and saucepans stained with spaghetti and chili sauce. "It's a mess but it usually is when she's gone. I don't mind much. She deserves a break." He pulled a nylon raincoat from behind the door and suggested they go out for a drink and something to eat. He'd been cooped up for four days. Corkery drove, following Tobey's directions.

Dudley had come out to see him the previous week. He hadn't mentioned a seventh-floor appointment, didn't have an attaché case with him, and had shown him no documents. "Something was bothering him, I don't know what. He couldn't sit still in the house so we took a walk, out along the creek toward the back pasture. He was asking me about a couple of Russians, what I knew about them, what I could tell him. None of it made much sense."

Corkery stopped at a small restaurant a few miles from the turnpike. Crossing the parking lot, he thought he could smell the Atlantic a few miles away but Tobey told him it was a marsh on the other side of the bridge. Inside they had a drink at a plain wooden table in the Pine Room. Three farmers in mackinaws and leather caps sat inside the door drinking beer. Waitresses were changing the tables for dinner.

"One Russian he was asking about I didn't know," Tobey said softly. "I couldn't tell Frank anything. All he had was his cryptonym, Pitchfork.

I'd never heard it before."

"A Russian, an Agency asset? Who the hell was he?"

"A Russian, but I couldn't tell him anything. It was stupid, what he was asking." Tobey's eyes moved away toward the couple coming in the door. "He wanted to know who this Pitchfork was, where he'd been recruited and when, who controlled him, the Agency or the FBI."

"Wait a minute. The FBI? Dudley thought Pitchfork had been in the U.S.?"

"Maybe, I didn't ask. It was crazy. I told him to shut up about it, whatever he was thinking. I didn't know and wouldn't have told him if I did. So he backed off a little, said he was working on this secret project for the seventh floor, a report on CI operations. The name Pitchfork had turned up. I didn't buy it. If he was working on this top-secret in-house study for the seventh floor, what the hell was he coming to me for? He dropped it and asked about this other Russian, a defector we picked up in Paris a couple of years back."

Two nearby tables filled. Tobey fell silent. A waitress in a red gingham dress brought a red tablecloth and silver wrapped in napkins. Tobey stirred restlessly, then got to his feet and suggested they find someplace quieter. "I wasn't meaning to chase you away, hon," the waitress said.

"It's all right," Corkery said. "It's our bowling night."

They stopped at a second restaurant a few miles away but Tobey thought it too crowded. They bought coffee and hamburgers at a drive-in window and sat in the car in the corner of the drive-in lot. Nearby a group of teenagers wandered about two nearly identical '60 Chevys with chopped tops.

"Ed Rudolsky was handling it," Tobey said. "He was Abbott's number one deputy at the time. I didn't know anything about it until Ed calls me in and tells me to pack a bag, we're going to Paris. Everyone else was cut out, the Sov Bloc people, the other deputies in CI, everyone. Just Ed and me. We leave National on the shuttle and by seven-thirty we're on the red-eye express out of Kennedy for Paris. The station number two picks us up at Charles de Gaulle and it's all arranged, a pickup in a little park up off Montparnasse on Tuesday afternoon. It's near this radiological clinic where this Russian goes once a month to have this growth on his neck checked out. First thing he wants when we get him to Frankfurt is a radiologist from the army hospital to look at his neck, then a cardiologist. He says he's under too much stress from the way we handled it. The guy's a hypochondriac, a nut case."

"What was his name?"

"Vadim Lazarev, a real bullshitter from way back. That's what I thought anyway."

"You debriefed him in Frankfurt?"

"Ed and some others did the first trick but the guy wore Ed out and he called me in." Tobey was watching a car at the illuminated island of the gas station next door. A woman in a raincoat

212

with a scarf over her head stood at the self-service pump. He sat forward to watch. His plastic raincoat crackled like cellophane and smelled like coal tar. After a few minutes the car drove away.

"He wouldn't come clean at first, wouldn't take a polygraph, wouldn't tell us anything except that he was a commercial officer, assigned to Paris. He said he wouldn't open up until we got him out of Frankfurt, said we were all second-raters, that Frankfurt had been penetrated, maybe a few of us too. He wouldn't talk to anyone except the number one back at Langley. Then one night he'd been drinking and opened up, told us about a few KGB operations in Paris and Vienna. He said he'd been sent to Vienna to clean out the *zarkhoz*, the housekeeping section, after a drunken brawl in the hall of one of the Soviet apartments. Some Lett got knifed. In Paris, the GRU had screwed up somehow at the Aeroflot office, some kind of embezzlement scheme based on false shipping manifests. This one GRU type tried to defect and they bagged him, drugged him, and trucked him out to Charles de Gaulle in a trunk. He gave us a lot of crap like that, right off the wall. In the meantime he wants all this medical attention, even asks for the key to the PX one night, then it's a woman, this blond American nurse he'd seen there at the hospital and wants for the night, a goddamn mattress party. Then he asks Ed to do a black bag job at the Paris X-ray clinic, steal his X rays, his medical history. The guy was a walking disaster zone, a nut case, like I said."

"What about his cryptonym?"

"AE/Crevice."

"Crevice. Did Dudley have both, his name and his cryptonym?"

"Yeah, both."

"So what did he want to know?"

"What I thought of him, whether he was bogus or not. I told him he was a con artist, a lightweight, like Phil used to say, the kind that can toe-dance on a chocolate éclair. I've seen too many of the bastards not to know."

He was in his late forties but to Tobey seemed younger, one of those men who never age: the smooth face, the thin shoulders, the slim hands. Someone had spoiled him, protected him too much as a boy from games and roughhousing, made sure his boots were dry, his nose wiped, given him his fear of germs, crowds, microbes, and contamination, given him that supercilious arrogance that lay on his face like a mask. His English was good, American English learned by rote; he slurred his words the way an American would. He had an annoying habit of using American slang: "piece'a junk" was one Tobey remembered. He was talking about the car that drove them from the airfield in Frankfurt. He irritated Tobey, who heard in his voice something else, disdain, even contempt. Everything he touched he debased. He'd hit him once in Frankfurt, knocked him out of his chair. Abbott was furious when he learned of it.

Tobey laughed. "The little bastard told Abbott about it after they set up housekeeping for him out in Maryland, told Abbott I'd beaten him up. He called me a criminal, one of the *'govnoed,'* the shiteaters." He laughed again. "Abbott called me on the carpet, really cracked the whip. Unprofessional, stupid, could turn Lazarev back the other way. I told Abbott the guy was a con, a fraud. He wouldn't listen. Neither would the rest of his second-floor acolytes. They thought he was the big haul they'd been trolling for all these years. He'd been a senior KGB deputy in Berlin, they said, watchdogging operations on the continent, some kind of special *Obergruppe* at Berlin-Karlhorst, running some East German networks. Had a villa at Ahlbeck, the resort there. Anyway, Abbott called me on the carpet. I thought he was going to sack me the way he did Frank."

Tobey drank the last of his coffee and took out a cigarette, turning to look out the back window.

"So you knew about that then, Abbott sacking Dudley."

"Oh, sure. I knew. They hushed it up, wiped the record clean, but I knew. Ed Rudolsky told me after he replaced Frank as Abbott's number one. They had a big blowup in Abbott's office one night, a real donnybrook. I dunno what it was about, something operational. The next morning Frank was gone, desk cleared out, everything. He went over to Congressional Relations, claimed they needed him over there, but that was bullshit. Abbott sacked him."

"This was after Lazarev defected?"

"Yeah, after. Ed Rudolsky didn't take over as

number one deputy until Frank left."

"Could the argument have been about Lazarev?"

"Maybe but I don't think so. Frank didn't know about Lazarev at the time. That's why he came to see me."

"Did Lazarev give us anything?" He watched Tobey's face as he frowned, leaning forward to watch the two Chevys speed away.

"Not when I talked to him. They say later he gave them some pretty good stuff, most of it collateral. He told them about a few KGB operations, one in Washington, some KGB nipshits running around the Hill, chasing congressional paper, intelligence committee staffers, one of them. A GRU operation too, I heard. Lazarev claimed the GRU was running someone in the Pentagon and over on the Hill, had been for years, but it was all scuttlebutt by then. I never heard the shoe drop. Abbott had Lazarev wrapped up by then and put him away someplace on the payroll as a consultant. I was out of it by then. For me, he was just what he was, an arrogant little bastard, maybe the new Soviet man the party was always talking about, a nice dresser, chain-smoker, Winstons or Marlboros, never anything else. Intellectually deprived but sharp the way a real smart kid is sharp. Liked American jazz. The son of a diplomat, someone said, the nice-looking little rich kid from Moscow's slums, two to a room and shared bathroom privileges." He pushed open the ventilator and flipped his cigarette out on the pavement. Hunched in his raincoat he watched it burn out.

"Fuck him. Who the hell cares?"

"Chambers told me you worked with him in Berlin. Dudley too?"

"Yeah. But Frank was never the operational type, never, not like Phil. But he was a decent guy, as decent as anyone I've ever worked with, and it broke your heart sometimes. Tricia's too."

"How is that?"

Tobey was silent for a minute. "He was in over his head. He didn't know the Sovs, how they worked. He just didn't know. What the Sovs were looking for in those days was when the West Germans would go nuclear, when we'd give them the bomb. The East Germans too. They did some pretty filthy stuff but so did we. Frank worked the FRG staff, the civil servants, the dinner party crowd. Barney McIntosh and his crowd worked the gutter, the faggots and pederasts, the blackmailers, the pimps and prostitutes. I don't like to think about it now, some of the bastards we used. The worst, a lot of them, in and out of prison camps, displaced persons lockups, people who had maybe a dozen names in their time, Germans, Poles, White Russians, who the hell were they? You didn't want to know then, now you don't care. It was all balls out then, go for broke, do what you had to do, and don't worry about the bodies you left behind. That's the way the East Germans had done it for years. The CIC too, those idiots. Now the kid lawyers over at Justice are crawling around on their hands and knees, picking up the audit trail. Like Klaus Barbie. You

217

know about him?"

"A little. Awful. You knew Tricia Dudley. What was she like?"

Tobey stirred, took out a cigarette, and pushed in the lighter. "Beautiful. Plenty of style, full of life. A little flaky. Used to come home with the chickens. Hung out with the Germans, not the U.S. mission crowd. Hated the military wives, the PX crowd. Some people thought she was wild but she wasn't, just different. Liked her gin neat, one ice cube. Went her own way, flew to Paris or London for her shopping, all by herself. She impressed the hell out of me. She had a beautiful voice, deep, real soft, like Jane Froman, the singer. She was a lush by then."

"Tricia was?" The car had grown cold. Corkery started the engine and turned on the heater.

"Yeah, a little. It was too much for her. She didn't like the Agency life, didn't like what it was doing to Frank. She wanted another kind of life, go her own way, wanted it for Frank. They didn't have a private life and it was eating her up. Some people had the wrong impression. Phil knows. Have you talked to him?"

"A little, not much."

"He'll never say. Some thought their marriage was on the rocks. McIntosh told me once Frank couldn't get it up for her, she was too much woman for him, that he'd be doing him a favor keeping her home in his bed, not someone else's. I would have hit the bastard except he was crocked at the time. He wanted Frank's job, that's what he was after. Tricia too. But you heard all sorts of crap in those days, not just the political and military stuff. Everything else got mixed in, the drinking, the sex life, who was sleeping with who, the drunks, the deviates, the fuckups at the British or French mission. The Brits had two gentlemen queers on the staff and the East Germans got to them. That's what happens when you've got too many people with not enough to do; everything gets mixed in. The East Germans and the Haupt-Ableilung picked it all up, those dimshits, all the gossip, all the sex, all the garbage. You had to be careful. I tried to stay clear of it. Christ, this car's cold. Let's drive back. It's getting late."

Corkery turned on the lights and drove out onto the narrow highway. "Do you remember the daughter?"

"Jessica, yeah. Bright little kid, as sharp as a tack. Pretty too, looked like her mother, spitting image. I spent a few days with Jessica and Frank at a place they rented every summer, an old farmhouse down on the Spanish coast. We had a great time. Belonged to Eric Prosser. He worked for us on contract in Berlin. I don't think Tricia ever went for some reason, just Frank and Jessica."

"This Eric Prosser. Where is he now? Retired?"

"Not Eric. Still there. Under deep cover, I think. Don't ask."

"Did most of the people at the Berlin base feel the way you did about Frank?"

"Yeah, the people I worked with liked him

whatever else they thought. Except for guys like Barney McIntosh, who was a gold-plated prick. I think he was responsible for some of the gossip about their marriage being on the rocks. I remember one night I was with Tricia, Frank, and a British couple in this crummy West Berlin night-club. We were slumming after a diplomatic reception. Barney and someone else wandered in after we got there. It was all smoky and dark with this small dance combo up front. The others were out on the floor except Frank and me. We're sitting there talking and this leggy platinum blond comes over and asks Frank to dance. So he does, gets up, gives me a wink, and goes off with her. So after a while the dance floor gets too crowded and the others come back to the table, but Frank's still out there with this blond dish, doing the Beacon Hill fox trot or whatever. So the music stops, he takes this blond dish back to her table and her two friends waiting there, all of them transvestites, and Frank comes back and sits down like nothing happened. Everybody laughed except Tricia, who was as mad as hell. Frank never said a word. He knew who she was all along. He didn't care what others thought, he had his own code, that's all. I always thought it was Barney McIntosh who put the blond up to it but I dunno."

They were in front of the house, the engine still running. Tobey got out heavily, grunting as he moved his heavy shoulders out the door. Two dogs were barking from the rear. Far in the distance a neighbor's dogs were answering. "Deer, probably." He looked toward the rear fields. "They move back to my pond at night."

"One more thing if you don't mind. Last question."

"Shoot."

"Did Dudley mention someone named Andreyev, Major Alexei Andreyev?"

"Andreyev?" Tobey bent through the open door. Corkery couldn't see his expression. "Not that I remember, no. Just the two names I mentioned. Don't think I ever heard. Who is he?"

"A Soviet defector. He disappeared."

"Can't help you there. Keep me posted if anything turns up."

"I will. Thanks again."

He moved toward the house, shoulders hunched in the beam of the headlights.

Corkery drove back to Washington, more confused than ever. Frank Dudley had driven all the way to Delaware to ask Tobey about two Russians, Vadim Lazarev and Pitchfork. He'd said he was working on a secret staff study of CI operations for the seventh floor, but he was lying; he was probably working on his Friday afternoon presentation to the seventh floor.

Tobey had told him Vadim Lazarev, the KGB defector, was a con artist who knew less than he claimed. But according to George Skaff the Agency backed Lazarev's claim that Andreyev was a dispatched GRU agent. As a result, the FBI dropped its pursuit of the mysterious "Comrade X" who'd tried to make contact with Andreyev at the bar on Pennsylvania Avenue and in the Senate office building.

Who was lying, who was telling the truth? Another mysterious Russian now, first "Comrade X," now Pitchfork. Tobey couldn't identify Pitchfork, probably because unlike Lazarev, he was still operational, a KGB officer Dudley evidently believed had once been in the U.S. but was now a shadowy name on a restricted BIGOT list known only to a few. What about Comrade X? Had both he and Pitchfork been in the U.S. at the same time? Both were unidentified. There was a curious symmetry there. He wondered if Comrade X and Pitchfork could be the same man.

A thatching of snow lay over the steep Maryland countryside. The brick house sat in a grove of oak trees at the end of the gravel lane. An overgrown fence lined with shaggy cedars and persimmon trees enclosed the lane on both sides from the surrounding pasturage and snow-reefed cornfields.

"It does seem a little desolate in winter, doesn't it?" Louise Dudley's footsteps echoed across the wooden porch as heavily as Corkery's in her thick-soled arctic boots. "Off the beaten path. That's why I love it so." She wore a dark blue wool parka with a green lining and a hood. Corkery wore no overcoat, just a rumpled tweed jacket and a blue and red wool scarf; he looked like a college undergraduate, dawdling between classes. An FBI agent had visited the house at Skaff's instructions and reported it empty. They'd seen his footprints in the old snow near the front steps.

A draft of wintry air greeted them in the front hall, touched with the tang of woodsmoke. She turned on the furnace at the thermostat at the end of the hall and led him into the old-fashioned kitchen. "It's terribly musty but a house has to be lived in, doesn't it." She brought a tin of coffee from the refrigerator, her gloves still on, and filled the automatic coffee beaker from the tap. "We have a three-hundred-foot well, which is quite deep, they say. Reassuring in a way." While they waited for the coffee she showed him through the house. Two large rooms lay on each side of the front hall and center staircase, furnished in heavy Victorian furniture. Upstairs were four bedrooms. He had the impression it was very much her house. "It's probably too much for us, I suppose. When we bought it we had the notion of something large enough for weekend guests. As it turned out, we seldom asked anyone out. I don't like apartments, I never have. I prefer small towns. Most of the furniture came from my parents' house in New York State."

She found nothing amiss in the downstairs rooms. The living-room grate was filled with wood ash. Corkery kneeled at the hearth. "Did you have a fire the last time you were here?"

"It was my idea. Frank didn't get to enjoy it. He was upstairs most of the afternoon. When it's raining in Washington, it's often snowing here, much like upper New York State. In the apartment I try to imagine, try to pick up the Frederick station on the radio in the kitchen, listening for the weather, but the reception isn't very good."

"Did he ever do any office work out here?"

"Not really. Occasionally he brought his briefcase with him but seldom opened it. He preferred to putter around, doing odd jobs. He planned to use a room upstairs as a study. That last Saturday we were here in October, he spent most of the day there, as I said. He was preoccupied that weekend for some reason." She led him upstairs, past two bedrooms and down the hall to a closed door but found it locked. "That's odd. Why on earth would he have locked it? I've no idea where the key is. Maybe downstairs."

She found a ring of keys in the kitchen drawer. The coffee was ready and they carried their cups back upstairs. None of the keys fit. Corkery went down the hall, removed the keys from the two bedroom doors, and kneeled in front of the locked door. "When were you last inside?"

"That last visit. He was working at something at the desk and I brought him a cup of tea. The keys are a terrible mishmash. He wanted me to throw them out but I couldn't, they seemed so much a part of the house."

One key almost turned the spring lever. "Almost but not quite. I can file it a little. Where does he keep his tools?"

Dudley's workshop was in the shed attached to a separate brick building across the small rear courtyard. It had once been the summer kitchen, she told him as she unlocked the padlocked door with a key from a hook in the kitchen closet. The light was dim. In the metal toolbox on the workbench he found a rat-tailed file. Among the cans on the shelf was a tin of black roof caulking. He dabbed some on a rag, put a thin coating on the key, and returned upstairs. He inserted the key, turned it against the metal tooth but didn't force it. She waited upstairs while he returned to the workbench and filed down the metal edge. She watched as he tried the key again.

"That's quite clever," she said when she realized what he was doing.

"Hit or miss. I'm not really a locksmith."

Three more trips to the workshop were required. She waited patiently upstairs, sitting at the top of the steps with her Audubon tree book open on her knee, her coat still on, lifting her head each time he passed with an encouraging smile. She'd changed in certain small ways since their first talk that Saturday in her apartment. She was less shy, more at ease, more spontaneous. Driving out from Washington she'd told him something about herself. She had an undergraduate degree in economics from Cornell and a graduate degree from Columbia. Her father had been a banker in upper New York State. She'd gone off to Ithaca with no idea of what she would do; mathematics had interested her but so had chemistry. After her mother's death she'd returned home for a semester to keep house for her father. Bored, she took a job at the bank, found it interesting, returned to Cornell, and took a degree in economics. With the encouragement of one of her teachers and her father, she'd gone on to Columbia. She came to Washington in the '60s as an intern at Treasury, a young economist with no experience and no friends. She enjoyed the work. After five years, she'd attracted the notice of a senior Agency economist she'd met and worked with at interdepartmental foreign exchange meetings who suggested she could do better at Langley. The Agency had hired her away.

She stood behind him as he tried the key for the fifth and final time. The key turned freely and the door swung open.

"You see, you did it," she said proudly.

"Lucky."

"Not luck at all, patience."

Inside the room a rollaway iron bed was pushed against the far wall. Against the other wall was a wardrobe and nearby two steamer trunks. An old-fashioned oak desk sat between the door and the window. On top of one steamer trunk were a chain saw and a 12-gauge shotgun in a sheepskin case. "That's probably why he locked the door," she said, kneeling to open one steamer trunk. "Old blankets, just as I thought." Corkery looked through the desk drawers smelling of carbon paper and ink. In the second drawer was a paperback German dictionary and beneath it a lined tablet with most of the pages torn out. The writing on the three remaining pages was heavily scratched over but some of the lines were legible. He held the tablet up in the light of the window. Down the margin were a dozen or so German words carefully printed in pencil. On the second page, the lines on the first page were repeated, but in a penciled print, not script. Two more pages were raggedly torn out, no text remaining; the final page was intact but blank. Folded between the last page and the pasteboard back binding was a Xeroxed text whose original had been typed by a poor typist. Between the typed lines were inserted the same words printed out on the second page.

Corkery held the Xeroxed page to the light of the window. The name on the top line was Alexei Andreyev.

"You've found something?" She was still kneeling behind him.

"I don't know. Remember the Tass article we found, the one from the newspaper?"

"The one he'd been carrying around in his pocket?"

"The same man. Do you recognize this tablet?"

She took it. "One of mine, I think."

"How about the handwriting?"

"Frank's." She frowned over the penciled text. "He's scratched most of it out."

"I think he was translating from German." He took the paperback German dictionary from the desk. "Using this. Is it his?"

"I don't know. I've never seen it. Maybe from his office. He had a larger German dictionary at home someplace. What's that?"

"Something he Xeroxed." The paragraph read:

One way or another every imperial capital ultimately betrays itself, imagining that nothing can escape its imperial edict, whether the motion of the planets, the drift of the stars, or the geography of the earth. This was as true of Athens, Rome, and Constantinopole as it is now of Moscow. The cartographers of the Chief Administration of Geodesy and Cartography in Moscow, directly responsible to the Council of Ministers of the USSR, are the most recent navigators aboard this ship of fools. The 1967 edition of the *Great Soviet Atlas of the World* whose falsifications I have just cited is a case in point. How can one abide a system that, among its crimes, would perjure your childhood memories? History is one thing: every age rewrites the past. But the systematic denial of the contours of the earth, maps that lie?

The inserted lines repeating the lines on the second page were identical.

"How odd." She reread it, half smiling. "It's Frank's printing. Strange. Do you know what it all means?"

"No, but I think he was translating something, something in German, comparing it to something identical in English."

The room had grown warmer. She stood and took off her parka. She was wearing a snug beige sweater that smelled of cedar chips and clung to her back and flattened her wide full breasts. She had the shoulders of a swimmer. Corkery moved aside the chain saw and shotgun case and she searched the second footlocker. He kneeled at the small green bookshelf under the window. The books were older, dusty and watermarked. A potpourri, she said from across the room; old novels, old travel books, a few college texts. Hers, he discovered, opening a copy of Samuelson. The linen cover was warped and faded.

LOUISE TOWNSEND read the delicate feminine handwriting. Seeing her maiden name for the first time, he was suddenly moved. He saw her as an undergraduate, tall, wistful, and solitary, walking along a campus path under the trees on an Indian summer day, the book under her arm. He saw the orange, yellow, and umber flaming on the autumn hillsides, felt the warm October sun on his shoulders, saw her face approaching, saw her eyes drop, and felt that peculiar lightness and exhilaration that comes with a Saturday afternoon in October after the final class. For some reason he knew it was Saturday, the weekend's possibilities limitless. She would be going somewhere, maybe to the house with the wide summer porch overlooking the lake. Would she drive, did she have her own car? What kind of coat did she wear?

"What is it?" She was watching him from across the room.

"Just thinking." He returned the book to the shelf.

She got up and moved to his side, had seen him

replace the Samuelson and now withdrew it. "One of mine."

"Funny, isn't it, what an old college text makes you think of?"

"It is. Sad sometimes. What were you thinking of?"

"A Saturday afternoon in October. Classes out for the weekend."

"Much too long ago." She returned the book.

In the steamer trunk she found some hunting clothes, a broken Thermos, and a pair of ice skates. He pulled the cover from the typewriter on the desk but the roller was empty and it had no ribbon. He searched under the desk and behind it, took out the drawers one by one, and reached in and groped along the wooden slides. She looked through the single drawer in the bedside table and they went through the blankets piled atop the rollaway bed, and unrolled the thin mattress, he grappling with one end, she trying to steady the other, unable to suppress a smile, her brown hair in disarray. "Do we know what we're looking for?"

"No. Do You?"

"No."

"Come to think of it, I think we probably found it."

They let the mattress fall and he rolled it up again and returned the bed to the corner. He picked up the tablet and they went downstairs carrying their coats. In the kitchen she emptied the coffeemaker and washed the cups. He searched the front two rooms a final time, thinking she'd join him, but she didn't. He called but got no answer. Returning to the kitchen, he realized how large the house was, how impossible it was to feel another's presence. He found her outside, walking the fenceline. She turned and waited for him, her hands deep in her pockets, her head bare. A solitary woman still, living with an elusive, unhappy man: separate bedrooms, separate beds. A proud woman too. "I always like to have a final look but don't often get the chance. He's always anxious to leave. That last time we were here in October, we were to spend the night but he decided not to."

They walked down the overgrown fence.

"Someone's been planting trees." He paused at a sapling, newly mulched.

"Me." She touched the dry leaves. "This is pin oak. The one ahead is white oak. I can't always tell, the differences are sometimes so small. Colonel Davenport, my neighbor down the road, has a woods full of oaks. He let me dig them up last spring. He raises black Angus. Horses too. He's asked me to ride but I don't, not really. I asked him about having a pond built. A lake would be better but a pond would be nice." They moved on. "It's quite a lovely life out here. I'd enjoy it."

"You think so?"

"Oh, yes. Very much."

"The year round, you mean?"

She looked up. "The year round certainly. Not you?"

"It's where I grew up." He looked off toward

231

the mountains to the west.

"And you decided to get away, is that it?"

"Far away."

They had reached the end of the fenceline and stood on the bank, looking west toward the mountains. A mud-splashed tan Bronco approached on the rural road below. A man in a tweed hat was bent over the wheel, looking up at them. She waved and he slowed, waved a hand out the window, and drove on. "Colonel Davenport," she said. Bales of straw were piled in the rear. On the back bumper was a blue sticker: HAVE YOU HUGGED YOUR HORSE TODAY?

The patches of snow disappeared as they droned back toward Washington in the fading autumn light.

"I haven't been in a convertible in years. I have a little Volkswagen."

"Volkswagens are okay but they don't say much."

"Really? What are they supposed to say?"

"More than I'll get you there. Amtrak and Greyhound say that."

"My Volkswagen is very dependable."

"Cars are like people. It's the metabolism. After a while, you settle down to theirs. Like with women." He turned apologetically. "I don't mean women, sorry. I mean spouses. They set the tempo, like cars do."

"So you know people by the cars they own. What about Volkswagens?"

"Like the Germans, some Germans anyway, the

way Volvos are like the Swedes. Dependable but not very exciting. Except for the Porsche or the BMW, but that's Bavarian — fat, well heeled, well cushioned. Corners well and you don't feel the bones." It hadn't come out the way he'd intended. She didn't seem to notice.

"And so what kind is this?"

"Italian."

"And what does that say?"

"Goes farther on less. Temperamental. Racy. Quick as a pickpocket, a Neapolitan pickpocket. *Scippatori*."

"*Scippatori?*" She laughed, the second time he'd heard her laugh. "What a marvelous word. What is it?"

"A thief on wheels. A motorcycle purse snatcher."

"It feels rather like Sunday afternoon," she said. "Dismal in a way. I always feel this way, driving back."

"So do I."

She turned in surprise. "I wouldn't have thought that. Why?"

"I work in a zoo." She laughed again. The traffic was heavier now. The headlights exploded past from the commuter exodus, outward bound, illuminating her face in the flux of white flashes. Her head was back against the seat.

"Have you talked to Jessica recently?" she asked.

"Not recently, no. I haven't had the chance."

"Me neither. I should, I suppose, but I haven't had the courage. She's totally unpredictable. You

233

never know what she's going to say. She can be very sweet at times, very difficult other times."

"When I talked to her the other day, she didn't seem too concerned."

"You can't tell. She's very good at hiding her feelings. She's never been particularly happy. Frank thought she was suicidal at one time."

"What's been bothering her recently?"

"Success, achieving something. Money too." She sat up. "She has an annuity and she runs out every autumn. Someone in Boston wants to marry her. I don't think she quite knows what to do about it."

"She told me she was afraid she'd wake up at forty and find she didn't have any talent."

"That's so foolish. She has so much talent and she's abused it so. I think it overwhelms her. Some talented people are like that, gifted people, I mean. It's as if they're so much cleverer or talented than everyone else they try to hide it, to disguise it, to pretend they're not."

"I've never had that problem."

"Neither have I. Jessica's problem isn't too little talent but too much, far too much for one person, whether languages, painting, stage design, scenery, acting, or making her own clothes. That's one talent I do envy her."

Corkery turned. "She was in theater?"

"Two years, I think."

"What? Painting scenery, stage design?"

"Both at the beginning, then acting. She's terribly quick at picking things up, a marvelous mimic. She can be so funny, but she can be frightening too. You aren't exactly sure who she is. She's a chameleon, she always slips away somehow, even from herself. Why? What did she tell you about her stage career?"

"Not a word. She's a mimic?"

"A marvelous mimic. She's very good when she goes into one of her little acts."

"I knew it." He turned onto the beltway ramp. "She was putting me on that afternoon."

She didn't seem surprised. "I wouldn't feel badly. You're not the first. But I wouldn't really call it a deception. It's just the way she is."

She was a translator, German, Dutch, and Danish, and overworked that day in her gray cubicle of an office in Language Services. Her door was closed. She lifted her brown head from her desk to gaze anxiously at Corkery through the glass as he knocked but he went in anyway. Linguists were women of some sensitivity, he remembered; most had graduate degrees and some came from literary backgrounds. There were exceptions. The worst were the European-born linguists and professors who took themselves so seriously, ranking themselves with ecclesiastics and high court judges at the bar of language, like the stiff-necked German-born philologist he'd spoken to three minutes earlier who told him he didn't handle Green Group miscellany and directed him down the hall to Mrs. Halleck.

"I'm awfully pressed right now," she said.

"Couldn't you come back tomorrow?" She assumed the paper in his hand required immediate action, like the documents stacked on her desk and overflowing on the nearby table.

He hadn't brought a document for immediate translation but a copy of the Intelligence Directorate's serial listing of articles on Soviet affairs for September and October, the ones Dudley had failed to receive and mentioned to Sterner. If Dudley had been translating something from German to English at his Maryland farm that Saturday, the most obvious source was the biweekly serial listing.

Puzzled, Mrs. Halleck studied the serial listing and handed it back. "I'm not sure I understand. What is it you're looking for? Something we translated, you think?"

"Something you might have been asked to translate but maybe didn't or couldn't. A request from Public Affairs by someone named Frank Dudley."

"Oh, dear." She didn't remember the name but got up from her desk, pencil in hand, and led him down the inner corridor to a set of file cabinets next to an empty desk. Here the correspondence files were kept, a copy of each letter or request, the date it was logged in, date of completion, and final disposition. "Was it classified?"

"I doubt it."

"Classified is handled differently. Do you understand the coding?" Corkery thought he did but Mrs. Halleck explained it again. The most urgent action requests were Red Group, followed by Yellow Group, and finally Green Group, the lowest priority, pushed to the bottom of the work schedule. Articles from the serial listing would probably be Green Group since the request usually had no operational priority but was prompted by someone's occasional or scholarly interest. Green Group requests were running three to four weeks behind. "If we had a Green Group request from Public Affairs, it would probably be in these cabinets here." She opened the top drawer of the first cabinet. "Red and Yellow Group requests are in that row over there. But we only keep action requests for six months. Do you have a date? A date would make it easier."

"October, I'd say."

"What was the subject?"

"I'm not sure. If you don't mind, why don't I just browse?"

She didn't mind. She glanced at her watch, said she was working against a four o'clock deadline, and hurried away. A minute later she was back. "One thing I forgot. We sometimes contract out unclassified material for translation, particularly when we have a backlog."

"Thanks. I'll go with what's here."

The action requests in the drawers were filed chronologically rather than by subject matter. Attached to each letter or action memo was a form giving the name of the article, the periodical, the name of the requesting office, and the date the translation had been completed. He began with the file for the first week of October, searching for translation requests from Public Affairs. He found three, all on the standard Agency forms, none dealing with Soviet affairs, none signed by Frank Dudley. He also found several requests from CI, five signed by Jay Fellows. "Bibliography of Soviet Central Asian Society Publications, 1951–59" was one. "Nationalities and the Mongol Dilemma" and "Kirghiz Balladeers: A Compendium of Ethnic Themes" were two more. Avid reader, Jay. What was his lovely wife doing those cold winter nights while her husband was tucked up in bed, his little AC/DC heater plugged into a volume of Kirghiz poetry? Worth exploring, he decided, maybe at the CI Christmas party. He worked his way through the October files and moved on to September. No luck there either.

Frank Dudley wouldn't have been able to justify a Red Group action request, but he was no shrinking violet either. He shut the drawer and moved to the cabinet where Red Group action requests were filed. October action requests were in three thick file folders. He pulled them out and carried them to the empty desk. He began with the files for the week prior to the Dudleys' weekend trip to the Maryland farm, the one Dudley had aborted after working all afternoon at the upstairs desk. Buried eight pages below he found what he was looking for. Dudley's request was neatly typed on an Agency form, requesting an immediate translation from the German of an article published in an obscure West German political quarterly. The article was entitled "Puzzling Irregularities in Soviet Cartography," written by someone named Yefrim Chernishevsky. The title of the article had been listed in the September serial listing. In justifying his request for an immediate translation, Dudley had claimed he would be delivering a speech at the meeting of the Explorers' Society in New York scheduled for the second week of October. According to a penciled note on the form, his request had been downgraded after Dudley's telephone conversation with the Language Services approving officer. It wasn't clear why the request hadn't been moved to Green Group.

With Mrs. Halleck's consent and her key to the Xerox room, Corkery made two copies of Dudley's letter. She couldn't understand what might have happened to the article in question and directed him down the corridor to the distribution office. The GS-8 clerk couldn't find a locator card for the Chernishevsky article. Lost in the system, she supposed. Corkery filled out a request for an immediate translation, took it to the division chief's office, and waited outside the door. Idle at her desk, the strawberry blond secretary invited him to sit down. They talked for a few minutes as she buffed her nails. The man at his desk inside was in no hurry to see him. Five minutes later Corkery went in anyway. After a brief discussion during which Abbott's name, Shaw's name, and the seventh floor were mentioned, he was promised a translation in two days. "If you want a fair trial of speed, use a pacer," he said to the secretary on his way out. She smiled, not knowing what it meant but impressed.

"Try me anytime," she said.

They walked along the Georgetown towpath through the windy winter twilight, tutor and pupil. The water below was as black as a Louisiana bayou, the bare trees shrieking skeletons above the broth, Halloween witches celebrating the short dark day's passing.

"Major Alexei Andreyev, yes." Chambers's breath was a faint vapor on the raw air. "A Soviet military officer, or so he claimed, a tank officer who'd spent six months with the Strategic Rocket Forces. God knows what he thought he was doing. You've seen the files?"

"No, just what the FBI showed me. CI claims no file, zilch."

"That's idiotic." He was hatless, his white hair a milkweed pod blown by the wind. A woolen hat was sticking from his overcoat pocket. He was carrying an umbrella and didn't quite know what to do with it, now a cane, now a saber and cutlass.

"Andreyev was assigned to East Germany when he decided to defect. There were some discrepancies in his story. A few were impressed but most of us had our doubts. I mistrusted him myself, could never persuade myself he was what he claimed. How can you know? You can't. He was careless." He stopped, inspecting a crumpled cigarette pack at his feet, nudged it, then speared it with his umbrella tip.

"Careless? That's an odd word."

"Careless. Not the exact word. Not laconic. That's not it. Something else." He paused to take a breath. Snow was nearby, blowing in from the Shenandoah before dawn. "Devil-may-care, casual, those may be closer. A very funny man, outrageous, especially when he'd been drinking, and he drank a lot. Clever, certainly." He hesitated, still searching for the right word.

"He's not easy to describe."

"Impossible to describe." He moved on. "Someone you simply couldn't get down on paper, and that's our culture, isn't it? The bureaucratic culture, Washington's culture, where words count for everything. Andreyev defied it. I suppose that's why he had us so confused. He was one of those people you find impossible to take seriously because he was so elusive, so damned quick. Always had this sly look in his eye. You were never sure he was taking you seriously. I mean, that's it, isn't it? People who don't give us the respect of taking us seriously destroy us. You see what I'm driving at? He was much too quick, a quick mind, too quick, a quick-change artist — an old song-and-dance man, that's it." He laughed. "Like most of us after a time, old song-and-dance men, all of us, still carrying these tired old tunes around in our heads. The feet move but the music's stopped. Julian Abbott too. That's what happens. Not you, not yet, anyway, you're too young."

He nodded to someone passing. Corkery, looking up, saw a delicate red nose, a bobbed head, and shining dark eyes. He caught the breath of warm perfume. She wore a belted blue coat and had nice ankles.

"Then there was the drinking. Drunks make me uncomfortable. He wasn't a drunk but he enjoyed drinking. Roast beef to him, roast beef and sack. You couldn't keep up. When he drank, he was very funny, very passionate. Insisted everyone drink as he did. Those who mistrusted him said that was part of his act, a watcher the GRU sent over, looking for DOD and Pentagon drunks. Preposterous." He looked at his watch. "I suppose he was a man of feeling as much as intellect and there's no doubt he was clever, no doubt. Brilliant, some thought. But there was something unique about him, no doubt. Whatever it was, it was genuine."

"Brilliant as an officer or what?"

"Every way. He spoke a half-dozen languages, which impresses most of us right off, the military especially. According to that, most Romanians would be absolute geniuses, wouldn't they?" He laughed and brought his collar up. He was enjoying himself, Corkery thought, too much; quick answers were what he'd come for.

"His English was very good. Rough at first but good. I remember one New Year's Eve at Roger Cornelius's house here in Georgetown. Roger was one of Andreyev's believers but couldn't persuade anyone else. This was a year after his defection,

I think. Andreyev was like a schoolboy come home for Christmas, all that feeling, all that passion, all those expectations. He wanted everyone to feel what he felt, to share his joy, to feel toward him the way he felt toward us. Love him, I suppose. We didn't. Like him? Yes. Be amused, be intrigued by him? Certainly. But trust him? No." Eyes downcast, he frowned, pondering the recollection. "No, not completely. Whom do we ever trust completely? It's difficult enough in Washington. In our trade, it's impossible. He was bound to be disappointed. When I saw him years later in the seventies, he'd changed. Something in him had died. Maybe he'd discovered nothing on earth would reciprocate all that feeling he'd brought over, that enormous passion he carried over the border with him — and the man just walked through, that was the most amazing part, just cut through the wire and walked through, half carrying this drunken NCO, left the lights on and the motor running behind him." He stopped again. "He said afterward he'd been trained that way, raised by some village halfwit. That if he'd been raised properly, he'd still be back in Moscow. So he had this passion for everything, God knows where it came from. Maps were another thing. He was a walking encyclopedia of Soviet topographical falsification, absolutely amazing. It was an obsession with him. He had all the cartographic skills, no doubt about it."

Corkery stopped. "Cartographic skills?"

"Superb. An expert, not only in cartography but geodesics, determining precise positions on the

243

earth's surface, all that. Brilliant at it."

Corkery caught up. "A Soviet cartographer?"

"One of their very best. He'd had all the geodesic training the Russians had to offer. Evidently he'd worked with Soviet geodesic teams in ICBM missile site preparation. Could tell just by looking at it when a missile site would go operational. Relative position of firing sites to targets, longitude, latitude, all that. Some thought that's why he'd come, a dispatched GRU agent. The Soviets were worried at the time about our Polaris program, whether we'd made any geodesic breakthroughs in underwater targeting systems. Too technical for me."

"So he was a professional cartographer." *Like Chernishevsky? Was that the key? What the hell kind of key? The key to what?*

The steps to the street were ahead. Chambers pointed to them with his umbrella. "So he had this fixation about maps, crazy about them. We could never decide whether he was pulling our leg or not. He said once other Russian boys read fairy tales when they were growing up, he read maps. So there you are —"

"You didn't trust him."

"No. How can you trust a man you feel intuitively isn't who he claims to be? It was my training, I suppose. He was too different. I mistrusted the passion, the exuberance that asks everyone to be a part of it. He'd rediscovered his life here, now he was asking everyone to rediscover theirs. How could we? We couldn't. That's a poor reason

244

to mistrust a man, isn't it?"

"He wore his heart on his sleeve and you didn't."

Chambers nodded, resting for a minute at the foot of the steps, his hand on the cold rail. He seemed winded. "I suppose you could put it that way. But I wasn't the only one."

"What about Abbott?" They climbed slowly toward the street.

"Never trusted him, not from the first. He had his own reasons. Not intuition, no. Julian has the intuition of a doorknob. He wouldn't touch him, wouldn't let anyone else at the Agency touch him. So all the apostles fell in line and Andreyev spent a few useless years at Defense, helping prepare war game scenarios, war game tactics for Soviet armor. He wanted to go to the army mapping agency but they wouldn't have him."

"According to the FBI file I saw, Andreyev failed a polygraph test in Munich. Maybe that's why Abbott didn't trust him."

"I doubt it. You can't flutter a man like Andreyev, never. No, Julian had something else. I don't know what it was, he never said."

At the corner, Chambers pointed at a pub across M Street. "We'll stop there, have a draft. English or so it pretends." He was still winded. "You have time?"

"Plenty of time," Corkery lied, looking at his watch. "The FBI said he disappeared, vanished into thin air. What do you know about that?"

"Not much. Austria, we thought, but we couldn't be sure. Left his hotel in Linz and didn't come back. A week later the Austrian border police picked up a report about a man being held in this little mountain village near the Czech border. They inquired, found a room, some blood, a broken-out window. Kidnapped, they thought. No one knew. He disappeared. A few weeks later there was a housecleaning over at the Soviet embassy, a half-dozen diplomats sent home. Later there was a trial in Moscow, the Tass item in your pocket, the treason trial."

The light had changed. "If they tried Andreyev for treason, how the hell could he be a dispatched agent?"

"That's the question, isn't it? Maybe a scripted trial, the final act in the whole masquerade. Julian thought so. He told the seventh floor *he* was the shadow defendant in the Moscow treason trial, not Andreyev. Since he'd doubted Andreyev, he was the one being accused. The KGB had been trying to destroy him for years. That's what he believed, anyway."

Corkery had stopped in disbelief in the middle of the street. Chambers, not noticing, hadn't changed stride. The crowd moved between them. "I told you a lot of it was farce," Chambers said as Corkery joined him on the pavement. "The feet still move but the music's stopped. In here."

The wainscotted bar with brass fittings was warm and crowded. The atmosphere was vaguely Victorian. They waited in the short queue for an empty table. Chambers shed his coat and carried his umbrella over his arm as the platinum blond hostess showed them to a table. A waitress in a short black skirt appeared; Chambers ordered two drafts of German beer.

"There were a couple of other names," Corkery said, "names I wanted to ask you about. Dudley asked George Tobey about them. One was a defector by the name of Vadim Lazarev."

Chambers nodded cautiously as the waitress brought the glasses. Anxious to get on with it, Corkery paid before Chambers could find his wallet. "Abbott's triumph," Chambers said after she left. "The voice behind one of his many masks. But don't get me started, that's gossip." He picked up his stein. "Cheers." Corkery, trying to read the hands of the old clock high beyond the bar, wasn't sure what he meant. The reflected lights from the bar hid the hands in the gold-leafed window.

Chambers didn't know the name Pitchfork. But it was odd that Frank Dudley had asked George Tobey about him, Tobey six years retired now. Very odd. Unable to raise the memory, he lifted his glass again. "What do you think?"

"The beer? Fine."

"Thought you'd like it. I don't much like to come here alone." He looked around at the young faces, the young singles, the young couples, the younger waitresses in their short black skirts. "It's very much a young man's bar."

So it was, Corkery thought, still brooding about Pitchfork and Chernishevsky as he drank his beer. Chambers was reminiscing about an operation he and George Tobey had worked during the early '60s. The principals were dead now. In 1961 the Soviets had intercepted an ICBM with an anti-ballistic missile over Lake Aral. Not until 1964 was the latter shown in Red Square, but they knew a lot about it by then. Corkery nodded, not daring to sneak a look at his watch. Chambers was right. It was very much a young man's bar, not a place for old men, creeping about through the nostalgia of a winter twilight in a confusion of names, past and present. For Corkery, impatient to be off, Chambers's memory had become an agony. He understood why so many thought Frank Dudley such a tiresome bore.

As they got up to leave, he said, "I wanted to ask you something. I don't know who else to ask or even whether it's important or not but I'd like to know. It's about Tricia. We've never talked about it. She died in England."

Surprised, Chambers nodded, pulling up his coat collar. "So she did. Does it matter?" They left the tavern and walked around the corner and up the street. "Don't believe the gossip," he said, breaking the silence.

"The inquest said 'misadventure.' Dudley was studying Mongolian at the University of Leeds at the time. She died alone in Kent, the Pied Bull Hotel."

"Alone, yes. A relapse, I suppose. A terrible thing."

"They'd gone to England from Berlin. So when you say relapse, you're talking about Berlin."

"Leeds was a sabbatical for both of them. They needed out and that was arranged. Tricia was an extravagant woman, unpredictable, full of life, but a woman very much alone. Frank's life didn't allow for the kind of life she needed. She was drinking quite a bit in Berlin."

"That's what George Tobey said."

"A symptom, not a cause. She'd had an affair in Berlin, a long and discreet affair. Frank never knew. The name doesn't matter. She needed to get hold of their life again, she and Frank both."

The Pied Bull Hotel was where she and her lover often met when she went to England for shopping in the summer and autumn. Now she was beginning a new life in Leeds. She had a bicycle and a garden, did her own cooking, no servants underfoot. She had stopped drinking and was proud of herself. She was starting over and wanted her lover to know she'd found herself, found the courage to begin again with her husband and daughter. She wanted him to see her as she saw herself, free again, wanted him to be proud of her, to let her go. They'd met for a final time in Kent. Jessica and Frank had gone ahead to the old Spanish farmhouse on the coast below Barcelona. She stayed behind to close up the house and was to join them before they returned to Washington. It was to be a solitary weekend in the English countryside for the two former lovers, nothing more, a farewell to the past. They visited the old Roman villa at Lullingstone and the chapel in St. John's Jerusalem Gardens the afternoon before. It was where they'd met in the past, the same hotel, the same gardens. He drove back to London. He called her to make sure she was all right but couldn't reach her. He called Chambers at his hotel in London where he was staying that week. The next morning they found her. It had all collapsed, the memories too strong, like the passion. She'd been drinking heavily that night, too much alcohol, too many pills. She didn't wake up, suffocated by the fluids in her lungs. A hotel employee found her. Chambers had driven down and identified the body.

They stood on the shadowy street near Corkery's parked car just below Chambers's house. "So you knew about the affair and who he was."

"His name isn't important."

"I'm not asking."

"I know you're not. Frank wanted too much, expected too much, of her and everyone else. He thought everyone was part of the family, bring them to the fireside, give them a few drinks, and everything was forgiven, sharing their liquor, their dinner parties, their affection. All part of the family. Sad. Frank was a gentleman. We weren't. We were ugly men doing ugly business." He looked up at Corkery. "Sorry. Why were you asking?"

"It bothered me. I thought knowing might help in some way. Louise asked me about her death. Frank Dudley never talked about it. I couldn't tell her anything. I can't now."

"So it is. You won't mention it."

"No, sir. Never."

"You're late," Jessica said, flinging open the door even before Corkery rang. She'd been watching from the bay window. Her dark hair was sleekly drawn back and she was wearing eye shadow, a black cocktail dress, and high heels; a loop of pearls was at her throat. "You said seven-thirty."

"I know. I got held up, sorry."

"I don't accept apologies." She slammed the door after him, shaking the window sashes, and turned back across the darkened gallery. "I rushed back from a reception just to get here. I even took a taxi. I despise Washington taxis. They're all Nigerians or Ethiopians. I don't like to go out late either. The streets around here are a war zone, in case you didn't know. Where do you live, in a Wasp bunker out in Great Falls, like Winston?"

She led him into the rear room, where bottles and an ice bucket were set out on the antique dry sink. "I was going to be very polite and offer you a drink but now I'm not sure. Say something to convince me. So what have you found out? Anything new?"

"Not much."

"I didn't think so." She fixed him a drink and sat down sedately at the far end of the sofa, a stranger again.

"We've had a few reports from people who claimed they've seen him. One was Paris. Did he say anything about going abroad?"

"No. Someone's obviously confused."

"Obviously. The apartment you mentioned in Paris, the one you wanted to buy, is that where you've been living?"

"Temporarily. I have a year's lease."

"Where in Paris?"

"Not that it matters but it's in the Fourteenth Arrondissement, off Boulevard Raspail."

"Who's living there now?"

"I am." She sipped her drink, her face expressionless.

"So it's empty."

"I know what you're thinking and it's very empty."

"How do you know what I'm thinking?"

"Intuition. I'm a cat person."

"Is it what I'm thinking or what you're thinking? You're not worried about your father, are you? You may even know where he is."

Her face lifted defiantly. "I certainly do not."

"But you know enough not to be worried. What did he tell you that day at lunch?"

"I've already told you. The rest isn't your business."

"Why the scatterbrain act last Monday, all that finishing school chatter? Because of something he told you?"

"You are a cheater, aren't you?"

"You know more than you've told me."

"*I hate being questioned! I do!* Why are you tormenting me?" She turned away, hand at her forehead, eyes shut, her arm on the back of the couch, a woman in anguish, giving him the benefit of her graceful neck and lovely silhouette. He got up noisily, topped off his whiskey at the dry sink, and sat down again. If she'd been waiting for tears, they hadn't come. She brought her hand down and picked up her glass. Her face was perfectly calm. "You're terribly stubborn, aren't you? You're also a pest. Now you're laughing."

"I'm not laughing."

"You are. You're always laughing. It wasn't an act, not completely. Anyway, it wasn't one of my best." She got up and turned to look at herself in the mirror above the couch, bringing her hand to her hair. "The clothes are the hardest part. If you get the clothes right, everything else follows. They were appropriately awful, weren't they? After that, it's more or less spontaneous. It was your fault. That 'Listen, Miss Dudley' bit. That was so smug, so condescending. You must have thought I was an idiot."

"I figured that's what you wanted me to think."

"Not really. Do you ever do it?"

"Do what?"

"Voices."

"No, I don't think so."

"Not even in your head? I think most people do, they're just not conscious of it. They have to, the world is so full of frauds. So you impersonate, hide from them that way when there's no place else. Like the brainless ones at the cocktail party tonight. Who saw Daddy in Paris?"

"Someone from the station. Hailing a taxi outside La Coupole."

"That was always one of his favorites. I don't know whether he's in Paris or not."

"What did he tell you at lunch?"

"That I shouldn't worry." She returned to the dry sink and put her glass down. "If I have another drink, I'll get snockered. When I get snockered, I get offensive. Why don't you take me out to dinner to keep me sweet, someplace quiet. I've got to get out of this goddamned mortuary."

The streets weren't quite empty, not congested either, just that ghostly hour when the rumblings from the evening rush hour still seemed to linger. If he'd belonged to a club, he might have taken her there, but he didn't. He drove down 23rd Street, across the Potomac, and out George Washington Parkway into Virginia.

At lunch that day her father had told her he might be going away for a short time and that she shouldn't worry. "A personal matter," he'd said, "a matter of conscience." She believed him. It was no one else's business. After Corkery telephoned on Monday she knew he'd ask questions. She hated being questioned, she always had; she despised it. It was easier for her to play a role than make up a story, so she had. She knew everyone would be making up stories about her father anyway, making it so melodramatic, like Louise, when it wasn't at all.

"So you decided to put me on," he said.

"I had to. You didn't give me any choice. My cocktail party drag, the Jessica Home-for-the-Holidays gig. I used to do it every Christmas."

"I heard you were on stage."

"I've always been on stage, ever since I was five." She spent three years in an English boarding school in Suffolk. It was once a priory. She hated the goddamned women there. They were murderers. They murdered her adolescence. Everything that happened they blamed her for. It wasn't funny. They were straight out of the Brontë sisters. It was always that way: official people, the official family, boardinghouse headmistresses, ugly English women in ugly shoes, coming to terrorize her at night. She always heard them coming. Their skirts smelled of coal sacking. There was a ghost in the orangery, a fifteenth-century nun who'd been brained by a falling tile. She saw her one evening after chapel, a gray little woman with evil eyes. She threw her clog at her and broke a pot. They said she had no business being in the orangery and was making it up. The headmistress flogged her with a switch and she cried herself to sleep. She saw the ghost two other times but never mentioned it.

At the sedate old country inn off Dolley Madison there were English sporting prints on the paneled walls of the second-floor dining room and a log fire burning in the stone fireplace. A group of boisterous middle-aged couples in the far corner was celebrating an anniversary. He ordered drinks.

She opened the menu and looked at it indifferently. "Even so, I was scared shitless when I went in the kitchen to get an ashtray that after-

255

noon. You probably didn't notice. My hands were shaking."

"I didn't. Why?"

"Why do you think? I was scared."

"You shouldn't have been. I'm harmless. I heard you were a mimic."

"It's compulsive. Isn't everyone? You forget. I was an overseas brat. I told you that the first time."

"I wasn't sure what you meant."

"Always on stage, always someone in the house. If they weren't houseguests there was always a cocktail or dinner party, even on Christmas Eve. Someone was always there, German, English, someone from Washington; then the servants, always snooping around. In Charlottenberg, we had a German *Putzfrau* with a glass eye. She was terribly evil looking, very Brechtian. Winston used to give her money to take it out." She put the menu aside and glanced out across the room. "That's what I had to put up with, the way my mother did. You don't understand, do you?"

"I'm trying."

"No privacy. You had to put on faces, like she did. I still do. One for the dinner party, one for your friends, one for your family, none for yourself. Being yourself, that's what's so painful, just being naked that way. I'm an actress at heart, even when I paint. That's a place to hide, painting, I mean, but not permanently. That's one thing about painting. If you're not totally honest in addition to being totally gifted, it'll find you out and destroy you. I could never make a career out of being second rate, never. I don't have first-rate talent, not truly and not honestly. What I told you on Monday was the truth, it wasn't an act. I don't know why I told you. Something in your eyes. I didn't intend to."

"You mean waking up at forty and finding you have no talent."

"I think about it every day. Don't you?"

"Not so much."

The waiter came. She ordered smoked salmon, quail with mushrooms, and a French Chablis at $27.50 a bottle. After he went away she lit a cigarette and said the wine list was second rate but what could you expect in antebellum Virginia. The horse prints were awful. The waitresses' costumes looked like they belonged in a ninth-grade operetta, like the costumes at Williamsburg. "What do you want to be at forty?" she asked.

"I don't know."

"That doesn't bother you?"

"Not much, no."

"Then you'll disappoint me like everyone else. You'll end up the way you are now, a government gofer on a government salary. My friends in Paris aren't any better off. They're pretty much the way I am, except richer. They all have these elaborate fantasies about what they're going to do with their careers but they're just living other people's lives, the people they read about. Winston's the same way. I can't learn from them. They don't have anything to tell me." The waiter brought the smoked salmon and uncorked the wine.

"What do you want them to tell you?"

"That I'm not one of them. Part of me is a snob, the way my mother was. I hate being second rate. I learned a lot from watching her. We didn't talk, never, but she taught me how to act just by watching her. At the end I don't think she knew one role from the other, sort of got lost in between. She drank herself to death in case you didn't know. Maybe no one's told you but she did. My father's not the person everyone's told you about either. I know what they think, have always known, the way a child does. That's another reason I didn't want to answer any of their questions. Yours either. It made me furious, it still does."

"What did you see?"

"What people thought, that he was a stuffed shirt, Mama's adoring dragoman." She moved her eyes away. "I don't want to talk about it. Why did you mention the painting of Les Baux? One of your interrogation techniques?"

"I liked it."

"No, you didn't. It's a fraud, an imitation of an obscure French painter no one's ever heard of except me. It's dishonest, the way a lot of painting is. I see it and know it but not many people do. An original painting is terrifying for second-raters, that's what genius is. It shows the second-raters the horrible vacuum they live in. Anyway, that's why I don't like it. I see it that way, my vacuum, no one else's. Louise had it framed, which was humiliating. She doesn't know the difference between Mondrian and Modigliani. Do you?"

"One draws lines, the other cadavers."

"That's not funny. You're not a Philistine, don't pretend you are."

"Maybe I am."

"You're not, I can tell. I told you. It's your eyes. They're terribly compassionate, maybe too much. Sometimes they frighten me. Anyway, I'm intuitive. I think you are too. Don't answer."

The quail arrived, followed by the headwaiter, who asked if everything was all right. Jessica ignored him. Corkery said everything was fine. "I know what I like and I liked your painting," he said.

She was watching a waiter pushing a cart with a flaming candlelit white cake toward the couples in the far corner. "Don't pretend. Just liking something is never enough. Liking isn't love, is it? Would you marry someone you liked? No. There has to be more. Marry someone with oodles of money, that's my aunt's advice. She did. You don't have any money, do you? I mean in the family."

"No."

"I didn't think so. It's your vowels. It doesn't matter but we might as well be honest with each other."

"Marrying someone for money is stupid advice."

"It's perfectly sensible if you've never been in love. I don't think I have. Have you? Marriage is just a contract, something arranged between lawyers, brokerage houses, banks, and family trusts. The nice thing about money is that it doesn't care about talent, it doesn't have to."

"Do you believe that or are you just trying on ideas?"

"Trying on ideas. What do you think?"

"I just told you."

"Being poor as well as stupid is worse. What consoles you? Religion? If you're poor and stupid, I suppose you have to be religious. You don't look religious. Maybe you've got some other secret you won't talk about." She gave a sigh and Corkery knew he was losing her again. "What are you laughing for?"

"I'm not laughing."

"You are, you're always smiling about something. I thought we were going to be honest with each other. Don't indulge me, please. If you insist on indulging me, I can be expensive. I'd like some brandy if you don't mind." Corkery called the waiter over and she ordered a snifter of Courvoisier.

"When are you going back to Paris?" he asked. She wasn't sure. She couldn't decide where she wanted to live, Paris, Provence, or Normandy. She described the villa near Entrecasteaux she thought might interest her father since it reminded her so much of the old Spanish farmhouse on the cliff above the Mediterranean he leased during the summers when she was growing up. Maybe she was thinking of herself, not him. She adored their summer vacations there. Ten years later she stayed there alone on two occasions, once for a few weeks, once for three months. She'd gone there to paint. The farmhouse was owned by a man named Eric Prosser.

"What was he like, this Eric Prosser?"

She wasn't sure. He was something of a mystery. She didn't know him and didn't remember him from her adolescence; he was just another name, a friend of her father's. He bought the farmhouse in the early '50s, retimbered the roof, rebuilt the old stone walls, installed a pump and a water system, and planted fruit and olive trees. In the early '70s she rented the house for a few months, trying to discover whether she had any talent. By then the encroaching tourist hotels and condominiums had swallowed the beaches to the north, but the old stone farmhouse and its ten hectares had remained undisturbed, protected against commercial inundation by the adjacent four hundred hectares belonging to an old Andalusian estate. To her recollection she'd never met Prosser and didn't see him that year. The lease had been arranged through correspondence in Vienna or Stuttgart, she'd forgotten which, through an address supplied by her father. Prosser wrote he was surprised she remembered the house and told her she was welcome to stay as long as she liked, rent free. She arrived in September after the French and Italian campers had abandoned the beach below. It took her a month to adjust to her solitude, and by October her work was going well. The autumn dove and pigeon hunters sometimes took shelter in the lee of the courtyard wall, waiting for the first light. The old stonemason who acted as a kind of handyman and custodian came three times a week to inquire about her. He came after the winter storms

261

to inspect the roof and tree damage. In late November the cold floors, smoking stove, and the days of relentless rain drove her back to Paris.

Prosser remained a mystery. She had the impression her father hadn't seen him at all during the intervening years. She was with her father in London some years later and he told her he'd written him to ask about again renting the farmhouse that August, a kind of sentimental holiday for the two of them. Prosser hadn't answered his letter. She had the feeling her father was hurt. She had always imagined a man her father's age, but during her stay at the farmhouse she learned from the stonemason he was a younger man. In the inland village six kilometers to the west she met a few people who knew him. One was the owner of the cantina, where he often went; the butcher and village carpenter who made frames for her canvases were also his friends. He arrived every July by train from Barcelona and stayed until August. They seldom saw him except for his trips to the village for supplies. Sometimes he came in the Volkswagen bus he kept at the farmhouse or sometimes he came on foot, trampling through the morning sunshine with the white mountains in the distance, a powdering of dust in his hair, like a stonemason, never in a hurry, always alone. He would sit under the arbor at the cantina for a glass of beer and afterward walk to the post and telegraph to collect his mail, then on to the shops. He was always civil, always had a word for everyone. After his purchases, he would hire a taxi to drive him back to the farmhouse; if he had bought mortar and lumber, he would rent the Siat truck belonging to the cabinetmaker and be driven back to the farmhouse. He was a strange man. She was sorry she'd never met him. It was the kind of life she thought she might like. No, her father wouldn't have gone there, not in winter.

It was eleven when they left the restaurant. The bill came to $114.84. She didn't want to go back to Margot's house in Foggy Bottom, not yet. She didn't know what she wanted to do. She wanted to go to Dulles and catch a plane. "Do you think I frighten people?" she asked. The question surprised him.

"No, not particularly."

"I have that reputation. I've been talking your ear off and you really haven't told me much about yourself except you were in the navy and play tennis."

"There's not much else to tell."

"There must be. If there isn't, I don't see much of a future for you. You didn't get a dishonorable discharge, did you?"

"No."

"I didn't think so. I've told you my secrets, tell me some secret, something terribly wicked, something *Grand Guignol* you've never told anyone else."

"There's nothing to tell."

"There must be something. Try to think."

A park police car passed, going very fast. He watched the taillights disappear. "Nothing much.

I got stoned once when I was in the navy, really stoned, banged out of my skull. Some bad grass an ensign friend of mine got from a West African. It was in Marseilles. I didn't know who I was for thirty-six hours. I woke up in this little park."

She laughed. "That's perfect. Two days, my God. And in Marseilles —"

"Yeah, but it wasn't much of a secret. There were three of us, another lieutenant and this ensign. The ensign disappeared. He didn't return to ship and we had to get the Shore Patrol to help find him. He was holed up in this fleabag hotel room, still stoned. We got him back aboard just before we sailed but word got out."

"Then it wasn't a secret. So tell me one of your real secrets."

"Maybe that's one of my problems, I don't have any."

"You must have. Everyone has secrets. I told you mine."

"Maybe it's what I just told you."

"You said you didn't have any."

"I don't. Maybe that's my secret."

"What?"

"Not having any secrets."

"That's your secret?"

"Probably."

"My God, you're definitely in the wrong profession. Everyone in Washington has secrets. It's unpatriotic not to."

"You're putting me on," he said. "You're doing voices again."

"Probably." She settled back in the seat. "How did you know?"

"I just did."

Her head was back against the cushions, her eyes half closed. "I have to be careful with you. You're much too clever for me. I sometimes think you haven't told me everything about yourself."

Maybe it was her intuition. His too. He hadn't told her about Otto Rauchfuss.

5

SHARING
THE SECRETS

The morning was luminous with winter sunshine, giving a crystalline clarity to the leprous old façades across the way. He stood at the telephone box fifteen feet from the Raspail métro entrance. A policeman faced the intersection from the curb, his back to him. If he turned in his direction, he would hang up.

The French woman answered the second ring, recognized his voice when he asked for Otto Rauchfuss, and told him to wait. He heard voices in the background, the echo of footsteps approaching, and then a man's abrupt voice. It wasn't Otto but the voice he'd spoken to earlier. Whoever he was he apologized for missing the appointment in the Marais; he'd wandered about for an hour, lost, unable to find the intersection and the restaurant. Dudley sensed he was a man unaccustomed to giving apologies.

He interrupted to ask about Otto. His voice,

so silent these past days, was husky and disagreeable, rusty spasms from an unused pipe. If they might meet and talk, the voice said, he would explain everything. Dudley said this was impossible; he was leaving Paris in the morning. The voice lapsed into anxious German. It was important they meet; he had received instructions from Otto Rauchfuss.

"Instructions? What instructions?" The policeman had stepped from the curb and was crossing the boulevard.

"To meet as soon as possible. Please, where do we talk? You will come here?" A long pause as Dudley clumsily searched his pocket notebook. "Hello? *Hello!* Are you still there?" Yes, Dudley was still there. He gave the German the name of a side-street restaurant between the Opéra and the Bourse; he was to wear a hat, carry a newspaper in his right hand as he entered at two-thirty that afternoon, and sit at a rear table with his hat atop the newspaper. He hung up and joined the crowds moving toward the métro.

Again he had changed hotels, again he felt better for it. After the theft, the hotel a few steps from Boulevard St.-Germain had grown intolerable. With its dark narrow staircase, damp linen, and knocking pipes, it had come to stand for something repellent, something sinister, blocking the light. His new accommodations were larger and brighter, high on a hillside in sunny Montparnasse. It was more expensive, of course, but worth it; a small fridge and a two-ring gas stove stood in the alcove, a small table in front of the high window. He booked in for a week, bought whiskey and gin, wine and fruit, magazines, even a few books from the stalls along the Seine, like a soldier on winter billet. He had acquired a suitcase and new shirts. He took his shirts out, purchased scissors and shoe wax at the local pharmacy, polished his shoes, and trimmed his hair.

He left his hillside flat wearing his Burberry and the pants and shoes he'd purchased in the flea market. In his shopping bag were a loaf of bread, the plastic raincoat, and the blue beret. He took elaborate precautions making his way to the restaurant across the Seine. At a large department store on the edge of Montparnasse he circulated through the crowd and left through a side entrance. Two blocks away he turned into a quick-service dry-cleaning shop, where he left his Burberry, and continued on to a métro entrance. When he reappeared on Avenue de l'Opéra he was wearing the plastic raincoat and blue beret. Two black Citroëns with official plates were parked in front of the Opéra; nearby stood three French policemen with silver piping on their caps, blocking the pavement. In front of the limousines were several parked motorcycles. Some sort of official visitor, he decided as he moved into the street. The shapeless gray raincoat hung from his shoulders; his waiter's trousers seemed wrapped to his ankles by bicycle clips above the ugly black shoes. Dangling from his right wrist was the white plastic shopping bag.

The restaurant was next to a residential hotel

on a side street two blocks to the east. An old couple sat alone at one of the two tables in front in full shadow, drinking coffee; a leashed wire-haired terrier crouched under the table between them. He was five minutes late. The restaurant was narrow and dark. A dozen tables lay to the right of the strip of rubber carpet that led to the bar halfway back the room, deserted at that hour, as he knew they would be. In the midafternoon silence a middle-aged man sat slumped at a rear table, his gray hat on a newspaper in front of him, gazing vacantly toward the street where an occasional car rumbled past, chrome flashing in the seam of afternoon sun overhead. Two-thirty had come and passed.

Dudley took a seat three tables away. He rummaged in his plastic bag, brought out a piece of bread and a pat of butter, left from lunch, returned them, and removed a packet of cigarettes. The waiter appeared. He ordered a draft, withdrew a cigarette from the packet, fussed about in his bag for a minute, and got up, the cigarette dangling from his fingers. He approached the man at the rear table and asked him for a match.

The face looking up was thick and sleepy under a porridge-bowl thatch of gray hair. He grunted, rummaged in his coat pocket, and brought out a pack of matches. Dudley guessed he was Saxon; *Plattfussler*, Otto called them contemptuously, the flatfooted ones, with their slow, clumsy gait and their slow adenoidal voices. Dudley lit his cigarette, returned the matches, and asked in German if he knew the métro line to Porte de Clichy. Then he sat down. "You had something to say to me," he said in English, "something about Otto Rauchfuss."

Two sleepy blue eyes inspected him curiously from beneath the shaggy brows. He was Otto's business partner from Interbahn AG in Bern. Klaus, he called himself. He'd come to Paris on business and now he was returning. He'd gotten an urgent telex from Otto in Bern that morning, summoning him. Dudley asked him the Bern Street address. He had it right: Weinbergstrasse 108.

"So Otto is in Bern. On the telephone, you said he'd sent you instructions. What instructions?"

Instructions to meet and talk to him. Talk about what? The young waiter stood uncertainly at Dudley's empty table holding a tray. Dudley beckoned him over and the waiter left the draft on the table. Talk about what? Dudley repeated. Talk about the business between them, obviously. "Then Otto must have given you my name." Klaus didn't answer. He called the waiter back and asked for his check. "If Otto sent you a telex," Dudley said patiently, "I'd like to see it."

Reluctantly Klaus fumbled in his inside coat pocket, brought out an envelope, and pulled on a pair of iron-rimmed glasses. He sat pondering the telex, sucking his lower lip. It was in German, he mumbled, putting it away. Otto was sending someone to talk to him. His name was Deutsch.

"I'd like to look at his telex if you don't mind."

270

Klaus let his gaze drift off toward the front window. Slow-witted, certainly, Dudley decided, repeating his request. The Saxon sighed, shrugged, brought out the envelope, and handed him the telex. Dudley scanned the two paragraphs, saw his name, then Deutsch's. Otto's instructions were clear enough; he was sending a man named Deutsch to discuss their "urgent problem." He would arrive in Paris in two days.

Dudley handed back the telex. The delay annoyed him, but he supposed it inevitable. How was he to make contact with Deutsch? The Saxon looked to the front of the restaurant, picked up his hat, gave a nod, and dropped it. A blond young man seated at the window came back to join them. He was slim and boyish, wearing a gray suit and blue raincoat. A flush of color lay on his pale cheeks; his lips were girlishly dark, as if he'd just come in from the cold.

The Saxon introduced him as Peter Dietrich, an accounting clerk in the Bern office on loan to Paris. He would be his contact. The young man flushed in embarrassment at the introduction but didn't speak. In the dim light both suit and raincoat looked pitifully threadbare; his shirt was wrinkled, his worn tie and shoes were those of a Harvard black shoes, the son of a Bronx tailor on a meager scholarship. His slim hand was very cold. Klaus didn't ask him to sit down, so Dietrich continued to stand awkwardly, as did Dudley who, for lack of anything else to say, asked Dietrich how he was enjoying Paris.

Dietrich flushed, smiled weakly, and said he was enjoying it very much. Dudley thought he recognized a Hamburg accent; yes, he was from Hamburg. The boyish color in his cheeks lay close to the surface. There seemed to be nothing more to say. Dietrich looked at the Saxon, who nodded, and he went back to his front table. A few minutes later, Dudley reclaimed his table, carrying his glass. He was still sitting there when the Saxon left.

Dudley watched them go, Klaus first, short and slow footed, followed by his thin German clerk. He thought he'd handled it well under the circumstances. He hadn't told the Saxon the nature of his business with Otto and he hadn't inquired, but then Otto was too shrewd to trust his partner with his offer to aid the federal prosecutor's office in New York. Otto had much to give, not only to the Department of Justice but to Langley as well, but first there were more urgent matters. He drank a cup of espresso, paid his bill, and left. At the door he remembered the white plastic shopping bag and went back to fetch it.

Two men watched him leave, one on the street, the other from a maroon Renault. Three blocks away Klaus and Dietrich climbed into the backseat of a waiting dark-blue Alfetta sedan and were driven off. As they turned along the Seine, the Saxon, swaying with the corner, reached down and gripped Dietrich's thigh with his strong fingers. Embarrassed, the shy young German tried to move his hand away but his grip was too strong. The

272

East German in the front seat watched, amused.

"Wie wars mit einen Tanz," the Saxon said, laughing and showing the discolored stumps of his teeth as he moved his fingers suggestively up Dietrich's thigh. "Let's go dancing."

The system was impenetrable, the whole un-knowable, the sum product of an institution whose memory was designed never to know itself. Adrian Shaw continued to insist Langley had no record of Major Alexei Andreyev. Corkery's search had found none, although he knew at least one document existed — the one hidden in Frank Dudley's basement footlocker, which had been given an Agency control number. But if classified files could be shredded, files in the public domain were something else. His visit to Burton Womack in Public Affairs failed to turn up a classified Andreyev file. Now he was visiting Congressional Relations to learn if an unclassified file had been overlooked.

His name was Tisdale, a GS-15 in Congressional Relations. Corkery wandered into his office a little after twelve and found him eating lunch at his desk. He was a tall man with carefully combed white hair, wearing a dark worsted suit and a starched white shirt, both as out of fashion as the thin rayon tie whose knot was the size of a peanut. He was a former House staff member who'd made a career of the House appropriations and budget subcommittees, a sly old sapper who helped the

Agency through the congressional mine fields each year. To Corkery he looked like a Tariff Commission clerk left over from the Hoover days, a young man out of shorthand school who'd come to Washington to make his fortune, lived in a Washington boardinghouse, commuted to work on a trolley car, and returned to Harrisburg or Norfolk on the C&O every weekend to have his mother turn his collars and darn his socks. The *Congressional Record* was open on the desk in front of him, and his head moved on his long neck as he watched the outer office for intruders. His secretary was at lunch. With the forks of stiff white hair sticking from the back of his head, he looked like an alligator-wise old heron, guarding his pond.

Tisdale's answers, fragmentary and elliptical, punctuated by long pauses over his vegetable soup, salad, and skim milk brought from the cafeteria, told Corkery to go away. He didn't know the name Andreyev, but after some prodding remembered Frank Dudley. He had worked with Dudley briefly after he'd joined the staff. Like a fish out of water, those first months; Dudley had no idea of procedures and knew no one on the Hill. Congressional liaison wasn't his style.

"Always talking about the old days." Tisdale paused to pinch slaw onto a plastic fork. "Had his own ideas, his own ways of doing things." He bent again to his plate, his gaze falling on Corkery's tie. "He was a walking clotheshorse too, George was."

"George?"

"Dudley. Isn't that who you were asking about?" Corkery waited as Tisdale finished his soup. He blotted his mouth with a napkin and moved his tray aside; but something in his visitor's presence had stirred old memories. His eyes wandered Corkery's face, blond hair, and tie. "Hippies," he said. The chair squeaked as he sat back.

"Hippies?"

"Sixties crowd. People your age, some of 'em."

"Where's that? Over on the Hill?"

"Staffers over there. Looked like it. Long hair, beards. McGovern crowd. Hippies." He continued to study Corkery as he brought out a toothpick. "Always poking around, asking questions. Spy stories. G-Man stuff. You ever work on the Hill?"

"No, sorry."

He probed a back molar. "Weirdos. Yuppies now." He put the silver toothpick in his vest pocket and got up.

"Sorry?"

"Sixties crowd. Sleeping on the couch, working late all the time, never see their wives. Dick 'em and dump 'em. A lot goes on. What'd you say the name was, the other name?"

"Andreyev, Major Alexei Andreyev."

"Write it down and I'll take a look."

Corkery waited near Tisdale's secretary's desk, watching the door while Tisdale searched the congressional correspondence files in the file room. Ten minutes later he returned with a thin folder. Inside were copies of two letters written to the Agency, one from an Ohio senator, one from

275

an Ohio representative, both inquiring on behalf of a constituent as to the whereabouts of Major Alexei Andreyev. The letter from the congressman included a copy of the constituent's letter. Her name was Christine Rawley, a name Corkery thought he'd seen before.

"His name's Frank, not George. Thanks." Corkery returned the file. "Frank Dudley." *We are talking about the same man, aren't we, old shoe?*

"Frank? Maybe it was. Frank Dudley. Sounds right, come to think of it. George sounds right too. What'd you say your name was?"

Corkery told him but doubted he'd remember. He would probably never see Tisdale again, one of those people you might spend twenty or thirty years with, sharing the same building, the same cafeterias, the same parking lots, and never see at all. Langley's woods was full of old possums like that.

Waiting in his in box in his second-floor office were four overnight cables reporting new Foxrun sightings. One reported Frank Dudley in Nicaragua in the company of a Cuban diplomat. Corkery glanced at them and swept them aside. Mrs. Halleck from Language Services had finished her translation from the German of the Chernishevsky article "Puzzling Irregularities in Soviet Cartography." A Xeroxed copy was on his desk, sent up by special messenger. Her note said the staff of the Berlin-based political quarterly in which the article had appeared was made up largely of Russian emigrés; the author was identified as a Russian

276

emigré now living in Western Europe. The fifteen-page document was maddeningly technical, filled with unfamiliar terms, unknown place names, rivers, villages, and mountains. As he was scanning the fifth page, a few familiar sentences leaped out from the text:

One way or another every imperial capital ultimately betrays itself, imagining that nothing can escape its imperial edict, whether the motion of the planets, the drift of the stars, or the geography of the earth . . .

He recognized the paragraph, opened his safe, brought out the Andreyev letter from the bottom drawer, and compared the sentences in the Chernishevsky article with those in the Andreyev letter. They were identical. So were a dozen other sentences; Chernishevsky might have been copying his text from Andreyev's letter. Frank Dudley had undoubtedly made the same discovery.

A knock came at the door. Susan Fern entered. Tall, willowy, with pale blond hair, pale skin, pale eyes, and a small chin, she was Jay Fellows's special assistant. Corkery thought the name about right: a hothouse plant if he ever saw one. Abbott wanted to see him at six o'clock.

"What about?"

"He assumes you know."

Five minutes later he was interrupted again, this time by a telephone call from Miss Fogarty. "I'm busy, for God's sake." It didn't matter; Shaw wanted him in his office immediately. He locked the two documents away in his safe.

Huggins and Underwood, the division's Latin American specialist, were already there, facing Shaw from the two armchairs near his desk. Huggins had been idle since his assignment to CI, awaiting the security clearances Elinor Wynn said would never come. He had been forced on Shaw in Abbott's absence. "He's just the latest nose of the beast," she'd said. "People upstairs have been trying to get their nose in Julian's tent for years." He was a retired lieutenant colonel who'd worked in Special Operations and the Training Division. Lounging in Underwood's office, Huggins had seen the incoming cables reporting Foxrun sightings in Latin America and reached his own conclusion, aided by gossip he'd picked up at the Pentagon racquetball court where he worked out twice a week with his semipro colleagues from the Defense Intelligence Agency.

"Frank Dudley a defector." Corkery heard Shaw scoff as he joined them. "Don't be ridiculous. That's simply not credible."

"You don't think so?" Huggins gave a small knowing chuckle.

"Certainly not. Defect where? Monte Carlo? Oxfordshire? Aix-en-Provence? The Catskills?"

Huggins sat hunched forward in his chair, nursing a cigarette, despite Shaw's ban on smoking. He toyed with the butt, turning it slowly in his thick fingers, head down.

"I notice you didn't say Moscow."

"Obviously I didn't say Moscow. If you knew Frank Dudley even remotely, you'd know how absurd it sounds even linking the two."

"I wasn't thinking of Moscow. One of its satellites."

"Where then? Sofia? Prague? Albania?" Shaw looked accusingly at Corkery, standing behind Underwood's chair. "Have you heard this ridiculous story?"

"No, sir, I haven't."

"Cuba," Huggins said.

Shaw looked at him blankly. *Cuba?*

"Cuba." Huggins sucked a final breath from his damp cigarette and sat back. "Gay old Havana."

"What in God's name would he be doing in Havana?"

"Not far, close to home, an easy boat ride. You don't hear much about it."

"That's as ridiculous an idea as I've ever heard."

Huggins was unfazed. He stubbed the butt in the shiny brown ashtray reserved for seventh-floor visitors. "Been talking to some Latin American types. The kind of big bucks the Cubans are offering. Narcobucks, a lot of it. Retirees especially. Put them on the payroll as consultants. Cabanas, beaches, plenty of good women. *Mulattas,* the best there is. That's the bottom line. Fixed up for life. Sanchez, he slipped away. Fred Costain, Al Elias. They found his skiff drifting empty down in the Keys, empty. Bonefishing, they said." He smiled his walnut-cracking smile, showing his teeth. "Bonefishing, my ass. Al never fished a day in his life. Where'd they go? No one knows. Now this guy Dudley. You remember the old Copacabana in Havana, the old Riviera night spot, the Havana Club on the sea. All fixed up now. *Mañana.* A guy could go down there and get set up for life. We oughta look into it."

Shaw's outraged face had crept across the desktop to suspend itself in unblinking silence, the serpent at last confronting the toad in his garden. "And you think Frank Dudley or anyone else in his right mind would have been tempted by something as obscene as that?"

"It's in the ballpark, sure. A lotta guys would go for it. Look at this guy Agee. Sold his balls to the Cubans and Sovs for a lot less. Some guys would. Buy a guy's balls, get his brains for free."

"And you imagine Frank Dudley has done this?" Shaw's voice was drawn to a whisper. "You imagine a little corner of prerevolutionary Cuba has survived, imagine a few retirees would be attracted by anything so absurd as that, to work by day for the Russians and spend their nights carousing in the nightclubs of gay old Havana. Is that what you're saying?"

"Sun City, sure. What they say, what some guys would go for."

"And you believed it? You're out of your mind!" Shaw stood up, sending his castered chair rattling crazily backward against the credenza. He pointed to the door. "Get out of my office! You too, Underwood! Get out of my office! Not you, Kevin. Out, both of you!"

Corkery remained, standing behind the chair. Shaw sat down at his desk again, cheeks flushed, his eyes downcast as he fussed with a few cables, but his mind was elsewhere; his hands were shaking. "Where do these people come from? Where in God's name do they come from?" His voice had the whispered huskiness of a man at prayer. When he at last looked up he didn't seem to know why Corkery was there. After a moment he remembered. "Needless to say, you're not to include this nonsense in your status report."

George Skaff was out that afternoon. Corkery spoke to Fred Rittenhouse from Skaff's office, who thought he remembered Christine Rawley and said he would look at the file and call back. Twenty minutes later, he telephoned. "Yeah, that was her name, Christine Rawley. After Andreyev disappears, we find out about her. She was one of his contacts up on the Hill. A secretary for some intelligence committee. Worked late. So did he, it looks like. A few drinks, okay, so one night maybe they wind up in the sack. We don't know for sure. Wait a minute." Corkery heard the rustling of papers. "Yeah, here it is. She'd been sleeping around for six or seven years is what we hear. So maybe Andreyev is punching her regularly. That's her business, his too, maybe, but what made her special is where she was working, on the staff of this House intelligence committee, that's where. What is it they called her?" He rattled through a few pages. Here it is. 'Libidinous,' an easy poke. They fired her."

"They fired Rawley?"

"Christine Rawley, right. Loose in the sack, real easy, they say. Some congressman's staff man from Ohio brought her to town, got lonely for her on weekends is what they said. He'd been punching her regularly. Same reason he lost out to someone else, who was sticking her better, bigger office, bigger stick, maybe. What'd you hear about her, anything new?"

Whether the subject was politics, race, sex, or women, there was a lot of institutional bigotry in the FBI. Fred Rittenhouse was no exemption. "No, nothing new, just backtracking. Thanks, Fred."

Abbott's office was in shadow, illuminated only by a pair of green-globed brass reading lamps on tables at each end of his ornately carved desk, an eighteenth- or nineteenth-century monstrosity, all oak leaf and acorn clusters along the massive leg near Corkery's chair. There were elves, wood nymphs, and satyric faces peeping out from the oak foliage too, so Elinor Wynn had claimed, but Corkery had never seen them. The desk had been presented to Abbott by a grateful German family whose rural manor house he had rescued from sequestration by the U.S. military government when Abbott was interrogating German detainees outside Darnhorst near Frankfurt. He had led a team screening witnesses for the Nuremberg trials. It was the rarest desk in the building, as was the man occupying it. His long androgynous face was half sculpted in shadow, as were his long hands and fingers, like a figure in an Egyptian bas-relief.

To Corkery's right along the far wall a dozen or so framed photographs hung, but he had never had the opportunity to look at them and never would. The least narcissistic of men, Abbott wasn't among them, so Elinor said. His biographers might have written his history from that wall, she claimed — the photographs taken in the Nissen training huts at Camp X in Ontario where Abbott had trained, the dim photographs of bearded Serbs crouching with their weapons in the stony passageways of mountain villages in the Balkans, of lean dapper men with bowlers and furled umbrellas on the steps of the OSS offices on Brook Street in London where he had spent the final year of the war after an eye infection in Yugoslavia had forced his evacuation. There were no pictures of Abbott hanging there to the right of the dehumidifying or fish tanks, whichever they were, both because of his elusiveness and because strong light pained his sensitive eyes. He wore tinted glasses indoors and dark glasses in the street.

During their introductory meeting months earlier, Corkery had difficulty hearing him. After a few polite questions, Abbott began talking about revolution, ideas, careerism, and hypocrisy. He talked of Khrushchev and Ivan Serov, the corrupt old Chekist who'd been replaced by Shelepin in

1958 as head of the KGB, but who'd remained loyal, even in disgrace. When the Presidium attempted unsuccessfully to depose Khrushchev in June 1957, Serov and Voroshilov, who'd sought Khrushchev's ouster, came to blows in the halls outside. Serov was loyal; Shelepin wasn't. A consummate bureaucrat, part of the bright new generation out of the Young Communist League, he represented a new breed, a new kind of duplicitousness, not in the service of an idea but of careerism and bureaucratism. When a revolutionary idea was dead, other motives substituted, most of them despicable; the careerists infiltrated the ranks, relativism flourished, hypocrisy most of all, duplicity for its own sake.

Abbott had spoken with passion and Corkery was bewildered. The monologue made no sense; a book Abbott had just read, some staff study he'd just finished? Unable to hear and unable to make sense of what he was hearing, he had crept closer, carrying his chair with him, wondering if Abbott was testing him, like his oral examination board, expecting him to ask questions and extend the dialogue. Or was he testing him in another way, some new device hidden in the cushioned brown chair, wired to the springs to monitor body heat, sweat, salinity, or blood pressure? Abbott had an obsessive interest in new gimmickry, was constantly poring over reports sent up from the technical staff and testing new devices in his office: new inks, new cellophane paper, new infinity mikes, new frequency-hopping microtransmitters, new phosphorus-bound papers impossible to Xerox. New technology made Abbott as paranoid as the Soviets, who could never tell what Bell Labs might come up with. Some supersmart young physicist started fiddling with his wife's microwave oven and comes up with a hand-held laser that could zap Moscow from Macy's basement.

No, he had been talking about loyalty, Elinor said later. A group of Young Turks from the clandestine services and the Soviet Bloc Division, supported by a handful of senior Soviet analysts, were out to unseat him, fed up with his paranoiac corruption of intelligence analysis. They'd been meeting secretly with the staffs of the intelligence committees on the Hill.

"You've been busy, I take it," Abbott began softly after an interminable silence during which he ignored Corkery and appeared to be reading something. Music was playing from somewhere near the front of the room, sentimental music from another ballroom in another decade, all strings and no percussion, the sounds of forgetfulness, as deadly as ether. Abbott dropped the pamphlet and folded his long hands together. Beyond the draped windows the short dark day was ending.

"Pretty busy, yes, sir."

"I thought we might have a quiet talk. The Dudley case seems to have obsessed you of late." He paused to modify the remark, correcting the impression he'd been personally monitoring Corkery's daily work schedule. "At least so Shaw tells me. You've been spending your time on little else."

"Pretty much."

The door opened. Jay Fellows came in, as silent as a cat in his crepe-soled shoes. He was carrying a stenographer's notepad. He took the chair to Corkery's right, crossed one leg over the other, removed a pen and opened the notebook. Abbott sat forward, toying with a ruler. "You have some definite ideas about the Dudley case?"

"A few, yes."

The eyebrows lifted as he again read something lying in front of him. "You asked Shaw for information about a man by the name of Andreyev."

"I did, yes."

He didn't lift his head. "Why?"

"I think Dudley's disappearance has something to do with Andreyev."

"And what's the connection?"

"I think he's looking for Andreyev."

Abbott didn't seem surprised. "Do you know who Andreyev is?"

"A Soviet defector."

"Do you know what he represents?"

Not sure what he meant, Corkery didn't answer. Abbott's chair creaked as he stirred to peer at another memo on his desk. "You also asked about one Vadim Lazarev. Who is Lazarev?"

"A Russian. He defected from Paris in '77."

"What is his connection with the Dudley case?"

"I don't know."

"Also someone with the cryptonym AE/Pitchfork. You asked about him. What is his connection with Dudley?"

"I don't know. A Russian, obviously. He's the mystery."

"You don't know. Why is Dudley looking for Andreyev?"

"I'm not sure."

"You don't know, you're not sure. What are you sure of?" Abbott fingered the pages of the document on his desk. In his contempt Corkery heard the echo of Shaw's taunting voice: "Well, what are you sure of?" How many times had Abbott accused Shaw in the same words, Shaw sitting here lacerated and ashamed in this same warm chair?

"I also asked for a file on Otto Rauchfuss," Corkery said. "I didn't get that either. It never got to my desk."

Abbott appeared not to hear, still reading something on his desk. With his finger he pushed back his tinted glasses and rubbed his left eyelid. The silence had grown enormous, pressing against Corkery's eardrums like the weight of the sea at fifty fathoms. Jay Fellows had stopped writing and was waiting. Gland-free, probably, like the Mediterranean lizards basking in the sun. Corkery had begun to sweat. Maybe a saline-sensor hidden here in the arms of the chair. He despised this room, this silence, the subversive babbling of the fish tanks, the strange smells, embedded in Shaw's pores now like a carbolic, in his worsteds, in his parchment skin and mouse-gray hair.

Poor Shaw. He felt sorry for him, that scurrying little dormouse with the sciatic limp, a frightened bundle of tremors and palsies scurrying secretly through the grass. Phil Chambers was right, all this dead, poisoned air: Get the hell out before it was too late.

"Have Dudley's daughter and wife been of any value?" Abbott asked, not lifting his eyes.

Corkery felt his face warm. "Quite a bit."

"Have they been in touch with him?"

"Not to my knowledge."

"Not to your knowledge. What is Mrs. Dudley's first name?"

"Louise."

"And the daughter's?"

"Jessica." They were strangers to Abbott or so he pretended, as much strangers as those frightened German wives and daughters who waited outside the barbed wire at Darmstadt or the young German girl described in Dudley's diary, searching for her lost brother at Gruenfeld where the German prisoners of war crossed the Oder. It was their two names that most angered him.

"I have yet to see a report incorporating all this," Abbott said. "I have yet to see a memo justifying your interest in these individuals. Do you think you could provide me with that? See that you do. I'll expect it tonight. That's all." He tore a page from his pad and held it toward Jay Fellows, who quickly rose to fetch it.

"I don't work that way," Corkery heard himself saying, releasing the lump of cold anger that had been welling up in him for days.

Abbott looked up. "Don't work that way?"

"Sorry, nothing personal. You haven't given me anything, neither has Fellows here, not even the Rauchfuss file, not even the FBI lab report, nothing from the D-staff either. You've let me walk around in the dark, rounding up stray cats from all over the alley, Andreyev, Lazarev, Pitchfork, the whole bloody conspiracy. Why should I tell you anything?"

"What conspiracy?" Fellows said. "It's Dudley we're asking about."

"Is it?" Corkery turned, in his face and voice the sudden savagery of youth. "Knew him well, did you? Tell me about it."

Fellows colored. "I wouldn't say that."

"No? What would you say? Sensible? Discreet? A gentleman of the old school? An old song-and-dance man, like Phil Chambers says, a wandering fuck-up like the rest of you. Come on, Fellows, let's hear it." He wanted to hear his mind work, hear divulged all the shabby little truths and half-truths that lay like dust in its forgotten corners. Face crimson, eyes flushed, lips drained ashen within his beard, Fellows said nothing. Corkery stood up, turning to Abbott. "If Fellows here or anyone else is working this case, let him write it. Screw it. I don't have anything more to say. Get another stalking-horse. I'm out of it."

Corkery slammed his office door and began clearing his desk drawers. He didn't know where

289

he would dump the Dudley material in his safe, but he wouldn't leave it for Jay Fellows or anyone else to pilfer. In the morning he would turn himself in to Personnel and request an overseas post; if he didn't get one, he would leave. The phone rang; he ignored it. A few minutes later Elinor Wynn came in without knocking, appearing as inevitably after office storms behind closed doors as thunder after lightning. "What the hell do you want?"

"My, aren't we abrupt these late evenings. What on earth is all this mess?"

"What it looks like. Shut the door. I'm packing."

"Packing for what?"

"Packing to leave." The phone rang again but he made no move to answer it. She reached to pick it up; he told her not to. She sighed and perched herself on the edge of the desk. "You are acting peculiarly."

"Nothing's peculiar for this place."

"Meaning just what?" The phone stopped ringing.

He emptied another desk drawer. "All the little secrets no one was sharing, all the files I can't get my hands on, all the cables and memos I didn't see, like the ones Abbott was looking at just now."

"Don't be so cryptic. You had a meeting with Julian?"

"Yeah. Always convenient to drop by when you've got a nose itch, isn't it? When someone else does, he can't find you."

"*Oh.* Is that how I work? What was the meeting about?"

"Loyalty. Shaw's gimpy leg, your stone-cold heart, Jay Fellows walking on his hind legs, fetching a bone. You three dream Abbott's dreams, don't you? Loyalty, that's what he was talking about, but loyalty's a two-way street. He wants me to give him what I've got on Dudley but won't show me his cards. Well, fuck him. He's not going to get anything from me. He has Fellows, he doesn't need me."

She stood up indignantly. "You told Julian *that?*"

"More or less. He wasn't het up, neither was I, just coolly professional." He banged a drawer shut. "I ask for files, I get stonewalled; I mention names, I get lies. You didn't trust me either, you and all the rest. People like me come and go, people like you stay. Now I'm gone, bagging it before you people breathe on me too much and I get embalmed or get sacked, like Dudley."

"Are you completely out of your mind?"

The door opened. It was Shaw, dressed for the cold, wearing his gray-green ulster and red scarf. "I've been trying to reach you."

"I've been busy. I've got to get my desk cleaned out."

"Cleaned out why?" Corkery didn't answer. Shaw looked at Elinor. "Is something the matter?"

"I haven't the foggiest."

"I just told you," Corkery said. "I'm leaving."

"What do you mean, leaving?"

"Just that. I've had it with this place, I'm transferring out. I'm going to turn myself in to Per-

sonnel and tell them to mail-order my ass overseas."

"You certainly can't do that."

"Can't I? Abbott wants a report on the Dudley
case, everything I know, and I won't give it to
him. That's a one-way ticket out of this place,
isn't it, telling him you think his little shop sucks
goose eggs? That's on my scoreboard, not yours,
Adrian. You know the old John Prine song, don't
you? 'Send my mouth, way down south, and kiss
my ass good-bye'? Well, I did, I have, and now
I'm out of here."

Shaw's eyes glistened feverishly. "That's ridiculous."

"Is it? Me and Huggins both." He tossed his
appointment book in his briefcase. "Maybe we'll
contract our services out, go bag a few. With my
brains and his muscle, maybe we can get some
big-bucks backers, narcobuccaneers, like he says.
Any missing skeletons in your closet, Adrian?" He
closed one drawer and opened another. "How
about you, Elinor? Anyone's shoes under your bed
you don't know where the body went?"

"This is idiotic!" Shaw cried. "You're obviously
mistaken in some way, it had to be a misunderstanding!" He turned on his heel and went out.

"He's right," Elinor said. "You're acting like
an adolescent."

"Maybe so. It feels better this way. Shut the
door."

"They won't let you walk out, you know that.
You're the stitch holding this Dudley search to-

gether, as idiotic as it is. Julian doesn't take bluffs."

"I'm not bluffing. It's not me, anyway. I'm not holding anything together. It's Jay Fellows. You ought to know. He sees your D-staff stuff, I don't. He's working the back channels, I'm chasing the wind in the street. I'm just the front man, Abbott's stalking-horse, the rube from the high shoe country they've been using to hold everyone's hand, make them feel good, wife, daughter, even the FBI, pretending we're all in the dark about poor wandering Frank Dudley but doing our best. Well, that's bullshit. Something else is going on." He sorted through the bottom drawer of his safe, brought out the Chernishevsky translation and the Andreyev letter, and stored them in his briefcase. "All I want now is not to get buried in your cold, cold ground, honey. That's the John Prine song, by the way. Electric guitar, two acoustics. He's got my kind of voice, trashy backyard, rusting old cars, refrigerators, beer cans, and bed springs, all lying out there in the high grass, like me, a Pennsylvania weasel. You wouldn't like Prine, Elinor. Like driving through the West Virginia panhandle on a winter afternoon, looking at all those trailer camps that fuck up your New England scenery —"

"I hate that word!" She slid from the desk. "It's repulsive and so are you. How can you be so deliberately vulgar!"

"Easy. It comes with the training. You wanna dance, a little go-go maybe?" He brought out his old navy photographs, laughed at the faces he saw there, and tossed them in his briefcase. "This is so goddamned stupid."

"It is and you don't make any sense!" She moved toward the door, hesitated, changed her mind, and returned. "Do you want to talk about it?" Her lids were lowered in that way he'd come to recognize, drawing the shades on the world. "You'll never work it out alone."

"No, thanks. It's too late."

"You never know until you try." He didn't answer, looking at two staff studies he couldn't remember why he kept. She lifted herself again to the desk. "In case you didn't know, Sherlock Holmes is dead. So are Bulldog Drummond and Inspector Maigret. We solve problems by committee here, the way physicists do. No one knows everything, just a piece here, a smidgen there. In the Jamesian sense, there's no Central Intelligence. It doesn't exist. Few people understand that but it's true. We're just a myth, CIA is Washington's biggest corporate lie. Sad, isn't it? All we are is a myriad of disconnected local intelligences, like Congress."

"Yokel intelligences, you mean. Are you talking about Jay Fellows or your pal Huggins?"

"I'm talking about the institution. Jay certainly isn't a yokel."

"Everyone's a yokel in some way. So is he."

"How on earth would you know?"

"I know. I've watched him. I've also seen his wife."

She laughed. "That's ridiculous. So are you,

Daffy Duck. Didn't you tell me he was your favorite movie actor when you were in the navy?"

"Those were my juvenile days. That's not what I said, anyway. You were talking about Woody Allen, your favorite nerd, and I said I liked my comedy pure, like Daffy Duck, not half-pint Manhattan neurotics." He took a few books from the bookcase. "Speaking of neurotics, where's Ed Rudolsky these days?" Surprised, she didn't answer. "That's what I figured."

"Retired. He works in Europe someplace. Why?"

"Just asking. What did you think of him?"

"He was very good. I was sorry to see him go."

"He replaced Frank Dudley, didn't he?"

"More than replaced, dear boy."

"What were you doing at the time, handling Special Projects?"

"It seems to me we talked about that once."

"So we did. If Frank Dudley is just a minor nuisance, why the secure-line telephone call to Abbott in London the Monday after he disappeared? Why the list of instructions you gave Shaw?"

"It's standard practice when Julian's out of the country. We always keep him informed. Anything else?"

"You ever heard of someone named Vadim Lazarev?" She didn't answer. "He was a Soviet defector. Rudolsky handled him. See what I mean?"

"Now that you ask, I may have heard the name."

"I'll bet you have. Major Alexei Andreyev, that

name ring a bell? It did once before, but you threw me out the door." Her face was cold. "That's what I figured. You're up to your neck in it, aren't you, honey, whatever this conspiracy is, all of you —"

Miss Fogarty was at the door. "Mr. Shaw would like to see you." Elinor Wynn slipped silently from the desk and went out.

"I'm busy, sorry."

"Now —"

"Go water your petunias, sweet pea."

The door slammed and he continued cleaning out his safe. A few minutes later the phone rang. He ignored it. On the fifth ring he picked it up angrily. "Look, don't bother me now —"

"Kevin?" a quiet voice asked. "Is that you?" It was Louise Dudley. She hadn't heard from him and was worried. She hated to bother him at the office but she'd found something.

"I've just talked to Abbott," Shaw said from the doorway. "It was all a misunderstanding, just as I thought."

Corkery went by him, coat on, carrying his briefcase. "We'll talk about it tomorrow. I've got a ballroom tango lesson, sorry."

The antique silver chest was opened at Thanksgiving and Christmas and occasionally at Easter, but seldom during the year. Louise had found bundles of felt-wrapped ancestral silver hidden under the lace and linen tablecloths in a highboy drawer and more in the drawers below. Their discovery led her to the cherry silver chest in the closet, unopened since last Easter. The cache she found worried her: a last will and testament to be found if he failed to return? Corkery said he may have been in a hurry, wanted to store the documents quickly and safely, had little time, and had thought of the antique silver chest.

There were bundles of old letters and postcards, faded and water-stained, bound with cord, and stored in two portfolios smelling faintly of mildew and probably brought from the basement footlocker. Also bundled inside were copies of his first wife's will and his will together with two codicils. Taped to the outside was a key to Dudley's safety deposit box. In a separate envelope addressed to Phil Chambers was a Xeroxed copy of the Andreyev letter and the remaining pages Corkery had been searching for.

"Does it make any sense?" Louise asked. They sat at the dining-room table as Corkery searched the documents.

"Pretty much."

"I'm tired of mysteries, I'm quite worn out with them. It's all a Pandora's box, isn't it?"

The postcards, arranged chronologically, were addressed to Dudley in Oslo, Copenhagen, and Washington and signed Otto. They came faithfully each year, posted from Berlin, each year repeating the same message. On *Totensonntag*, the Day of the Dead, West Berliners were allowed to visit the Stansdorf Cemetery in East Berlin. One Sunday each year Otto Rauchfuss visited the two graves in Stansdorf Cemetery, left the two arrangements of Michaelmas daisies brought from a West Berlin florist, and made arrangements with the grounds-keepers for the graves to be attended. Each time he sent Dudley a postcard.

In a white linen envelope were four black-and-white photographs, yellow at the edges, taken during the winter of 1946–47. In one standing next to a jeep was a young girl, tall, blond, and lovely, wearing a GI field jacket and woolen trousers. Two other photographs were taken on a gray afternoon with the frozen lake in the background; she sat on a snowbank, lacing her ice skates and smiling, wearing the same GI jacket, woolen cap, and trousers. In the fourth she stood on the steps of a dark apartment house, the woolen cap in her hand.

"She's lovely," Louise said. "Do you know who she is?"

She was Nina von Winterfeldt, a girl Frank Dudley had known in Berlin, the young girl who had haunted his diaries in Berlin and later at Harvard. She died of diphtheria in 1948 when Dudley was in Cambridge. She was buried in Stansdorf Cemetery in East Berlin; her grandmother died the following year. Otto had arranged for the burials and described the church services and the funerals in two of his early letters. Corkery knew the month of her death and was familiar with other details from Dudley's Berlin and Harvard diaries. He had long suspected Dudley knew Otto Rauchfuss, but not until he read the postcards and the letters at the cherry table did he realize how close their friendship had been.

298

"You knew about her?" Louise said.

Corkery nodded. "I knew. He wanted to marry her and bring her and her grandmother back to Boston. His father said no."

"How awful." She studied the three photographs. "I never knew. Never."

"No one did. There were a lot of things about him no one knew."

She looked at him, still holding the photographs. "But you knew."

"I knew. It's my business, I suppose."

The first letters, sent to Dudley at Harvard, were awkward and self-conscious, scrawled in poor English and signed Otto Kippensammler, the name in the army handbook. It had been under Corkery's nose all that time. Since *Kippe* was the German word for cigarette butt, it followed that *Kippensammler* was someone who scavenged cigarette butts from the Berlin streets. Cigarettes were a local currency in Berlin 1945–46; twenty Camel cigarette butts were worth thirty German marks. Otto Rauchfuss was Otto Kippensammler; a rubble rat, a fourteen-year-old street orphan when Frank Dudley first met him.

He looked up. Louise hadn't moved, still watching him. "You didn't tell me you knew all this. How did you know?"

"About Nina von Winterfeldt? I found his Berlin and Harvard notebooks."

She looked at him in astonishment, let the photographs drop to the table, and got up. "You amaze me sometimes, absolutely amaze me."

299

"Why? Where are you going?"

"To get a drink. Would you like one?"

"Beer's fine." He thought she was angry.

The voice in the other letter Corkery recognized. It was unmistakably Andreyev's.

I have described many times my decision to leave the GDR and see no need to repeat it now. On a rainy night in October I had accompanied an East German army NCO by the name of Werner to recover some transits and mapping scopes from a truck that had broken down along the border. We were drinking vodka, Werner was in difficulty with his captain, and I was bored with my assignment. One thing led to another and we soon found ourselves cutting through the wire.

I will instead introduce the Rudyev family and my mother's brothers, a subject I've never discussed before. Four years after I arrived in Moscow as a boy to be taken into the household of my mother's brother, Mikhail Rudyev, he was arrested. No official charges were ever brought. He was taken away one evening in the custody of two men. I never saw him again. Six weeks later his wife, a seamstress in a Moscow parachute factory, learned through a party official he was being held in a prison camp in the Urals. My aunt was anxious, quite naturally, not knowing what her husband had been accused of, but insisted to her friends he had been transferred to the Ministry of Geology in the main administration for the Urals and Siberia. My cousin, Vasily, told the same tale to our friends at the Semiletka Gymnasium. This was my first experience with lies. Like all lies, it altered in a minor but important way my relationship to the truth. In time both my aunt and my cousin came to believe this lie; for Russians that is the secret illness of their times.

After attending the Semiletka Gymnasium in Moscow, my cousin Vasily and I became students in the Technical/Geodetic Institute. One day in 1944 we arrived in class to find ourselves conscripted into the army. I saw no action during those last months of the war but spent my time with an engineering brigade in the Caucasus, repairing bridges. After the war I returned to the university and was later assigned to the Institute of Geodesy, Aerial Photography, and Cartography in the old Demidov Palace on Karl Marx Street. Here I made a reputation for myself. Given my fondness for maps, the studies came easily. I was eating my own bread, so to speak.

Five years later I was recruited into the GRU in the 5th Directorate's map procurement division. I shared a small office on the third floor of GRU hqs near the Khodinka airfield; my window looked out on the Institute of Cosmic Biology whose mysteries I often pondered. Cosmic biology made no sense to me. I was no closer to the mystery when I was posted to Berlin-Karlhorst in the German Democratic Republic.

Louise returned with the drinks and sat down. She said she wasn't angry, just disappointed. "You're not aware of it, I'm sure," she said, "but you're probably the most single-minded individual I've ever met in my life."

He heard a coolness in her voice he'd never heard before. "I take it that's not a compliment."

"In some ways, it is, in a professional way. In other ways, no, not in a personal way. I don't suppose it occurred to you that I'd be interested in anything from Frank's past that might shed light on what's happened."

"You mean the Berlin and Harvard notebooks? As a matter of fact it did. I thought about it."

"But you didn't share them with me."

"No."

"Why?" The gray eyes were unsmiling.

"Because they violated his privacy. Since they did, I knew that if you'd found them here in the apartment, you'd never have read them, never."

She didn't answer for a minute and finally shook her head. "You astonish me. You do, constantly. So matter-of-fact about everything. Maybe I wanted to be angry. I'm sorry. I'm not angry, not at all. Just terribly disappointed." She looked away. It was a long time before she spoke again. A sadness he'd never heard before was in her voice. "I haven't done anything for days, just walking around in a fog. And then there's that lovely old house, just standing out there in the country. I'm afraid I don't quite know what to do about that either. More indecision. The utter sameness, day after day." She got up abruptly. "Get on with your work, please. I'll only distract you. I have things I can do."

Andreyev's letter may have begun with his boyhood days in Moscow, but the purpose was to describe for Langley an attempt by unknown Soviet intelligence officers to recruit him during a trip to Montreal.

In addition to my uncle Mikhail Rudyev in Moscow, my mother had a second brother, Grigory Rudyev, a civil engineer who was working in Tadjikistan in 1938 when he escaped to Afghanistan with his wife. This was the secret whispered about the kitchen table in the small flat on Mockva Street in Moscow: Uncle Grigory had "escaped" to Afghanistan. "Escaped from what?" we children wondered. Knowing only the familiar world around us, we didn't understand the mystery. Uncle Grigory worked for the Kabul municipality waterworks. A son Mikhail was born there and in 1939 or 1940 the family moved on to India where Uncle Grigory was eventually interned by the British as an unwanted foreigner. In 1949 a letter was received from him at the flat on Mockva Street sent from the British camp at Valivade, India, saying his wife had died and he was considering returning to the USSR. No mention was made of his son, Mikhail. We heard nothing more. Then in 1953 or 1954, another letter was received, this one from an International Relief Organization camp in Lebanon, telling us he had applied for resettlement in Canada as a landed immigrant. This letter was postmarked Yervan in the USSR. At the bottom of his letter Uncle Grigory wrote that it would be hand-carried from Aleppo to Yervan by an Armenian friend who worked in a Beirut gold suq. Scribbled across the back flap of the envelope were a few words in Armenian, which was typical; an Armenian must always have the last word. In the same way Armenians imagine their final history will be written by them. The truth is the final word will be written by others in another language, as with the Persians, the Greeks, the Romans, and the Mayans. This was the last word we received from Uncle Grigory Rudyev.

With these necessary details dispensed, I can now take up the matter at hand.

Just a few days ago while I was attending a Slavic Studies Association meeting in Montreal, a stranger introduced himself to me as Mikhail Rudyev! We were standing under a brightly lit chandelier outside the mezzanine conference room of the hotel where the meeting was being held, waiting for one of the opening sessions to reconvene. A colorless little man with gray hair, blue eyes, and an unhealthy pallor, the consequence of those long maritime winters, he said his name was Mikhail Rudyev, a Canadian citizen and a professor of history at a small Canadian college.

You can imagine my astonishment! I laughed. Coincidences always strike me this way, and this one was too preposterous to credit. I asked his father's name. Grigory Rudyev, he said, a Canadian citizen who had died in New Brunswick in 1960. And where was he born? In the USSR, of course. Did he have any sisters and brothers? He seemed to remember he did. The sister's name was Margarita, my mother's name. The brother was Mikhail, for whom he had been named.

I felt light-headed at hearing this, as if I'd blundered by chance into another man's dream. Intrigued, he asked why I'd inquired about his family. I said I'd once known a Russian named Rudyev but this was in Europe years ago and I'd forgotten his first name. My comment interested him. His father, he continued, had left behind quite a few papers in his native Russian. Perhaps if I remembered this Rudyev's first name and where we'd met, he might look at them.

This was even more preposterous. Did he expect me to believe he had so little curiosity about his father that he'd had no interest in his papers until a remark by a stranger provoked it? I said I doubted the name would come to me; I'd met him long ago, and it was of little consequence now. Shortly afterward, the meeting reconvened. I took a seat far away from cousin Mikhail, but his remarks troubled me during the long, dull, scholarly afternoon.

Avoiding the crowded lobby and coffeeshop, I took a walk before dinner. Dirty snow was piled high along the curbs; the wind was bitterly cold. Taking refuge in an underground shopping arcade, I strolled about, looking in the windows and thinking about my chance encounter with a lost cousin who had vanished years earlier in Kabul, Afghanistan, only to miraculously materialize under a Montreal chandelier, a ghost from my childhood. Was it possible? No, it wasn't possible. It occurred to me we might be related after all, but in an official rather than a maternal way. I suspected he'd been sent to make contact with me. My self-esteem was renewed: Moscow had taken notice of my case.

Vanity again! Let's be honest about it. All of us despise anonymity and I despised mine. That's an understandable emotion, isn't it? What did Napoleon say? "Vanity made the revolution. Liberty was only a pretext." I felt flattered, like the crippled old soldier a laughing young girl nods to in the street, bringing a fresh tingle to all those forgotten wounds. But by the time I returned to my hotel room after a lonely dinner, the excitement had worn off. Was this man Rudyev GRU or KGB, an official cousin or not a cousin? Nothing of the sort, I decided. I had seduced myself. I was back at being myself again, a very meager, threadbare role. Barely

306

able to afford my airline ticket, I'd come to Montreal from Washington to beg a financial grant or two, cadge some translation work, perhaps a minor teaching position. Why would anyone take notice of me?

On the following day, I avoided cousin Rudyev during the morning meetings, but the coincidences continued. Having decided the afternoon colloquium didn't interest me, I took advantage of the empty lounge to refill my coffee cup from the table thermidor. I was standing to one side, considering how I might spend the remainder of the afternoon, when a man joined me from the nearby conference room. He took a fresh coffee cup, filled it from the thermidor, and lit a cigarette. He nodded and spoke to me in Russian. These are his exact words:

"You are enjoying the conference, Citizen Andreyev?"

Citizen Andreyev! Not Comrade, but *Citizen!* No wasted words, you see, no polite preliminaries, no ambiguity, no pretense, like that of my accidental cousin. He came straight to the point: "Citizen Andreyev!" Here was my predicament in a nutshell. He'd tracked me down in Montreal and in a single word condemned me to a prisoner's uniform in the far-off Gulag, stripping me of the dignity even the poorest peasant knows in being called "Comrade."

I said nothing, put down my coffee cup, and walked toward the coatroom. He followed me. "I didn't come here to insult you," he called,

"I came to talk to you."

Putting on my coat, I asked him what about.

"About you and your situation."

"My situation?" What did he know about my situation? Even I knew nothing about my situation. If I had known my situation, seen it clearly, the way Tolstoy or Chekhov would have seen it, I might have been redeemed. I would have said, "Well, this individual, who is obviously me, must do such-and-such to save himself and his situation," and I would have done it. But my situation wasn't that of books but of life. In books and novels, which are meant for our pleasure, we know whom we would pretend to be, but in life we have no clear idea of who we are. Few bother to find out. Instead, we read of other people's lives; we sneak into their villas and aboard their yachts, creep into their closets and dress in their clothes, climb into their beds, sip their champagne, and make love to their wives and mistresses. Maybe if we talked to the author — and authors esteem themselves these days, knowing the rich, the powerful, and the beautiful — we'd learn that we're not esteemed after all, that we're not the hero or the heroine, not Prince Andrey or Pierre, but instead are one of the faceless shadows on the ballroom floor, the ones playing whist in the drawing room where Anna and Vronsky meet, the nincompoops whose lives are so trivial and pointless Tolstoy doesn't bother to describe them at all. Such was my own life at this stage of my existence; yet this stranger was telling me I might be redeemed. No doubt the Serpent spoke the same words to Adam and Eve in the Garden.

"Your situation is not as desperate as it seems," he said, pulling on his own coat. "Things might be done. We're prepared to help if you're prepared to listen."

Fair enough. This was strictly business, as we Americans say, no vanity involved. I was no longer flattered but curious. "We?" I thought; who was *we?* He was a tall man with a pock-marked face, as thin as a spade, blue eyes, and brown hair with a soft wave. He washed it often, which struck me as odd for a Russian of his crude situation, but what did I know of his situation? His name was Boris.

We met outside the hotel that evening and walked along Mount Royal Street. What he said as we strolled was simple enough. I had been twelve years in exile and had nothing to show for it; thus certain lessons had been learned. Moscow was prepared to make a new beginning if an understanding could be reached. If I wished to return to the Homeland, that would be arranged but a price would have to be paid. I could expect no less than five nor more than eighteen years imprisonment for my crime, a generous concession given the fact that I was still condemned to death under article 64a by the Military College of the Soviet Supreme Court. We entered a little side-street restaurant, where he told me my entire history, beginning in the small village where I was born and continuing on to the present day. An incident occurred shortly after we took our seats that struck me as odd, but I'll return to that in a moment.

It is a curious feeling to have your history told you by a stranger. It is also depressing; the facts are there but they're trivial. You keep waiting for more but then you realize there isn't any more. It is like having your obituary read to you or looking at a corpse in a coffin, like that snowy morning in Moscow when I waited for forty-five minutes with Colonel Bulakov from the Soviet Army Academy to file by General Dolgin's coffin. When we reached the casket the old woman ahead of us pointed an accusing finger at the shrunken figure lying in the flower-filled crypt: "That's him? That's General Dolgin!" She stood gaping at a weasel face as shriveled as her own. I thought she was going to seize his shoulder, wake him, and demand he tell her more; but there wasn't any more and that was why we were standing there in that long sad queue.

We had ordered drinks and the waitress confused Boris's order with that of another customer. Her French-Canadian French confused him even more. It may be he was also confused by my lack of enthusiasm, which brought disorder, or *otsutstvie portadka,* to his instructions, the chaos every apparatcheki dreads. Recognizing his bewilderment, she graciously spoke in

English, but her thick accent so cleverly disguised the change he was unaware of it. He asked her to speak in English, which she did, very slowly, as if speaking to a child, a humiliation that annoyed him even more. After she brought him his whiskey and left, he began to curse. Here is what he said: "These goddamned Canadians, these f—king goddamn Canadians!"

Since he said this in English, not Russian, I knew my suspicion was justified: never trust a man who swears in anything other than his native tongue. This is especially true of the crudest Russian: Does the barnyard cock atop a Ukrainian pigsty crow like an English nightingale? Indeed not. He may wear a French shirt, a German suit, a Swiss watch, and smoke American cigarettes, but when he swears in the presence of a countryman, he will swear in honest, down-to-earth Russian, for which, like our own Russian poetry, there is no substitute on the face of the earth.

So this nonsense told me something of Boris. Had he been true to himself he wouldn't have sworn in English; if he wasn't being honest with himself why should I believe he was being honest with me? In this way I knew he'd come to deceive me and that his offer of repatriation in exchange for certain "tasks" I was to perform was a deception. If I were to meet with him abroad in Bern or Vienna to further discuss "my situation" as he hinted, he would smash me and my ambiguous predicament to pieces and drag

311

what remained by the heels over the border where there would be nothing left to discuss.

Dinner arrived. I was a condemned traitor, what more needed to be known? But Boris was nevertheless curious about me. Such men usually are. They want to know about the broader aspects of life. Being sent straight from the kennel to do their work, where they'll soon be returned, they must take advantage of their opportunities for cultural improvement in the great world. They're like the party official from the provinces come to Moscow who gives the prostitute her rubles in his hotel room and as he pulls on his pants asks if she has any children and if she enjoys her work; or the little party bureaucrat I once heard ask the legless soldier sitting on his castered board outside the Dynamo Stadium in Moscow if he sometimes felt an itch in his toes. Such information is stored away in that little compartment in his skull reserved for nonofficial scientific information.

Boris asked me why I had decided to leave East Germany that cold night so many years ago. What were my thoughts?

"Comrade," I said, "my situation was very complicated at the time. I was half stewed, I owed Comrade Drukov two hundred and twenty thousand Deutschmarks I couldn't repay, I had been sleeping with the wife of Herr Dummler, an East German diplomat serving abroad whose daughter wrote him of her infidelity, and my map was wrong. I made a very serious mistake."

"Of your own volition? An act freely done?" It seemed to amaze him. "An act freely done," I admitted, "but one I have regretted every waking moment of my life." We returned silently to our plates, each trying to decide whose lies were the most shameless.

We finished our dinner and left. In the dark street Boris hinted he might soon be assigned to the Soviet embassy in Washington and mentioned a few names — x, y, and z, currently assigned there. Did I know them? No, the names meant nothing to me. We turned a corner. With the icy wind biting at our naked ears Boris was anxious to bring our talk to an end. He told me I would soon receive an invitation to a reception on March 18th at an Eastern European embassy in Washington. The day before the reception I was to drive at a late morning hour to a certain Safeway grocery store in the Virginia suburbs near Arlington Boulevard. Inside at aisle number 2 at a precise time I would see a man wearing a gray overcoat and a red scarf pushing a grocery cart holding a single sack of oranges. I would ask this "Comrade X," as Boris referred to him, a Russian well and favorably known to me, for help in finding the health foods section. "Comrade X" would then give me further instructions. If the invitation to the Eastern European embassy didn't arrive, I was to wait. Sometime that spring I would be invited to an international Slavic studies conference in Vienna. Air tickets would be provided.

Boris asked me to repeat what he had just told me. I did. I also questioned him about this unknown "Comrade X." In what way was he "well and favorably known to me"? He assured me all this would be revealed in due time. He left me on the next corner and I returned to my hotel. I saw nothing of Boris or my fictitious cousin during the remaining two days of the conference. I had no doubt that the two approaches were related, one wet, one dry. But on the final morning something happened that made me believe someone had been rethinking my case.

At breakfast in the hotel dining room that last morning, I was sitting alone at my table near one of the high windows overlooking the street when a man carrying an overcoat seated himself a few tables away. It was late, the dining room had almost emptied, and I was one of the few diners left. I'd grown tired of the conference by then and had decided not to attend the closing sessions on the mezzanine. I took little notice of him at first. He had written his breakfast order on the card on the table, the custom in Canadian hotels, but service was slow at that hour and no one came to retrieve it. He seemed impatient, glancing in my direction several times as he searched for a waiter. I was the only diner in his vicinity and ignored him. I assumed he was late for the meeting upstairs. Abruptly he picked up his overcoat and left. As he passed behind my chair, he stopped and bent to retrieve something from the carpet. "Excuse me," he said in accented English, "you must have dropped this." He left the envelope on my table and hurried out. It was all done very quickly. My name was written in pencil on the envelope. Inside was a hand-printed note, also in pencil, and a postcard. The note read: "If you wish information concerning your uncle Mikhail Ivanovich Rudyev, mail the enclosed card from the hotel lobby post box at 10:10. Details will be supplied." The note was unsigned. The postcard was a view of Quebec City on a snowy winter day. It was stamped and addressed to a woman named Erika Witte, Kolnerstrasse 75, Dresden, German Democratic Republic. The single-paragraph text proclaimed the raw beauty of the Quebec hinterlands and promised to send an envelope of Canadian postage stamps bought from a local dealer. It was signed "Hulga."

It was all very puzzling, puzzling but not puzzling, simple but not simple. Had Boris's instructions been revised on higher authority? At 10:10 I mailed the postcard in the lobby box. That afternoon I caught my Air Canada flight and returned to Washington.

So this is my tale as I await the invitation to the East European embassy here in Washington. I am forwarding this letter to Langley, Virginia, through the intercession of a friend in whom I have total confidence. If you find my situation intriguing enough to discuss further, I am at your service.

Respectfully yours,

/s/ Alexei Andreyev

At the bottom of the last page, Corkery found a final comment written in Julian Abbott's unmistakable handwriting: "The man is obviously insane."

Corkery hadn't slept well and his throat felt raw. In the Library of Congress's Madison Building that morning he reread Andreyev's congressional testimony and afterward stood looking in the windows of the small storefront office on East Capitol Street where Andreyev had his translation service. A Quick Copy franchise was next door. A FOR RENT sign was taped to the unwashed front window, glazed gray by the seasons. On the sill inside were a few copy machine brochures. A metal typing table stood abandoned in the center of the front bay. The unpainted ribs along one wall showed that the interior had once been divided into partitions. They'd been removed. A broom leaned against the wall near a pile of rubbish. It was another abandoned station on the road to nowhere.

Dudley's obsession had become his own. He didn't know why Dudley wanted to find Andreyev. He didn't understand Andreyev's importance, not to Dudley, not to the Soviets. He was an unknown quantity from the beginning; no one trusted him, not then, not now. He was washed up, a has-been, an out-in-the-cold defector doing $10-an-hour translations. Why did he matter to Dudley? Why would the Soviets have made an approach in Montreal, instructing him to meet with a Comrade X in Virginia, a Russian well and favorably known? Was he lying about that, trying to reinvest his career, like Frank Dudley? Who was the friend who delivered Andreyev's letter to Langley, the friend in whom he had total confidence? Corkery didn't know. He'd been rounding up stray cats from all over the alley. One more remained.

It was a Capitol Hill basement apartment with the entrance under the side steps in a dim areaway. Dried leaves and scraps of yellowing newsprint scraped and fluttered in futile convulsions above a leaf-clogged drain, trying to escape, like the last hatch of summer mayflies dying on the lake. A ceiling light burned overhead, although it was midmorning. Snow flurries appeared, danced crazily in the cold wind, and vanished. There was another basement apartment across the patch of bare earth where a screen door was ajar. The mesh was discolored and torn from the frame, sullied and ballooned out by small sticky hands.

The young woman who answered his knock was tall and large boned, wearing a loose black sweater and paint-stained gray corduroys. Her wide-set blue eyes were expressionless under straw-colored bangs. She might have been sleeping. Her face had the petulance of a lonely child on a rainy day, imprisoned in her own boredom. "What do you want?"

"Christine Rawley?"

"Maybe. Who are you?"

"My name's Corkery. I'd like to talk to you about someone you may know. It's important."

"Yeah, well, I don't feel like talking. Bother me some other time."

"I don't have much time, that's my problem. Just a few quick questions, that's all I'm asking."

She hesitated. A middle-aged woman left the screen door opposite, looked disapprovingly in their direction, and pulled a scarf over her head. "Okay, but make it quick. I've gotta go out."

The narrow hall inside was used as a dining room. A few breakfast dishes lay on the table. Three steps away was a tiny living room filled with secondhand yard sale furniture. The unpainted bookshelves were filled with paperbacks. An electric typewriter sat on a table under the front window. Next to it was a new tin footlocker with the lid lifted. She was packing. Someone had started to paint the pale green walls with white paint but had stopped a few ragged inches below the low ceiling. On the back of the couch were a blanket, sheets, and a pillow. He could smell the rot of copra rugs, latex paint, and decaying plasterboard.

She moved aside a few magazines to make a place for him in a corduroy-covered armchair. "Make it quick. What'd you wanna ask?" Her breasts swung freely within the loose black sweater.

"His name's Andreyev. I think maybe you know him."

She glanced at him contemptuously as she opened the curtains above the typing table to let in more light. "Jesus. Another one. Are you FBI types ever a joke. I've been through all this before."

"I'm not FBI. Did you know Andreyev?"

"Sure, I know him. I did some typing for him. Is that a crime?" She sat down heavily on the couch, lifting her long arms to gather in her hair. Her eyelids had dropped as she measured him, as if she found his curiosity as trivial as his face. Her own was shiny and pale, large pored and waxen, like a grapefruit.

"Where did you know him?"

"When I worked on the Hill, then after."

"You work on the Hill?"

"Don't be stupid. Not anymore. If I did, you wouldn't be here. Make it quick, I've got things to do."

"You wrote a letter to an Ohio congressman and senator asking about Andreyev. Why did you write the letters?"

"Why do you think? Go read your phone taps. If you think I'm going to tell you more than you know, you're even more of an asshole than those other FBI guys I talked to."

Her voice was perfectly flat, without irony, just the ugly calm of someone stating an ugly fact in a damp, ugly basement apartment on Capitol Hill

319

where the walls had to be sponged off and the floors mopped down after a heavy rain. The light dimmed as someone passed along the areaway. Overhead footsteps were descending the stairs; a heavy piece of furniture was being dragged down a hall. The wind gnawed at the window.

"I don't know anything about phone taps —"

"Look, I've been through all this once, I don't want to go through it again, okay —" She moved as if to get up.

"Neither do I. I'm in this thing cold turkey. I'm not from the FBI." He took his laminated Agency identification tag from his pocket, got up and handed it to her. "I think someone's got it all wrong, that's why I'm here. I'd just as soon no one knew about it."

She sat studying it, glanced up at him, looked again at the color photograph, and handed it back. "What makes you think I believe you?"

"I'll take that chance."

"Yeah? Why should I? You're not the one taking chances, I am. What you guys say and do are two different things. You tell me one thing, you write down another. You know how an FBI report reads, don't you? I'll bet you've even written a few. I've read what you guys wrote about me, FOI stuff. It took me two years and three hundred and fifty bucks to get it. I talked to the FBI, not here, another apartment I had. Two very nice FBI types, nice manners, nice smiles, and I fell for it. I even made them coffee. Then two years later I read what they wrote. I didn't know the stuff. It all

320

sounded weird, someone I didn't know doing weird things, that's how it read. That's why the FBI keeps it all confidential, the FBI's adult bookstore, that's what their files are. Ask me. I wake up one morning, cold turkey, like you said, and all of a sudden I find out I've got a shitty reputation. All of a sudden I'm not just a secretary but a security risk, a real easy poke, this yuppie staffer over on the Hill tells the FBI, this junior staff yo-yo I never said boo to he was such a shit. Why should I talk to you? You probably think you know all about me, what those FBI idiots wrote." Angry, she got up impatiently. "I've got things to do."

"I'm trying to find Andreyev. I thought maybe you could help."

"Yeah, well, that's not my problem. Maybe he doesn't want to be found. I wouldn't blame him. He was a nice man, better than anything this goddamn town deserves."

"Why did you write the two letters to your congressmen?"

"He owed me a little money, if it's any of your business. Not much, not enough to matter, not enough to make a difference to the IRS either, although those FBI characters claimed it did. The IRS auditors said so too. I thought he could put the FBI straight on how much money and what it was for. But that wasn't the only reason."

A door slammed upstairs. She went into the kitchen to bring a package of Kents from the table, moving with the awkwardness of a large woman who'd spent a lifetime trying to make herself a size smaller. "I didn't report it on my income tax, the typing I did for him. It was stupid of me, but I didn't. Then the FBI tried to make it into something big, like our relationship, which was an even bigger joke. I never slept with the guy, he didn't even try to come on with me. It was strictly business, that's all it was. After he disappears, I get these FBI guys poking around, making it into something big and I'm holding the bag. I lose my job, I lose my reputation, I get an IRS audit, and I'm in hock for all this money the FBI tells the IRS I earned but didn't."

"So you thought if you could find Andreyev, he could clear it all up."

"He would have too. I know he would. I don't care about getting my job back. Fuck the job, fuck Washington too. I've had it with this goddamn city. I'm leaving. The other reason I wrote the letters was he interested me."

"Who else typed for him? Did he say?"

"I've said all I'm going to. Anything else is my business. His too. I don't wanna see anyone else get hurt the way I was. Like I said, why should I talk to you?"

"I'm trying to find him."

"Yeah? That's what the FBI said. Prove it." She got to her feet. "I've gotta go."

"Prove what?" He got up. "What do you want me to prove?"

"That you're not just another FBI bullshitter."

"So what do you want?"

"Those FBI reports I was talking about. The stuff I got through the FOI act was sanitized, the names cut out. If you could get me some of the raw stuff, the originals, maybe we could talk some more."

"I could get them, have them in a few hours."

"Yeah, sure. Don't break your arm."

"I'll get them. I can have them this afternoon."

She was watching him suspiciously. "On the level?"

"On the level."

"Okay. Tonight's better. Maybe at Yu's. He closes at nine. Yu Kum-song. His restaurant's a couple of blocks over on Pennsylvania. I've got a week's work over there, keeping his books. He's fouled up and the IRS is on his ass. So are the Social Security people." She opened the door. "About nine. If the door's locked, knock on the glass. And it better be good. Don't try to screw me over."

The smell of winter was in the air as Corkery and Shaw walked out through the front entrance after lunch, their lacerations healed. A feeling of brotherhood prevailed; Corkery had been welcomed back into the family.

"I'm somewhat familiar with naval tradition," Shaw said, drawing himself up in his ulster. "Decisiveness, the impatience with paperwork and fiddle-faddle. Florence's brother was that way. He was in the navy, just as you were."

"Florence?"

323

"My wife." Cells of sunlight alternated with snow flurries and gray shadows, like washed and unwashed windows. To the west the clouds were thickening. "Her father was an Episcopal minister." His voice had dropped to a cathedral whisper, the tone he used for the more sensitive office routine, the result of which made his annual meeting to schedule summer leave requests sound as though he were dispatching officers, staff and secretaries to infiltrate the Sikhs of the Punjab, the emirs of Bokhara, and the lobstermen of the Maine coast.

"Florence's?"

"Florence's, yes."

During lunch, an intimate affair in the executive dining room that Shaw had paid for, he'd explained that Julian Abbott had not been presenting him with an ultimatum the previous night. He had been preoccupied with other matters that had nothing to do with Frank Dudley, matters in which Jay Fellows was also deeply involved. If Corkery had misunderstood his distraction during their meeting, that was regrettable. He was disappointed Corkery hadn't shared his conclusions. He had told Shaw to give Corkery whatever help he needed.

"He has complete confidence in you," Shaw repeated, drawing his scarf up, "complete confidence. He considers last night an unfortunate misunderstanding, nothing more. He'll explain this evening." He looked at his watch. "Six-thirty."

"Six-thirty." Corkery reminded him of the Andreyev file.

"Andreyev, yes. I'll see what I can ferret out."
He stopped to offer him what appeared to be a
mint, his ridged fingernail carefully pinching it
from the silver-papered tube. "He was at Omaha
Beach on D Day but that was long before your
time. He later converted to Catholicism. Then he
became a Trappist."

Corkery stopped in his tracks: "Andreyev?"

Shaw continued on. "Florence's brother. A
dreadful affair. He was the only son." He stopped
again, his eyes drawn to a small tractor pulling
a leaf mill under the trees. During the summer
his face bloomed primrose pink from his gardening
weekends, but on this autumn day it was as colorless as winter rain. "That's much larger than
mine, but not so dependable a model."

It wasn't a mint at all, Corkery discovered as
the mentholated vapors frosted his lungs. It was
the same medicinal lozenge with which Shaw lu-
bricated his throat before staff meetings and gave
such a tomblike breath to his deliberations. Turning his head, he pursed his lips and shot it off
into the shrubbery.

"The war did something to him. He was an Episcopal minister. Later he became a Trappist, as I
said."

"The father?"

"The brother. Ralph. His monastery name was
Brother something-or-other. Trappists take vows
of silence. Since her father was an Episcopal priest,
it was something of a family tragedy. He's buried
at Gethsemene in Kentucky."

"The father?"

"The brother. It's still discussed. Florence's mother never got over it. She lives with us." The wind carried seeds of snow to his ulster. He stopped to meditate on a copse of newly planted white spruce, mint green against the autumn foliage, their trunks still wrapped in burlap. "The wind can do as much harm as ice. I once gave her some books by Thomas Merton. They didn't help."

"Help what?"

"Help her understand." Corkery heard him sigh, the sigh of an older generation relieving itself of the past. With Shaw emotion was rare, but grief remained a need, as redeeming as rain. He wondered whom he grieved for. Not Frank Dudley certainly. The white-haired man from Personnel who sat near his cafeteria table each morning turned first to the *Washington Post* obituaries over his buttered toast and tea, searching for early deaths to sigh over. Shaw's sorrow was probably similar, a dignified groping for excuses for pain. Corkery wondered about his domestic life, what his wife looked like, whether he'd ever thought of walking out, slamming the door, hitting the road, leaving everything behind, like Frank Dudley. Not everything either: he drove a ten-year-old Dodge with a clicking valve.

Corkery listened and nodded. They now shared an intimate bond, their lacerations healed. His wife's name was Florence, they were childless; his invalid mother-in-law lived with him, so did his sister-in-law. His brother-in-law had been a Catholic monk, his father-in-law an Episcopal minister. Pondering the painful secrets just disclosed, it occurred to him that Adrian Shaw was never intended for the clandestine service.

An hour after he returned from the FBI office, Susan Fern brought him a copy of the Andreyev letter, identical to the one he'd already seen. She didn't say where it had been miraculously found. "Do you have anything for him before your six-thirty meeting?" She waited, as spectral as ever. He said he had nothing but changed his mind; it was now or never. "He might look at this," he said, handing her a copy of the Chernishevsky translation.

At six-thirty Abbott's secretary closed the door behind him. Alone in his office, Abbott rose from the shadows behind his desk, indicated a chair, and moved out to join Corkery in the brown armchair opposite. "Tell me about this," he said softly, holding out the translation of the Chernishevsky article. "I don't understand it, not in the slightest. Tell me what it means."

He listened as Corkery told him Yefrim Chernishevsky's article on Soviet topographical falsification used language identical to that used by Andreyev in his congressional testimony and most recently in his letter to Langley. In all likelihood Dudley was in Europe, searching for Chernishevsky, whom he believed to be Andreyev or someone known to him. Perhaps he was mistaken; the paragraphs might have been borrowed by both men from some other article on the same subject, but as improbable as Dudley's search, he was a man obsessed. In finding Chernishevsky, Dudley had probably sought the help of his old friend Otto Rauchfuss, who had many friends in the Soviet emigré community. They'd first met in Berlin in 1946 near the Bahnhof Zoo, the black market area of the British zone where fourteen-year-old Otto had tried to flog Dudley a Leica II camera with a 1.2 lens. Later they'd met outside the antique shops on the K-Damm. "Otto Kippensammler," Dudley had called him in his diary. Otto pinched cigarette butts off the pavement to survive; Dudley became his surrogate father. He didn't know whether Otto had been summoned by Dudley or had come on his own to persuade Dudley to help plea-bargain his indictment by a federal court in New York. Both may have realized Washington wasn't a secure place to plan their next step. Now Otto was lying in the D.C. morgue, but Frank Dudley was still on the loose, a man whose judgment was impaired, a man running on his rims, badly in need of finding.

Corkery had expected Abbott to offer some comment, but he had nothing to say until Corkery confessed he didn't understand Dudley's reasons for wanting to find Andreyev.

Andreyev, Abbott said, was a dispatched GRU agent whose assignment to the GDR and his later defection had a specific purpose: alarmed about the Polaris submarine threat, the Russians dispatched him across the border that night to learn as much as possible about new U.S. geodesic techniques essential in ballistic missile targeting.

Having said this, which explained nothing to Corkery, he sat slumped in silence, gazing at the Chernishevsky translation on his knee. "Otto Kippensammler, indeed. You have remarkable energies. Quite remarkable."

"It was a mystery I couldn't solve. I still can't."

He lifted his head. "You've also cast a remarkably large net, if I'm not mistaken."

Corkery wasn't sure it was a compliment. "True, I suppose."

"You've talked to a number of former officers who once worked in this building."

"True too, yes. I didn't have much choice."

Abbott raised himself to retrieve a brown enamel cigarette case from his desk. "Now I'll tell you something apart from all this, something so fundamental to my own thinking I can't escape it, just as it's something so alien to yours that you won't believe me, but it's important. Always keep it in mind." He fitted the cigarette in his holder and lit it. "You should never accept anything I say at face value."

Astonished, Corkery wasn't sure he heard him correctly. He leaned closer. "Sorry?"

"You should never accept anything I tell you at face value. Remember it, never forget it. You should never credit anything a professional intelligence officer tells you about an operation or the personalities involved, never. It doesn't matter whether an operation took place twenty years ago or yesterday, whether an operation is blown, re-tired, or made to seem officially closed. There's always someone or something left to protect. In that sense people waste their time chasing down intelligence sources. Whatever they tell you, what-ever missing piece you believe you've uncovered, you'll be mistaken in some minor but basic way. Khrushchev once said 'The grave straightens out the hunchback.' It's true. Never ask a professional intelligence officer to straighten out his hunch-backs. He can't. In any case, you're right about Dudley. He's a threat to us and to himself. I'm also convinced we'll find him shortly. It's inev-itable that he be found. I think that was part of his intention. That doesn't surprise you, does it?"

"No, sir. Not really."

"I didn't think so." He got up, stooped and creaking. "It's been very interesting. I also think you're completely right. Keep me informed. Every evening, I should think. At six-thirty or there-abouts."

Corkery left. Abbott hated publicity, hated leaks, hated the press, and hated anarchy: *"Never believe anything I tell you,"* he had told him. He might have been telling him he despised the mob and mob history, its perversions, its distortions, its chaos and bastardy, its smell of the streets where Corkery had been so long wandering. The truth, always secret, wouldn't be found there. Where then? Inside the citadel? *"Always someone or some-thing left to protect,"* he'd said. Whom was he still protecting? Corkery didn't know. Abbott did. He had discipline, he had faith; Corkery had none. Elinor was right. He could have led an army, a thousand armies.

Capitol Hill was a misty orange fog ahead, as forlorn as a night railroad yard under the vapor lights. The Alfa pounded over an unseen bump, sped through an amber caution light, and streaked up the hill. The front windows of Yu Kum-song's restaurant were dark and the shade drawn. Corkery rapped at the glass, waited, and rapped again. A hand moved aside the shade and a Korean woman appeared, pointed to the nine o'clock closing sign, and went away. He rapped again. A lantern-jawed Korean appeared, staring menacingly through the glass. "Christine Rawley," Corkery called. "Is she here?" The Korean let the shade drop. A minute later Christine Rawley unlocked the door.

"I thought you weren't coming." She was wearing blue jeans, down-at-the-heel boots, and a turtleneck rag sweater. Her blond hair was drawn back in a ponytail. The front dining room was in shadow except for the light at the cashier's desk where a Korean woman sat, totaling up the receipts. In the smoky room beyond the overhead lights were on and five Korean waiters, cooks, and scullery boys were silently eating dinner. She led him to a table in the rear in front of the metal-clad doors to the kitchen. A cigarette was burning in an ashtray. Open on the table were a set of ledgers, government questionnaires, and Social Security forms.

"Did you bring them?"

"Right here." He gave her the manila envelope. Inside were a dozen Xeroxed copies of FBI reports, some as brief as two pages. She brought them out and glanced through them. "Jesus. They talked to all these people?" She paused over the name of an FBI informant. "Edna Parsons, that goddamned bitch. No wonder. What did she say?"

"Sometimes it's better not to know. After a while they all read the same."

"She never liked me. What's 'Barnswallow'?"

"The FBI's code name for Andreyev."

She glanced up. "Sounds bad. Is it?"

"It could be if we don't find him."

She continued searching through the pages. Two Korean cooks passed through the swinging doors, carrying their dishes. "That prick," she said, recognizing someone's name. "I knew he was out to get me. I wonder if I could take him to court." He waited. "I don't know half of them." She put them aside. "Maybe I need a lawyer. Okay. Where did we leave it?"

"Why don't we begin at the beginning? How did you happen to do this typing for him?"

She had met him at a Greek restaurant on Pennsylvania Avenue. She was having lunch with a secretary from the Hill, an older woman he knew, and he'd stopped to say hello. He'd needed some typing done and asked if her friend could recommend anyone. A week later she saw him at the same restaurant; he remembered her face and stopped on his way out; he had a deadline and still hadn't found a typist. She could use the money and offered to help. Over the next six months she typed fifteen to twenty manuscripts for him. Most were translations from Russian publications on file at the Library of Congress, some were for the Congressional Research staff at the Library of Congress, and others for House subcommittees and other government agencies. None was classified. She usually dropped the typed manuscripts at his office on East Capitol Street. On several occasions she'd given him the typescripts over lunch. He always paid in cash, never by check.

"It was strictly business, that's all it was. Then after he disappears, I get these FBI guys poking around, making it into something big. They ask me about the times I had lunch with him, what was in the envelopes I gave him. They even want to know the dates. They had copies of his bank account by then, the dates he made these cash withdrawals, five to six hundred dollars at a time. Sure, I gave him envelopes, translations of articles about lake pollution, virgin lands, deforestation in Siberia, health care delivery systems, putting a pipeline through frozen soil or tundra, whatever they call it, you name it. He paid me, sure, that was what was in the envelopes, but not two or three thousand, never."

"How much?"

"A couple of hundred at a time, that's all. Do

they think I'm an idiot, passing this secret stuff from the House intelligence subcommittee to Andreyev right there in a restaurant full of congressional secretaries and staffers? I couldn't believe it. Then he disappears, leaving me holding the bag, like I said, no job, no reputation, in hock to the IRS for this money I never even earned, and him owing me two or three hundred besides."

"So you thought Andreyev could clear it all up."

"If he knew about it, sure he would. He never wrote checks and never used a credit card. The other reason I wrote the letters was he interested me. I used to wonder what happened to him. Every time I'd pass his little hole-in-the-wall office on East Capitol Street, I'd get sad. A couple of times he gave me books to read because of what he thought I'd missed out on, never finishing college. Russian novelists; Chekhov, Pushkin, this Russian poet. I think he was a poet. I never read it, the paperback he gave me. To know someone like that and know you'll never see him again, that's real sad."

"Who else typed for him? You said you were having lunch with this other secretary when you first met him. Had she done any work for him?"

"No. She knew him from the time he'd testified on the Hill and she and some staffer had gone over some of the edited transcripts with him. He'd asked her but she didn't have time."

"So you were his only typist."

"As far as I know. He wasn't getting much work

that last month. At the end he wasn't getting beans. Sometimes I think maybe he got fed up and cranked off to start a new life. That makes me feel better. He was pretty much a loner. I thought maybe he'd found someone."

"Found someone? Why do you say that?"

She shrugged. "Just a feeling. I was going to drop some work off one Friday afternoon and I was across the street from his office and saw him getting into a station wagon. A woman was driving. They were both laughing as they drove away. I kind of figured she was his girlfriend, which was maybe why he never tried to come on with me. I thought that was nice. Then when I dropped by his office the next Monday during my lunch hour, he seemed pretty happy. He didn't have any new manuscripts to type and so I asked him if he was two-timing me, if he'd found a new typist. He laughed and said no. He was a private person that way. I never asked."

"Did you mention this woman to the FBI?"

"Are you kidding? I didn't remember when I first talked to them. By the time I did, I'd made up my mind not to tell the jerks anything. It was his business, not theirs."

"You saw them together just this one time?"

"No, another time, not long after, just before he dropped out of sight. It was on a Saturday morning, I think. I saw him from across the street. He was coming out of this bagel place on Pennsylvania in the block next to the Madison Building. She was in this station wagon with D.C.

335

tags, waiting at the curb."

"Had you ever seen her before, around the Hill someplace?"

"I don't think so, but I didn't see her real good. She was in the car both times. She was dark haired. That's about all I could see."

"But you remember the tags, the license plates?"

"D.C. tags, yeah. I know because I was kind of wondering if she worked on the Hill and was looking for a congressional parking sticker."

"You said a station wagon. Do you remember the color?"

"Maroon. It was Swedish, I'm pretty sure, only not new, maybe five or six years old. My old roommate back in Marietta had one just like it, a maroon station wagon, kind of boxlike."

"Volvo?"

"Volvo, yeah. A maroon Volvo, that's what it was."

6

A CONSPIRACY
OF FOOLS

The wind smelled of rain and the streets were wet, whether from an afternoon shower or the African sanitation crews Dudley couldn't tell. He crossed the Seine with Dietrich at his side. On his head was a blue beret, over his shoulders was his Burberry, worn continental fashion, like a cape. His baggy gray flannels and brown fiber shoes with thick rubber soles had been purchased two days earlier. An observer might have taken him for a tourist, probably English, and no doubt eccentric, possibly a retired teacher of Romance languages from some soot-blackened factory town in the north.

They turned east and passed a newspaper kiosk. Dudley took no notice of the afternoon headlines. Dietrich was limping. "What is it now?" He glanced down at Dietrich's right shoe. The heel was loose. "They're old shoes?"

"Yes, old shoes."

"You should get them repaired." Dietrich stopped again to fiddle with his right shoe while Dudley waited patiently. "You can't economize with shoes. Shoes should be bought to last ten or twelve years. You should buy shoes the way you do municipal bonds, a long-term investment." He wondered again what Otto paid him; a pittance, he supposed.

Dietrich had told him his mother was a Hamburg seamstress. She'd once been in theater and now sewed theater costumes, sitting in a little back room offstage to mend and stitch during dress changes. As a boy Dietrich often accompanied her. His visits had inspired an interest in theater. He'd intended to go on stage. Dudley had advised him to save his money and seek formal training if that was his talent; he certainly shouldn't waste his life as a bookkeeper if that wasn't his talent.

"It's all right now." Dietrich stood up, his pale cheeks flushed.

"You should find a shoe shop," Dudley said, "buy yourself some decent shoes. Look for heftiness. In Paris that's not easy to find. But you should look." A block beyond he left the young German to fend for himself and strolled on. The decrepit old hotel near the end of Rue de Rivoli had seen better days. Inside was an Ottoman courtyard with a fountain and hanging balconies filigreed with pieces of opaque orange glass, many cracked or broken; the mosaic floor was patched over in places with untiled concrete. A pair of ugly blackamoors with piano-key teeth supported an orange canopy that led to the dim bar where a few shadows gathered, figures outlined by the pale glow of a television set behind the bar. It was a little after four and he was early. The lobby was idle at that hour except for a pair of businessmen who appeared to be Egyptian standing at the check-in counter. Dudley had brought a newspaper in his attaché case, opened it, withdrew the newspaper, and sat with it on a lopsided green armchair near the elevators. The cushion felt damp. The stone urn to his right held a plastic fern and was littered with cigarette butts. A few Algerian waiters in kepis, Turkish trousers, and carpet slippers limped back and forth carrying pots of tea and coffee to the few loungers in armchairs in front of the high windows.

At four-twenty he took the lift to the fourth floor and walked down a flight of stairs to room 318. The door was ajar, as Dietrich had said it would be. He knocked twice, waited, and went in. A small dark-haired man was bent over a luncheon cart in the gray light of the window across the room. He turned and came to meet him, his hand held out. "Welcome. I am Deutsch."

"Frank Dudley." They shook hands, Dudley, a foot taller, moving the attaché case to his left hand. Deutsch, still smiling, gestured him to the armchair near the window. "Please. Some coffee?" He wore a dark blue double-breasted suit with wide lapels; the shirt might have been denim; the tightly knotted tie had lost its color. He brought Dudley a cup of lukewarm coffee, offered a cig-

339

arette, which he declined, and brought a stiff-backed chair from near the bed. It was unmade and littered with newspapers; some had fallen to the floor. The room had the smell of foul sleep and sour linen. "Otto tells me you have some very interesting documents to show me."

Dudley lifted the attaché case to his lap, opened it, and withdrew a sheaf of papers. "As you probably know," he began, "Otto has quite a few friends in the Russian emigré communities, Berlin especially. I mentioned this article to him. As a matter of fact I wrote to him in confidence about it, asking his help in locating the man who wrote it. It appeared in a West German emigré publication last August."

The phone rang, Deutsch quickly rose, excused himself, and went to answer it as Dudley watched. His dark hair was thick at the back of his head. There was something illicit about him; the egregious smile, the woolly hair, the seedy clothes. He might have been an out-of-work musician, a man who worked the piano bars of shabby hotels and lived on the run.

Deutsch returned, glanced at his watch, and sat down again. Dudley handed him the Xeroxed article. He studied it silently, turned a few pages, frowned, and returned to the title page. "The name here is Chernishevsky. A Russian emigré?"

"Yes, but I have reason to believe the article was written by someone else, a man using the name of a Russian emigré. He's the man I wrote and spoke to Otto about. His name is Andreyev, Major

Alexei Andreyev."

Deutsch's confusion immediately disappeared. "I understand, yes. Yes, that is the name Otto mentioned, Andreyev. I have made certain inquiries for Otto, in Berlin and other places. Alexei Alexovich Andreyev, yes. So that is it. What is it you wish to know about this man Andreyev?"

"My hope is to find him."

Deutsch nodded, still smiling. "Good. So we have found him."

"You know where he is? You know where to find him?"

"Of course. He is in prison in the Soviet Union exactly. In Dubrovlag Prison in Moldavia."

Dudley's mind went blank. "In prison?"

"Yes, in prison." Deutsch's expression changed as he watched Dudley's face. He leaned forward sympathetically, touching Dudley's knee with his small hand. "I'm sorry. I'm very sorry."

Dudley couldn't imagine it. He could hardly breathe. He felt moisture crawling on his upper lip and temples. An enormous weariness had crept over him.

"I am sorry. Otto doesn't like bad news but it is true. In prison. I asked Otto who was interested in Andreyev. He wouldn't tell me. Who is interested in this Andreyev person?"

"I can't go into that at present." He couldn't comprehend it: Andreyev in prison and he in Paris, trapped in this awful hotel room. His mouth was as dry as paper.

"I understand. But if he is in Dubrovlag Prison

now and that surprises you, then what is next? We make our own surprise, we find how to make his release." He searched his jacket pocket for cigarettes, found the package and held one out. "Please." Dudley declined, barely moving his head. Deutsch bent forward, his fingers again touched Dudley's knee. "I told Otto we must be clever. An idea happens to me. Do you know Karl Eigner?"

"Eigner?"

An old and respected trade unionist, Deutsch explained. His office was in the Free German Trade Union building on Unter den Linden in East Berlin. A humanitarian, a man of principle.

Dudley vaguely remembered the name but what difference did that make? It had all come to an end.

In the past, Deutsch explained, Eigner had negotiated certain sensitive East–West prisoner exchanges. Last February, three East German agents and a Russian imprisoned in West Germany had been exchanged for five West Germans held in the GDR. "I tell you this between the two of us," he said softly, sitting down again. "Not for Otto or no one else. Otto's business is his business. This business, I know. Eigner is negotiating for the return of a certain Russian and East German being held in Bonn. Bonn has instructed a list of names to be drawn up in secret. My sources tell me there will be at least three names on each list." Deutsch's voice was a whisper. "In two days Eigner will be in Geneva for the ILO conference. We could discuss this with Eigner in Geneva. He would consider it, I'm sure."

Dudley stirred himself uneasily and leaned back. Deutsch had brought his face too near. His breath stank of bitter coffee and carious teeth. "Consider what?"

"Andreyev's name on the list of prisoners to be exchanged, an East–West exchange."

Dudley looked at him as if he were mad. "You can't be serious."

"I am serious. It is very sensitive."

"They'd never agree —"

"Of course they would never agree. This is what everyone thinks. But everyone is wrong and they do agree. So what I am saying is this: Is this man Andreyev important or not?"

"Yes, of course." The man was raving mad.

"So there you are. Probably you need to seek instructions. Lists of names would have to be drawn up, exchanged, and agreed to. A protocol drafted and signed." He moved to the bed and retrieved a newspaper. "There is one other idea that occurs to me." He folded the paper, found the item he was looking for, and moved to study it in the gray light of the window. In a few days a delegation from the Soviet Human Rights Commission in Moscow, part of the International Helsinki Federation, would be visiting Paris. The Soviet delegation was now in Rome. Perhaps the Andreyev matter could be raised with the Moscow delegation through the embassies in Rome or Paris. But a direct approach to Karl Eigner in Geneva was preferable. He could arrange it.

The phone rang again. He thrust the paper at Dudley and moved to answer it. In five minutes, he said in French: "Wee wee." In five minutes. "Wee wee." He put down the phone and looked at his watch. "Shall I talk to Eigner or would you prefer to speak to the Soviet Human Rights Commission? I have only one more day in Paris."

Depressed, confused, and anxious to escape the unwholesome hotel with its sour smells of foul sleep, sordid dreams, and lewd passions, Dudley said he would like to think about it. No doubt about it, the man was a fool. But he'd come all this way from Bern after all, and Dudley, with great courtesy, thanked him and promised to call him at his hotel in the morning with his decision.

She drank a glass of water at the kitchen sink, left it on drainboard, and slipped the dead bolt on the back door. She made her way down the darkened hall and tried the front door. Looking through the cut-glass window, she saw a faint orange glow from the areaway. The interior lights of her Volvo were on. The battery would be dead in the morning. She took her raincoat from the closet, slipped it over her shoulders, and opened the door.

"How come you don't answer your bell?" said a familiar voice from the shadows.

"Oh, God!" She shrank back, terrified.

"It's okay, it's me." Corkery moved into the light from the door. "How come you didn't answer your bell?"

"I didn't hear, I was in the kitchen. What are you doing here?"

"I've got to talk to you. Something I brought, something I want you to read."

"You've been drinking. I know you have —"

"Not this time. Five minutes is all. Just five minutes and I'll go." She hesitated, sighed, and stood aside.

"All right. Five minutes."

They sat at the table in the kitchen alcove under the cone of light from a hanging pewter lamp. He took the Chernishevsky article from his jacket pocket. "Read this. The paragraphs marked in red pencil. Read them and tell me if they mean anything."

She sat forward to read the translation, still wearing her raincoat over her bathrobe. He watched her face, saw her frown as she read the first paragraphs. "Where on earth did you get this?"

"Read the rest."

She turned a page, read another paragraph, and turned back to the title page in bewilderment. Where did this come from?"

"Translated from the German." He brought out a copy of the original article. "Published in West Germany last August."

"August? Impossible." Confused, she looked from one copy to the other. "It's impossible.

Chernishevsky? It couldn't be." She searched the middle and final pages, returned to the paragraphs marked in red pencil, and traced out the date line on the German original. "August? It couldn't be. Where is he? Where's the man who wrote this?"

"We'll talk about that. Moscow destroyed his memory, slandered his childhood recollections. You knew him, didn't you?"

"Where is he?"

"You knew him, didn't you? You knew Andreyev. You were up to your neck in it. You knew why Abbott fired Dudley. It was because of Andreyev, wasn't it?"

"I can't talk about it! I can't! How much does Abbott know?"

"Forget Abbott. What are you afraid of? What's everyone so afraid of?" He took back the two articles, thrusting her hand away as she grabbed for them. "You've answered my question. That's all I came for."

"It's not simple, for God's sake! Don't you understand!" She ran after him down the hall. "Where's Alex? Tell me!"

He turned at the door. "Why did Andreyev write that letter to Abbott? Who was the friend he mentioned, the one he had absolute confidence in? Was it Frank Dudley or someone else?"

"I can't, I really can't —"

"The hell you can't. Who was it? Who did Andreyev give that letter to?"

She backed away. "How much does Julian know?"

"Nothing. I wanted to talk to you first."

"It's not that simple, don't you understand! It isn't! Julian didn't understand, Frank didn't, none of them did. It was more than just Dudley and Julian, much more!"

"Who did he give that letter to?"

She didn't answer. He opened the door. She slammed it closed and backed against it, face lifted. "*Me!* It was me! I told him to write it! *I had to. Please!* Tell me what's going on!"

"You have to come clean first. Otherwise no deal."

It was a long story. She didn't know where to begin so she began on a blustery autumn afternoon in Vienna when an American diplomat returning from lunch to his parked Volkswagen found a manila envelope on the front floor. Inside was a smaller envelope sealed with gum tape and addressed in crudely inked letters "To the Necessary American CIA Authorities, Embassy of Vienna, America." The second secretary returned to the embassy more intrigued by the hapless address than the envelope's contents. In his office he typed out a whimsical note addressed to "The Agency of Intelligence, Central" and sent the package upstairs to a CIA colleague. The documents were in Russian, the official report of a committee of inquiry reexamining the cases of a handful of prisoners in the Gulag. The pages were in terrible condition, tattered, watermarked, and food-stained, as if carried to Vienna in a bag of dirty laundry on one of the trains carrying Jewish emigrés. Many of the Gulag prisoners were Jewish, so it was thought the source was a Jewish emigré. The Israelis usually watched for that kind of thing in Tel Aviv, then peddled it back to Langley, a little quid for all that quo, usually through Julian Abbott, but this bundle ended up in a diplomat's Volkswagen, wrapped up like a wad of Chinese laundry.

Few at Langley paid much attention to the eighty or ninety pages of the committee of inquiry's report, just archive material, but Julian Abbott had seen a summary prepared by the Intelligence Directorate and asked for more. One name he remembered, no one knew quite why, an old topographer who'd been in the Gulag for years; he'd been released, given back his old rank and his pension, but not his position in the Ministry of Power Stations. He was too old. His name was Mikhail Rudyev. There was quite a bit of information on the old man's family, including a nephew named Alexei who'd been adopted and had taken the Rudyev name. He'd joined the GRU and was posted to East Germany at the time the committee of inquiry had made its report. At Abbott's instruction, a staffer had gone back over some military intercepts, monitoring East German military traffic; the name Rudyev had turned up there. Abbott believed Andreyev's real name was Alexei Rudyev, a name he'd never mentioned during his interrogation at Frankfurt and in Maryland. A few years later, a Soviet KGB defector told Abbott the same thing, or so he said, that Andreyev was Rudyev.

"Vadim Lazarev," Corkery said. They sat at the kitchen table.

She lifted her eyes. "Vadim Lazarev, yes." She hesitated. "How much did Julian tell you?"

"I'll get to that. Go ahead."

"Lazarev said Andreyev was a dispatched agent under GRU control. His operational name had been Viktor. He claimed he'd worked with Andreyev or Rudyev at Berlin-Karlhorst, that he knew his cousin, Vasily Rudyev."

"George Tobey thought Lazarev a liar, a con artist."

She nodded. "Julian too. He never trusted Lazarev, never —"

"Sorry?" He leaned over the table.

"He never trusted him. Few people knew but it was true. He was a useful peg on which Julian could hang sensitive intelligence from assets still under deep cover. He attributed a lot to Lazarev, put words in his mouth Lazarev never uttered. The Rudyev background may have been one, I don't know. I had my own suspicions. Anyway, then the FBI very stupidly got into the act —"

"Wait a minute. You had suspicions about what? What he attributed to Lazarev?"

"Some of it. I think it actually came from someone else before Lazarev defected, someone who'd known Andreyev years ago. I suspected that's why Julian never trusted Andreyev. He never said why, not to the clandestine services directorate, not to our own Soviet people. It finally dawned on me from something he said one night when we were working late. I thought he had a Soviet asset under deep cover at the time of Andreyev's defection, maybe at Karlhorst in East Berlin, someone who was still operational and knew Andreyev. But he wouldn't say anything, not a whisper."

"Pitchfork," Corkery said suddenly. "A Soviet asset still in place." She looked at him blankly. "Sorry. Did you ever ask Abbott about it?"

"No, never. But that's what I thought."

"What about the FBI? You said they got into the act."

"An unknown Russian tried to approach Andreyev in Washington, a 'Comrade X.' The FBI thought he'd been sent by Moscow under instructions and told Andreyev that if he made another approach, he should show interest. Julian was furious when he heard about it. He said the whole thing was a KGB operation concocted with Alex's help and we'd be playing into their hands. The seventh floor wanted to go along with the FBI, but Julian kept dragging his feet. Then one night he called Ed Rudolsky and me in and told us he thought he had the answer. Alex had gone to Copenhagen for a cartography conference. Julian proposed we tell the FBI we couldn't agree to the FBI operation because Alex had contacted us during the Copenhagen conference and we'd already begun working with him on an operation in Europe."

"He told the FBI that? That Andreyev was his asset?"

"I know it sounds crazy. He told them I was Andreyev's case officer."

"Here on FBI turf? Doing what, for Christ's sake?"

"Nothing. Julian was desperate. He was stalling for time, that's all, anything to get the FBI and the seventh floor turned the other way. He told me to get to know Andreyev and we'd see what happened, take it from there."

"Jesus, you were in deep, weren't you? That's a federal offense."

"I know. Too deep, much too deep. So was Julian."

"Who knew about it?"

"Julian, Ed, and I, that's all."

They learned Andreyev was taking an evening investment class at George Washington University, and she began attending a few days later. It was a small, informal class, only twelve or so students, most of them government civil servants. Four or five stayed after class to talk to the instructor about the current market. They had formed an investment club; Andreyev belonged and she joined. They met at a nearby restaurant after class, sometimes at different houses. The stock market didn't interest her and neither did the others in the investment club, but Andreyev fascinated her. Everything she'd read about him was wrong. He was at loose ends but had the idea he might get a broker's license. He had an office on East Capitol Street. He did translations: technical papers from Soviet journals for trade associations, engineering magazines, the National Institutes of Health, the National Academy of Sciences, and the Library of Congress. It was contract work and he was bored. Photogrammetric engineering interested him more, reconnaissance and remote sensing systems from space, mapmaking and mineral surveys, what satellites might do. He'd once spent an evening describing for her the NASA Laser Geodynamic Satellites launched in 1976. *Lageos,* it was called; it would revolutionize geodesic techniques. He had an application with NASA and the Earth Satellite Corporation but couldn't get on. "They never gave him a reason. He thought space satellites not only revolutionized mapmaking, but began a new age, a new kind of global consciousness, and he wanted to be part of it. It broke his heart when he couldn't."

"Wait a minute. Began a new age how?"

"Photographs of earth from space. He said they'd revolutionized our awareness of planetary existence, given us a totally new consciousness of earth, continents, and people far beyond anything we'd known in the past, a new unitary consciousness that transcended borders, nationality, and culture. He thought the nation-state was an anachronism. All those old finite constructs had been swallowed up by space."

"Jesus. So you fell for it."

"I didn't say I fell for it," she said angrily. "We talked about it."

"Okay, so you didn't fall for it. How was he living while he was dreaming up this new utopia?"

"Barely. Living in rented rooms, moving from one place to another. He had a room not far from the Library of Congress, just four blocks from here. He had an application in there as a translator. Old-age insurance, he said."

"Andreyev wasn't what you expected. That's what you're telling me, isn't it?"

"Yes, not in the slightest."

"You thought Abbott was wrong about him."

"Completely." She told Ed Rudolsky one night that she understood why he'd left the GDR that night, that she could see him doing it. There he was, riding in a Russian jeep with a German driver on the frontier, talking about hunting boar in the Trans-Caucasus, and suddenly through the rain he saw the partially downed fence where someone had tried to escape and failed, and there up the hill through the trees was Hesse, and so he'd done it, just to show it could be done. "He was so terribly restless, that's what you have to understand, always searching for more, even as a boy. His fascination with maps began there. It was genuine. It was all he had, his maps and his imagination —"

"Did you tell Abbott about all this?"

"No, not then. I was going to. I think Ed Rudolsky suspected but I wasn't ready to tell Julian."

One night she and Andreyev had a long talk at her house after an investment club meeting. She'd been the hostess and he'd remained behind to help clean up. By then he was as bored with the group as she was. At the sink in the kitchen, rinsing the glasses, and later, sitting in the living room, he had told her everything: where he was born, the problem about the date of his birth, the name of his uncle, Mikhail Rudyev, imprisoned in the Urals, the uncle who'd escaped to Afghanistan and was detained by the British in India. He'd never talked about this with anyone but it didn't matter, just as his childhood recollections didn't matter.

"Did you write it up?"

She was slow in replying. "Yes, but not then."

"Did he have any idea who you were?"

"Not in the slightest. He thought I worked at the National Academy of Sciences. By then Lazarev had defected in Paris and claimed Alex had been a dispatched GRU agent, or at least Abbott reported that's what Lazarev said —"

"But you didn't think it came from Lazarev. You think Abbott got it from his Russian asset still in place."

"That's what I suspected, yes. Anyway, the FBI believed it and backed off."

"So what did Abbott have up his sleeve then?"

"As far as I knew, nothing. Julian's stall had worked and the FBI and the seventh floor turned Andreyev over to Abbott. I thought that would be the end of it but it wasn't. Julian and Ed Rudolsky had gotten another idea. Ed managed to smuggle a forged letter to Andreyev's ex-wife in Moscow telling her he was homesick and was thinking about returning home." She put her head in her hands. "It was preposterous, all of it. They didn't tell me. Maybe they thought I couldn't carry the load, I don't know. They thought the KGB would pick it up and make another attempt to contact Alex —"

"It did. They sent Boris to Montreal."

"It's not that simple. Boris wasn't sent by the KGB —"

"No. Who then?"

"Just wait. Frank Dudley found out about the forged letter. He was furious. He'd met Andreyev someplace, at Roger Cornelius's house, I think, and thought maybe we should find a place for him, not the operational side, maybe the intelligence directorate. When he found out about the forged letter he was absolutely livid. He told Ed Rudolsky he'd lost his mind, that Alex was everything he claimed to be, and attempting to betray and entrap him was criminal, exactly the methods the KGB would use. He threatened to go to the seventh floor with the whole story. That's when he and Julian had their argument. Julian sacked him, put him on administrative leave, and told him he was going to have him fired."

"But he didn't."

"No, but he could have. You have to remember, these were hard times. Vietnam had collapsed and the Soviets were on the march in the Third World — Angola, Afghanistan, and Ethiopia. The seventh floor wouldn't have backed Frank. His old friends had left by then. So they reached a gentleman's agreement. Ed Rudolsky brokered it. He persuaded Frank his career was worth more than his trust in Andreyev. If Alex was whom he claimed to be, he would report any covert contact by the KGB. If not, Frank had sacrificed his career for the sake of a dispatched Soviet agent. Ed convinced Abbott to forget the incident and recommend Frank's transfer without prejudice. It took a lot of convincing but both finally agreed. Both were to keep their mouths shut."

A week later, Andreyev went to Montreal for a Slavic Studies Association meeting. He called Elinor the second night from his hotel. He'd met someone, a strange little man from a Maritimes college, a man who claimed to be a relative, but he wouldn't say anything more. He called her again the third night. Someone had approached him during the coffee break, someone odd. They'd gone out to dinner and had a long talk. He was a Russian. He said he would tell her more when he returned.

"It's hard to express what he felt, a forgotten man, an exile, a failure all those years, a man who suddenly had a home again. He never wanted what he got, the notoriety, the man made over in a dozen different images those first five years, the defector, the publicist, the Pentagon's mouthpiece at the closed hearings on the Hill, the armor expert, the tank tactician, a man they'd given whatever face was fashionable those years, none his own, a man who didn't really exist —" Her head was down, her hand at her forehead. "He was a man ahead of his time. He'd always been."

"You didn't believe he'd ever been under GRU control."

She lifted her head angrily. "You're not even listening!"

"I am listening. You didn't believe he'd ever been under Soviet control, what Abbott or some asset under deep cover had said about him."

"I thought everyone was wrong, yes, all of them, completely wrong, Julian most of all —"

"Then why in the hell didn't you tell them? You had to be right. Andreyev told you everything about Montreal."

"Everything, yes, but he was confused. He thought Boris might be from the Soviet consulate in Montreal, maybe the embassy in Ottawa. He didn't know what to do about the instructions Boris gave him. I said I could help. I had some contacts in the intelligence community. If he would write it up, I'd pass it along to someone who could advise him. That's when he wrote the long letter. He wrote some of it here at the kitchen table. I typed it for him —"

"And gave it to Abbott."

"I gave it to Julian and Ed both. They didn't say anything, neither of them. Not a word. They were too stunned. I couldn't understand. It made no sense. Then a week later, everything changed. I didn't see Alex again. He wouldn't return my calls, wouldn't walk over in the evenings, the way he'd been doing. He just dropped out of my life."

She knew something was terribly wrong the afternoon she stopped by his office on East Capitol

357

Street. They had planned to drive up to Deerfield that weekend where he was to be interviewed by the headmaster at the academy for a teaching position. She saw it in his eyes as soon as he got up.

"He'd changed, completely changed." She shook her head miserably. "He didn't trust me. It was all over. He wouldn't see me after that, wouldn't return my calls. He moved out of his flat and took a room in Foggy Bottom. Then he left, went to Europe. Ed Rudolsky told me they lost track of him in Vienna. They found his passport in this little Austrian village near the Czech border. I knew the only way he'd have gone back was if they tricked him in some way, kidnapped him. Julian and Ed were wrong but they didn't care about the damage they'd done, the wreckage they'd left behind. They didn't care about me, care what Alex thought, none of them."

"Care about what he thought? What the hell did he think?"

"*He thought it was me, don't you understand!* He thought I was the one who told them about his uncle Mikhail, about the Rudyev family, the uncle who'd gone to Afghanistan! He thought I was the one who set up that ridiculous meeting in Montreal! It was Ed Rudolsky who sent those Russians to Montreal, Ed and Julian! It was their operation —"

"*Their* operation? Montreal was? Abbott's?"

"It was a CI operation. Julian was behind it. Ed got hold of some ex-Agency contract people,

358

Russian emigrés, like this Boris. They sent them to Montreal pretending to be KGB, trying to recruit Alex, a false-flag operation. They had something else planned. I didn't know what it was, I never knew! Then when they read his Montreal report, they realized everything had gone wrong. They hadn't expected the Soviets to contact Alex."

"What Soviets? You said they were Ed Rudolsky's Russians."

"The other Russian, the strange man in the dining room who gave Alex the postcard to mail. He wasn't part of Ed's operation. He must have been someone sent to contact Alex. He probably had him under observation and then at the end of the conference gave him this postcard to mail to East Germany. The postcard was probably returned to Alex here in Washington by someone who told him the other Russians were Agency or FBI, sent to entrap him. He thought I was part of it, that I'd told them about the Rudyev family, that I'd been in on it from the very beginning."

Looking at her anguished face, it finally made sense to him — why Frank Dudley had the appointment on the seventh floor, why he was in Europe, searching for Andreyev. It was Julian Abbott he was after, to destroy the man who had ruined his career; not only Julian Abbott but everything he stood for. When CI's crazy conspiratorial world came tumbling down, Abbott's would lie in ruins with it.

"Jesus Christ, where in the hell does this string run out?" He got up stiff-legged and moved to the sink, carrying his beer glass, feeling terribly, helplessly beaten, hardly hearing Elinor's voice.

"Where is he? Where in Europe? Is he Chernishevsky? Tell me!"

He rinsed his glass under the tap. "Why would Abbott send those two Russians to Montreal? What kind of operation were they planning? It doesn't make any sense."

She didn't know. They never told her. "Where is he? Where is he in Europe? You have to tell me!"

He took the brandy glass from her hand, filled it and returned it.

"It's going to take a little time." He sat down again. He knew she would feel cheated and so she did. She put her head down and he lifted her chin, told her to drink, and so she did as he told her what he knew. She asked him about the FBI reports Ed Rudolsky had shown her after Andreyev's disappearance, detailing his womanizing on the Hill. He told her about Christine Rawley. The FBI reports were probably similar to those written about Christine, all provided with the idea of persuading Elinor her lover wasn't the man she'd thought him to be.

Corkery got a telephone call from Abbott's secretary that afternoon a little before three o'clock. Two minutes later he was in his office. "You were quite right," Abbott said, handing him a telegram.

360

"He is in Europe. In Paris." It was inevitable that Frank Dudley would make a mistake and so he had. He'd broken his silence and telephoned Otto Rauchfuss in Bern.

Dudley's conversation had been winnowed from the hundreds of thousands of international telephone calls made during the same period by the NSA Menwith Hall Station in the Yorkshire countryside and relayed by satellite to NSA hqs at Fort Meade, Maryland, for scanning. The call might have gone unnoticed except that Otto Rauchfuss's name, like Frank Dudley's, had been added to the NSA Elint watchlist. The conversation appeared on a computer printout behind the doors of an analyst's office where it was given a caption, six numerical references under a Top Secret Codeword classification, and relayed to the CIA cable secretariat at Langley. The Agency's D Division passed it to CI. The hard copy read:

FIRST VOICE: "Hello? Hello? Sorry. Mr. Otto Rauchfuss, please."
SECOND VOICE: "Excuse, please. Rauchfuss? Who is calling, please?"
FIRST VOICE: "Frank.* Tell him it's Frank. Sorry, but I must speak with Otto. This is his Bern office?"
FRENCH OPERATOR'S VOICE: "Who are you calling in Bern? Technica Klemenz?"

*Believed to be Francis Eliot Dudley (SFNG7 2–NE–300560).

FIRST VOICE: "Oui. C'est ça."
SECOND VOICE: "This is Technica Klemenz, yes."
FIRST VOICE: "I would like to speak to Otto, please."
SECOND VOICE: "Is not here, Mr. Otto. N'est pas ici. Is in Dresden."
FIRST VOICE: "Dresden? I understand. Is this his secretary?"
SECOND VOICE: "Who is speaking please?"
FIRST VOICE: "An old friend. I have a message for Otto. Are you his secretary?"
SECOND VOICE: "Mr. Otto is in Dresden on business. He will come after tomorrow."
FIRST VOICE: "I want to ask Otto about his friend Deutsch, Nicholas Deutsch.** It's important. Is Deutsch known to Otto's Bern office?"
SECOND VOICE: "Deutsch? Who? I don't know."
FIRST VOICE: "Would you ask Otto? Would you tell him his friend is asking about Nicholas Deutsch. I need information. Tell Otto 'Es geht um die Wurst.'*** He'll understand."
SECOND VOICE: "Who is calling please? From where you call?"

_____

**Also known as Nicholas ("Nikki") Karl Herz and Nicholas Rosengoltz. Known intelligence fabricator in service of GDR and Soviet intelligence services.

***"Es geht um die Wurst" : "The sausage is at stake."

362

FRENCH OPERATOR'S VOICE (indecipherable): ". . . the room number? What room is this? Hello? Hello? Room 402? Mr. Schofield? This is the operator. Mr. Edward . . . excuse me, Mr. Frank Schofield? Is your call to Bern finished? Who is speaking now? Hello? Bern?"

FIRST VOICE (indecipherable): ". . . waiting for this call for two hours. Room 402, yes. Sorry. Bern? Hello?"

FRENCH TELEPHONE OPERATOR: "The connection has been broken —"

The previous October the State Department had issued a passport to a Mr. Frank Schofield of Carlyle, Maryland. The application had been received and returned by mail. Mr. Schofield had claimed to be a marketing specialist with the Department of Agriculture. A Mr. F. E. Schofield had been listed as a passenger on a British Airways flight from Kennedy to London the Friday of his disappearance. The passport photo was of Frank Dudley.

"It's gone on too long, don't you think?" Abbott said with a wintry smile, taking back the D-staff file. "Let me know as soon as possible what support you need. Talk to Jay and then we'll talk again first thing in an hour. We want to keep it completely in-house for the time being, not a word to anyone. You'd better pack your bags."

"To do what?"

Abbott didn't look up. "To go find Dudley and

bring him back. That's what we've been talking about, isn't it? We've no time to lose. If the East Germans are on to Dudley and know who he's looking for, the Sovs aren't far behind. Can you leave tomorrow?"

The bay windows of the detached brick house on New Hampshire Avenue were dark as Corkery made his way up the brick walk. The azaleas, rhododendrons, and Japanese holly rattled in the wind. He thought he'd come too late but then saw a light come on and a shadow cross the gallery. A stout woman with blond hair answered the door. She'd called him an hour earlier.

"Thank God you've come. I'm Margot. She's in the rear. Come in, please. It's been terrible, just awful. I can't understand why anyone would do something like that. I just don't understand." They crossed the dark gallery. "She keeps calling him Uncle Otto, that's all she can talk about. She said he was a close friend of the family, hers especially. Her Uncle Otto, her mother's Mr. Fixit. That's why I had to call you. She's terrified to death about her father. I don't understand why anyone would do such a thing."

Jessica was lying on the couch in the sun room, covered by a black and orange afghan. Through the bay window behind the couch the rear garden was illuminated with security lights as white as snow. She turned toward him, her face deathly pale.

"Why didn't you tell me! Why in God's name didn't you tell me!"

"I couldn't, I'm sorry. I couldn't bring myself to —"

"Couldn't bring yourself to!" She tore the afghan from her shoulders and sat up. "I must be going crazy. Am I completely crazy? I trusted you! You of all people! You share something with someone, you share everything, don't you? Didn't I share everything? Didn't I? What more could I have given? What more did you want from me? Where were you last night? You said we were going to dinner! Why didn't you come, why didn't you tell me!"

"I intended to —"

"You didn't! All that time you knew, you knew and you didn't say a word! All that time he was lying there. You could have told me, we could have talked, you could have made me understand. You didn't! Why did you leave it to them, why them? Why that terrible man, why him?"

Carl Vitale from Security, two weeks behind in his own investigation, had been there that afternoon. He'd brought photographs of Otto Rauchfuss lying in the D.C. morgue.

"I don't know why he came. He had no business being here." But he knew why he came; Vitale had been left out in the cold, ignored by CI for the last week. Margot stood behind Corkery, silent and frightened.

"What did he do wrong? He was just a simple man. Why Uncle Otto? Why him? Can you tell me? What did any of us do wrong? I don't understand! Why Uncle Otto was here, why he came,

365

what happened to him! Do you know? Tell me! What happened to us, not just Daddy and Uncle Otto, all of us!" She searched his face. "Tell me, please! Can't you please tell me —"

"It's not simple. It never was. I'm sorry —"

"You're not sorry! How could you be sorry! You lied to me from the first! You said we didn't have any secrets and I believed you! From that first day you came here, you lied to me! He was already dead, lying in the morgue. That very first day! That night we drove out to Virginia and had dinner, you knew then! You lied to me!"

"I didn't. I swear I didn't —"

"Just go! Go!" She wrapped herself in the afghan and collapsed back against the couch. "Go! Get out!"

There was nothing more he could say. Margot walked with him to the door. Like Jessica, she didn't understand any of it.

7

RUNNING WITH THE JACKALS

Corkery was met at Charles de Gaulle in Paris by Morgan from the Paris station, a large affable man with an untidy sheepdog mustache, wearing rough English tweeds and smelling cleanly of shaving spice. Gritty and sleepless, Corkery felt like a stray dog creeping into the dawn streets after an all-night lockup in a parking garage.

It was a gray morning but the overcast was breaking up to the east. Morgan, humming to himself from time to time, thought it would be a fine day. They sped toward Place de la Concorde in Morgan's dark blue Peugeot through interminable gray streets, past endless blocks of gray buildings whose façades might have been interesting in the bas-relief of sunlight and shadow but at that hour were indistinguishable one from the other. African street sweepers flogged their brooms through the gutters; a few elderly men and women crept along the pavement, walking their dogs. Schoolchildren

367

trooped their way to the lycée.

The station chief was Tom Glanville, a large blond man with a square face, square shoulders, and eyes as blue as a Norwegian fjord. He'd played tackle at Yale and now walked with a cane, the result of a recent hip operation. Not the sort of man from whose tongue the French would trip lightly, Jay Fellows had said. He knew no more than Abbott intended, which was very little; Dudley was a CI matter, a problem to be kept in the family, and Corkery was very much family now. Glanville, who wasn't, may have suspected he was less than completely informed; doubt had left an indelible shadow on his face. Corkery saw it as they shook hands, and saw it trouble his silence as he sat in front of his desk and read the two immediate "Eyes Only" cables just arrived from Langley and brought to him in a sealed envelope by the commo chief.

The first cable was a repeat from Munich. The editor of *Ukrainski Samostinik*, a magazine published by Soviet emigrés in Munich, had told a base officer he had received an article identical to Chernishevsky's "Puzzling Irregularities in Soviet Cartography" four months earlier but had rejected it. The editor thought the article had been sent from Vienna. The second cable reported Nicholas Deutsch's arrival at Vienna's Schwechat Airport twenty-four hours earlier, his entry recorded by the Austrian alien control police. Corkery was to proceed to Vienna the next day. Further instructions would be waiting.

He told Glanville of his change in plans and they listened to a middle-aged station officer by the name of Meade who had been assigned the case. A cautious little man who enjoyed something less than Glanville's full confidence, Meade kept the details of his inquiry in a notebook rather than memory, and read from his notes in a hesitant voice made even more uncomfortable by Corkery's too many questions and Glanville's troubled silence. Corkery thought his mind so cluttered by dates, names, and secondhand facts he was dead to the chase.

A Mr. Frank Schofield of Carlisle, Maryland, had arrived from London on an Air France flight and stayed for two days at a small hotel off Rue des Saints-Pères on the Left Bank. He'd moved to a hotel near Boulevard St.-Germain and five days later to a suite in a residential hotel in Montparnasse. It was the telephone call from room 402 in Montparnasse that had been intercepted by NSA's eavesdroppers. The same day he booked a flight from Paris to Bern on Swissair and bought a Eurail pass at the Gare du Nord. A receipt was found in a dresser drawer at his hotel room. The following morning he paid his bill and checked out but hadn't appeared at Charles de Gaulle to claim his seat. So where had he gone? No one knew. Hospitals, private clinics, police stations, and jails had been visited but without success.

According to the desk clerks at the three hotels, Dudley left early and returned late each day; he'd made no phone calls with the exception of the call to Bern from his Montparnasse hotel, had no visitors except for the hotel on Montparnasse, where a young man had called for him each afternoon those last three days. He had waited in the lobby, Dudley had joined him, and they'd gone off together. The clerk believed he was German. Whoever he was, he wasn't Nikki Deutsch, who'd left Paris for Geneva aboard Air France two days after his arrival. Dudley had cashed four traveler's checks at a bank on Rue du Bac, a total of $3,500 in all.

This was all Paris knew. Glanville and Meade waited to learn more but Corkery had nothing to add. Disappointed, Glanville invited him to dinner that evening, as Jay Fellows predicted he would. Corkery collected his suitcase from Morgan's office and Morgan drove him across the Seine to the little hotel on Rue de Lille Abbott had recommended; very small, very discreet, and very inconspicuous, it was one of his favorites. He registered, left his bag in his room, and returned downstairs; Meade drove him on toward Montparnasse.

Jessica's apartment was on the fifth floor of a nineteenth-century building off Boulevard Raspail just north of Boulevard du Montparnasse. There was no lift. The door on the fifth floor was open; scaffolding was in place in the front room where two plasterers were working; in the kitchen some of the flooring had been pulled up and a plumber was adding new piping. Amid the debris Jessica's furniture and paintings were stored under dropcloths in the bedroom. No one had been living there. On the way out Corkery stopped at the concierge's office and asked if anyone had looked at the flat. Yes, an official from the municipality had been there. The tenant owed 20,000 francs in parking tickets; the municipality was threatening to impound the furnishings.

At the embassy Corkery made reservations for Vienna for the following day and spent an hour going over his notes in Morgan's office. Why had Dudley reserved a seat from Paris to Bern on Swissair? Why had he also bought the Eurail pass at the Gare du Nord? Had something made him suspicious, or was he fed up? Where would he have fled now, north to Bern or south by rail to the secluded old Spanish farmhouse half hidden by cypress and pine trees on the cliff overlooking the Mediterranean? Or did Abbott have some reason to think he was in Vienna?

Corkery declined Glanville's offer of a car and left the embassy on foot, crossed Place de la Concorde in the dimming afternoon sunlight, and walked along the Seine. On the footbridge over the Seine near the Tuileries he stopped, leaning against the iron rail looking east toward Notre-Dame and thinking of Jessica. She had been in and out of his thoughts all day. Her father might still be here, somewhere in Paris; but now he was on his way to Vienna. Who mattered most to him? Jessica? Louise? Frank Dudley? Jessica mattered most, he supposed, but for how long? They lived in two different worlds.

He wandered back to his hotel, took a shower,

shaved, and at six-thirty sat down on the bed and picked up the telephone. He would call Glanville at home, tell him something had happened, and he would miss dinner. He would explain in the morning. Then he would get his bag and take a taxi to the Gare du Nord. Ten minutes later he would be on the train speeding south toward Lyon, Aix, and Marseilles. In the morning he would be in Barcelona, by afternoon at the old farmhouse overlooking the Mediterranean.

He sat looking at the telephone number Glanville had given him. "Once Abbott trusts you, that trust is absolute," Elinor had said. He put the telephone down and finished dressing. At seven-thirty he was downstairs waiting for the car to take him to Glanville's flat on Isle St. Louis.

At Schwechat in Vienna, darkness had fallen. The luggage was delayed and the passengers had to wait an additional twenty minutes. Corkery recovered his single bag and moved out through the glass doors past a handful of Austrians waiting for passengers and out through the lobby. A taxi was just pulling away. He didn't see the man join him and only turned at the sound of his voice.

"We have a car for you. Corkery, isn't it?"

"Corkery, that's right." The voice surprised him. He was a middle-aged man, heavy in the jowls and shoulders, wearing a rumpled corduroy jacket with elbow patches and a brown knit tie.

"Whose keeper are you?"

"Murphy. I met you once, Rome, a couple of years back. Holder's with me. You don't remember, do you?"

"I don't think so, sorry."

"It was at the residence, a dinner. I was with the EUR division chief from Langley. You were with the DCM's daughter."

"I remember the dinner."

At the bottom of the ramp below the taxi and bus stands a black Plymouth was waiting, its engine running. A pair of jet turbines shrieked from an access runway. Corkery waited until the din had passed before he dropped his head to nod to the man in the storm coat in the backseat.

"We haven't met," he said. "Paul Holder. I thought maybe we could talk, get our ducks in line."

"I didn't expect anyone." Corkery got in the backseat; Murphy got in front with the driver.

"We're a little confused," Holder said. "We're not sure who we're looking for. Dudley, Nicholas Deutsch, or this other chap. What's his name?"

"Chernishevsky," Murphy said from the front seat.

"They're all in the same bag," Corkery said. "Find one and maybe you'll find all three. Is Deutsch still here?"

"So far as we know but we don't know where," Murphy said. "He's dropped out of sight."

"Anything on Chernishevsky?"

"An address, that's all, but we wanted to talk to you first."

Holder said Murphy was as familiar with Vienna as anyone and would be working with Corkery. He'd been assigned to the 430th CIC detachment in Vienna in the '50s; after the Austrian peace treaty he had been transferred to Munich where the Agency had recruited him. They passed the chemical plants, their towers outlined in white lights. "I never worked with Frank Dudley but I knew him socially," Holder said out of the darkness. "A nice chap. I liked him. I don't understand it. I don't understand it at all." Murphy turned from the front seat.

"He's sure whipped up a storm, hasn't he?"

"I suppose he has." Corkery was looking out the window. He hadn't been in Vienna for years. They drove into a dimly lighted square where the bus lines terminated.

"What happened?" Holder said. "Does anyone know?"

"No. No one knows."

At the embassy on Boltzmanngasse they met in Holder's office. Holder's short dark hair was peppered with gray, but his face was youthful behind his tortoise-rimmed glasses. Judging from the photographs on the credenza behind his desk, skiing was his passion. A young station officer brought coffee and Holder thanked him. "That's a good chap."

Murphy told Corkery what they knew. The Austrian Alien Control Police had no record of Nicholas Deutsch's departure from Vienna and no record of a Frank Schofield. Yefrim Chernishevsky was also unknown, but a name check at the Canadian embassy had turned up a Y. Chernishevsky who'd made a nonimmigrant visa application two years earlier. He'd listed his profession as journalist and given the address of a pension across the Danube canal. The visa had been refused. A notation in the visa file referred the case to the Vienna office of the High Commission for Refugees.

"Interesting," Corkery said. "A journalist. Canada too. The Austrians don't have any record?"

"Nothing," Murphy said.

"Maybe an illegal entry. But you've got an address."

"Yeah, from the Canadians, but we haven't checked it out yet."

"We were told to wait for you," Holder said. "Apparently the lads back at Langley thought we might queer the pitch."

"We wanted to see what the UNHCR turned up," Murphy said. He had an appointment at the UNHCR in the morning if that was all right. Corkery said it was. He had also begun name checks with the other Viennese refugee agencies — Caritas, Russian Relief, the Tolstoy Foundation, the Hebrew Immigrant Aid Society, the World Council of Churches, even the Jewish Documentation Center on Rudolphplatz — but had nothing yet.

There wasn't much else to say and Corkery had nothing to add. As they got up, Holder said he had to admit he was expecting someone older. In

Murphy's office a desk had been cleared for him. Murphy would have put him up at his apartment but Langley's instructions had been specific about that too. He had made reservations at a hotel two blocks from St. Stephen's. The car was waiting downstairs, an old motor-pool Plymouth with worn shocks, slick seats, and a Manhattan taxi cab sway to the backseat.

The next morning Corkery talked to the station's Soviet expert, Gregory Rudin, a middle-aged man with thin dark hair and a midwestern accent. His parents were Russian born; he was from Ann Arbor, Michigan, where his father once taught at the university. He didn't know the name Chernishevsky but thought it might be Ukrainian. From his safe he produced a copy of a Soviet enemies' list published in Moscow the previous year by the KGB and stamped SOVERSHENNO SEKRETO: ABSOLUTELY SECRET. The Soviet watchlist contained an alphabetical listing of Soviet defectors but no Chernishevsky; five Andreyevs were given, none with the same initials. Corkery had been shown the same watchlist at Langley by Jay Fellows.

Rudin said he could put out a few feelers among the more recent Russian emigrés in Vienna, many of them across the Danube near Mexicoplatz. He suggested Corkery talk to Dr. Alfred Freyberg, formerly a Soviet analyst with the Vienna bureau of Radio Free Europe who ran a research service and published a newsletter from his bookshop on Mariahilferstrasse. Freyberg was a scholar, like his wife, an old Comintern member, but had good contacts with the Russian emigré community and was sometimes useful. It was a long shot but worth pursuing.

Corkery and Murphy had lunch in the embassy cafeteria. Murphy didn't think Dr. Freyberg would be of much help. "They're old Comintern types, living in the past, him and his wife both, groundskeepers in the old Comintern graveyard." He'd had no luck that morning in tracking down Y. Chernishevsky at the UNHCR offices. But something had struck him as odd.

He'd met with a senior UN resettlement officer, a Miss Faversham he knew from the cocktail and reception circuit. Her secretary had found a locator card for Y. Chernishevsky. A downy-cheeked Englishwoman of advancing middle age, Miss Faversham had summoned her assistant, a pint-size Hungarian refugee named Jozef Biros, and asked him to fetch the file. He told her the file had been retired. Surprised by his quickness, she asked him to make sure. After he left, she explained the search would take time; retired files were kept in an adjacent building where they awaited final disposition. She offered Murphy tea while they waited, but to her dismay Biros returned before the tea arrived to say the file had been destroyed. She was embarrassed but concealed it with that graciousness with which a gently bred Englishwoman copes with a better informed and more strongly willed subordinate. Murphy thanked her and left. On his way out, he stopped by Biros's desk and asked the date the file had been retired. Biros had risen high enough in the UN ranks to claim an office, a desk, and a solid brass nameplate identical to Miss Faversham's. He resented Murphy's presence as much as his questions. His French cuffs were neatly turned back over his wrists, his small white hands freshly scrubbed with hand cream, a rubber cap on his thumb as he reviewed the police records for an immigrant family in the waiting room next door.

Murphy asked Biros to try to remember and stood blocking the light, polluting the smells of Biros's tidy little office with his cigarette smoke as he waited, annoying Biros as much as the squalling infant whose screams could be heard from the waiting room. He'd told Murphy he couldn't recall the exact date but thought the Chernishevsky file had been retired two years ago. Having also ascended high enough in the UN humanitarian relief hierarchy to despise the particular case, he abruptly picked up the phone and told the receptionist to remove the squalling infant instantly.

"I know these goddamned UN clerks," Murphy said as they walked toward his car, "known them for years. Most of them are useless. They think they've got a lifetime annuity. Holier than thou."

"He didn't say why he remembered Chernishevsky?"

"No, just that he had a good memory for names and he remembered the name."

"Two years ago? Curious. Maybe we should talk to him again."

Murphy drove a tan Volkswagen convertible with a discolored canvas top patched with strips of cloth along the ruptured seams. The summer heat and the winter rains had turned the rear isinglass window a sulfurous yellow. The streets were cold, the sky the color of tarnished pewter as they climbed the hill toward Mariahilferstrasse.

The windows of Dr. Freyberg's bookshop on Mariahilferstrasse were dusty and forbidding, discouraging the casual walk-in. Scientific and medical texts were lined up in the left bay, historical and philosophical works in the right. On the shelf in the back of the left bay were volumes in Russian and Hebrew. They were greeted at the rear counter in the front room by Freyberg's daughter, a small gray-haired woman with eyes as large as a lemur's behind thick black-rimmed spectacles. She and her mother had opened the bookstore while Freyberg was working in research and analysis at the Vienna bureau of Radio Free Europe on Walnerstrasse; the bookstore and its second-floor cottage industry had become an extension of the old man's scholarship. He was a Galacian Jew, like his wife, who had once been a member of the Communist Party and worked for the Comintern. They published a mimeographed monthly book list of articles and books of interest to Soviet scholars, available by subscription; every three months they published a list of Russian samizdat that had surfaced in Western Europe.

Murphy introduced himself as an embassy officer, Corkery as a visiting publications procurement specialist with the Library of Congress working in the Russian language section. She took Murphy's card and led them up the stairs past the rare book gallery and on to the second floor. Dr. Freyberg was alone in his book-lined office, sitting at a table to the right of his desk, reading and taking notes from a tattered Soviet periodical. A reading lamp on a double pivot, like a dentist's drill, hung just above his right shoulder. On the corner of the desk was a stack of similar periodicals. He was in his mid-seventies, as small as a gnome; his elongated skull, fringed with white hair, was dented like an old copper kettle. He wore rimless glasses; around his neck was a black cord from which hung a magnifying glass. He didn't lift his head until he'd made a final notation on a card.

He looked at the copy of the Chernishevsky article Corkery gave him, read a few paragraphs, holding it up in the light of his reading lamp, nodded, and turned back to the first page as Corkery and Murphy waited, facing him from the horsehide sofa where he napped in the afternoons. Two bottles of dark liquid, a spoon, and a water glass sat on the small table at the head of the couch where two indented plush pillows lay. Freyberg nodded again as he continued to study the text. Behind him on the wall hung two dim portraits in ornately gilded nineteenth-century frames. One might have been the elderly Tolstoy; the other was the young Trotsky. A gas heater hissed from a far dark corner. Dr. Freyberg put the article aside. Yes, he vaguely remembered it. He hadn't read all of it at the time of publication and couldn't comment on its technical accuracy but he remembered the title.

Chernishevsky's subject was obscure except to specialists, and Chernishevsky was obviously an expert. Soviet topographical falsification was well known, beginning in 1937, if not earlier; borders, lakes, rivers, waterways, all duplicitously misplaced. Not only were strategic areas like the Leningrad region, the Soviet coastline bordering the Gulf of Finland, and the Chinese frontier region systematically falsified, sometimes by as much as forty kilometers, but hundreds of obscure villages in Siberia as well. Hydrographic charts of Soviet waters were so distorted as to be useless for navigation. What was the purpose? Military? To deceive invading armies? To frustrate ballistic missile and multiple warhead targeting? No, not entirely, not when obscure villages in Siberia were also misplaced. Paranoia, the Stalinist sickness that had corrupted every instrument of national existence, the illness of their times.

Having disposed of the theoretical issue, Freyberg turned with less interest to Chernishevsky. The name meant nothing to him. Apart from this single article, he wasn't familiar with the name, which wasn't on his subscription list or in his card files. He took off his glasses and handed the article back. Murphy was already on his feet, buttoning his coat. Corkery was slow in getting up.

"But you know the name Chernishevsky isn't

in your files or on your subscription list. You know that."

Freyberg nodded. Yes, he knew that. He was quite sure. How did he know? Because he had asked his daughter and research assistant to search their files.

"Because you were curious about the article in the German quarterly?"

Freyberg had put on his glasses. No. He had no interest in Chernishevsky. Because a few days ago someone asked him the same question. He could tell him no more than he could tell them.

"Someone here in Vienna asked you about this article?"

"No, not the article, the name. A specialist from the National Library, the scientific periodical room. He telephoned."

"Did he tell you why he was asking about him?"

Freyberg's eyes dropped indifferently to his notes and his magazine. "He said someone was organizing a scientific congress. They were interested in this Chernishevsky. That's all he said."

He didn't remember the librarian's name. His wife did. She entered the room a moment later in a squall of cigarette smoke, as small as her husband and as shriveled as a winter crabapple. "Lausacker," she shouted, leaning on her heavy cane. Her ankles were thickly wrapped with gray surgical stockings. She stood in the door, her dark eyes fixed intently on Corkery, two tiny black holes in a time-ravaged face. "Why do you ask?"

"She's a little deaf," her husband said, not looking up. Corkery told her he was a publications procurement officer with the Library of Congress, interested in Soviet topographical falsification.

She smiled suddenly. "You're a liar, young man," she shouted, still smiling.

At the embassy Murphy's secretary told them none of the other Viennese refugee agencies had a record of Chernishevsky, not Caritas, not the Hebrew Immigrant Aid Society, not the World Council of Churches. The communications watch officer was waiting in Murphy's office. He handed Corkery a sealed manila envelope. It was a cable from Abbott: "For Boswell from Glasgow, Eyes Only."

Someone would be arriving in Vienna within twenty-four hours. He would fly into Schwechat at 1530 hours, wasn't to be met, wouldn't call at the station, and wouldn't require any support. He would meet Corkery at 1930 hours at a flat in the Inner Ring and fly out of Schwechat at 1145 Zulu the following morning. The detail was obvious but the meaning opaque and in its very blankness Corkery lost for an instant all sense of horizon, like a man in a whiteout.

"Trouble?" Murphy asked.

"I don't know."

It was midafternoon when they left Murphy's Volkswagen in a reserve area behind the Austrian National Library on Josefsplatz. Dry leaves scraped and rattled across the pavement as they walked around the building to the main entrance. They waited in silence at a table in the corner of the scientific periodical reading room. Only two tables were occupied. Five minutes passed, then ten. They took off their coats. Corkery watched the afternoon light dim through the high windows, looking out at the skeletal tree limbs against the sky. It was the waiting more than anything, always the waiting: static surveillance posts, apartments, vans, train stations, phone booths, hotel lobbies, parked cars. Men came and went, planes arrived and departed, train windows were washed, glasses rinsed and put away, filled and set out again, emptied again, washed, rinsed and put away again. People went to bed, made love, and got up; women had babies, men had heart attacks and went to hospitals. Bars, air terminals, and train stations emptied and filled; newspapers were read and thrown away; washrooms filled and emptied; so did department stores, bookshops, bordellos, corners near bus stations, telephone booths next to taxi stands, and you continued to wait as the emptiness gathered in the mind like soot on a winter sill. He was thinking of Jessica, and it suddenly occurred to him and so powerfully he knew it was true: Frank Dudley wasn't in Vienna and never would be.

Murphy stirred next to him. "What happened to the girl?" he asked, his voice a hoarse whisper.

"What girl?"

"The one in Rome, the tall one that night at the residence."

"The DCM's daughter? She's in Cairo, studying Arabic. She sends me postcards."

At last they were summoned. The inner corridor was lined with steel shelving filled with boxes of documents. At the door of his small office Lausacker welcomed them with a smile, shook their hands, and asked them to sit down. He rarely had visitors, as they could tell from his office. His gray hair was parted in the middle and cropped close on the sides, Junker style. He wore a gray cardigan over a gray shirt.

Yes, he had called Dr. Freyberg a few days ago. Two men had visited him that afternoon. Both were German, one a visiting professor from Humboldt University in Berlin. He found a scrap of paper under a paperweight and read the name: Dr. Guenther Flegel, an associate professor of physics. He was helping organize a conference under the auspices of the university's Committee for the Propagation of Scientific Knowledge. Chernishevsky was on the list of scholars invited to the conference, but they'd been unable to locate him. They had only a few days before the invitations were to be sent out and had asked for his help. The man accompanying him was a cultural attaché from the East German embassy. No, he didn't give his name. Lausacker, unable to help them, had called Dr. Freyberg and a professor at the university; neither had been able to supply an address.

"We're running with the jackals," Corkery said as they walked toward the car. "Humboldt University in East Berlin. It has to be the East Germans. They're on the same trail except a couple of days ahead of us."

"Deutsch, you think?"

"No. Someone else. I think the goons are in town. Deutsch is out of it by now."

In Murphy's office Corkery drafted a cable to Langley, telling Abbott the East German Haupt-Ableilung knew what Dudley knew.

The address Chernishevsky had given on his Canadian visa application was in the old Soviet sector of Vienna across the Danube canal. The pension was a soot-streaked building of weathered stone with gabled windows high on the steep roof, steep steps in front, and a heavily scarred door worn with passage. On the ground floors of the neighboring buildings were electrical parts shops, automotive supplies, and wholesale plumbing equipment outlets. A light snow was falling, whitening the narrow street lined with vans and trucks. Just inside the lobby the middle-aged *Hausbesorger* sat at a small table in his office behind a pebbled glass partition, spooning soup from a bowl on a tin tray as he browsed through the pages of *Krönen Zeitung*, a napkin around his neck. He heard them enter, looked up, saw Murphy towering in the door, Corkery taller behind him, and didn't move, still holding the lifted spoon. His hair was gray above his ears but reddish brown on top, like a fox squirrel. He was wearing a toupee.

Murphy said they wanted to ask about Yefrim Chernishevsky, a previous tenant. At the name, the damp blue eyes glistened and the slippered feet began to move, rolling the castered chair away from the table and soup bowl, away from the electric fire at his feet, and away from the door where the two strangers stood.

Murphy repeated the question.

The *Hausbesorger* hesitated but then continued to roll himself backward against the desk. He stopped, hand lifted awkwardly over his left shoulder to reach for the telephone, or try to, but the phone lay two feet beyond his reach. He couldn't lift the receiver without turning his back to the two men in the door, and this he was reluctant to do.

"What's wrong with him?" Murphy said.

"Maybe he thinks he's seen us before. Ask him who he's calling." Murphy asked him. He didn't reply. "Tell him to call the Alien Control Police," Corkery said. "Give him the name of your contact there." Murphy gave him a name and the telephone number. The *Hausbesorger* hesitated, his hand still groping for the telephone he couldn't see.

"American?" He spoke for the first time. "You are American?"

"American," Murphy said. The *Hausbesorger* sighed, nodded, and slowly rolled himself back to the table.

Two men had come the previous morning, two men in overcoats, like them, both foreigners, asking about a man by the name of Chernishevsky who'd occupied room 502. He'd told them he'd never had a tenant named Chernishevsky and knew no man by that name. Room 502 had been rented by a Russian emigré but his name was Moskvichev and he'd stopped renting it six months ago. The *Hausbesorger* thought he'd emigrated to Canada but he wasn't certain. The two men had asked to see his registration books; he refused. He attempted to call the police but one had put his foot against his castered chair and sent it spinning against the wall and ripped the telephone from his hands. They'd forced him to show him his books.

He brought out the leather-bound registry and showed Murphy and Corkery the names. No Chernishevsky was listed. V. Moskvichev had occupied flat 502 when Chernishevsky had made his visa application at the Canadian embassy. Corkery showed him a photograph of Andreyev taken from his passport application. He couldn't identify the photo. Whoever it was, it wasn't Moskvichev.

Corkery left the two of them below and climbed to flat 502 at the top of the house. It was a garret room under the steep roof now used as a lumber room. A pair of narrow dormer windows looked out into the snow-filled sky. The floor was dusty and rugless; a white hospital cot with an old mattress rolled up on the frame was pushed under the eaves. Scraps of carpeting, a few rusted fire grates, plumbing fixtures, and an ancient humpbacked steamer trunk with a Lake Geneva tourist seal on its side lay there too. Under a cracked oilskin cover was a small letter press and a typewriter. A scrap of paper was stuck in the roller at the back of the letter press, and he tore it free. The paper was watermarked with red, green, and blue threads running through it, the kind used in official documents. He kneeled to look at the typewriter. The ribbon had been removed. The white glare from the blowing snow filled the room and made it seem smaller. He looked for a gas line but found none. The wind gnawed at the gables, drafts of cold air trickled across the bare floor. He wondered how the room had been heated.

Downstairs he asked the Austrian about the letter press. It belonged to Moskvichev, who said he'd send for it but never had. Had Moskvichev rented the room to live there or to work? To work. He had a flat across the Danube in the Old City.

"An accommodation address probably," Corkery said as Murphy drove back through the narrow street. "Maybe a mail drop too. We're still walking in someone's footsteps."

"Looks like it."

"Someone a couple of days ahead of us. Chernishevsky or Andreyev is here somewhere, whoever he is. Illegally, probably."

"You're sure of that?"

"If the East Germans think so, so do I." Shrouds of white smoke lifted in the sky above the rail yards. A train whistle shrieked nearby.

"John Doe," Murphy said. "Sure. Any one of a million John Does, take your pick. I'd say that makes our chances of finding him slim to nothing and Slim's left town."

Corkery watched a flight of pigeons sweep from a nearby roof, frightened by the locomotive. "If

Chernishevsky got phony papers somehow, who'd know?"

"Whoever papered him."

"Yeah, but if no one papered him. If he came to Austria on the run, hiding out, grabbing at whatever he could, claiming refugee status, who'd know? Whoever was handling his case would know. If not directly then indirectly, inferentially."

Murphy thought for a minute. "The clerks, the caseworkers."

"The clerks, right. They work the cases, they see these poor bastards every week out there in the waiting room, waiting it out, waiting for the police checks, waiting for medicals, waiting for sponsors. They know the names. When someone disappears or a file goes cold all of a sudden, no visa issued, they usually know why."

"That figures. Okay. So what?"

"This clerk at the UNHCR office knew Chernishevsky's name right away, like Freyberg and the Austrian concierge back there. He didn't have to look."

"Off the top of his head, yeah."

"A file two years retired and he remembers. What was his name, the clerk with the IBM memory?"

"Jozef Biros. Yeah, but people like that get to know names, that's what they're paid for."

"Maybe. Either he remembered because there was something odd about the case or because someone reminded him recently, someone who talked to him before we did, the way they talked to Lausacker or the concierge back there, someone who asked him the same question. One more thing. If these two Germans show up at the pension back there asking about Chernishevsky, where the hell did they get the address if not from the UNHCR? Except for the Canadians, that's the only audit trail Chernishevsky's left in Vienna, a locator card at the UNHCR with the file missing."

"You want to talk to Biros yourself?"

"No. We don't have time. We're a couple of days behind. We need quick answers."

"Quick and dirty. Someone on contract, someone who doesn't have a name. It's worth a try. Let's talk to Holder."

The apartment was on a narrow street behind the Academy of Sciences, a short walk from Stephansplatz through the shadows of medieval Vienna. Corkery left his hotel a little after seven. The wind was punishing, lifting him across the intersections, whipping at his coattails, stinging his ears and bringing water to his eyes. By the time he reached no. 6 his face and jaw were as numb as if deadened by novocaine.

Inside the dimly lit foyer an old man in an olive green trench coat sat on a chair near the glass door. A crutch was across his knee, a black transistor radio on the floor beside him. He lifted himself to his crutch and opened the door to the iron-caged lift, nodded and closed it after him. As the lift ascended Corkery saw him cross the floor and take a key ring from his belt and lock the street door. There were two apartments on the fourth floor. He knocked at the paneled door nearest the elevator and waited. He was about to knock again when a man in a tan raglan opened the door. He was of medium height with dark eyes and dark hair thinning above a high forehead.

"Steiner?"

"Steiner. Come in. I just got in." He led Corkery down the hall and into a front salon where two lamps were lit on an ornately carved table between the two high windows. A second salon off to the right was in darkness. A radio was playing from a console; a leather suitcase and an attaché case sat next to the sofa. The two chairs and tables at the far end of the room were covered with white dustcovers. "The flat's a little chilly still. Corkery, is it? How's Langley these days?"

"Pretty much the same."

"Never changes, does it?" He took off his raglan and dropped it across a chair. The raglan was old but well kept, recently dry-cleaned; the buttons didn't match. He closed the drapes as Corkery waited and turned on a third lamp next to an armchair. He was neither tall nor short, not heavily built and not slight, a man you might stand next to in a ticket queue and not notice, someone you might sit next to during a transatlantic flight and have no reason to remember and find impossible to describe. His hair was brown, not black; he wore an inexpensive gray suit and a blue workman's shirt with a gray woolen tie. His shoes were

English, sturdy and heavy soled, meant for walking; Rhenish cobblestones, Hamburg quays, steep narrow streets along the Spree.

"Something to drink? Scotch? Rye? Beer, maybe." Corkery said Scotch would be fine. Steiner opened his attaché case and took out some papers. "I brought you these. They're not much, but Abbott wanted you to see them as soon as possible. I'll have a look in the liquor cabinet." He went out the door and Corkery sat down on the sofa. One document was the original typescript of the Chernishevsky article, heavily marked up by the German typesetter and soiled by the linotype operator's fingerprints. Attached to it was the envelope in which it had been mailed. It bore Austrian stamps and a Vienna postmark but no return address. Beneath it was a statement by an editor at the Institut Zur Erforschung Der USSR in Munich who remembered receiving the same article in July or August, as well as several other pieces by the same Yefrim Chernishevsky, all posted from Vienna. They might have published one of the earlier essays but it was too long and needed editing. The institute had been unable to contact him to suggest changes. The editor was convinced he was Russian, no doubt a scholar and genuinely so, but probably a crank as well. Corkery studied the smudged typescript and wondered how Steiner found them. A black bag job?

Steiner returned with bottles, ice, and two glasses. A third document described Dr. Guenther Flegel, the associate professor of physics at Berlin's

Humboldt University Dr. Lausacker mentioned. Included was a Xeroxed copy of the first pages of a dark-blue passport with a gold eagle on the cover: Deutsche Demokratische Republik, issued to Flegel a week earlier. The passport photograph was identical to that of Hans Ritter, an East German intelligence officer from Normannenstrasse in East Berlin. He had traveled to Vienna three days earlier and claimed to be making arrangements for an upcoming conference at Humboldt under the auspices of the Committee for the Propagation of Scientific Knowledge.

"So he's a ringer, this Flegel?" Corkery took the drink Steiner offered, trying not to look at him too closely. "Looking for Chernishevsky, is he? If the East Germans know what Dudley knows, they've gotten to him. Now the pros are in town."

"I think so."

"How long have you had this?"

"Three days."

"Abbott got worried, did he? What was it, the East German connection?"

"Deutsch, yes. The Haupt-Ableilung owns him." He spoke so quietly Corkery could barely hear, spoke in a voice you wouldn't recall, an American voice marked by no accent, no mannerisms, and no identity. Who was he? A quiet professional who worked without passion and didn't change his suits with the fashion or his shirts with the season, a man with time and patience and a face that defended its solitude. Where was he from? Someone on contract, running an Agency proprietary in Berlin; someone who had an asset in the East German Staats-Sicherheits Dienst?

"What about Otto Rauchfuss? The Haupt-Ableilung owned him too?"

"Not completely, no. They used him but didn't control him. Otto was too unpredictable, too much his own man. *'Waschecht,'* a dyed-in-the-wool Berliner. They're often that way. Deutsch is different, completely treacherous. Otto wasn't. Ugly the way he died. But Julian didn't take Frank's disappearance seriously until Deutsch's name surfaced."

Corkery hesitated, looking up at him. "Frank, you said."

"Frank, yes."

"You knew Frank Dudley."

Steiner nodded. "I knew him, yes."

"Phil Chambers, George Tobey?" Again Steiner nodded. "Berlin?"

"Berlin, yes. A long time ago."

"How long since you've seen him?"

"Frank? Not for years. I got a letter from him years back but it was about something else." He turned to take the ice bucket and two bottles to the table. Not much for small talk either. But something in the way he moved recalled Jessica's description of someone similar; a man with time and patience, a stranger who defended his privacy but had a polite word for everyone, a man walking through the Spanish sunshine with the white mountains in the distance.

"I don't suppose you have a house in Spain, do you? An old farmhouse."

Steiner smiled in quiet surprise. For the first time Corkery had a sense of the man within. "I did, yes. Who mentioned it? George Tobey?"

"Jessica. You're Eric Prosser."

He smiled again but didn't acknowledge the name. "Abbott said you'd cast a large net. Strange, meeting this way. You know Jessica?"

"Jessica, Phil Chambers, George Tobey too. Jessica told me she rented your farmhouse a couple of times and wanted to thank you but never got the chance. You've never met her? I mean since Berlin?"

"Once, but she didn't know." He sat down, refilling his glass.

It was the autumn when she'd first rented the old house. He hadn't seen her in years, not since Berlin where he'd glimpsed her a few times but always at a distance; she was a youngster and his face was one among many. He was hunting in Spain and staying with the old stonemason who acted as custodian. He was dove hunting and after the morning shoot stopped to see if she needed anything. She was standing in the open courtyard. He hadn't seen her in years and suddenly there she was. He thought she was Tricia. He couldn't imagine she could be anyone else. He left without meeting her.

"You still have the house in Spain."

"I don't go there, not for years." It was up for sale, an agent in London was handling it.

"How is George, how's Phil Chambers?" He seemed grateful for company, a little like Phil Chambers that way. He hadn't seen either man for years. He was fond of both and often thought about both, envying the quiet life they led. One day he'd look them up. What about Corkery? How long had he worked in CI?

It was after ten when Corkery left. Returning through the cold streets, he wasn't thinking of Andreyev or Chernishevsky but Tricia Dudley's last weekend in the English countryside, the one Phil Chambers had described: the old Roman villa at Lullingstone, the chapel in St. John's Gardens, the Pied Bull Hotel. Her farewell to the past, he had said; it had all collapsed; the memories were too strong.

Prosser no longer visited the Spanish farmhouse. He had seen Jessica in the courtyard that autumn morning, thought she was Tricia, and had turned away. Why? His own memories too strong? Did he remember the same hotel, the same garden, the same terrible farewell? Was he the one who'd called Phil Chambers in London to say he was worried?

Looking up and seeing the hotel entrance across the street, he stopped, not knowing where he was. He was in Vienna. Steiner was the mysterious Eric Prosser, still in Germany after all these years, as George Tobey had said, but who else he was, he didn't know. He would never know.

The face that peered back at Frank Dudley from

the tattered book he'd picked up from the bookstall on Quai St.-Michel along the Seine that afternoon seemed curiously familiar. The stalls were banging shut, the old French woman was moving her books inside; but Dudley had been transported. At that moment he might have been that boy whose photograph he'd found, wearing a white sailor suit and stretched out at his parents' feet on the green lawn of the summer house on the Massachusetts shore. His head was in his hand, elbow in the turf, eyes lifted toward the sea. His left hand held a willow switch with which he coaxed forward the small pony about the grounds in the pony cart that had once belonged to his father. His father's portrait in the same cart hung in an upstairs bedroom in the house in Boston. His mother, father, and grandmother were seated behind them in white wicker chairs, figures in a triptych.

His father, spade-bearded after his return from a voyage to Labrador, was wearing his blue yachting jacket and white flannels, his hands on his hips, elbows turned out, his left hand holding his yachting cap. The pose, faintly Edwardian, might have been for his grandmother's benefit, a facsimile of Edward VII to whom she'd been introduced when her brother was posted to the Court of St. James as naval attaché. His mother sat in the chair to the right, thin and pale in a white dress and white hat, holding a white parasol and a book bound in white linen.

He felt the texture of the image clearly, was absorbed in it so completely that his wrist tingled with the touch of the grass. He smelled the salt from the sea and heard dimly in the background the sounds of cups and saucers from the deep side porch where the photographer would later join them for tea. He was eight when the photograph was taken. The emulsion had fixed him forever, suspended him eternally in infinity's gray light even at that moment standing at the stone wall overlooking the Seine.

The portrait capturing the timelessness of that August afternoon would soon stand on the mantel of the fourth-floor nursery of the house in Boston, there to remain until that dark January day after his discovery of Miss MacIntosh's dismemberment when he would rip it from its frame, tear it in a dozen pieces, and burn it in the grate of the nursery fireplace, an act of patricide that was never discovered but which he recalled vividly now as he studied the photographs of the Romanoff family in the musty book he'd found on Quai St.-Michel, a family later murdered by their Bolshevik captors in the dark cellar at Ekaterinburg on July 18, 1919. The Romanoff family portraits were similar in many ways: the boy in the sailor suit, a hemophiliac; Frank Dudley, a lonely, vulnerable young boy left to his own devices those early years and in his own solitary way struggling for air.

Memory again, the terrible tomb of memory. The shadows of late afternoon, the hint of mist downriver, and the pinpricks of light in the distance sped the transfer, returning a sense of personal loss at events over a half century past.

Young Dietrich, who had sat down on a nearby bench to again fix his shoe, now rejoined him. Dudley showed him the title page. The book was in German, an account of the final weeks of the Romanoff family at Ekaterinburg, spiritual cousins of that gathering of Dudleys on the green lawn on the Massachusetts shore, all victims now, all dead.

In the house in Boston, Dudley's mother was as much a stranger as his father. A diabetic with a weak heart complicated by a late, unwanted pregnancy, she kept to her shadowy bedroom and sitting room two floors below the semi-Victorian fourth-floor nursery. At four every afternoon he was taken to be received as she lay on a damask couch, fresh from her nap and toilet. Her kisses were cold, her hands dry. Her skin had the feathery nap of the dead white moths lying under the lamp of his summer bedroom. Her questions were uttered with a dry medicinal breath, the finely lidded eyes awaiting his reply held the cold fixed pupils of the reptiles in a zoological garden. The simultaneity of darkness and light, coldness simulating affection, death disguised as life, struck terror in his heart and sent him fleeing up the servants' stairs as fast as his short legs could carry him to find comfort against the warm bosom of Miss Harkness, his Scottish-born nurse, or her successors, surrogate Miss Harknesses.

She was a young woman of indeterminate age (at Harvard he realized she must have been thirty when she joined the staff) and his constant companion during his early years. She was as much a stranger to the women inhabiting the lower house as he was. The rooms below were a museum, a repellent hodgepodge of nineteenth-century furniture, cold floors, unlit hearths, and dark rooms. Her comfort was in Robert Burns, Sir Walter Scott, Robert Louis Stevenson, and the Bible. She read to him in the evening and would sometimes send him down the servants' stairs to unlock the kitchen door to admit one of her nocturnal guests. He had no recollection of her lovers. He remembered more vividly her warm embrace as she lifted him from his bath, her bedtime stories, and the first afternoon Miss MacIntosh came to tea.

Miss Harkness had seemed tired that week. Someone had left, sending a letter saying he wouldn't be returning. Gray hairs had begun to sprout in her thick dark hair. She spent long periods at her dressing table seeking them out, her small breasts sagging within her petticoat, her white shoulders dolefully slumped. A maid from a neighboring house was to join them for tea one rainy afternoon but had failed to appear. Miss Harkness brought Miss MacIntosh instead, a creature of pure presence, able to lift the saddest of spirits, as she had Miss Harkness's that afternoon. She was never required to speak; her thoughts were always known. You never had to move your eyes to know she was looking at you; she was always looking at you. Her smile never dimmed, as gracious that first afternoon as it would remain for two years thereafter. Her skin was café au lait, her lips carmine, her hair bushy black, her eyes fragile white shells, her spiny nose a crude angle cut with a machete from the most prominent ridge of the Pacific coconut that made up her head. The coconut had been brought back from Tahiti by Dudley's grandfather after a South Seas voyage. For years it had lain forgotten on a dark closet shelf in the first-floor billiard room. Brought from its tomb that rainy afternoon to the fourth-floor tea party, the coconut was given a body made from a dressmaker's dummy with a full cotton bust and a wire skirt draped with bright calico. Her arms were Miss Harkness's black stockings stuffed with rags, her hands a pair of white doeskin gloves. She wore a shawl, a straw hat with a fresh flower in the band, and a cameo brooch.

She came to tea that afternoon and remained for two years, kept discreetly at the back of the closet, her head and shoulders concealed by a quilted bird cage cover. She survived Miss Harkness, who left the house one weekend to visit a seafaring cousin from Glasgow staying at the Seaman's Institute on the Battery in New York and never returned. She didn't survive Miss Harkness's successor nor his father's return from the Arctic the following February. His father met Miss MacIntosh for the first time that evening as she stood next to the couch, listening to Dudley and Miss Harkness's successor as they read together. Three cups of cocoa sat on the table. His father was dressed for a formal dinner and ball, wearing his cutaway, sash and medals, his beard neatly trimmed. He'd been surprised to find Miss MacIntosh there. The governess, unfamiliar with the protocol of Miss MacIntosh's clandestine visits, had introduced Miss McIntosh as a Scottish cousin of Miss Harkness. His father stiffly shook her hand and immediately sent his son downstairs with the three cocoa cups. When he returned, Miss MacIntosh and his father were gone.

The nurse said his father had taken her to the ball. The time had come for both him and Miss MacIntosh to make new friends. She never returned. The nurse didn't mention her again but by the end of the first week he knew something was wrong. He had grown tired of the game by then; Miss Harkness had been Miss MacIntosh's spirit, her fragrance Miss MacIntosh's fragrance, all she'd left to him, but now she smelled only of the dust of the closet. In early March he was in the rear basement, searching for lizards and toadstools with his magnifying glass and flashlight in the dark earth of the old cellar behind the boiler room. The walls were of stone; there were no windows in the front of the basement. Old bottles lay in boxes, old radiators, old pipe snippings, a pair of lobster traps and rusting fire grates. As he stooped to explore a damp patch in the seam of stone wall his flashlight cast a moving shadow against the partition behind him. Fixing his beam there he saw a familiar figure. The wire skirt was rusting now, leaving an orange smear on his fingers; the cotton bodice was damp and discolored. A damp clump of crushed straw lay on the earth nearby and led him to the decapitated head, smashed by the walnut hammer that still lay nearby, the eyes missing, the smile splintered in two halves by the same blow that had split her skull.

Upstairs on the same afternoon, he had torn his father's picture from the frame, torn it in dozens of pieces, and burned it in the nursery grate.

"My father was in the navy," Dudley said, returning the book to the bin. "I think I told you. More trouble?" He glanced down at Dietrich's right shoe. The heel had come off again.

"I think it's all right. Sorry. Was your father always in the navy?" They walked on toward Place St.-Michel.

"The navy was his career. He spent most of his time at sea. I didn't see a great deal of him when I was growing up. I missed him of course, although I didn't realize it at the time."

Dietrich didn't know his father, who'd disappeared when he was two. He had been raised by his seamstress mother and older sister. Dudley wasn't surprised. The lack of a masculine figure in the Hamburg household had long been apparent to him.

He'd again changed his lodging, his new one in an ugly little pension in a twisting cul-de-sac near Rue de la Goutte d'Or in Barbes-Rochechouart, a Muslim neighborhood. Dietrich's flat was a few blocks away. Karl Eigner, the East German trade unionist, was coming to meet him in Paris. Word had arrived from Deutsch through Dietrich two days earlier; the modalities for a prisoner exchange would be explored, a protocol agreed upon.

"His ambition was to be the naval attaché in London," Dudley said, "like my great-uncle. As I recall, they offered him Havana. That sounds right, Havana. He ended up at Newport." He paused, looking at the wet light fading from the river. "He was an absolute bastard but I forgave the old goat in his old age. I'd wanted to marry a young German girl but he was opposed. I was foolish enough to agree. I'd always intended to have a son and share with him what I'd never shared with my father, but it didn't work out."

"I'm sorry. You have just one daughter, Jessica?"

"Just Jessica, yes."

"She's artistic?"

"*Artistic* isn't the word." Poor Dietrich. He'd told Dudley he had artistic tendencies and had once danced in a cabaret. "She's a painter. I intended that she have a father even if she had nothing else." Dietrich had stopped again, again fiddling with the heel of his shoe.

Dudley waited patiently. "You should really stop wasting time with those shoes. They're totally worn out. Throw them in the rubbish bin. We'll find a new pair for you."

"It's all right now. I'm sorry." Dietrich straightened, his pale cheeks flushed. "Let's go this way." He led the way down Rue de la Hachette, a narrow lane lined with small restaurants and crowded with early-evening shoppers where the smell of cous-

cous, roasting lamb, and frying fish filled the evening air. Dietrich enjoyed walking through Rue de la Hachette because it reminded him of an Arab souk or as he imagined an Arab souk might be. He had never been to an Arab country but had a Parisian friend who spent his summers in Tangier. Dudley had never met him but could well imagine. From the way Dietrich's froggy-go-a-wooing eyes wandered so tenderly after the young men they passed during their afternoon promenades, it was obviously a sad lonely liaison of some kind.

He again waited as Dietrich lagged behind to examine the bins of fresh fruit in front of a small grocery, his eyes on a black-haired Lebanese youth weighing oranges in a scale. Patience was what Dietrich needed, the poor fool. He lacked a strong father figure. "If you want to go on stage, do it," Dudley had told him. "Don't stay with office work or bookkeeping if it doesn't suit you. Quite frankly, I have doubts as to whether bookkeeping suits you."

Dietrich had welcomed the advice.

"I wish my French was better," he said wistfully as he caught up, his shy advances no doubt ignored. He took out his pitifully worn wallet to search for franc notes. "Shall we have a glass?"

Reluctantly Dudley agreed, although he would have preferred to dine alone. The young man needed not only friendship and compassion but encouragement of a firmly masculine kind. In due time he intended to tell him to give up these sordid indulgences, that it wasn't entirely a matter of hormones.

His name was Kleiber, an Austrian, so Holder said, but Murphy was dubious. He was a man of medium size with a thick neck, goat shoulders, gray hair so closely cut it showed the pink of his scalp, and eyes so pale they seemed without color or depth, like a shallow sea drafting white sand. Murphy didn't think he was Austrian and wasn't sure who he was, maybe someone out of Munich, a man with no name and no nationality, but quick and dirty was what they wanted, no questions asked. He remembered the rabble he'd worked with during his 430th CIC days at the old tobacco building on Porzellangasse when Vienna had been crawling with gallows-birds like Kleiber: Hungarian, Romanian, and Croatian fascists, ex-Waffen SS killers, ex-Abwehr agents, Belgian, Dutch, or stateless and on the run from denazification courts, extradition, prison, and God knows what else. At one time Kleiber had been an investigator for the Byelorussian National Public Committee based in Munich, so Holder said, and had some dealings with refugee agencies. "A good chap, a quick study," he had told them. "Comes highly recommended." He didn't say who recommended him and disappeared quickly into his office before Kleiber arrived.

Murphy briefed Kleiber as Corkery listened, giving him the barest details. He said they were looking for a man named Yefrim Chernishevsky and thought Jozef Biros knew something about him. Kleiber had only a few questions and suggested he visit Biros at the UNHCR office. He had no better luck than Murphy. Biros was lying, he said from the backseat after they'd picked him up a block from the UNHCR offices. Corkery, intrigued, asked why he wanted to visit Biros at his office. Technique, Kleiber said. It was important Jozef Biros recognize him the next time they met.

The next time? Where would that be? That night. They would visit Biros's bachelor flat on Turkenstrasse in Vienna's 9th District and talk again, this time privately.

"So you've worked the refugee crowd," Corkery said, turning from the front seat. "You know how to handle them."

Men like Biros? Yes, he'd worked with them. On the pavement a wedding party was leaving an Orthodox Catholic church. Corkery saw Kleiber cross himself as they drove by. "What other kind of work do you do?"

"Excuse me?" Kleiber leaned forward.

"What else do you do these days, what kind of business?"

Kleiber sat back, his head turned on his thick neck as he looked out the window. "I am putting milk on the fire, like a good housewife, making sure the fire to stay hot, making sure the milk not to boil. What work you do?"

Corkery said he was a document procurement specialist from the Vatican Library, looking for a lost papal diary.

"Good." Kleiber smiled, showing his gap teeth. "Very good." His pale eyes vanished between thin slits under the massive brow bone. Corkery thought he looked like a Mongol assassin at the court of Genghis Khan.

It was after nine o'clock as Kleiber and Corkery climbed the stairs of the old apartment house on Turkenstrasse to the fifth floor. The illuminated glass panes leaked amber light to the landings; the smells of simmering stew meat and vegetables still lingered in the stairwell. In a fourth-floor flat below a television set was turned on very loud; Corkery heard the sounds of gunfire and the TV sound-track of "Bonanza." At the top of the stairwell Kleiber rapped softly at the door to the left as Corkery waited on the step below. Jozef Biros answered; thin and small-boned with a head of thick black hair, he was wearing a white shirt and carpet slippers. "Excuse me," Kleiber said. "I am Herr Kleiber. I visit you today, remember —"

Biros remembered and tried to slam the door. Kleiber blocked it with his foot and smashed it open with his forearm. The door was still quivering as Corkery followed. He had no idea what Kleiber had told Biros that afternoon at his office, but he'd made an impression. Biros's eyes were as bright as candle flames dancing in the wind as he backed away. His mouth had trembled open but no words came.

"I have gentleman with me," Kleiber said. "Tell us where we find Chernishevsky, okay? We have no time to talk, you see. Tell us." The room was small and uncomfortably warm, parched by a gas heater against the rear wall. An old gas fixture hung from the ceiling. A small black-and-white television set was on but the sound was turned down. The walls were hung with strange paintings. Beyond the single sagging armchair was a draftsman's table on which a model boat lay on a newspaper. Biros had been assembling the rigging when Kleiber knocked. At the end of the table was a jar filled with brushes, surrounded by wrinkled tubes of oil paint.

"You make boat models," Kleiber said. "Very good." He lifted the three-master in his thick hands. "A boat maker, very good. '*Seelig sind die da bauen, denn sie werden Sohne Gottes heissen.*' Blessed are they who build, for they shall be called the sons of God." He studied the delicate rigging and smiled his demented Mongol grin. "You know the words of Christ?" He lifted the boat toward Biros. "Very good, yes." He examined the keel, fingered the mast and rigging, smiled again, and savagely brought it down over his lifted knee. His expression unchanged, he scattered the smashed pieces of balsa and torn rigging to the floor and moved on. Biros, still retreating, threatened to call the police.

Kleiber laughed. "Call police? Yes. Call them."

He walked boldly past the quivering Biros, glanced in the small kitchen, crossed to the double-hung window, and pointed down to the street. "There is car there, black car. That is the police. Come call them. Open window. Call them." He lifted the bottom frame of the double-hung window and rattled it to the top of the casement. "Come! Call police."

The cold air blew across the room, scattering the newspapers on the table, the torn rigging, and the broken balsa. Biros, his bright eyes as large as saucers, looked at Kleiber, looked at Corkery, at the window, at the littered floor, thought better of it, and bolted for the door. Kleiber caught him, hoisted him by his belt, stunned him across the nose with a short hammer blow, and smashed him against the wall. The goosenecked lamp on the drafting table crashed to the floor. Corkery lifted it and in its glare saw that the two pictures above the table were both muddy oil portraits copied from magazine photographs; one seemed to be of Margaret Thatcher. Kleiber lifted Biros from the tangle of cord. "Why do you make business worse?" He carried the limp Biros across the room, feet dangling, and slung him down on the windowsill. "Where is Chernishevsky?"

The drop was five stories down. At the bottom was a stone wall razored with broken bottle shards. Biros sat perched on the sill, like a finch on a wire, his small fingers trying to grip the casement on each side. Summoning a weak breath, he tried to stand. Kleiber thrust him back and lifted a wooden chair from the floor to cage him within the four legs, the bottom two resting on the sill. "Where is Chernishevsky?"

Cold air poured into the room. A train was passing nearby, drowning every noise except its own, like the roar of the sea, rattling the glass in the window and shaking the casement. Biros sat in its tumult, quivering with the cold, balanced on the windowsill, fingers holding desperately to the casement, the chair rungs pressing against his chest.

"Where is Chernishevsky, little bird?"

Biros didn't answer. With a quick thrust Kleiber lifted the back of the chair. Biros's feet lifted, his carpet slippers flew off, his head and shoulders disappeared out the window. *"For Christ's sake!"* Corkery cried. Kleiber kept the chair rungs pressed against Biros's chest as he moved aside to put his head through the window.

"When the chair goes, you go, little boat builder. Where is Chernishevsky?"

Corkery couldn't hear the answer. Still holding the chair, Kleiber moved to the other side and again put his head out the window where Biros dangled, clinging in terror to the chair rungs to keep from pinwheeling backward. "Still there, little bird?"

Corkery heard weak sobs from the darkness: *"Chernishevsky!* Yes! Chernishevsky!"

Kleiber waited another two minutes, talking to Biros through the window. Satisfied, he brought the chair back to the horizontal and they pulled him in. His knees were as weak as water, his mouth was open, and saliva drooled down his chin. His thick Hungarian hair was standing on end as they carried him between them to the armchair.

Chernishevsky had Austrian nationality now but Biros didn't know under what name or how he had gotten his papers. He had once applied for resettlement in Canada but abandoned his application after he received his Austrian papers two years ago, probably illegally and under his new name. He didn't know the name or where he lived but thought he was still in Vienna. He had seen him a month ago in the UNHCR offices with another refugee, a Czech woman awaiting resettlement in Canada. Her name was Eva Lausman and she worked as a laundress at a hotel on Wolfengasse near the old Fleischmarkt. That was all he knew.

Corkery asked about the Chernishevsky file at the UNHCR. Biros claimed the file had been stolen. Two men had come to see him, asking the same questions they were asking. He had gotten the file and was telling them what little he knew of Yefrim Chernishevsky when Miss Faversham had summoned him. When he returned both the file and the two men were gone. Kleiber said he was lying; the two Germans, whoever they were, had bought the file, wasn't that true? What had they paid? He asked for Biros's bank statements.

Exhausted, frightened, and still trembling with the cold blowing from the open window, his handkerchief to his bleeding nose, Biros began to weep. Kleiber comforted him as Corkery closed the win-

413

dow. "Don't weep, little boat builder. Your secrets are our secrets until next time. Courage, little bird." He patted him affectionately on the shoulder. "Be mindful of the words of Christ."

Murphy picked them up out front and they dropped Kleiber off in the darkness near the Volksgarten and drove on to the Innerstadt. "The guy's a sadist," Corkery said, watching the shadow disappear through the arc lights.

"Kleiber? What'd he do?"

"Dangled Biros out the window, a parachute jump and no harness."

"Quick and ugly, wasn't that what we wanted?"

The hotel Biros described was on Wolfengasse, a narrow lane in the old city. The personnel office was closed and the night manager didn't know the Lausman woman. Neither did the bell captain. Corkery suggested they find the laundry. They took the elevator down two floors to the sub-basement but the laundry was closed. In a half-lit tunnel nearby smelling of steam, fuel oil, and baking bread, Corkery stopped an electrician pushing a repair cart and asked if there was an employees' canteen. He pointed over his shoulder. They followed the corridor past the generator room, cold storage lockers, and bakery to a pair of metal-clad doors. Inside the white-tiled canteen two men in white service jackets sat at an aluminum table, drinking coffee, their faces lightly powdered with flour. One of the men knew Eva Lausman. He thought she lived in a flat behind Mariahilferstrasse toward the railroad tracks. He got up and moved

414

to the house phone against the white-tiled wall to the rear and telephoned a dough cutter in the bakery, a Hungarian woman who gave him her address.

It was after eleven. The apartment building was a few blocks from Dr. Freyberg's bookstore; Murphy couldn't find an entry to the street from Mariahilferstrasse and had to circle back along the railroad tracks. A few snowflakes floated through the headlights. The street was a cul-de-sac, ending in a set of stone steps that led to Mariahilferstrasse. The Lausman flat was on the third floor. There was no lift. The light from the pebbled glass door fell like moonlight across the floor as Corkery rang the bell in the door panel.

The woman's face was in half shadow as she opened the door, wearing a heavy gray cardigan, gray stockings, and white shoes. She nodded as Murphy spoke her name and nodded again at the name Chernishevsky. She opened the door farther. A Slavic face, Corkery thought: she had high cheekbones and a full wide mouth. Small shadows lay like bruises under her eyes. Her light brown hair was tied in a bun at the back of her neck.

"Something has happened?"

"We'd like to talk to Mr. Chernishevsky. Do you know where we could find him?"

A girl of eight or nine appeared at her side in a blue flannel nightgown; a blue ribbon was tied in her butternut hair. "Please, Gretchen, go back, please." The girl only pressed herself against her mother, looking up.

"We're friends," Corkery said. "We don't have much time."

Her hand moved to her daughter's shoulder as she looked at them uncertainly, her eyebrows so colorless she seemed to have none at all. At last, she nodded toward the door across the landing. "There, but he is gone, all day now. I didn't know what to do. He never is gone like that, never."

Corkery crossed the landing and rapped at the glass-paneled door.

"He is not there. Just a few minutes ago I go in. I have a key. He hasn't come. I not know what to do."

Murphy asked if they could use her phone. She had no phone. There was a pay phone in the hall at the bottom of the stairs.

8

A PRISONER
OF EXILE

In the three-room flat opposite Eva Lausman's
they found Andreyev's unmade bed, his cluttered
bookshelves, his Olympia typewriter, his notebooks, and dozens of letters stuck away haphaz-
ardly in desk drawers and binders. On the floor
near his typing table was a pile of yellowing newspapers. Among the books on the shelves above
were four Soviet atlases, dated 1937, 1939, 1967,
and 1969, all bought secondhand in Vienna or elsewhere in Western Europe. The letters were to
newspaper editors, emigré journals, and scholarly
quarterlies, but most often letters to himself, like
the fragments Corkery found in the notebooks, to
the man betrayed, the man fallen between the
cracks; Andreyev, the mapmaker, now wandering
the antipodes of his own vast but increasingly eccentric imagination.

He'd left quickly, taking nothing with him.
Holder thought they'd kidnapped him off the

streets. Murphy agreed, saying it had been quick and ugly. Corkery wasn't sure. A quick-change artist, Phil Chambers had said, an old song-and-dance man. A single threadbare gray suit hung in the closet alongside two shirts, both blue. A plastic laundry basket filled with freshly washed clothes sat on a chair in the bedroom. In the refrigerator were cartons of milk, bottles of cider and beer, butter, and orange juice; in the vegetable bins were onions and potatoes. A bowl of fresh fruit sat on the enamel table. A pot of African violets sat on the windowsill and a bowl of ivy above it.

Holder sent a team in. They went over the flat, searching for paraphernalia, exploring the books, the file folders, probing the closet walls and ceiling, the pots of African violets, the cans of baking powder and flour, the bed, mattress, and chairs, the wall receptacles, the lamps, the ceiling lights, and the tins of foot and tooth powder in the bathroom. They found nothing. It was a mystery, a small matter, a minor footnote in a dossier long retired. Andreyev wasn't in a Moscow grave and not in prison, but living another man's life in Vienna. Why?

For Corkery there was a kind of madness in those three rooms, a man living so futilely amid the smells of tobacco, coal smoke, carbon paper, dust, and stewing vegetables that hovered about the little crypt where he sat late into the night, like a pensioner in perennial twilight, in composition under a dim mezzotint of St. Stephen's.

Hanging on a nail from the bookshelf was a NASA color photograph taken of the earth during the first Apollo moon landing; a small brightly veined planet, almost translucent, like a turtle egg, swam in an infinite ocean of blue. Such photographs had revolutionized our age, Andreyev had told Elinor, created a new unitary consciousness of planetary existence, of earth, continents, and people beyond anything known in the past.

Eva Lausman had shown them two photographs of her own, taken a year earlier during a weekend picnic outing down the Danube. Andreyev had rented a car, an American car, much too grand for her. Gretchen had been delighted. The two photographs showed a large man with heavy shoulders, a badgerlike face, and thick curly hair beginning to gray. She knew him first as Yefrim Chernishevsky, a Ukrainian refugee she'd met one morning in the overheated UNHCR waiting room. They'd become friends. Later he'd acquired Austrian nationality; she wasn't sure how. He'd taken the name Alexander Andronov, that of a Volga German, and moved to the flat across the hall. He told her he'd had no choice. He worked four days a week at an office supply shop owned by a man named Grosz, selling Japanese calculators and copy machines. Gretchen, who often visited his flat in the evening and liked to explore its rooms, had once found an American passport lying in a drawer. He said he was keeping it for a friend. Whoever he was, he was a good and kind man, an unusual man, trapped by ugly circumstances she knew nothing about. Her own situation was similar. Her maiden name was Barzak. A print shop clerk in the basement of the Ministry of General Engineering in Prague, she'd fled four years earlier during a holiday in Hungary but had been unable to immigrate because of a spot on her lungs. She couldn't resettle until the last signs of her tuberculosis had been cleared up. Her most recent X ray was encouraging.

She suspected something had gone wrong the Sunday before his disappearance. That day Andreyev had taken Gretchen to the zoo; she seemed upset after they returned. On Sunday night and again on Monday she'd left her bed to crawl into bed with her mother, frightened by something she wouldn't explain, saying simply she'd had a bad dream. Then on Tuesday she had come directly from school to the hotel in the Innerstadt to wait for her mother, something she never did. Corkery questioned her as her mother watched; he didn't want to make too much of it. He had no success. Whatever had happened on Sunday was something only she and Andreyev shared.

Eva Lausman said he spent many of his free afternoons at the Austrian National Library, the Osterreichische Nationalbibliotek on Josefsplatz or the Bibliotek der Weiner Universitat at the university. The librarians confirmed his visits. He had a habit of clipping pieces from the local press. Among the clippings were articles describing the latest discoveries in particle physics, biology, archeological discoveries in the Caucasus, the latest debates in the Austrian or German parliaments, the most recent museum scandal, a bogus Rembrandt identified in some European museum after so many decades of awesome reverence: "Another historical swindle!" were the words scribbled in English across a clipping from *Die Welt* reporting a fake Vermeer found in a Munich gallery.

Next to his typewriter was a page from an article he'd been transcribing from his notes the night before his disappearance, prompted by a newspaper article describing the visit to Vienna of an imperial Arab head of state, a visit that had summoned all manner of uniforms and masquerades from the old Austro-Hungarian costume closet, so his note read. He had passed the imperial cavalcade of limousines near the Staats Opera, on its way to hear a Handel opera.

The subtlety of manners in the imperial capital, as well as their cultural and technological complexity, makes it difficult for us to suggest, much less propose, that our most eminent heads-of-state, politicians, diplomats, generals, and publicists be taken by the hand and gently led off to that secluded sanctuary where they so rightfully belong. Judged by any civilized standard, by the museums they endow, the concerts they dutifully attend, the astronomical observatories they dedicate, the libraries to which they leave their papers, and the grandeur of the distant planets whose atmospheres they probe while remaining indifferent to the poisons of their own, the lunatic asylum is where they all belong.

In one of the blue-green accordion files on the shelf above the typewriter they found his four-hundred-page treatise describing forty years of Soviet cartographic deception, 1937 to 1977, which he'd begun in Washington. He'd once made a metaphor of the subject, the disease of our times; now it had grown tiresome. Did the lies of the Administration of Geodesy and Cartography in Moscow matter? Did the fact that Moscow's cartographers might one night pack up a sleeping village in its wooden carts and resettle its huts and pig sties twenty-five kilometers to the east affect in any way the lives of the villagers? Did it matter to them whether the earth was a sphere, a trapezoid, or a blueberry pancake?

He had become an epistolary intellectual, he wrote in one of his notebooks, a feuilleton essayist; he had become clever with words, the most pathetic insult of all. To grow poorer in life, feebler in action, darker in thought, and yet richer in words the way a Polish cow pond, denied sunlight, grows thicker in scum; the way a Petri dish breeds mold in the vacuum of its laboratory culture. No wonder exiles were the most prolific of journal keepers, recording their daily temperatures in the solipsism of exile. This was the shabbiest trick life had played on him.

His evening meals he often took alone in a large

cavernlike cafeteria on Mariahilferstrasse a half-dozen blocks away. It was as large as a trolley barn, Corkery discovered the evening he ate there alone, smoky and poorly lit. High overhead were dusty steel joists and above them a dim roof where the light never penetrated. The customers didn't remove their coats. They were working men and women for the most part, come to eat the way they lived, simply and sparingly at the zinc-covered tables. Curiosity had brought Corkery there. He sat among them with his tray that evening, watched as they broke their bread carefully, ate silently and deliberately, scrubbed the plate clean with the last pinch of bread, and then drank a cup of coffee and smoked a cigarette. It reminded him of a railway station. It wasn't merely the bundled anonymity of the customers or their harsh cigarettes, but had something to do with their transience as well, strangers sharing a meal in passing, the illusions of trains waiting somewhere nearby, the smell of coal dust, steam, and wet wool, a winter vastness beyond. "An immensity too vast to understand its destiny," Andreyev had written of Russia.

Corkery knew he wanted to return. It was everywhere in his notebooks, in his memories. Why hadn't he?

Late the following afternoon he stood at the window of Andreyev's flat, looking across the street toward the fourth floor of the building opposite where at his request Holder had set up a static surveillance post. He hadn't been enthusiastic. Corkery asked for three days. The embassy sedan that had brought him waited in the cul-de-sac at the top of the stone steps leading to Mariahilferstrasse. The madness in the three rooms might have been his own, a man living so futilely with questions he couldn't answer; it was his fourth visit. He saw nothing in the window of the third-floor flat opposite to reveal the watcher inside. On the floor above a toilet flushed; water hammered through the pipes. On the windowsill were two African violets. Next to them lay a few drops of water. Curious, he touched the drops with his fingers. Watered that day? In the kitchen the counter was empty, no watering pot there. The cold cock was still dripping. He waited as the drop formed and fell to the stained yellow basin. He felt the towel hanging on the rack next to the stove. It was still damp. He went across the landing to the Lausman flat, knocked but got no answer. Eva Lausman seldom returned from the hotel laundry before six-thirty. And what did Gretchen do those long winter afternoons? She often studied her lessons with Andreyev in his flat. He crossed the landing and stood inside the door, listening. There were few places to hide, none in the front room or the kitchen. He went back to the bedroom. The closet was empty. She was under the bed. *"Guten Abend,"* he said gently.

Her smiling face was partially hidden behind the watering can. *"Guten Abend."*

Her mother was cross with her at first, but then

held the quiet blond head against her shoulder as she sat on the worn sofa. On the wall behind her hung a silver and walnut crucifix; to the left was a tinted Sunday supplement photograph of Pope John Paul under glass and behind it two dried palm leaves. "I am understanding if you are mad with her," she said. She promised to keep the key to Andreyev's flat in her purse. Corkery said he wasn't mad at all.

Childhood was a secret country, he remembered. Why an eight-year-old girl might suddenly change her mind and admit to secrets she'd refused to share forty-eight hours earlier he didn't know, but Gretchen had. A pale winter sun lay over the walks and grass and flower beds at the Vienna zoo that afternoon, drawing out what little brightness remained as Gretchen led her mother and Corkery away from the taxi, through the front entrance, and along the walks she knew so well. The trees were leafless now except for the evergreens and the oaks, unevenly clad in rust-colored leaves.

If she was now willing to share her secret, she was telling the tale in her own way. Her mittened hand was in her mother's but quickly she broke free and bounded on, leading them with quick backward glances at first and then the bobbing white ski cap with its white pompom. The animals that had so fascinated her during her first visits with Andreyev two years earlier did so no longer. Exotic plumage, eccentric shape, or mammoth size weren't enough to hold her attention; liveliness interested her more, especially the gibbons. In the reptile house she stood with her hand in her mother's, staring transfixed at the small poisonous vipers draped over their bare tree limbs like coral necklaces. The sedentary zebra and oryx got only a passing glance. Then she was off again, insisting they buy peanuts at a concession stand. They opened the peanuts and stood watching the camels. Gretchen thought they looked very cold, standing there in their shaggy woolen coats. They had come from Africa, she told Corkery, like Hannibal's elephants; they had walked over the Alps.

She noticed things, her mother said, little things only a child notices. Eva wore a drab brown coat and brown wool stockings. "She is caring for how I look." Gretchen was in tears that Sunday morning because her mother wouldn't let her wear her new blue wool jumper and blue coat, the one she wore to Holy Innocents.

By four-fifteen she had shown them everything she and Andreyev had seen that day but hadn't shared her secret. She led them to the green bench a hundred yards from the main entrance where she and Andreyev rested and finished the last of the peanuts before the long bus ride back to the flat. Behind the bench was a grassy terrace with a circular flower bed in the center and beyond that another main walk. After a minute Gretchen left the bench and skipped down the asphalt walk, stopped and stood motionless, looking out over the grassy terrace. Then she turned, her right knee lifted, eyes closed, as if in a trance, waited motionless until two elderly visitors passed, and continued down the path away from them. At the bird building a hundred yards away she turned to face them, motionless again, as if watching someone behind them.

One of her games, Eva Lausman said. Often left alone in the apartment, she had a repertoire of secret games; some she knew, some she didn't. Some ended with her eyes closed, right or left knee lifted, something hidden in her right or left hand or her jumper pocket. Gretchen had moved on, not returning by the same walk but by the path angling off under the trees on the other side of the terrace. She had taken off her white ski cap and was walking very fast. A few minutes later, she rejoined them on the bench and fell across her mother's lap, breathing heavily, her cheeks stung by the cold, her mittened hands held tightly closed against her mother's brown coat. Slowly she opened her right fist. She was holding a silver thimble. In her left fist was a single peanut. "Two Elkrings," she said. "Don't look."

Elkring was king of the bad elves, her mother said, the troll who frightened children left alone in lonely apartments on rainy nights. Elkring might also be a frightening face she'd seen on her way home from Holy Innocents, on the bus, or even at the zoo.

She had seen two men at the zoo that Sunday with Andreyev. She had first noticed them near the front gate as they entered, then saw them through the windows outside the zoo restaurant where she and Andreyev had cocoa and biscuits. As they sat on the bench, finishing the peanuts, they had walked behind them on the far side of the terrace.

She closed her mother's hand over hers and got up, leading them toward the front gate, her hand in her mother's, the thimble shared between them. On the windy pavement outside the entrance she gave her mother's hand a squeeze just as she'd done that Sunday with Andreyev as the two men approached, their faces growing larger and uglier as they towered over her. They spoke to Andreyev. No, they didn't speak in German. She thought they were asking him to come with them and bring the little girl. Andreyev talked to them. The two men followed him to the curb afterward and stood watching as they crossed the intersection and waited for their bus.

One was tall, the other short; both wore overcoats and hats, both spoke a language she didn't know. Had she ever seen them before? No. But she had seen one of the men the following evening, standing in the dusk at the stone balustrade at the top of the steps, looking down into their street. He smiled as she passed, the same smile he'd given her outside the zoo entrance. Terrified, she had fled through the winter twilight as fast as her legs could carry her.

Why had she waited so long to tell them? her mother asked as the taxi drove them back to the flat. Gretchen only shook her head, but for Corkery vagueness would no longer do. He had questions to ask, but needed an interpreter for a child replying through her mother's imperfect English translated from her native Czech, the language of mother and daughter at home.

Murphy recommended her, a Czech woman who worked in a senior position in the embassy administrative section. A diminutive, well-bred woman with bobbed gray hair, she was born in Prague, where a sister, a university lecturer, still lived. An embassy car brought her the same afternoon. Corkery told her they were trying to identify two men of unknown nationality who dealt in stolen passports.

Gretchen was shy at first as she sat on the worn sofa in the small living room, her eyes downcast. The interpreter, wearing a green wool jacket and skirt, had taken inventory of the flat in a few quick glances, most conspicuously the poor furnishings and the ecclesiastical Slovakian bric-a-brac on the walls. Sitting on a stiff-backed chair in front of the sofa, she asked Gretchen to describe meeting the two men that Sunday at the zoo. Gretchen was silent. Corkery suggested she rephrase the question: Did her friend Andreyev know either of the two men? The question provoked a frown and was rephrased: What was Andreyev's reaction when they spoke to him? Did he ignore them? Was he frightened, as she had been? Again Gretchen remained silent. Corkery suggested a simpler question: Had they shaken hands?

Gretchen nodded. Yes, they had shaken hands. With both men? She held up one finger: no, with one man, not the other. Which man had he shaken hands with? The tall man. So the tall man had shaken hands with Andreyev but not the other man. Yes. He hadn't shaken hands with the other man. Had Andreyev talked to both men? No, only the tall man. While the two talked, what was the smaller man doing? He was watching. Watching? Yes, watching. He had stood to one side as Andreyev and the tall man talked. Gretchen screwed up her face, her lower lip stuck out; this was the way he looked. While Andreyev was talking to the tall man, the little man had reached for her hand and suggested they have an ice cream while the two friends talked. Gretchen had snatched her hand away, clinging to Andreyev. Andreyev and the tall man had laughed and looked at the other man.

Something tugged at Corkery's memory. "Just a minute," he said to the Czech woman. "Is that what the smaller man said, 'friends'? Did he say it in German?" Yes, he had said "friends." He was speaking German, not the other language.

So Andreyev knew the taller man. Someone sent from abroad to search him out, someone well and favorably known? Sent from where? The same pattern or the same man? He asked how long they talked together. Again troubled, she gave the question some thought. "As long as we've been talking?" the Czech woman suggested. Yes, as long as they'd been talking. What happened when they left? Did they again shake hands? Yes, Andreyev had again shaken hands with the tall man, who

430

gave him something from his pocket. A letter? No. A piece of paper? No. A card. A card like a birthday card? No, a small card. Andreyev put it in his pocket.

The following evening she'd seen one of the men standing in the dusk at the stone balustrade at the top of the steps, looking down into their street; which man was he?

The tall man.

But another question had begun to trouble Corkery as he watched and listened, the same question her mother had asked earlier: Why had she waited so long?

After the interpreter left, Corkery showed Gretchen the photographs. He doubted the station's rogues' gallery of the Soviet diplomatic staff would help her identify the two men she'd seen at the zoo; the collection was incomplete and the faces imprecise, photographed or Xeroxed as they often were from a diplomatic passport. He had brought a dozen with him, including a photograph of Nikki Deutsch.

Lips pursed, chin on her chest, she was curious at first, but soon lost interest. She passed over Nikki Deutsch's photograph without a word. After the pictures were put away, he sat for a few minutes and asked her about Holy Innocents, her teachers, and the subjects she was studying. Finally he asked her when she'd last seen her friend from across the hall. She looked up, surprised, her lips moving as if silently counting back the days. She said she'd last seen him on Sunday.

431

"Sunday. The day you went to the zoo?"

She nodded, looking up expectantly.

"I am thinking she is liking it very much, all this questions you are bringing," her mother said.

"I think you're right," Corkery said, pulling on his coat.

Gretchen had been terrified on Sunday, Monday, and Tuesday. Instead of returning to the flat alone, as she usually did, she'd gone to the hotel to wait for her mother. By Thursday her fears had disappeared. Not only had she returned alone to the apartment, but she had found the courage to enter Andreyev's flat across the landing where she had spent so many evenings waiting for her mother's return from the laundry. She'd watered the plants and waited there alone and then hidden under the bed when he had entered. Today she'd given up her secret and taken them to the zoo. Now she sat on the small sofa, pleased with herself as she had every reason to be, and it was her accomplice's smile that answered his final question. If someone had reassured her, told her everything would be all right, who could that have been except Andreyev himself?

Holy Innocents School was a four-story brick building in an open courtyard enclosed by a low wall and an iron paling fence behind the church and parish house. The iron gate at the street entrance was still closed as Corkery drove past; a few women bundled in overcoats with scarves over their heads were waiting on the pavement. He turned around in the narrow alleyway next to the chapel, drifted to the curb fifteen meters from the front gate behind two cars, and turned off the engine. The afternoon was gray; the ceiling lights were on in the classrooms inside. Snow flurries danced across the hood and windshield, vanished and reappeared. He read the *International Herald Tribune* from Paris and waited. The previous afternoon a body had been taken from the Danube, bobbing in the choppy current a few meters from shore. Two boys had seen it and shied clods at it; the wind shifted and drove its mass toward them, the eyes empty mollusks under a sea urchin's pod of matted hair. The skull showed a few lacerations and the pockets were empty; the body had been in the water for some time. The autopsy would be slow and difficult. Holder doubted the body was Andreyev's, still convinced the Soviets had picked him up off the street. Why else would he have left so much intact in his flat?

A few more women had joined the mothers on the pavement. A custodian in a gray jacket appeared and opened the front gate. Ten minutes later a nun led the first group of girls out the door and down the walk to the front gate. Another taller group followed, all carrying book satchels. A third group departed, marching three abreast, dressed in blue jackets over blue jumpers, blue stockings, and blue berets. Corkery wasn't sure he'd be able to recognize Gretchen. He had opened the door to stand in the street and saw her among the girls on the steps in the fourth group. He got back in the car as the group reached the gate and started the engine. As they dispersed outside, he saw her face clearly as she turned and spoke to a classmate. She walked with two girls to the boulevard a block to the west, where they stopped and stood together on the corner. Her two friends crossed the street to the south; she turned north toward Mariahilferstrasse. A hundred meters beyond she pulled off her beret and put it in her pocket. At the next corner, she paused to look in a shop window, gave a glance in Corkery's direction at the oncoming traffic, ran across the boulevard without hesitating at the curb, and disappeared down a side street, away from the direction of her flat. He had to wait for the oncoming traffic to pass before he could follow. The narrow cobbled street had a high curb and no clearance between cars; he had to move behind a parked car to let an appliance van pass. She was crossing the busy intersection by the time he reached the stop sign at the foot of the hill. As he turned into the traffic, she disappeared behind a bus. He maneuvered into the right-hand lane as the bus pulled away, searching the wide sidewalk ahead of him. He thought he saw her passing under the canopy of a florist shop. He accelerated, looking for a parking place ahead of her, but at the next intersection the cars were five deep at the stoplight. The chase stalled. Two blocks ahead an English Ford was leaving a parking place and he moved in behind it, left his car, and walked back along the wide pavement through the growing pedestrian traffic. Bus and tram queues were forming and he paused to look at the route signs, wondering if she'd slipped aboard a bus or a tram. By the time he reached the florist shop canopy, the street lamps were beginning to come on. He'd lost her.

He trotted back to his car and drove to the Innerstadt and the old hotel on Wolfengasse. The service door on the alleyway couldn't be opened from the outside; he walked around front and went in, bought a newspaper, and sat in the lobby reading and watching the front door. It was after six o'clock when he saw the slight figure wearing the blue jacket and blue beret come in and cross the lobby and take the service stairs to the basement.

He went back to the embassy and on to his hotel. After dinner an embassy car picked him up and drove him to the Lausman apartment building. Gretchen met him at the door in her bathrobe, a towel wrapping her head. She'd been drying her hair at the electric fire in the corner of the sitting room. Eva Lausman put the kettle on the gas ring and told Corkery Gretchen had been waiting for him. "Are you bringing more pictures?"

No, he wasn't bringing more pictures. He wanted to ask her how she spent her afternoon.

Gretchen had disappeared into the bedroom and returned with her school satchel. She brought out an orange exercise book, turned the pages, and held it out to him with a smile. The note was printed in English below the conjugation of the verb *to see* but in an adult hand. Corkery knew that she had kept her rendezvous. "God help us,"

435

Eva Lausman said when she saw the handwriting, her hand over her heart. The note read:

> You are obviously a clever man. Being weaker than you, I ask for my freedom because that is according to your principles. Others would deny me that freedom because that is according to their principles. Let you and I resolve this matter as gentlemen in the currency of our times, so to speak. I ask for $50,000 to close out this long overdue account. $40,000 will be deposited in the Banque d'Indochine in Bern in account number 78-952 to the credit of Eva and Gretchen Lausman. The remaining $10,000 will be in US dollars in small denominations. That being done, in 24 hrs I will telephone you at your hotel at 7:25 pm with further instructions.

> A. Andreyev

The lights were on early that dark morning in the suite of offices on Boltzmanngasse. Corkery thought he would be the first to arrive, but Holder was already in his office. From the unfamiliar faces in the corridor and the passage of the NSA communicators and technicians along the inner corridor, he assumed something else was going on.

In Washington, Abbott hadn't hesitated after

receiving his cable. Within two hours of the opening of business the $40,000 was deposited by the Bern finance office through a Luxembourg bank to the Banque d'Indochine. Holder summoned him with a few questions. Andreyev had asked for $50,000 but hadn't said what was to follow, only that they would resolve the matter as gentlemen. What did that mean? "What's this chap going to do, just hand himself over?"

"I think that's the idea."

"You know him better than I do but it doesn't smell right." He asked what additional support Corkery might need. He had little to give and wondered if they might close down the surveillance post opposite Andreyev's flat. He was shorthanded and had a problem of his own. Late the previous night the station watch officer had gotten a hurried telephone call from a Czech claiming to be a member of a Czech delegation led by the vice minister of interior visiting Vienna. In broken English he asked for political asylum but refused to give his name: he was under close watch and mistrusted the Austrian authorities with whom the delegation had been meeting. He thought his opportunity might come the next evening during the formal reception and state dinner. At that point he broke off saying he would call the following day to arrange a time and place. A special communications watch was being set up. On Holder's desk was a list of the Czech delegation, their names and passport numbers obtained from the Austrian Ministry of Interior. The anonymous caller would be among them. Holder was cautiously skeptical about the call.

In late morning a finance officer from the admin staff brought Corkery $10,000 in U.S. currency in small denominations in a canvas satchel. The bills were loose, shabby and worn in their new wrappers. Murphy thought they looked like mob money, crap table stuff. Corkery planned to carry the $10,000 in his overcoat but changed his mind. He went down to technical support and had the bills recompacted in a currency press. He asked for a briefcase, was shown three, and chose the smallest.

The afternoon passed slowly. Murphy was restless and uneasy, leaving his desk a half-dozen times to prowl the corridors. He thought they might need some additional equipment, maybe night-optical binoculars. He went to see what he could find. Corkery began a long cable to Langley, typing it himself but after thirty minutes tore it up and began again. You had to be careful about words these days, like everything else, not be betrayed in little ways, not be tricked into believing the facts and what you knew, words and reality, were in every way the same; that was Washington's illness.

At four-thirty Murphy pulled on his overcoat and said he was going to check the car, leaving behind a cup of fresh coffee and a cigarette still smoldering in the ashtray. Fifteen minutes later the officer on watch opposite the Lausman flat called and said his replacement hadn't arrived.

Corkery told him to hang on.

"What ho! Who's this?" a voice bellowed from the door while Corkery was on the phone. "New staff?" He was a tall man wearing a double-vented jacket; an inch of starched cuff showed. His gray hair was damply combed, ruffled along the back of his neck like grouse feathers. Holder, at his side, introduced him. Corkery, still on the phone, didn't catch the name. After they left, he again told the watcher to hang on. Holder returned and stuck his head in the door. "Any developments?"

"Not yet. Who was that?"

"The deputy chief of mission."

"How much does he know?"

"Who, Binky? Not a twitch. Prowling his empire."

Ten minutes later Murphy called from heavy traffic eight blocks away. The car was a dog; he thought he'd better pick up something quicker. At six Corkery left the office and dropped by Holder's suite but the door was closed and the commo chief was waiting. He went back to his office, locked his safe, picked up the briefcase, and left.

Murphy joined him downstairs in the hotel bar, as restless as one of Abe Runyon's pointers before the hunt back in Pennsylvania. They had a drink and went upstairs and ordered club sandwiches and coffee from room service and watched Austrian TV with the sound turned low. At seven-fifteen Holder's secretary called and asked if they could drop the surveillance watch for that night.

439

Corkery told her no. Ten minutes later the telephone rang again. He thought it might be Holder's secretary again but it wasn't. The voice was muffled and low:

"Is the ticket to Bern ready?"

"It's ready, but I'd like to talk first —"

"There's no time. The Sudbanhof, you know it?"

"I know it, yes."

"You go there now, you buy a paper at the north stand. You go to the taxi queue and take a taxi to Karlplatz. At Karlplatz you wait for the tram to Meidling-Hauptstrasse. You understand?"

"Karlplatz to Meidling-Hauptstrasse." Corkery wrote the names on the telephone pad. "Meidling-Hauptstrasse, right."

"On the east corner is a tobacco shop and a phone box. You wait at the phone box. Between eight-thirty and nine, the phone will ring. You will answer after the third ring. If something happens, tomorrow, I don't know. That's all now."

"Just a minute —"

The connection was broken.

They left the hotel by the freight dock and walked back the alley where Murphy had left the gray Plymouth sedan. "Why not just drive straight to Meidling-Hauptstrasse?" Murphy said. "Scout it out and wait there. Why not?"

"Because that's not what he said."

"Who's to know?"

"He is. Maybe Meidling-Hauptstrasse isn't it, maybe he'll show up at the Sudbanhof. He's probably on the move, taking his chances on the run. We'll move with him."

"You think it was Andreyev?"

"I don't know but I'd say the odds are with us."

"You said he doesn't know you. How's he going to make contact if he doesn't know you? You're just another guy carrying a briefcase."

"Maybe he's seen me come and go. We'll find out. The newsstand and the taxi queue at the Sudbanhof. Maybe there."

Murphy dropped him off in the darkness at a side entrance to the Sudbanhof train station. He walked through the smoky terminal with the briefcase, moving with the crowd, bought a paper at the newsstand, and stood aside for a few minutes, reading the front page, ignoring the crowd around him. The floor trembled with trains moving in the sheds; a whistle sounded, a gate rang closed. He folded the paper under his arm, looked at the clock above the information desk, and followed a baggage dolly toward the taxi queues. Again he stood aside, waiting under the overhang; no one approached. Twice prepared, twice disappointed, he joined the queue. He gave the taxi driver an address on Karlplatz to the north and sat back in the rear seat as the taxi sped away. The driver had the radio turned on and was hunched forward, one arm draped over the wheel, the other fiddling with the radio dial. He drove too fast. He must have been a very short-legged man to drive as he did. When they reached

Karlplatz he turned to ask Corkery the address; Corkery told him to drop him at the next corner. As he paid him through the window, he saw he had only one leg. He was ten minutes ahead of schedule and walked to a tram stop two blocks ahead. Ten minutes later he boarded the tram and stood at the rear, swaying in its motion, watching the dark street behind him. At Meidling-Hauptstrasse he followed an elderly couple out the rear and crossed the deserted intersection under the arc lights. The dark tobacco shop was on the opposite corner; the iron grating was pulled down. Against the wall just to the east was a telephone call box in an illuminated white plastic crypt. Two trams passed as he waited. Steam lifted from an iron manhole in the intersection. Murphy drove by, saw him, circled the square, and eased to the curb a hundred yards away, lights out. He waited against the wall in the cold, shoulders hunched, the briefcase at his feet. A woman walking a dog crossed under the arc light on the corner. Cars drove by at long intervals and droned off in the distance, leaving the square emptier than before. At eight forty-five the telephone rang, a shrill ring that shattered the silence. He waited for the third ring and picked up the receiver.

"What is her school, the little one's?" a voice asked.

It wasn't the same voice that had spoken to him earlier. "Whose school?"

The voice hesitated: "You came from where?"

442

"From Karlplatz."

"And before?"

"The Sudbanhof."

"And the little one's school?"

He felt like a fool. "Holy Innocents."

"Good. The street to your left from where you stand, continue for one block east. The fourth house from the end. Third-floor front." He hung up.

Corkery picked up the briefcase and walked to the corner under the arc light where Murphy could see him, stood for a minute, and turned back past the tobacco shop and the illuminated telephone shell. The narrow street was lined with semidetached three- and four-story brick houses. A ragged little front garden stood inside the iron fence of the fourth house from the end. Through the window of a barely furnished front room on the first floor he saw a white-haired woman bending over a gas grate; two floors above on the third-floor front a pair of curtained windows was dimly lit. At the top of the front steps was a wooden enclosure, like a wet-weather room. A few flowerpots and coal scuttles sat on the concrete floor. The frosted glass door inside was ajar. He pushed it open and entered the empty foyer, paused, and climbed the carpeted stairs to the third floor. A crack of light showed under a door at the front. As he moved along the banister the door opened and a short middle-aged man stood facing him. Corkery walked toward him but as the face came into focus he stopped. He wasn't Andreyev. He

443

had seen too many photographs not to know.

Lost again among shadows and delusions, lies and half lies, fraud and deception, he knew he'd again been deceived — by Langley, by Dudley, by Andreyev, by his own cleverness, and now by the stranger at the end of the hall. Standing in the shadows of an ugly Viennese pension smelling of dust, cabbage, and stewing chicken, holding a briefcase stuffed with ten thousand worn-out American dollars, he'd been drawn too far beyond the limits of belief. He no longer believed in any of it: Andreyev was a fraud, a fiction, a cause he no longer believed in. So was Abbott, so was Frank Dudley, that delirious wanderer; so were they all, the whole bloody circus.

"Who the hell are you?"

He smiled, embarrassed, a short plump man with thinning gray hair and a small paunch below which drooped a pair of dark worsted trousers. On his feet were a pair of fiber slippers.

Corkery moved closer. "I don't know you."

The man shook his head. "No, you don't. And I don't know you. Come in." His accent was thickly Russian. "Andreyev will be coming soon." The room was in partial shadow, lit by a single lamp on a green table near the double windows looking down into the street.

"Who are you?"

His name was Moskvichev. He was a Russian, like Andreyev, but from Odessa. They'd met four years ago in a Bierstube across the Danube canal near Mexicoplatz where the Russian emigrés gathered. They became good friends, both Russian, both emigrés, both men who'd quarreled with their times.

"The Moskvichev from the pension across the Danube canal?"

Yes, the Moskvichev from the pension across the Danube canal, the man who had once rented the top-floor room under the eaves and whose letter press was still there. At the time the *Hausbesorger* was an old friend. He once kept his letter press and a supply of inks, papers, and plates there, his workshop at the time, but the old *Hausbesorger* died. His replacement was less sympathetic. Not Jewish either. Still angry, Corkery had nothing to say.

Moskvichev led him through a cloth-hung doorway and into the adjacent room where a small German-made stainless steel printing press stood against the wall. On the table stood an enlarger and boxes of photographic chemicals and paper. The darkroom was in the closet. He was an engraver by profession. He could manage them all: police certificates, identity papers, birth certificates, even passports, although passports were the most difficult. He opened a drawer in a steel cabinet and showed Corkery a collection of foreign passports and engraving plates, pressed between sheets of rubber membrane.

He was a passport forger, a counterfeiter in the currency of nations. He corrected mistakes of birth, errors of nationality in which Vienna abounded. Most Eastern Europeans would have

445

preferred to be born American, English, French, or Canadian — even Austrian, God forbid, but instead were Romanians, Poles, Lithuanians, Croatians, Serbs, Russian Jews, or Czech Slovaks, like Andreyev's friend, Eva Lausman. Everything was relative. He spoke slowly, mixing German and English, his eyes wickedly bright as he glanced up at Corkery, whose suspicion amused him. In his youth he'd been just as suspicious. He'd also been a Marxist; now he didn't know what he was, except that he was still a socialist. Would socialism survive the martyrdom of the Russian peoples? He didn't know. Christianity had survived the martyrdom of Galileo in 1642. Or had it? He'd immigrated to Israel but remained only eighteen months. To be a Jew was to be outside. In Tel Aviv, what could he be, an engraver and printer? To be a forger was to be a criminal. In Vienna, to be a forger was perfectly respectable. In Vienna, in some little way every man was in some way a forgery, hiding himself, disguising his past. He knew nothing about Andreyev's past.

They returned to the front room. Moskvichev brought a bottle and two glasses from a cabinet. "We'll drink, all right? You're a cynic, I see that." He was still amused. "Why so cynical? You're too young." Corkery coolly declined the brandy, still holding the briefcase. A deck of cards and a newspaper sat on the table between them; in the distance through the windows the blue and yellow lights of Vienna flamed like gas jets. Moskvichev pointed to the newspaper headlines with a stubby

446

finger. "Counterfeiters," he said, moving the papers aside. Everything you read in the papers was false, all written by counterfeiters of a certain kind. "Do you doubt me?" He smiled again.

The phone rang from atop the bookcase. Moskvichev glanced at his watch and got up to answer. He bent forward, frowned, said something, and turned. Andreyev was having trouble. Did he have a car?

Corkery nodded. In English, Moskvichev said yes, he had a car. He listened, and nodded again, looking at Corkery. "Near the Sudbanhof? Yes. Kapelle Park, near the Sudbanhof. Thirty minutes. Yes. The south side of Kapelle Park, the square. Park the car opposite the south entrance. Wait there, yes. Fog lights? The fog lights twice? What color?" He lowered the receiver. "What color?"

"The car? Gray."

"Gray, he says, yes. Blink the fog lights twice. Yes, thirty minutes." He hung up and moved quickly to the door. "Kapelle Park. 'Trouble,' he said. Be quick now. Blink the lights twice when you see him. Good luck for you." Corkery was past him, bounding down the corridor. "Good luck for both of you."

Murphy was waiting in the darkness three houses away. "Kapelle Park? I think I know it but check the map." The car jolted away. He turned on the dash light, braked at the corner but didn't stop. "He said trouble?"

"Trouble." Corkery searched the street map

447

under the dash light.

"He screwed it up, what?"

"I don't know."

"You're sure it was him?"

"I'm not sure of anything." He found Kapelle Park on the map. "Here it is. Three blocks west of the Sudbanhof. You know it?"

"I know it. It's a half-assed way to do it, completely half-assed."

"He's on the run." Corkery was watching the long slalom of red, amber, and green traffic lights on the long boulevard ahead. "Can we make it?"

"Thirty minutes, sure. But it's still half-assed. What about the ten thousand?"

"Here, in my briefcase."

Kapelle Park was a ghostly island under the foggy arc lights. They were ten minutes early. Murphy slowly circled the square as Corkery scanned the park with the night-vision binoculars. Pebbled walks lined with flower beds entered from each side and met at a fountain in the center. The wide circular pitch was surrounded by benches and flower beds and illuminated by amber arc lights mounted on high posts along the outer perimeter; shrubs and trees lay in each shadowy quadrant. "See anything?" Murphy said.

"Nothing. Empty, it looks like."

Murphy drove on. Two blocks beyond he turned down an alley and returned to park on the deserted side street opposite the south entrance. They waited in silence, the engine turned off. From time to time a solitary taxi from the Sudbanhof rumbled around the square and disappeared. An empty Mercedes truck rattled past, its tailgate clanging. A light in the apartment window above them went out. "What's that?" Murphy asked. Corkery told him it was someone going to bed. Five minutes passed. They sat in silence. Corkery lowered his window, took a cigarette from his pocket, but changed his mind. Murphy slumped deep in his seat. "It's screwed up. Jesus —"

A sedan entered the square from the north, slowed, and drew to the curb on the north side of the park. A few minutes later the lights went out. Corkery moved his binoculars. A figure left the rear door and entered the park.

Murphy roused himself. "Can you make him out?"

"Not yet. He's in the trees. Tall, maybe. Hard to tell."

He watched as he reappeared, tall and long legged under the arc lights in the park's center. A second figure had emerged from the far shadows. "Someone's there, someone waiting." The two men embraced and stood apart again on the south side of the fountain, visible down the corridor of shrubs.

"Queer place," Murphy said. "Right out in the fucking open. What the hell kind of tradecraft is that?"

"What he wanted, queer as a twig, like everything else."

"Did he say he'd be alone?"

"I assumed it."

449

"It's half-assed."

"It's always half-assed. It was born half-assed." Corkery bent forward with the binoculars, straining to see the two men, two blurred gray shadows against a field of electric green. "Like looking through an aquarium tank."

"Anything yet?"

The two men were still talking but the taller man was gesturing. The shorter man pointed in their direction; the tall man turned toward them.

"Blink your fog lights."

"Now?" Murphy blinked the lights. "You don't suppose one of them is Dudley, do you?" he said suddenly.

"I don't suppose anything." The taller man hesitated and turned back, his gestures more emphatic. The other man pulled something from his coat collar and held it out. The taller man took it and turned quickly in their direction. "Blink your lights!" Corkery's heart was racing. "Something's wrong."

"I did."

"Blink them again!"

Murphy blinked the lights. The tall man walked quickly toward them. "What's he doing?"

"He's coming —"

At the north entrance the headlights of the waiting sedan flooded on. Someone left the front seat and called out. Corkery moved his binoculars but the headlights from a third car entering the square flashed across the windshield, blinding him. The car veered into the square and slammed on the brakes.

Murphy turned. "What the hell is this circus, what's going on?"

"Christ knows." At the north entrance the waiting sedan was in motion. It came careening around the square, engine roaring, high beams on. Corkery was out of the front seat, running across the cobbled street. Caught in the full glare of the oncoming headlights, the tall man dodged aside, the sedan braked; a door was flung open, the car accelerated and the door caught him, smashed him forward a few yards, and flung him savagely aside. The sedan sped on. Cornering out of the square, it spun on a patch of ice that had lain there all that winter day in the shadow of the cathedral, bounced off a wall of yellow stone, regained speed in a shriek of stripped gears and smoking rubber, and was gone.

Two men had leaped from the third car. Corkery heard Holder's voice. Holder first reached the figure broken against the curb, then Corkery, Murphy at his heels. The head was turned queerly aside, one knee was raised, flexing and unflexing in agony. Corkery kneeled to look at the bloody face, heard the strangled breath in his throat, and prodded Holder aside. "Don't move him. Get an ambulance."

Holder looked up. "What in God's name are you doing here?"

"Same reason you are, a phone call." He studied the narrow face and the stiff straw-colored hair as he felt for his pulse. The right hand still held

451

a scarf Andreyev had given him. He took the scarf and below it saw the dark stain in the fabric of the right-hand pocket of the raglan; a vial had broken. He leaned closer and smelled chloroform. "The Czech who called," he said to Holder. "Where were you to pick him up?"

"Here. He called thirty minutes ago. Why? What in Christ's name is going on? Do you know this man?"

"I'm not sure."

"Andreyev?"

"No, not Andreyev." Corkery stood up, still holding the woolen scarf, looking through the shadows toward the arc lights at the center of the park where the two men had met. He walked down the pebbled path to where they had embraced and stood talking as they had that Sunday at the Vienna zoo. It all made sense now. Here in Kapelle Park they'd finally met alone, two old GRU colleagues renewing an old friendship, two men well and favorably known to one another, Andreyev and "Comrade X": the same pattern, the same men. He looked at the scarf in his hand. It was a red scarf.

The park was deserted. He heard nothing, no retreating footsteps, no car moving away, only the sound of the klaxon far in the distance. Andreyev was gone. He walked back to where Holder, Murphy, and two other men were waiting. Murphy had thrown his coat over the figure against the curb and wadded his own scarf behind his head. He looked down at the unconscious face. "It's a

452

long story. I don't know his name but he's a Russian, like Andreyev."

Abbott would tell it in his own time and in his own way. The Russian lying in the gutter was Abbott's man and had been all those years. He was Pitchfork, the agent Abbott had been protecting in Moscow, Berlin-Karlhorst, and later in Washington, where he'd frustrated the FBI's clumsy attempt to compromise him after he'd seen Andreyev in the Connecticut Avenue bar and the Senate office building. Comrade X and Pitchfork were the same man, the man Abbott's bogus Russians in Montreal later had tried to deliver Andreyev to at the Safeway store in northern Virginia and failed. Why? He didn't know. It was an operation only desperate or stupid men could have conceived, and Abbott wasn't stupid.

As Andreyev's old GRU colleague, he'd probably been sent by the Russians to persuade Andreyev to come home, first that Sunday at the Vienna zoo, now in Kapelle Park; if not by persuasion, then by more violent means. But Andreyev must have told him what he couldn't tell him at the zoo, that he knew he was the Russian Andreyev was to meet in the Safeway store in northern Virginia. The evidence was as simple as the red scarf he had given him. How would the CIA's Russians in Montreal have known Comrade X would be found at a certain hour pushing a grocery cart and wearing a red scarf unless the CIA had sent him?

Andreyev had given him the scarf and his choice.

Either go back to his KGB or GRU posting or go home to the Americans waiting in the car across the square. What choice did he have? Andreyev had flummoxed them, Washington as well as Moscow. But how masterfully he'd done it. Now he was gone again, a man ahead of his times, just as Elinor had said.

9

A CONFESSION
IN THE COUNTRY

It was midafternoon when they left Paris and drove west across the dun-colored countryside. The old carriage road was narrow under rows of poplars, sycamores, and plane trees set too close to the crumbling asphalt. Dietrich had rented a car, a maroon Fiat hatchback he had difficulty managing, too quick and lively for his feet and hands. For someone who'd once danced in a cabaret, he drove clumsily and erratically, drove miserably in fact.

"Don't use second gear so much," Dudley said. "You can shift now." The passing fields were barren under a toneless gray sky.

"Sorry."

"Shift more quickly, more fluidly." Annoyed with Dietrich's driving, he consulted the road map that lay between them to conceal his nervousness but it brought no relief; an uncertain destination, a strange car, a hapless driver. They were on their

455

way to meet with Deutsch and Eigner at a château in the countryside. Feeling himself a prisoner, he looked out the window. A few hayricks stood in the distance. Black and white Guernsey cows grazed along a fenceline. He felt the car grind down and turned. "Why are you shifting?"

"There's a lorry ahead."

"Use your brakes then. That's what brakes are for."

"I'm sorry."

"Stop being sorry. You don't have to be sorry. We've plenty of time." Poor Dietrich. His endless apologies, like his haplessness, exhausted him. He pitied him, pitied his romantic hopes and his graceless ineptitude. Disgraced in every way, even in the smallest things, he was unlikely to change. Now he was in love with a brown-eyed Tunisian busboy in a Tunisian restaurant.

They passed the farm truck, bounced over a railway crossing, and turned southeast through a village of a half-dozen houses set close to the road. Their gardens and fields were deserted in the afternoon vacuum. The villa was five kilometers beyond at the end of an unmarked lane, once a carriage road, lined with the gnarled trunks of ancient trees too often pruned. A gatehouse stood just inside the crumbling stone pillars, half hidden by shaggy cedars and poplars. A small Frenchman emerged listlessly from the gatehouse, pipe in his mouth, opened the sagging gate to what had once been a feudal estate, and beckoned them through.

The twisting drive passed over a narrow bridge

near an abandoned pond filled with dead cattails and brackish green water and ascended past the rotting wharf and up the hill toward the château. Radio masts lifted from the circular turrets at each end of the stone-and-stucco villa. An antenna field and a microwave dish sat on the high slate roof; the third-floor shutters were closed. In the center of the pebbled courtyard was a stone fountain. Three cars were drawn up nearby. Dietrich parked next to a black Citroën with diplomatic plates. To the east of the courtyard stone steps descended to a formal garden or parterre, now a patch of worn brown turf where a volleyball net hung forlornly from two portable stanchions. To the side were open fields and in the rear a misty woods. A rest house, Dudley decided as he left the car. Stiff legged, he paused to look up at the communications field on the roof. It was a weekend villa like the ones owned or rented by Paris embassies for their diplomatic staffs. He saw no flag.

Dietrich admitted his nervousness and asked if he could remain in the car. They were ten minutes early. Surprised but not displeased, Dudley agreed. A stout man in a gray worsted suit had left the massive front door and waited on the stone steps. He bowed and greeted him in German, like an innkeeper in some remote hotel in the Taurus. *"Komm,"* he called. He led him inside, where a second man waited, took Dudley's coat, and led him down the carpeted corridor to an oak door. He opened it and nimbly stepped aside. Dudley entered alone.

It was a large room, once a chapel, paneled in dark wood. Two stained-glass windows lay in an alcove behind a green Ping-Pong table. Above the stone fireplace was a faded tapestry and above it two crossed pikes. On the walls were Interflug travel posters. One, circa 1937 or so, showed an old corrugated-sided Fokker transport lifting itself into the nullity of a blue Tyrolean sky. To the side was a recent Olympic poster; a statuesque East German Isolde in blond braids was crouching, a shot putter's ball at her ear. Facing the fireplace was a couch covered in brown plastic flanked by lounge chairs with metal arms. Two metal-rimmed cigarette urns sat nearby; cigarette butts littered the hearth and fireplace.

At the far end of the room in front of a bay window two men sat behind a long table separated by three empty chairs. One man got up and came to greet him energetically, motioning toward the single chair drawn up opposite the three empty chairs.

"For you, please. Just a few minutes. We are still waiting." Since he didn't introduce himself, Dudley assumed he wasn't Eigner.

He sat down and the German returned to his chair. The second man, smaller and grayer, continued to watch him silently with sad blue eyes. As Dudley met his gaze, he stirred and looked away. With nothing else to do, Dudley studied the high-beamed ceiling and the stained-glass window, thinking of the von Winterfeldt estate in East Prussia. The manor house had been built in 1715;

in the great hall had hung portraits of Frederick the Great, and Frederick William II and IV. He looked again at the East German Olympic poster. The Prussian kings had visited there, down the long drive sheltered by lindens and three-hundred-year-old oaks. Now what? A Polish hostel for the lumpen proletariat, a party retirement home? Depressed, he opened his letter case and sat looking at his notes. A moment later he heard the sound of a car crunching across the pebbled drive, the sounds of doors slamming, muted voices, and sudden laughter. When the door behind him opened, the two men at the table stood up. He remained seated and didn't lift his head. Three men moved swiftly across the parquet floor and filed behind the table, bringing with them the bracing smells of the winter outdoors. Hearing their voices, he realized they were Russian.

What on earth did Deutsch and Eigner think they were doing?

He looked up, prepared to be angry, but the slim, dark-haired Russian at the center of the table nodded agreeably. The Russian to his left, older and grayer, also nodded. The short brown-faced Russian to his right ignored him. Deutsch wasn't among them. He wondered which one was Eigner.

The dark-haired Russian in the center, obviously the senior diplomat present, if diplomats were who they were, looked at a few typewritten pages he'd taken from his attaché case.

"For what is it you bring us here for, Mr. Dudley?" he began, still looking at the document in

459

front of him. "For what is it we are to help you with?"

"Bring you? I'm here to talk to Herr Eigner, Herr Deutsch and Herr Eigner."

"Who is Herr Eigner?"

The short brown-faced Russian next to him leaned toward him and whispered something. The older Russian nodded, glanced at Dudley, and turned a page. "Someone in prison, to be released from prison. You ask that a man be released from prison."

"Well, yes, to put it crudely, but —"

"What is this man's name?" Again the younger Russian interceded, this time to turn a page in the document his senior was reading. Dudley observed that the senior Russian was certainly poorly briefed, to say the least. The older Russian nodded, found the name, and looked at Dudley. "Andreyev?"

"Andreyev, yes."

"He is why you are here?"

"Not completely. I mean, these were to be exploratory discussions with Herr Eigner, purely preliminary discussions relating to the possibility of having Andreyev returned. I emphasize here the word *possibility*, the possibility of such an exchange, not the —"

"Exchanged? How exchanged?" His voice was quick and abrupt.

"An East–West exchange. We're talking theoretically, of course. Selected prisoners on our side exchanged for certain individuals you might be holding. The modalities would have to be worked out and that would take time —"

The Russian looked at him blankly. "Modalities? Explain, please."

"Yes, certainly. To begin with, lists of names would have to be drawn up, exchanged, and agreed to. A protocol would then be drafted to be signed once the signatories were in agreement on all particulars. Absolute secrecy would be essential —" Dudley's dry mouth, the sweat gathering on his forehead, the uncomprehending look on the face of the senior Russian, and the words he heard himself uttering gave way to the sudden knowledge he was speaking absolute rubbish. He was forced to pause. "Andreyev would be the most important name on our side," he heard himself say. "We would not consider any exchange unless his name was on the list. My superiors were quite explicit on that fundamental point."

"Superiors!" the brown-faced Russian broke in impatiently. "What superiors?"

Coloring, Dudley looked at him. "My superiors."

"Superiors? Tell us their names." In his words he heard a contemptuous echo of his own slightly nasal New England drawl and reddened even more. The Russian in the center raised his hand for silence without looking at the small Russian.

"And this man you say is in prison, he is Andreyev?"

"Andreyev, yes. The same man who wrote this article." He took the document from his letter case

461

and slid it across the table.

"And these superiors, who are they?" the Russian asked calmly as he looked at the Xeroxed article.

"At present, I'm instructed not to be any more specific than that. As a matter of fact, I've gone quite beyond my brief already, even in being here. My preliminary discussions were to be with Eigner. Is he coming, by the way? Anything else would be inappropriate, to be discussed only at the proper time."

"Proper time!" the young Russian broke in. "What proper time? To talk in more riddles!"

Shocked, Dudley ignored him. A German woman in a pale green nylon dress appeared at the end of the table, bringing tea, coffee, and fruit juice. A smaller woman, similarly dressed, followed with a tray of cups and saucers. Dudley asked for tea. The one housekeeper set out the cup and saucer, the other poured it out from a brown-and-black plastic carafe. Standing quite close to Dudley, her arm lifted, she smelled sourly of dried sweat. The Russians took coffee.

After the two women left, Dudley said, "The man who wrote the article in front of you is now in a Soviet prison in Moldavia. I do not call that a riddle."

"Preposterous," said the brown-faced Russian with contempt. His English was without an accent and far better than his senior's. "That is completely preposterous."

"It isn't at all preposterous. The man who wrote

that article is now in a Soviet prison in Moldavia. His name is Major Alexei Alexovich Andreyev. He was a Russian army officer who crossed into West Germany in the sixties, immigrated to the United States, and is now being held in a Soviet prison. I have been sent to set in motion the negotiations that might lead to his release. That is all I'm willing to say at the moment."

The gray-haired Russian to his left spoke for the first time. "He is a traitor then." He sat forward, his veined hands together, his sad blue eyes fixed on Dudley. "For us is clear, Russian traitor in Russian prison. For you is not clear, American citizen in Russian prison. You come and say we must talk, we must release this man —"

"Not must, not *force majeure*. To discuss, that's all."

"To make propaganda, to make scandal —"

"Not at all."

"Not at all? So you know. And because you know, is all right." The gray-haired Russian unfolded his hands, shrugged, sighed, and sat back.

The senior Russian had leaned forward to question the dark-haired man at the foot of the table who had been transcribing the conversation. "Secrecy," the stenographer said, consulting his notes. "Yes. He said 'secrecy.' "

"Secrecy," the Russian repeated, looking at Dudley. "In greatest secrecy, you say. Secret. No one to know. No one but you, Mr. Dudley, all alone. No embassy peoples, just you. So what is this, Mr. Dudley? We will talk honestly. What is it you want from us?"

"I've told you."

"But no, no. You don't tell us. You don't say nothing." He lifted the papers in front of him and dropped them aside. "Is no one named Andreyev, no Russian major, no one who leave German Democratik Republik the night you say, no one at all. Is no one in Russian prison in what you say, Moldavia? So why this make-believe, for what reason? So tell us now in secret, no one to hear. Tell us now, what is secret game you play, what is it you want?"

"I've told you."

"And I tell you too, I tell you everything. There is no Major Andreyev. No. So what is it, what is it we do for you? We are businessman too, Mr. Dudley. We do business. We come here to do good business with you, yes. Secret business, yes, if you like. So tell us."

"I've come for the reasons I've said. If you doubt me, why have you kept me waiting all these days?"

The senior Russian smiled. "Kept you waiting? Is you who have kept yourself waiting. Did we bag you to come? No. We not bag you to come. Is not us. Is you. Why are you come here, Mr. Dudley? For what reasons? We have something you want? Or you, you have something we want? So tell us. Tell us something so we can be serious, so we can say, 'Yes, this man, he is serious man, he is man we can talk to.' Tell us something serious, Mr. Dudley. We listen now."

Dudley searched his memory for something to

say but could think of nothing. The room was silent except for the ticking of a clock from somewhere off to the right. Dusk was gathering outside beyond the high windows. The voice came again. "You were in Vienna, Mr. Dudley. Tell us about Vienna. Were you serious man in Vienna? When were you in Vienna?"

Dudley stirred. "In 1957, 1958."

"And who was your station chief in 1957, 1958?"

He watched the mist lifting from the pond. "A man named Tyndall. Ralph Tyndall."

"And what was your work at the station?"

Dudley cleared his throat. "I had certain operational responsibilities."

"Was this Tyndall also known as Noel?"

"Noel? Yes, I think he was."

"Good. Now we are serious, Mr. Dudley. You were in Berlin?"

"Yes. Yes, I was."

"Who was station chief?"

"The station was in Bonn. I was at the Berlin base."

"The Berlin base, yes. Who was chief of Berlin base?"

"Phil Chambers."

"Who?"

"Chambers, Philip Chambers."

"Where is Mr. Chambers now?"

"He's retired. He lives in Washington. In Georgetown. He has a very lovely home in Georgetown, a lovely home."

465

"So tell us something about your work at Berlin base. What was your title?"

"I was a deputy chief."

"Deputy chief. At the Berlin base?"

"Yes, at the Berlin base."

"How many men, how many men you have in Berlin?"

Dudley hesitated. "That's hard to say. Twelve or fifteen, I suppose. We were always bringing people in —"

"You speak German?" It was a different voice; he was still looking through the window.

"Yes."

"You speak Russian, Mr. Dudley?"

"A little. I haven't kept up, although I try to keep up with the literature. I studied Mongolian once —"

Someone spoke to him in Russian. He didn't reply. He heard laughter. The senior Russian raised his hand.

"Tell us something about Berlin, your operations there. You had interesting operations there, successful operations? That was a long time ago but maybe something interests us."

He could think of nothing to say.

"Too long, you think, too long ago? So tell us something from last year, from this year. Tell us something. Tell us about Mr. Julian Abbott, for example. He interests us." Dudley didn't reply. "So Mr. Abbott later. Is all right. Tell us now about Otto Rauchfuss then. You do business with Otto Rauchfuss all these years? He had certain contacts, he has told you things? What things did he tell you?"

They waited. He heard someone sigh, heard a chair being moved back, heard the creak of leather as someone shifted, heard it like the creak of new snow underfoot. When he dreamed of Berlin it was always winter there: the grid of black streets, black canals seen through a curtain of snow, tiny crow's feet on a blanket of white, oaks with crowns as fine as black brushes against a horizon of medieval gray. Closer by, men were moving; he remembered windows, the smell of coal dust, midnight vespers at the smoky church in Nicolskoi, Nina kneeling alone at the altar rail, the broken fresco of sunlight on a baroque doorway near the Wall, the smell of burlap and oil, the deep scratches on the counter of passport control at the Friedrichstrasse crossing, the two students shot to death in the Saint Sofia cemetery after a night tunneling escapees under the Wall near Bernauerstrasse. George Tobey thought one was McIntosh's *Tunnelgraber;* McIntosh said they were someone else's students. There was a fearful row in his office, a dreadful row, and no one knew whose students they were. Someone telephoned to ask about travel orders and Jessica's Pan Am ticket, and suddenly he was in the rear salon in Charlottenberg and Tricia was bringing him a whiskey-soda and telling him how Otto's friend with the little garage in Kreuzberg had found the short circuit in the electrical system, an erratic wire in the starter, so now she could drive without fear of the Mercedes failing to start each time she stopped, and then she kissed him and said she'd let the servants go and they would dine alone that night, thank God, but from her luminous voice, eyes, and touch he knew what she knew, knew she'd again been with Eric Prosser all that long afternoon, its miracle still illuminating everything she saw and touched. Who could ever deny her that? When he dreamed it would always be winter, like his memories of St. Paul's, the dark afternoons ice-skating in the Grunewald, Nina at her high window, snow dusting the rubble where so many still lay buried in 1946. For a moment, watching the mist beyond the windows he lost all sense of time and place, lost in a mystery deeper than the one that had brought him here. But then a voice broke from deep within and he found himself unable to speak, not knowing what he had come to find, what he had come to recover: *Tricia! Nina! Tricia! Why you? Why did it have to be you?*

Lifted away, still not knowing, he heard the terrible heartbreak of another voice in another time: "I'm here to ask for his freedom, can't you understand that? Can't anyone understand that! A man falsely betrayed, falsely accused, and falsely punished! By you, by us, by everyone! Why in God's name did it happen! In the name of decency can you answer that? Can anyone answer that?"

He heard the terrible force in his voice, saw the shocked faces staring up at him, felt the tears warm on his cheeks, and realized he was standing, towering above them. No one spoke, no one moved, looking up at him as if he were mad. Only the old Russian with the sad blue eyes finally stirred, breaking the terrible silence. "For whose freedom, Mr. Dudley? Whose freedom do you come to ask for?"

He sat down very slowly, very painfully, and they watched from across the table as he rattled the teacup from the saucer and brought it to his lips, watched with a certain fascination, the three Russians, the blond German who had entered late, and the German stenographer; the Russians not knowing what they had come to learn but now, having learned nothing, disgusted with themselves for allowing the East Germans to deliver them there, ashamed for themselves and for this pathetic man sitting there in his ugly shoes, this preposterous man the East German services had been monitoring for so many years, this short-peckered New England gentleman who would be a Bismarck, as Otto Rauchfuss had told them over the years, this rosy-cheeked pansy who lusted after girls dressed as boys and boys dressed as girls, this stiff-necked American puritan with the tears drying on his cheeks.

"Is finished, I think," the senior Russian said softly, gathering up his papers. They stood up and filed out silently from behind the table, followed by the German stenographer, leaving Dudley alone except for the blond German who had entered late. Outside he heard voices, some angry. A door slammed. A few minutes later two cars drove away. Only then did the German get up, move down the table, and drop the paper in front of Dudley in disgust. He left, slamming the door behind him. It was an obituary clipped from an East German newspaper. Otto Rauchfuss had been buried two days ago in Stansdorf Cemetery in East Berlin.

From his hotel window Corkery watched the winter dawn dissolve the Vienna darkness and in the first gray light discovered it was snowing, a thin slanting snow that swirled at the window and reappeared like frost on the street below. Passing trucks blew it like ashes over the cobblestones. In the distance a small figure limped across an empty square, an old woman carrying two bags. He watched her silhouette dim and fade into the distance like winter smoke above the rooftops.

He called the station watch office, which had nothing to report, and shaved and dressed, listening to the BBC. The landscape had shifted during the night. To the east morning had already arrived: mortar shells in Beirut, a car bomb in Athens. Everywhere to the east the night was being recovered, the rubble cleared and trundled away, and even as it was people were coming awake to haul away the dead limbs, like charcoal makers, readying the faggots for tomorrow's fires. Washington was asleep. Reagan had addressed a newspaper editors' convention.

It was a small matter that would never see the headlines. Andreyev was gone, Abbott's Russian

470

had come home. The cable had come from Langley at two o'clock Zulu following the altercation in Kapelle Park; he was Major Nicolai Glushkov, a senior KGB officer once posted to Washington with the GRU, now assigned to East Berlin. He had a concussion, a broken arm, and a broken collarbone. He had been evacuated to Frankfurt. Corkery still didn't know why Abbott's Russians in Montreal had tried to deliver Andreyev to him during his Washington posting. It seemed senseless, but Abbott had made a career of improbabilities. He wondered what bizarre operation Langley's dean of determinism had been cooking up.

Thinking about it, or rather speculating about it, he decided he didn't care. Recent events had opened up crevices in his professionalism. The Cold War moraine was giving way under his feet. He felt like a man on an ice floe, watching a continent disappear, and wondered if cynicism was an occasional occupational hazard or the ultimate career reward.

A little after ten o'clock he got a call in Murphy's office from Paris over an open line. Morgan couldn't tell him much. They'd found Dudley's hotel room. The whole affair had taken an ugly turn.

"Ugly, very ugly. I sent you a cable. Glanville's working with the French on it. He wants you here, quick as you can make it. He thinks you guys have hung him out to dry. Just a warning, okay?"

He went up to the commo center to wait for

471

Morgan's cable. It was already there, one of a dozen yellow tapes, looped, tied, and hanging from the wire in a commo room. He watched as the communicator fed the yellow tape into the crypto teleprinter and read it off the roller. Three paragraphs were enough. He turned away in disgust. He went downstairs to travel and reserved a seat on a morning flight to Paris. Upstairs again he cleared his desk and shredded his cable file. Murphy was with an embassy crew sent out to box up Andreyev's personal possessions, tag them, and ship them to Langley. In the inner hall he met Holder, on his way to a meeting someplace. "Still here? What's up?" He thought Corkery was on a plane to Frankfurt. He had a lab report for him from Technical Services. The scrap of paper he'd sent them was identical to that used for Austrian passports. What was that all about? Corkery told him to send it to him at Langley.

Late that afternoon he managed to do his only shopping in Vienna. Not far from his hotel on a street lined with expensive shops he found the one Holder's secretary had recommended. There were velvet cushions in the window, gilt cupids over the archway, and a thick glass door with a gold-leaf medallion in the center. Inside were illuminated cases attended to by women in gray smocks. The shop's artifice was arranged in gold and silver wrappings, like cubes of boullion. Corkery chose a box of chocolates for his mother in Pennsylvania and had it gift-wrapped. Around the corner was a gift shop where he prowled for thirty minutes, trying to find something for his father. He finally left with a Bavarian beer stein made in Czechoslovakia, the sort you could pick up in any airport souvenir shop, army PX, or K mart.

An hour later he was waiting for Eva Lausman in the gathering twilight of the hotel service entrance. She came out alone, wearing her thin brown coat and rubber boots, a scarf over her head. It was windy and they had difficulty talking as they walked along the street. Passing a pair of cellar steps that led to a small restaurant, he suggested they have a drink. She looked at the menu under glass beneath the miniature chalet roof next to the leaded glass door and said it was very expensive. She was reluctant but he told her he was leaving the following morning. The interior was warm and crowded. Wrought-iron lamps hung along the stuccoed walls below the beamed ceiling. They squeezed into a table for two at the rear. A young waiter in a burgundy jacket appeared with two dinner menus.

No dinner, Corkery told him. Eva Lausman didn't know what to order. Corkery suggested sherry.

"No sherry," the waiter said, suddenly bored as he saw her worn cloth coat.

"Campari, maybe," Corkery suggested.

"No Campari." The waiter looked away toward a couple just entering. There were no tables. The woman was wearing a fur hat.

"How about some wine, maybe vermouth?"

She asked for vermouth, if only to send the

waiter away. He had spoken to the budget and fiscal officer at the embassy about her case and how she might transfer the money from Bern to her account in Vienna. He'd given her his name and telephone number and suggested she call. The waiter brought the drinks, setting them down carelessly. She found the vermouth bitter and didn't touch her glass after the first sip. No, she hadn't called the man at the embassy but promised she would. He was probably a very busy man. She was sorry Corkery was leaving, sorry about Andreyev, sorry about the money, which she didn't think of as hers at all. She would talk to the Reverend Mother Maria at Holy Innocents. These were very confusing times. The couple at the next table got up and the woman in the fur hat sat down. As her heavy scent reached them, she looked anxiously at the well-dressed woman in the fur hat, then at the queue beginning to form inside the door. Aware of her uneasiness, Corkery finished his drink and called for the bill. Standing outside, he offered to call a taxi. She declined. He said he'd try to keep in touch with her. She turned in surprise. That would be very nice, she said. She hurried away. Watching her go, he wondered why he had wanted to talk to her.

He left Vienna the following morning. The plane lumbered down the access runway, creaking ominously, buffeted by the blasts of crosswind whipping out of the cloudy sky. As the jet sprinted down the runway, he watched the dipping wings, not certain the shuddering aircraft would ever lift its cargo of Austrian, German, and French businessmen from the tarmac. A few flecks of rain darted across the window, flagellate and long-tailed. As much as most men, he occasionally thought of himself as a coward, not in his fear of pain or violence, but in his dread of loneliness, that palpable gray nothingness that now lay only a wing length away. Maybe Andreyev feared the same thing. *Byezbozhnik,* the third page of his Russian military paybook had read so many years ago: Without God. Vienna drifted in fragmentary patches through the broken clouds, vanished in a thimbleful of space, and they were lost in gray.

Morgan met him at Charles de Gaulle in Paris.

"Busy man," Morgan said as they drove away. His eyes were bloodshot. He'd come from a two-martini lunch with two visiting straphangers from Washington. The afternoon traffic was heavy and slow. As they waited at a stoplight, Morgan yawned and scratched his mustache. "There was this fruit I heard about in the navy," he said. "A pathetic guy when you think about it, real pathetic. You felt sorry."

"I read your cable," Corkery said, watching the cars move out of the side street. "Dudley isn't a fruit."

"Maybe not." They drove on. "He was sure mixed up with a couple of fruits." Corkery said nothing. After a minute's reflection, Morgan said, "This guy in the navy was a pharmacist's mate. Used to twit around the chaplain's office. Then one night during General Quarters a couple of old-timers jumped him in an ammo locker. They found him under a tarp with an eggbeater stuck up his keister, no shit. Had to get a surgeon in to cut it out."

Corkery studied the faces passing along the sidewalk as if searching for someone. "What was an eggbeater doing in an ammo locker?"

"Beats the hell out of me."

"You didn't see it, just heard it."

"Just heard it, yeah."

"So did I. It's an old bullshit story, like the ones Reagan tells at his press conferences. I heard the same story in the Med a hundred times."

"No kidding."

"No kidding. That shit's been around the Med longer than the Phoenicians."

Morgan pondered this for a minute. "How come you're so touchy? I wasn't calling Dudley a fruit, just making a comparison. This German with a busted skull was a homo. They find him with another guy, both as queer as queens. Add it up. The French police tell us this Dietrich had been putting Dudley to bed for weeks."

"Who said?"

"This concierge, this Algerian. Didn't you read my cable?"

"I didn't get that far."

"All I can say is you better read the reports."

Corkery turned. "I've been reading too many reports, that's the trouble. Too many of them. Langley's papered with them, so is Washington — the FBI's, DIA's, State's, Reagan reading the

White House funny papers to the White House press corps, your cables, mine, everyone else's, end to end and wall to wall. That's Washington for you, everything in words and on paper, but it never happens that way, never did and never will. It's always something else. So is Dudley."

Morgan tried to digest this but gave up. "Jesus Christ," he said finally. "I was only telling you."

At the embassy Glanville had gotten a cable from Langley, wanting to know where Corkery was. They'd expected him in Frankfurt. What was he to tell them?

"Tell them I'm in Paris," Corkery said. "What the hell else?"

Late that afternoon he visited the ugly little hotel in a narrow cul-de-sac near Barbes-Rochechouart where Dudley had been registered. Along the sidewalk at the corner Algerians and Africans sold secondhand clothes from cardboard cartons and metal racks. The alleyway was littered with paper, cans, broken glass vials, and an occasional hypodermic needle. Inside the hotel a drunken African sat on the narrow stairs moaning to himself, his woolly head in his hands. His scaling feet were shoeless despite the cold. Nothing in the second-floor room suggested Dudley had been there. It was a small foul room with a single window, a narrow iron bed, a dresser and a table, both heavily scarred with cigarette burns, a room that so completely denied Frank Dudley Corkery could only conclude he was now locked in a surrealistic nightmare completely his own.

In Dietrich's room a block away evidence of the melee was still there — a smashed TV set, a broken lamp, and a broken window. Sheeted with plastic, it rustled with the wind blowing along the alleyway and leaked a constant trickle of cold December air. Sometime after midnight two nights earlier the Algerian concierge had heard the glass splintering, angry voices, and sounds of violence. Climbing the stairs to investigate, he had been savagely assaulted by the two men running down. Both were foreigners; one was carrying a camera. In the room above he found Dietrich bloody and unconscious on the floor, attended to by a hysterical young Tunisian. He summoned the police, Dietrich was rushed to the hospital and on the following day was interrogated by the French police. There the whole bizarre tale began to unfold. He was an unemployed cabaret performer from Hamburg who'd been given a large sum of money by an employer in Berlin, a man named Vogel, and sent to Paris with certain duties to perform. Sexual entrapment may have been the purpose, but Dietrich, by then unshakably loyal to his paterfamilias, Frank Dudley, had refused to be more specific. In a suitcase in Dietrich's room the police found copies of telex messages from Bern. These led them in turn to Frank Dudley's room nearby, to Otto Rauchfuss's freight forwarding office in Paris, now abandoned, and finally to the West German and American embassies.

Morgan had questioned Dietrich in his hospital bed. He hadn't seen Dudley since seven o'clock on the evening after their return from the château, identified by the station as a rest and recreation villa rented by the East German embassy. He didn't know what had happened there. Dudley was like a man anesthetized afterward, not his usual self at all. He barely spoke and had asked Dietrich to drop him off in the Marais. Dietrich returned the rented car, met his Tunisian friend at the restaurant, and they returned to the pension. Just after midnight, rude rough hands had wakened them. Dietrich wept as he told the story. Both men were German but he didn't know them.

"Limp as an oyster by then, I suppose," Morgan said as they ascended in the embassy elevator. "A lovely pair. Climb anything, some of these Arabs. What now?"

Corkery said he wasn't sure. He wanted to think about it during the evening at his hotel on the Left Bank.

It was midafternoon when the train from Barcelona pulled into the rural station. The rain had passed through an hour earlier, the day was waterlogged, and the beach deserted. At sea the horizon was walled by an ugly squall line. Two nuns, a crippled old fisherman, and a conductor in a worn blue suit carrying an oilskin portmanteau departed the coach ahead of Corkery, moving cautiously down the steps, their bow legs moving them like crabs.

Twenty meters away a small brown-faced Spanish taxi driver in a gray rainslicker studied the five arriving passengers as he leaned against the bat-winged front fender of his polished thirty-year-old Mercedes, probing his teeth with a twig. The fisherman would walk, the two old nuns would be driven away by the elderly priest who had come to fetch them in his battered old Deux Chevaux, and the train conductor would wait in the tiny station for the evening express to return him to Barcelona. This left the tall foreigner, whom the taxi driver's sharp eye now settled upon disagreeably.

He was wearing a beige raincoat and carried a calf briefcase. His blond hair was unkempt and his beardless face Nordic pale. The taxi driver saw not a tourist fare but a penniless vagabond from the North, a hiker or beachcomber, like the Swedes and Germans who came in June to camp on their beaches, find work in their hotels to the north along the sea, and make love to their daughters and sisters, their blond legs sticking shamelessly from their little nylon beach tents until autumn drove them north again.

Corkery turned, searching for the car from the Barcelona base he'd asked to meet him. The damp sea wind smelled of brine and kelp. A dory drifted in the light swell; gulls floated among rafts of seaweed. The dark beach, as black as volcanic ash, reminded him of Iceland.

Esta loco, the taxi driver thought as he removed the spice-flavored toothpick. Crazy, this long-necked German come to sleep on the beach. He turned his head derisively to spit with the wind. He'd wasted his time and petrol meeting the afternoon train from Barcelona but still he waited, reluctant to admit defeat and leave the station with his rear seat empty in full view of the despised priest and two nuns who still sat in the Deux Chevaux admiring the new church linen brought from Barcelona. His eyes moved toward the dark smoke of squall line as he waited for the Deux Chevaux to leave. He heard something thump against his automobile, turned, and saw a suitcase resting upon his polished front fender. He scrambled indignantly around the car. *"Un minuto, ahi, muchacho!"*

"Scuzi." Corkery removed the suitcase.

"Sabe con quien esta hablando?" Carefully he dusted the front fender with his pocket polishing cloth. Do you think I'm Italian, stupid one?

"Pardonnes. Casa Prosser, sabes ir desde aqui?"

The driver didn't reply immediately, still examining his polished fender, suspicious of the foreigner's strange Spanish and his menacing German size. Yes, he knew the Prosser villa but it wasn't called the Prosser villa but the Hallstein villa. It was a long way and the road was miserable. Picking up a fare hadn't entered his mind. To tell the truth, he'd come to meet his wife's cousin but she'd missed the train. He should go tell her the bad news. He bent over to give the crown of the fender a final buff and mentioned a fare. Corkery hesitated, looked behind him toward the high hills, and agreed. The taxi driver pocketed his dust cloth and smartly opened the door, but the old Deux Chevaux had driven away by then, the old fisherman was out of sight, and no one remained to witness his victory.

The climbing road was roughly paved. The inland village was perched high on the slope, a cluster of rooftops and white plaster houses six kilometers to the southwest. The lights were on in the butcher shop and bakery, making the afternoon seem even darker. A tin sign clattered in the winter wind above a restaurant. The second-floor hotel was closed for the season. They circled the fountain in the main square where a horse drawing a rubber-tired kerosene cart was being watered. The twin-towered church stood among ancient rocks on a promontory above the town. Farther along were the post and telegraph and a cantina shaded with cypress trees with an arbor to one side. A mud-splattered new Renault was parked in front. They continued out the tarmac across the high plain where the fields were divided by stone fences and an occasional olive tree, the sea again visible in the distance. A seam of apricot light showed below the curtain of clouds to the west.

The taxi driver said fine weather would soon come. His father was a fisherman and he knew the sky as well as his father had known the sea. Corkery asked him if he'd taken any fares to the farmhouse recently. No, he'd taken no one there for years. He knew the man named Prosser. He once arrived every July and stayed until August but he no longer came. He was a strange man, a gentleman, but his hands were rough and callused, his knuckles raked with saw or stone scratches, and he didn't own a fine German or American car. He was always civil, always had a word for everyone, even the old priest who was suspicious of him for reasons only priests know about, and who gave him nothing in return except a cold nod.

He turned his small head and spat out the window.

He turned off the highway across the coastal highway and onto a narrow gravel road where pools of water lay in the potholes and depressions from the afternoon rain. On the rise ahead Corkery recognized the plantation of pines and cypresses Jessica had described, concealing the high stone wall enclosing the courtyard. The road ended in a turnabout in front of the high double doors. In the shed across from it was a rusting orange-and-gray Volkswagen camper, tires gone, resting on blocks.

Corkery banged at the heavy door as the taxi driver watched from the Mercedes. Chained and padlocked from inside, the doors yielded a few inches but no farther. The driver told him it was just as he said; no one was there. Corkery walked up the road toward the sea and saw fresh tiremarks in the damp roadbed where a car had turned in, backed out, and driven off. He walked along the high east wall, searching for a way in. The stone wall was eight feet high, crowned with a mortar beading ornamented irregularly with green wine-bottle shards. In some places the beading had crumbled away. The courtyard wall gave way to the stonework of the farmhouse on the east where two high windows looked toward the sea. The shutters were open. He tried to lift himself to the sill but failed. Through the trees behind him he could see the sea and hear the surf pounding on the beach hidden below. The wind blew through the cypresses, a faint siffling sound Pennsylvania pines made, but the wind smelled of the sea and the smell of the old stonework, pine nuts, even the earth was different. He circled the rear and returned through the trees to the west. He paid the driver and told him to come back in two hours. If he hadn't come in two hours, he would begin walking toward the village.

After the Mercedes drove off he searched the shed for a ladder but the only timbers he found were a few short lengths of roof joist. Under the rear seat of the Volkswagen camper he found a set of rusting tire chains and untangled them in the road. Shackled together they might carry the wall but he needed an anchor; a concrete block might do. In the corner of the shed he found a tireless truck rim. He shackled the four chains together and wired them to the tire rim through the bolt holes. Lifting the chains and rim, he thought the contraption too awkward. He tried a hammer throw, the chain swung slowly, rotated 360 degrees as he rotated with it, but technique was everything and he had none. The truck rim banged off the stone wall two feet short. He finally settled for the old high school gym set shot, all thirty pounds together, heaved straight up; on the second try the rim cleared the wall. He grabbed the trailing chains to keep them from following and took in the slack until the rim seated itself against the rough stonework on the other side of the wall. He tested its strength, worked the chain back and forth to break away a section of the mortar and glass beading, and hauled himself up. As he approached the top he was tiring fast and the tire rim had begun to work itself free. His right hand found the top, then his forearm; with a final heave he pulled himself atop the wall, releasing the chain. It rattled across the stonework like an anchor chain rattling out of its locker as the whole jerry-rigged contraption went crashing to the flag-stones below.

Exhausted, he lay atop the wall, feet dangling. It had begun to rain, a misting rain he was unconscious of until he felt it against his face as he raised his head. His sweater was ripped in the sleeve; blood leaked across the back of his right hand. He lifted his right leg, kicked a crumbling section of beadwork away with his heel, straddled the wall like a vaulting horse and dismounted, right leg, then left, turning as he slid from the top to grip the stone edges with both fingers before he dropped to the flagstones below. In the center of the deserted courtyard was a small pool littered with leaves and storm-broken boughs; a blue glazed statue of St. Francis stood at one end. A single canvas camp chair was nearby. A long-handled minnow seine leaned against the far wall. Nearby lay a half-dozen discolored blue snorkel masks and rubber swimming fins.

The kitchen door was unlocked. It was a large room with an adobe-and-stone oven and a stone fireplace where a wood fire had burned recently. The smell of pine still lingered. Lying among the burned and charred pine nuts were mounds of black ash and shreds of paper. Copper pots and vessels hung from the whitewashed wall above a counter near a white metal butane gas stove. In the center of the room was a long table that might have once been a refectory table. On it in front of a chair under an oil lamp was a pannikin from a mess kit holding a piece of chicken and a mound of cold beans. Nearby lay the basket with the roasted chicken and the pot of beans, both half wrapped in a Spanish newspaper. In another basket were five eggs, two unlabeled bottles of Spanish wine, a water jug, and a bottle of olive oil. On a second chair was Dudley's brown attaché case, standing open. It was empty.

An airline ticket envelope was next to the kerosene lamp together with a ballpoint pen. He had torn open the envelope to use as notepaper, but whatever he had started to write he hadn't finished. In addition to the fragrance of recently burned pine nuts there was another smell in the room, the smell of musk, most powerful near the gas stove where a coil of copper tubing dangled, disconnected from the missing butane cylinder.

Corkery went down the stone corridor between the two bedrooms. In the first the bed was empty, the mattress rolled back, but in the second a mound of shadow lay on the pallet beneath the window. On the floor nearby was the butane cylinder. A length of rubber tubing coiled up across the mattress and lay on the pallet below Frank Dudley's jaw. Stuffed into the end of the tube was a cloth, now dry, still touching the corner of his chin. Down the unshaven cheek ran a dried stain from his mouth; the vomit had dried like a crust of porridge. His mouth was half open, his neck corded and hollow, his face something battered by the sea. His open eyes stared past Corkery as he touched the cold hand and continued to look past him as he lifted it, not in shame, not in anguish, not in sorrow, not in any emotion Corkery could recognize.

He let the hand drop and pulled the counterpane over his face. On the Moroccan rug at the foot of the pallet was a nylon suitcase. Kneeling he zipped open the suitcase, found a bundle of clothes and caught the smell of soiled linen, bitter medicines, and the foul little hotel room in Barbes-Rochechouart. The room was in full shadow. He went back the corridor to find the generator room, passed a glass-paned door, and looked in. The ceiling was of skylights set at angles in the roof. Where Jessica had painted, he supposed. The generator tank was empty.

He lit the oil lamp and went back to the bedroom and carried the nylon bag to the end of the pallet

487

where the body lay. Inside were a soiled shirt, socks, and two pairs of underdrawers. Lying in the bottom was a silk-lined leather writing case, empty except for a manila envelope, a Eurail pass, and two prescriptions from a Dr. Alain G. Mollet at a Paris medical clinic on Rue de Tolbiac. *Medicine for what?* He held the prescriptions under the lantern; Mollet was a cardiologist. The manila envelope was empty. He replaced the prescriptions in the writing case, put the clothes on top of it, and returned it to the floor. In the airless little water closet down the corridor, he found a wash-basin and a dop kit. Inside were a razor, a tin of French shaving cream, and two vials of pills from a Paris pharmacy. On the kitchen mantel was a ring of keys.

He crossed the courtyard and unlocked the padlocked double door, stood for a moment in the road, listening for a car, changed his mind and went back to the bedroom. He lifted the butane cylinder and hose from the floor next to the pallet, carried them back to the kitchen, and reconnected the stove. He left the lantern burning on the kitchen table, crossed the courtyard, and stood looking back toward the high plain. He saw nothing, no car lights at all, and turned toward the sea. Beyond the shed was a pile of lichen-covered stones. Down the track toward the cliff he came upon a pair of metal columns topped by a filigreed metal arch; under the arch was a rusting gate with a ducal crest locked by a rusting iron chain. There was nothing on either side of the columns and nothing beyond, just a copse of pines, vines, oleander, rosemary, and wild grasses. The old Andalusian estate, he supposed, the one Jessica mentioned.

He walked to the top of the cliff and stood looking out over the Mediterranean where the light was passing. Far down the beach a Spanish farmer was pulling a cart piled with dried seaweed. Gulls floated like gray chips on the sea below. Here they had come, summer after summer, Jessica waiting here in her swimming suit, hugging her knees, waiting for her father to take her to the beach below. So many summers ago, so many years during a time that would never come again, not in Jessica's lifetime, not in his. *"Jessica sent me,"* he would have said a week earlier. *"I've come to take you home."* Now he'd come too late.

There was something decent and honorable about Frank Dudley, but something terrible as well. He'd seen the consequences of the most shameful experiences of his age, yet had remained unchanged in certain ways, enjoying its privileges as if they were God-given virtues, blind to its arrogance, blind to its madness, blind to its nightmare surrealism as dark as his own these last weeks. He'd always been protected by something, some vein of self-righteousness that had always protected men against self-discovery; not quite faith, not quite belief, not quite religion, Elinor Wynn had said. What was it? Whatever it was, there was something in Frank Dudley he pitied, something in all of them he pitied, feared, and sometimes despised. Because he despised it, he supposed he feared it in himself as well.

The sound of a car roused him. He turned in the fading light and saw the headlights approaching the cliff from the coastal highway. The headlights flicked down as he walked toward the car.

"Corkery!" he heard someone call.

He waved his hand and continued on. It was the Renault he'd seen in the village. The two men were from the Barcelona base and had brought the stonemason, Prosser's custodian.

"Dudley's here someplace," one called. His name was Phillips. "He told the mason here he was going to meet his wife and daughter here for the holidays."

"That was twenty years ago," Corkery said. "Where have you been?"

"You found him?"

"Inside. Go get the local coroner. He's probably the doctor. We've got to get the body out of here."

10

A COLD WAR REQUIEM

On his Saturdays Adrian Shaw prepared his own breakfast at his house in Alexandria, a ritual he'd followed for years although he didn't fancy himself a cook. He enjoyed his solitude in the kitchen, especially autumn and winter when the light in the garden was as gray as the Maine coast where he spent his annual holiday, investing the kitchen with the primal mystery of the earth's beginning. Never good at sports as a youth, he'd had a passion for geology. Rainy New England weekends sent him upstairs under an attic dormer to pass the long morning in uninterrupted seclusion with his microscope and mineral collection. Now he recovered his privacy in the early-morning kitchen or on his hands and knees in the rear garden. Roses were his specialty.

On this December morning a fine Atlantic mist shrouded the garden; the patio flagstones were damp from an overnight rain. The coffee was perking, two strips of bacon sizzled in the frying pan, and a single egg was cracked and waiting in a salad bowl. He had just returned from scattering nuts for the patio squirrels when the phone rang. Annoyed, he waited for a second and third ring before he lifted the receiver from the wall above the kitchen counter. He disliked receiving telephone calls before seven in the morning. His mother-in-law, asleep upstairs, was an invalid. It was another of those dreadful Saturdays. Abbott was in Europe.

"Shaw here." At the sound of Susan Fern's voice he drew his robe closed. "Good Lord. Found him where?" He heard the door open upstairs. "What's his condition?" A soft tread crept down the back stairs. "I'm sorry, I'm terribly sorry." He ignored the furious scratching at the door opposite leading to the basement. "Yes, I know it's confusing. No, it's not the time to say anything, not yet. Where's Corkery now? I need to talk to him. Of course I'm coming in. Thirty minutes or so. Get hold of him. But Spain! What on earth was he doing in Spain?"

The iron skillet was beginning to smoke. He hung up and took the skillet off the range. A moment later his wife joined him. She was small and plump, wearing a quilted bathrobe. Her pitifully thin hair was pinned up in a white skullcap, like a Shaker's cap. "What was that about?" Her voice was hoarse. They'd been out late the previous night, one of those tiresome little office retirement dinners that begin awkwardly and end deliriously

492

as the wives continue the talk begun at the dinner table, picking bare the bones of their common ignorance of their husbands' professional lives.

"The office. You're down early."

"I couldn't sleep. Your toast is burning." She ignored the smoking toaster, took a cup from the cupboard, and shuffled to the coffeemaker. He salvaged the burned toast, scraped the embers into the compost pail, and carried his plate to the breakfast table in the alcove where the *Washington Post* lay in its plastic wrapper. His wife had coffee and smoked a cigarette sitting opposite, bathing him in the smoke of her Pall Malls as she yawned herself awake, eyes shining with tears. They were childless. At certain moments as she sat in inert self-indulgence, the glandular fat on her neck and jowls so conspicuous, the loss seemed to him especially pathetic. Her name was Florence.

His sister-in-law joined them, also in a bathrobe. In appearance she was very much a younger fascimile of her older sister, including the sparse hair and the dress and shoe size. Daughters of an Episcopal clergyman who'd ministered to small-town parishes in the Pennsylvania coal fields and New England factory towns, they'd intermingled their wardrobes since childhood. She typed letters for an obscure historical society on F Street run by a sisterhood of Anglican spinsters. Most were futile appeals to the National Endowment and other foundations for the restoration of old churches and rusticating graveyards. The histories were endlessly described at the dinner table.

"Did I hear the phone?"

"Adrian has to go to the office."

"Already? Poor Adrian." She gave a small pout as she opened the basement door to free her Yorkshire terrier. "Poor Gypsy." A furious scraping and scratching followed as the little dog raced hysterically about the tile floor. She opened the back door and a raggedy cannonball shot out into the mist. The patio squirrels fled for the trees.

"Is Mother awake yet?" asked Florence.

"I don't think so. And what time did you two pets get home?"

"A little after twelve, I think. Wasn't it a little after twelve, Adrian?"

"Twelve-twenty-two, yes." He didn't move his eyes from the newspaper, although his mind was elsewhere. Poor Frank Dudley. An incomprehensible mess, all of it, a total mess, utterly and absolutely. How in God's name could it be salvaged?

"So tell me about dinner?" his sister-in-law asked. "Who was there?"

"Everyone," his wife said. "Everyone except Abbott." She gave the name a mournful whisper.

"Oh, dear. Where was he?"

"Frankfurt, someone said, didn't they, Adrian? Poor Adrian." Another pout. "He never goes to Frankfurt."

"Poor Adrian."

Silently he gathered his dishes and escaped upstairs to dress.

At Langley dirty snow lay along the access road and was humped along the verges of the parking lots. Susan Fern was anxiously waiting for him in his second-floor office, avoiding the two visitors waiting outside in the second-floor suite, her chinless face even paler in the wintry morning light. One was from Personnel, the other from Public Affairs. Both needed guidance. Five phone messages lay on his desk.

She was at wit's end: was it heart failure, death by suffocation, or suicide? There were two cables from Madrid. Personnel, the seventh floor, and Public Affairs wanted immediate clarification. Where had Frank Dudley been all these weeks? Whom had he been in contact with? Dudley's wife hadn't yet been informed; neither had his daughter. Both had called and left messages the past week, asking for Corkery. What were they to be told? Inquiries were bound to follow.

Abbott had added a more ominous possibility in an eyes only cable from Frankfurt: death by foul play. Any of these possibilities might be raised in the aftermath of a terribly confusing case soon to grow sinister if steps weren't taken; it was only a matter of time before someone leaked the story. Abbott had left Frankfurt and Glushkov to fly on to Paris to meet Corkery, but Corkery had vanished. The Paris station didn't know where he was. Glanville was livid: "A loose cannon on deck," he'd reported twenty-four hours earlier in a cable complaining to the DCI, typical of Abbott's counterintelligence division high-handedness. Now Corkery was in Spain. He had sent a four-line cable. He was at the U.S. airbase outside Madrid, where he had brought Frank Dudley's body.

"Get hold of Corkery for me," he told Susan Fern.

"I have a call in. He's in Madrid."

"I know he's in Madrid, dear girl. Please get hold of him. Track him down immediately. Tell the people outside to give me an hour. Where are the Madrid cables?"

Corkery's cable reported finding the corpse, nothing more. According to a longer cable, the death certificate signed by a Spanish doctor in the village concluded death by unknown causes. Since he had no facilities, no autopsy was performed. In a personal comment, he said Dudley might have suffocated, possibly by his own hand; lung congestion was also a possibility. The air force pathologist at the U.S. airbase outside Madrid thought the forensic evidence unmistakable: Frank Dudley had died of a heart attack. From vials of nitroglycerine in his suitcase and two prescriptions discovered in his letter case written by a French cardiologist, it was clear he'd suffered two attacks of angina in Paris. Corkery had found the body, fetched the local Spanish doctor, watched his examination, witnessed the death certificate, and accompanied the body to the Madrid airbase for an autopsy. What were his conclusions?

Thirty minutes later Shaw reached him. It was three o'clock in the afternoon in Madrid. Shaw was at his desk, alone in his office except for Elinor Wynn, who had entered a minute earlier, ignoring the closed door. Now she sat in the brown leather chair opposite Shaw's desk, listening. Corkery was in a vaulted commo room in the embassy in Madrid.

"Heart attack," Corkery said. "I don't think there's any doubt."

"You're sure of that. I mean, there's no doubt in your mind."

"None at all."

Shaw hesitated. "The way he was found, did that suggest to you any other possibility —"

"No. He died of a heart attack, Adrian. He suffered two attacks of angina in Paris. I found vials of nitroglycerine in his dop kit and a couple of prescriptions written by a French doctor."

"Good. I don't mean good. It's tragic, of course. I mean, we have to be absolutely clear about this. The relatives have to be informed." Again Shaw hesitated. "This Madrid cable mentioned suffocation, maybe strangulation, possibly suicide."

"That wasn't mine. Just guesses. Phillips put it on the wire before the air force autopsy."

"I didn't think it was yours. Splendid. I don't suppose you've seen Julian's cable from Frankfurt, the suggestion of foul play —"

"Panic. A shot in the dark, that's all —"

"Panic? Julian? But Julian's always —"

"A shot in the dark. Forget it. He's right here. Do you want to talk to him?"

Shaw was bewildered. "Julian's there, with you now?"

"Sitting here with me. You want to talk to him?"

"Yes — well, I mean, if he wants to add anything —"

Corkery paused and then his voice came back. "He has nothing unless you have —"

"No. Heart failure, all right. That's definite, you're sure. Good. Heart failure. You'll bring the autopsy, of course. Now, about the body."

"It'll be at Andrews tomorrow evening, six P.M. local. I'll be coming too. Personnel needs to find out what's to be done with it."

"Yes, that's something Personnel was asking about. Good, we can go ahead and inform the relatives now." He paused, not knowing quite what to say. It was Corkery's voice more than anything. "You're all right then, are you? I mean —"

"I'm all right. Just one thing more. I don't want to see or talk to anyone, you understand. No one. Can you send a car?"

"Yes, certainly." Shaw put the phone down, looking at Elinor in amazement.

"It's over. Dudley's dead, heart failure. Corkery found him. He was in Spain."

"Julian's with Kevin?"

"Yes, Julian's with him."

She got up. "Then we'll never know, will we?"

They sat at a heavy walnut table in a vaulted grotto in a Madrid cellar restaurant, both drinking, Corkery listening as Abbott unburdened himself. The tables in the nearby crypts were deserted at that early-evening hour. The air was thick with the fragrance of wine and wine casks, of candle wax, dampness, and moldering wood. The cellar had the smell of a medieval cathedral at the hour of vespers. Like the old Gothic Quarter of Barcelona, Abbott had said approvingly.

At the hospital in Frankfurt two days earlier, Major Nicolai Glushkov had told him he'd written his own orders in Berlin when word came that the East Germans had located his old GRU colleague Andreyev in Vienna. The initial KGB plan was to kidnap him off the street. Glushkov persuaded hqs he could fetch him home without incident. He carried chloroform if he failed.

" 'Old friends' still doesn't explain it," Corkery said. "Why would you try to deliver Andreyev to Glushkov in Virginia? I still don't understand that."

Abbott smiled cryptically through the twilight as his long fingers fiddled with the stem of his wineglass. It was his fourth glass. Corkery had the feeling he might be light-headed.

It wasn't easy to explain. A strange case, very strange, and just as complicated. As Corkery had guessed, Major Nicolai Glushkov's cryptonym was Pitchfork. He had been recruited in Brussels years earlier. He'd been very good those first years, very reliable, no hint of his later indiscretions, the braggadocio, the recklessness, the alcoholism, the womanizing.

After postings to Brussels, Warsaw, Prague, and Berlin, he'd returned to Moscow and the First GRU Directorate on Arbatskaya Square, handling GRU illegals abroad. In Moscow again after those years abroad he'd had difficulty adapting. There had been a nasty divorce. He'd inveigled an overseas post, this time to Washington, much to Langley's dismay. There he ran afoul of the GRU rezident, a sour little GRU officer who thought him not only a swaggering braggart but a drunk. At two successive national day receptions, he had been loud, vulgar, and rowdy. He'd insulted the Czech and Polish ambassadors and their wives, or so it was reported. He'd taken liberties, acceptable at his earlier postings in Eastern Europe but not in the U.S.; he'd hunted in the Shenandoah and sailed at Annapolis without permission. The GRU rezident put him on a short leash and considered asking GRU hqs for his recall.

A few weeks later an embassy attaché reported seeing his old GRU colleague Alexei Andreyev up on the Hill. Old friends, they'd once shared a third-floor office at GRU hqs in Moscow near the Khodinka airfield. Glushkov had been in Warsaw when Andreyev had crossed the border into West Germany. He'd never had any reason to doubt Andreyev's loyalty and told Langley Andreyev must have defected under GRU control, a dispatched agent.

He decided to scout Andreyev out on his own. He waited for him one evening in a Pennsylvania Avenue bar but Andreyev ignored him. He saw him a second time outside a Senate hearing room, spoke to him but again had been rebuffed. Having twice failed, he sent a message to Ed Rudolsky asking Ed to arrange a meeting with Andreyev.

Rudolsky refused. A few weeks later he repeated his demand. He claimed he was being returned to Moscow for assignment to the lowly Fifth GRU Directorate, working with GRU units in Soviet military districts, an assignment that would effectively end his value to Langley. Bringing Andreyev home would rejuvenate a career that was erratically in decline. He gave Ed Rudolsky an ultimatum: either arrange a meeting with Andreyev or he would act on his own.

"He'd become impossible by then," Abbott said. "Vain, rash, and dangerously impulsive. He was drinking more than ever. Like most egomaniacs, he took very stupid risks, not courage so much as bravado. He thought no one cleverer than himself. He may have been lying about his Fifth Directorate assignment but we didn't know. He was grasping at straws, and so was the FBI, which stupidly planned to entrap him once they discovered who he was." Abbott's voice droned to a whisper with the passing of the waiter along the stone floor. "Perhaps it was vanity, nothing more, a coup de theatre. But by then his usefulness was becoming questionable. He wasn't only a nuisance but a liability."

With little to lose, Abbott decided to have a run at Glushkov's rabbit. Ed Rudolsky came up with the Montreal false-flag operation. They didn't tell Glushkov all its details since they weren't sure how Andreyev would respond. He'd refused to acknowledge his old GRU colleague when they met on the Hill, but he had shown a puzzling loyalty

501

in failing to identify Glushkov from among the photographs shown him by the FBI.

In the meantime the KGB had begun to reconsider Andreyev's case on the basis of the GRU's sighting in Washington. He had been a long time in the U.S., knew a number of personalities at the Pentagon and elsewhere, but had failed professionally and fallen on hard times. The KGB routinely monitored Slavic studies meetings. When Andreyev went to Montreal a GRU or KGB officer identified him, reported his presence, and may have put him under surveillance.

On the final day an unknown Soviet officer, obviously under instructions, dropped a postcard near Andreyev's restaurant table to be mailed to Dresden. The postcard was probably returned to Andreyev in Washington by another Russian — who, when, and where, no one knew. It must have been as a result of that meeting that Andreyev was told Boris and his accidental cousin weren't who they claimed to be. Andreyev may have suspected his old friend Glushkov was somehow involved.

"So the whole thing fell apart," Corkery said.

Abbott nodded. "A very agile mind, Andreyev's, very agile. An intuitive mind as well. He'd known Glushkov for many years, going back to their early student days in Moscow. He apparently considered him an opportunist, nothing more, vain and impulsive, but with a certain romantic swagger. But whatever his weaknesses, Glushkov was a man difficult to dislike. Andreyev, much more the intellectual, may have pitied him, I don't know —"

"He wouldn't compromise him."

"No, he wouldn't compromise him."

Andreyev apparently told the Russian who'd returned the Montreal postcard nothing of Boris's instructions for a meet in the northern Virginia suburbs. On the chance Andreyev might show up, Rudolsky sent Glushkov to the Safeway store but didn't say who he would meet. Andreyev failed to appear. He may have come early, identified Glushkov, and left. They didn't know. Two days later Andreyev vanished. After his disappearance the Soviet embassy in Washington was in turmoil; several diplomats were recalled, including Glushkov and the GRU rezident. The GRU rezident was retired. Glushkov survived hqs suspicion, transferred to the KGB and spent three years in Moscow, assigned to the First Directorate, and was again posted to Berlin. He never knew he was to meet Andreyev at the Safeway store until Andreyev told him in the meeting at Kapelle Park.

"So you were wrong about Andreyev," Corkery said, "wrong all along. So was Glushkov. He wasn't a dispatched GRU agent at all and never had been."

Abbott gave him a wintry smile. "Possibly. I'm not sure. But it wasn't only what Glushkov told us. In the late fifties we began to see a new type of Soviet defector. Andreyev fit the profile. A new kind of agent who represented the duplicitousness you found in the post-war generation of Russians. They'd risen through the ranks that way, not through murder but through hypocrisy, a kind of murder of the self. Like the czar's, the Soviet system has always been based on duplicity and deceit, hypocrisy too; any totalitarian power structure always is. It's the sickness of a bureaucracy that can never cure itself until the old tyrant is dead. But it never does, you see. All those who consented to their own degradation are contaminated too. On their faces they see the dead king's pox. They murdered their selves yet lived on. I thought Andreyev one of them."

He lapsed into silence, the long pharaonic face, the sculpted fingers, the breath from the tomb. He roused himself again. "I suppose this is what psychiatry, what psychology is all about —"

An entire body of modern knowledge didn't exist for him, Corkery thought, but said nothing, waiting.

The carafe was again empty. Abbott looked at his watch, decided reluctantly not to ask for another, and sighed. Madrid was one of his favorite cities, Barcelona too. "Madrid, Barcelona. You breathe it in, don't you? Its long history, its memory." He rose stiffly, hobbling for a moment, as if his legs troubled him, stooping in a twilight still thick with the fragrance of corrupt wine casks, medieval candle wax, and rotting wood. He breathed in again. "History is the memory of states, someone said. So it is. Always."

History the memory of states? As the words echoed through his mind — what states? — Corkery found the answer and at last recognized the simple truth

504

of this sad, tormented man. It all finally made sense. No wonder his morbid secrecy, his contempt for the bastardy of the streets, his fury at popular protest, whether the Vietnam student insurgents at home or Third World guerrilla insurgency abroad. He understood neither. How could he? By tradition, culture, and intellect, Abbott was a European, not an American. *Raison d'état* and the sanctity of the great European nation-state were sovereign in his imagination. The small and the weak, whether individuals or nations, would be ruled, deceived, manipulated, or coerced into carrying out the will of the strong and the great. However sterile, corrupt, or tyrannical, the status quo must be preserved. Abbott was a cabinet diplomatist of the nineteenth century, a historical fossil, a man who didn't belong in the rowdy, vulgar, egalitarian twentieth century at all. The Cold War expressed as perfectly as an ice crystal the frozen symmetry of his mind. Its end would destroy him.

"You've done a remarkable piece of work," he murmured as they approached the waiting car. "One last word, something you shouldn't forget. You and I work in a world of mediocrities, don't forget it. You're not one of them. Remember that, never forget it." He paused a little unsteadily, putting his hand on Corkery's sleeve. "You have remarkable energies. Quite remarkable."

So there it was: they were both intellectual royalists. Corkery opened the door for him, shut it, and went around to the other side. "Never believe anything I tell you," Abbott had told him. Recognizing the source of that corrupt loyalty Elinor had so often talked about, he didn't believe him now.

How many planes had come home? Adrian Shaw asked himself, standing nervously in the shadows outside the operations room at Andrews Air Force Base as he waited for the Air Force DC-8 to descend to the tarmac out of the dark December sky. Planes bringing crippled pilots home from Hanoi prison camps, hostages from Tehran, from Lebanon. Now this one. Twenty yards away waited the Agency sedan and driver that had brought him.

He stood alone, wrapped in his gray-green ulster, his gray head lifted, keeping apart from the small group waiting near the two cars and the hearse sent from Bethesda Naval Hospital that would carry Dudley away. Louise Dudley, taller than the rest, wearing a black Persian lamb coat, stood with someone from Public Affairs. Jessica Dudley was accompanied by a tall dark-haired young man in a dark blue overcoat. Shaw hadn't intruded, hadn't even introduced himself.

A mystery still, much of it. He had been a part of it, had played a minor role. There were no TV cameras, no newsmen, no photographers, no yellow ribbons tied to mailboxes or front yard trees. Unlike politicians, Pentagon weapons systems publicists, and the White House Press Room, intelligence chiefs couldn't hold instant press conferences to proclaim a covert operational victory.

In time Andreyev's name and Glushkov's might surface in the press and elsewhere, perhaps Dudley's too, their stories told but only in fragments, all three to become subjects of popular curiosity. Their mystery would defy explanation. They should expect that, young Corkery especially. He made a mental note to himself to raise it with him.

An air force officer came out of the operations room and looked off to the east. A DC-8 was descending gooselike toward the tarmac. Shaw turned, saw it lumber onto the runway, and again felt a moment of exhilaration.

The three names would surface but the details would remain murky. An article or two might get written, relying upon erroneous sources and drawing false conclusions. If more questions were raised than answers were available, as would happen, the three names would inevitably come to stand for Soviet stealth and their own dreadful incompetence. Every conspiratorial bureaucracy views its failure as its antagonist's victory, whether the State Department in combat with the Pentagon, the Pentagon with the Office of Management and Budget, CI with the FBI, or Washington with Moscow.

As the mystery deepened the entire episode would give way to what Abbott called the "Third Man Complex," an aberrant and diseased state of mind to which the popular imagination and popular journalism were susceptible. The Third Man might be a Russian, an Englishman, or an American, but whoever he was and whatever his nationality he was always lurking about when inexplicable events occurred, that unknown figure standing far off in the shadows who personified everything we don't know at any moment in history. He might seem as real as Philby, that palpable old fraud, as Abbott so often said, proof of the unfathomable duplicity on the other side, but in truth he was only the long shadow cast by the lamp of our common ignorance and just as insubstantial, the doubt that haunts our uncertainty, the fear that despite our heroic pretense we're only too weakly human after all. Easier for the popular mind to explain the mystery in that way than to confess that the complexity of institutions, people, paper, and events has outgrown our capacity to understand what we know. The world had become too infinitely complex to be knowable in all ways, like history itself and the unbearable mysteries of the human heart. In that sense, Andreyev, Major Glushkov, and even Frank Dudley, poor soul, would all remain unknowable.

The DC-8 was there, wing and tail lights blinking, turbines whining down after long, long flight. The hearse and the two cars drove forward along the concrete apron. Shaw followed in his own black sedan. The two dozen military passengers left first. Most were officers and their dependents returning home from U.S. military bases for the holidays, some with arms filled with PX packages, oblivious to the sad cargo carried in the rear. After they moved away, a hydraulic lift rolled into position at the rear cargo door. Two flight nurses in gray nylon flight uniforms stood in the door and then moved aside. Three enlisted flight attendants moved the casket onto the lift and held it as the lift lowered. The casket was moved into the rear of the hearse, which drove slowly away, followed by the two cars. Neither the wife nor the daughter had left the sedans.

The flight crew had begun to leave the plane. Shaw continued to wait. Corkery finally appeared in the cabin door, stood talking to one of the flight nurses, and came down the stairs. Shaw left the rear seat and signaled him. Corkery came to join him.

"Been waiting long?" he asked.

"Not long at all. Are you all right?" He was rumpled and unshaven, looking very much the vagabond, carrying a suitcase and a calfskin brief-case.

"Not bad. A little tired." He put his bags in the front seat and they got in back. The driver drove away.

"I have to tell you what remarkable work you've done. I've no doubt Julian told you."

"In his own way. Thanks, but one stray's still missing."

"Stray? What stray?"

"Andreyev."

"That's right, yes." Taken by surprise, Shaw settled back in his seat. Andreyev was the least

509

of his concerns. As the car left the gate, he said, "There's one thing I wanted to ask you while there are just the two of us. It's about the autopsy, and how you found him. I mean, his physical and mental condition, precisely what you found there in the farmhouse —"

"He was dead. There's nothing to ask."

"I realize that, but at the same time —"

"There's nothing more to ask, Adrian. He's dead. There's nothing I can add to that. It's over."

Frank Dudley was cremated and buried in a private ceremony in Boston. Four days later a memorial service was held in an Episcopal chapel in northwest Washington. Decorated for the Christmas holidays, the church smelled of spice, greenery, and the heavy fragrance of lilies. Louise Dudley, wearing black, arrived early and sat alone in the front pew. Jessica arrived late and was accompanied by her aunt from Boston, several cousins, and a tall dark-haired young man in a dark-blue overcoat. Her passage down the center aisle was followed by a rustle of movement, like a warm wind through a summer wheat field, but her face was hidden from the turning heads by a black veil. Phil and Eva Chambers were there and so were Roger Cornelius and a handful of Dudley's retired colleagues. Adrian Shaw came alone. Most of those in attendance were from the church congregation. Frank Dudley had been a vestryman. This explained why Adrian Shaw, looking about from a middle row, saw so few people he recognized.

The organist played Bach, Buxtehude, and Praetorius during the prelude as the church continued to fill. After a long pause, during which a police klaxon could be heard wailing in the distance, two Anglican priests began the procession, swaying down the center aisle in their long white robes. The taller of the two, thin and silver haired, mounted the oak pulpit and in a sad, sepulchral voice read the Opening Sentences from the Forty-sixth Psalm. Entering the church at the last moment was Colonel Davenport, Louise Dudley's neighbor in rural Maryland. A shy man and the sole companion to her grief these last days, he knew none of the mourners and had waited outside out of respect. He would have stayed away but was reluctant to leave her alone after the service, as he knew she would be. Now the sight of her distant figure stirred in him such feelings he found it difficult to imagine this sad ceremony had anything to do with her.

After a song and the First Lesson, the Episcopal priest, who'd studied at the Yale drama school, read from the Book of Common Prayer. A second priest read passages from Robert Lowell telling of the sea and drowned sailors and from Anglo-Catholic T. S. Eliot's "The Dry Salvages":

There is no end to it, the voiceless wailing,
No end to the withering of withered flowers,

511

To the movement of pain that is painless
and motionless,
To the drift of the sea and the drifting
wreckage . . .

Sitting in the back row was a middle-aged *Washington Post* writer who reported on intelligence subjects. He was drawn there uninvited because he'd been intrigued by Dudley's obituary and suspected the full story hadn't come to light. He'd learned from a contact in Public Affairs that Frank Dudley had been missing for weeks. From a source in the FBI he'd learned a worldwide search had been under way, and that Julian Abbott had been in Madrid the day Dudley's body was returned to the U.S. He was convinced something was seriously amiss.

He'd been given Kevin Corkery's name, supplied through a contact at the Defense Intelligence Agency who had put him on to its source, who'd confirmed Dudley's disappearance and mentioned Kevin Corkery. During lunch at a Crystal City restaurant, the source had said he should talk to Corkery. "CI's bird dog," he'd told him in his loose, rumbling voice. "He's the guy they sent after Dudley. Talk to him, he'll tell you. He's a straight-up kind of guy." He was an ex-army lieutenant colonel, a former Agency operative from the Special Operations Group recently transferred to the Pentagon's Latin American task force. "Europe? Forget Europe. That's all old pussy," he'd said. "Latin America's where it's at these days."

512

His long, rambling tale made no sense, his crudeness had disgusted the reporter, but he'd drawn out the colonel on certain U.S. military operations being conducted out of airbases in Honduras which proved useful. He said he'd get in touch with him again. His source's name was Earl Huggins.

Searching the condolence book on the table in the alcove a few minutes earlier, he'd found and identified a few familiar names, but not Corkery's. From the last pew, the congregation in full view, he felt more strongly than ever that Dudley's death was a mystery worth exploring, more so than the eternal one the Anglican priest was now invoking from the altar. In the cool glance Adrian Shaw had given him as he took his seat — he'd tried unsuccessfully to meet with him — he felt a momentary gratification. His interest in intelligence matters wasn't based purely on the public's right to know. He struck through the curtain of official secrecy not merely to inform the public but to draw blood from an arrogant, entrenched bureaucracy whose power denied his own. Truths concealed, disguised, or falsified were inevitably stupid and shameful ones, or so he believed; yet he didn't serve justice. His triumphs were personal, revelation a form of revenge, but he wasn't a fantast.

His attention was drawn to the whispers of a couple seated in front of him. The man was tall and broad shouldered; the woman was plump with graying hair. Her comments were in German and so were his replies. He knew neither her name

513

nor his but decided George Tobey's wife must be German.

The eulogy was delivered by the husband of Jessica's aunt. Long and rambling, delivered in a flat New England voice by an investment banker unaccustomed to public performance, its message wasn't immediately apparent; it proved to be a secular tribute to public service. To the congregation, most of them active or retired civil servants, his words had a tiresome and slightly fraudulent echo, like a retirement toast heard too many times. There were more readings from the Bible and the Book of Common Prayer. Louise Dudley's head and shoulders remained upright; Jessica's sagged from time to time, her grief audible. The tall young man in the blue overcoat, innocent of her multiple voices, tried to console her.

All that long evening Phil Chambers, still wearing his mourning trousers, shoes, and shirt, waited for the visitor who hadn't come. Now he lingered near the front door, peering into the evening darkness. His wife saw him as she came up the stairs with the cocktail pitcher. "What is it now?"

"Nothing. Just checking."

"He said he'd come when he could. Are we going to have a drink?"

"That was two days ago." He followed her up the stairs and back the hall to the sunporch. The three glasses he'd set out sat on the tray next to his chair. "He wasn't at the service."

"I know he wasn't at the service. I imagine something has come up. I'm sure you'll hear from him. He's a very dependable young man." She gave him the pitcher.

"He learned his manners in the navy."

Shocked, she turned to look at him, expecting his face to deny it. He refused to look at her, not trusting his defenses against those penetrating blue eyes. She took the glass he handed her. "And you have the manners of a hypocrite."

She left the room with her glass, carrying it down to the kitchen. Sitting there in front of the fire, miserable and ashamed, he knew he'd ruined her evening as well as his. With nothing to console him, he would find solitude in his book, a toothless old lion, fouling his cage.

11

LAST TRAIN FROM BERLIN

The taxi left him under a wrought-iron and smoked-glass hotel marquee on a narrow street two blocks from the Kurfürstendamm. He entered the lobby, walked past the desk and the elevator, found a service exit, left by the door on the alley, and walked back toward the Kurfürstendamm. Traffic was heavy on the wide boulevard; the winter clouds hung low over the rooftops, tinted rose and lavender from the shimmering neon pools below. Not a sunset at all, he thought, head lifted, as he threaded his way through the early-evening crowds. From time to time he stopped, hands in his overcoat pockets, moodily studying the expensive gentlemen's shirts and suits in the bright windows.

"Like Tiberius's Rome," he had told his American interrogators during his Frankfurt debriefing. "Rome or Capri, an exotic sporting house." Now even more so. He paused to review a regiment

516

of English shoes arranged in a window. His own needed replacing; his socks were damp from the rainy Frankfurt streets he'd wandered yesterday, but he had little money left. He turned away. The shop next door stopped him. Looking at the fresh flowers in the steam-hung window, he remembered Frau Dummler's fondness for roses. She smiled rarely those last days in Berlin so many years ago, pretending sadness at her husband's posting to Aden, where wives weren't permitted. She lived in a small flat on Leninallee. Her dining room smelled of the roses he brought, her bedroom pillow of the little German barbershop where he had his hair trimmed. Inside the shop he bought four white roses in green tissue.

On the pavement again he looked at his watch, calculated the time, and continued on. A few minutes were still left. He found a vaulted rathskeller in the block beyond, entered, and took an empty table just to the left of the door. He ordered a whiskey and brought out the paperback novel and the pocket notebook he'd bought in a Frankfurt bookstore two days earlier. The notebook was the only one he had left; the others had been left behind. He'd purchased it to carefully calculate his expenses, having so little money, but inevitably other messages began to intrude. He studied the pages he'd written the night before but the lively conversation at a nearby table drew his attention away. The tables were rapidly filling; he saw no women in the warm smoky room except the two harried waitresses.

"Capitalism makes a man reserved and solitary," he'd told his FBI liaison officer, his feelings at that moment as he sat among German businessmen in the crowded Berlin bar. At the time he'd been quoting Khrushchev, but the FBI agent didn't know that. "He must rely on himself because there is no one else he can rely on." He had been drinking heavily at the time, was disappointed in love, in his profession, in life. He supposed those words, entered in a dossier in Washington, were thought to be his own. What would they make of them now? He looked at the notebook, looked again at what he'd written the previous night, and tore out the page. Why pretend? He had nothing more to say. He smoked a cigarette, watching the lights from the boulevard move across the lozenges of thick window. He finished his whiskey, stood up, picked up the paperback and notebook, and pulled on his coat. The waitress caught him in the outside vestibule, holding out the white roses. Her hair was the palest blond, her lips brown, her cheeks damp with moisture; there was a dimple in her chin. Frau Dummler? The old trot would be sixty now, smelling of tooth powder, hair dye, and her husband's cigars.

"For you," he said. "Please."

The crowds thinned as he walked, one dark street emptying into a darker one where the shops were beginning to close, the metal shutters banging down. A damp wind blew through the alleyways. He stopped at an ash can outside a closed shop and emptied his wallet of its papers and tattered pictures, the photograph of Eva and Gretchen, now a tatter of cracks and wrinkles. He tore them into pieces before he dropped them among the refuse. His notebook too? He hesitated, standing in the shadows, notebook in hand, ready to rip it to shreds. To be left without even a scrap of paper was to be left with no memory at all. No, he would keep it. He looked at his watch and knew he'd dawdled too long. It was time to go. He trotted across an intersection and into the underground twilight of the U-bahn.

Twenty minutes later the train surfaced in the Friedrichstrasse station. Blue-uniformed guards stood along the platform, farm boys, most of them. Their faces were fish gray in the submarine light. Greased carbines were slung over their shoulders; some carried machine pistols. He entered the East German checkpoint, gave the guard a name, and was led along a narrow corridor to an overheated office where a German in a tan topcoat sat waiting. He stood up as Andreyev entered, still talking to the clerk. He took the passport the Vopo handed him, opened it, studied the name and photograph, looked again at Andreyev, nodded, and left. The clerk behind the desk continued to study Andreyev, who waited inside the door. "Where is your home, Comrade?" Andreyev asked, conscious of his curiosity. "From what proud German city?" The clerk flushed, looked down, and didn't answer. Five minutes later the door opened and the German in the tan overcoat beckoned.

They went down the corridor and climbed the

steps to the S-bahn platform. The wind swirled in sharp gusts, punishing their faces and snapping at their coats. Andreyev stood with his hands in his pockets looking east through a twilight as gray as a winter sea stretching toward some unknown headland beyond the Oder and the Vistula. He remembered the yellow lantern in the old woman's crooked window, fetching him home safely through the snow.

The German in the tan overcoat followed as he boarded and stood with him at the back of the coach. The iron S-bahn swept them eastward and ten minutes later left them at the top of a steep iron staircase. The German pointed below as they descended; a black sedan waited at the curb, drifting clouds of exhaust over the cold pavement. A small man wearing a gray hat and overcoat left the rear seat of the sedan, called to him, and opened the door. A second car waited in front of the sedan. The German escort got in the front seat.

"We have no time," the little Russian said as they drove away. "You're late." His tone was severe.

Andreyev didn't know him. He was from the KGB Second Directorate, probably of the new generation. "I know, Comrade. It's the rotten weather. There were floods in Antwerp. Have you heard about the floods in Antwerp? Like Venice —"

"We've been waiting since your telephone call, all of us. Then you come late." He wasn't of the new generation at all but sourly middle-aged.

520

"Ten minutes late."

"I'm not speaking of today but last week. After the second phone call and the postponement, some said you wouldn't come at all."

"I had several bank accounts to close out. Then there were the floods, Comrade, but I'm here now, I telephoned, I came."

"Ten minutes late." They drove in silence as the small Russian looked out the window. "How is your health, Citizen? Good?"

"Good enough, yes."

"Some said, 'Well, he must be ill.' "

"No, I'm not ill."

"You're not a young man."

"No, I'm not young. For a man my age, ten to fifteen years will be a long time. I suppose it will be ten to fifteen years."

"That is not for me to say."

"I came freely, of my own volition. I came the way I went, my own decision, no one else's. I should think that would be in my favor."

"That's for the Military Tribunal to decide."

"I'll have to give testimony, I suppose."

"Of course. You'll tell them everything there is to tell."

"That's impossible." The small Russian turned. "But if it's my memory they want, they're welcome to it. I have no more use for it. I'll tell them what I can."

"About Vienna above all. About Glushkov."

"About Vienna, all I remember is that it was very confusing. The Americans found my flat, they were everywhere in Vienna, looking for me. Would you mind if I smoked a cigarette, Comrade?"

"Of course they were looking for you —"

Andreyev settled back in his seat. "A quiet talk, Glushkov tells me, so we meet in Kapelle Park, very discreetly, you see, but suddenly the cars come, cars everywhere. Did I know Glushkov would bring the Americans?"

"Of course he brought the Americans —"

"I didn't know. I have to be honest about this, Comrade. I was confused, I have to admit it." He studied the dark buildings they were passing. Little had changed. Very somber, very monotonous.

"He is a traitor, this Glushkov. That isn't confusing. You will not be confused about that."

"No, certainly, thank you, Comrade, thank you for not confusing me." A light in a second-floor window drew his attention. A woman was talking and gesturing to someone hidden. Her child or her husband? "I'm not confused about that, Comrade, thank you very much."

Poor Glushkov, his old GRU colleague who'd greeted him so warmly that Sunday at the zoo, Glushkov, that swaggering nincompoop who'd said he'd been sent from Moscow to fetch him home. Poor Glushkov, his boyhood friend who'd always worn his school and military uniforms so well. He pitied his elderly parents, living in the little flat on Mockva Street, so proud of their ambitious gallows-bird of a son who took them on holidays to the Black Sea coast. He pitied his lovely sister with her pale cheeks and her dark hair, shy in adolescence, shy at the university, shy as a young mathematician when he'd last seen her, quicker in every way than her reckless brother. At the time all would have ended up in the Gulag, or so he thought. What could he have done?

"So you decided to come home."

"As I said, Comrade, I was frightened. Not knowing what to do, I remembered General Bulakov, my old tutor from the Soviet Army Academy on Narodnogo Opolchenia Street. He'd understand my situation. You know him?"

"General Arkady Bulakov, whose daughter married Doronov of the Central Committee secretariat?"

"Doronov? Did the old trot finally marry? Fancy that."

"Ivan Ivanovich Doronov, yes. An older man."

"I don't recall." They sped through an open square. Andreyev didn't recognize it. "Finally married her off, did he? Well, the general would understand my situation, I told myself. He has friends, General Bulakov, even in retirement, friends in high places. So I said to myself, Well, seeing my situation is such-and-such and that the old general was once fond of me, even to the point of suggesting I become a member of the family, his daughter then being unmarried, a fish biologist, as I recall —"

"General Bulakov is dead. His daughter is married." The little Russian abruptly rolled down the window. "What kind of cigarette is that?"

"Danish. Bulakov dead? I'm sorry. Would you like one —"

"I don't smoke."

"Don't smoke. Then I apologize. Does the smoke bother you —"

"No, it doesn't bother me."

"To tell you the truth, smoking helps my nerves. But if it bothers your nerves, Comrade, I'll put it out —"

"No, it doesn't bother my nerves. Continue to smoke if you like."

"Thank you, Comrade." They were passing a cinema. Andreyev studied the young faces in the long queue along the sidewalk, wondering what movie would draw such a crowd.

"Try to be calm, Citizen. You have made the right decision, no doubt about it."

"No doubt whatsoever, Comrade." He watched the retreating queue through the window. Probably an American movie.

"To be nervous is normal. Homesick too. You missed your homeland so you came."

"Yes, to be homesick is normal. To think about your homeland is normal. Does that mean you want to be a child again? No. To be a child again is to suffer it all again in the same way. I wouldn't want to live my life over again. How about you? Don't you agree, Comrade? Is your life worth living over?"

"Of course it is." And then this sourly middle-aged Russian with the imagination of a dog, living each day as he lived the day before, this little man you could talk to without thinking, told him why he had made the right decision, told him what Glushkov told him so often when they shared the same small office at the airfield in Moscow, two young officers who'd grown up together, two young men with similar backgrounds, told him that however small his role each was indispensable to the whole. If they couldn't change the Party, they could change their relationship to its true strength, the central core from which would come the future leadership. The Party was more than the sum of its parts: it was the energy that flowed from its fusion, the power to mobilize men, institutions, nationalities, and continents. There was no avoiding the future and no escaping history. In returning now, Andreyev would be making his own contribution, however meager.

So there it was, the same lump of cold cabbage dished out on the same cold plate. No doubt about it, in one way or another every imperial capital was a brotherhood of lunatics, never mind that the subtlety of manners and the complexity of its technological and bureaucratic protocol kept the secret safe from public disclosure.

The car had stopped. They were at the Schlesischer station in East Berlin or what Andreyev took to be the Schlesischer station. He wasn't sure. When he had last passed through it at the end of an interminable twenty-eight-hour journey in the dead of winter from Moscow via Brest-Litovsk, its reconstruction hadn't been completed. Through the gaping holes in the towering

525

dome of roof the stars could be seen. Rather like a planetarium, he'd thought at the time.

"No bags," the little Russian from the KGB Second Directorate said to the three Russians who met them. "He came with no bags." Two fell into step behind Andreyev and his escort; the third ran ahead to the departure gates. In the dimness of the old station a scattering of East German civilians and soldiers waited for their trains, their bundled possessions at their feet. They turned, young and old, to watch the strange procession as it passed. Beyond the iron gate the Moscow express stood on track three where it had been kept waiting for fifteen minutes. On the platform next to it an East German trainman leaned wearily against his staff with the red disc, a lantern at his feet. Andreyev remembered the old Express D. 4 for Moscow as a ramshackle collection of ancient railway rolling stock. Little had changed: the two third-class coaches were from the Polish national railway; the combined sleeping and dining car may have been Russian, like the Russian diesel locomotive with the Red Star on the cab.

They boarded the fourth coach whose origin may have been French. The blinds were drawn; the interior was paneled in larch and smelled of scouring powder and faded lavender. Andreyev found a seat in the front of the carriage, facing forward, took off his coat, and sat down. Somewhere behind him the three Russians found seats. His duties done, his escort lingered for a minute in the aisle. He wouldn't be accompanying Andreyev. In the thin light of the coach lamps, the little Russian from the KGB Second Directorate saw clearly for the first time the man he'd spoken to in the shadows of the sedan — the badger face, the quick brown eyes, and the thick gray hair. Andreyev wasn't quite the man he knew from the photographs or the voice from the shadows of the car. The gray summer suit was rumpled, as if he'd recently been caught in the rain; his wrinkled gray shirt was missing the collar button; the tie holding the collar loosely in place was as thin as a shoelace, ten years out of fashion. He'd come from the West not like most Russians, dressed in the latest fashion with the latest models of Western consumerism in their suitcases, but like someone out of a displaced persons camp.

It occurred to him Andreyev might be a little mad. His own thin face betrayed his uncertainty, confronting some doubt, some void in his own memory. "All that time, Citizen, all those years. You must have had reasons."

Andreyev nodded. "I must have had reasons, yes. The truth is I've forgotten what they were." He felt very stupid, all this official bustle on his behalf. It was a boy's game and this middle-aged Russian was a boy, like Glushkov, but there was a little of Glushkov in all of them. One had to forgive that.

The Russian nodded and left.

Relieved, Andreyev stood up again, removed his jacket, and made himself comfortable in his faded green plush seat. It would be a long journey, twenty-five to thirty hours, depending upon weather and circumstance. He wondered how much had changed in the intervening years. Would the Leningrad and Varoslyvl stations be the same? Would the holes in the roof through which we study the stars be patched by now? Probably not: the same smell of coal smoke, jetting steam, and sweeping compound. Would Moscow be the same? Would existence taste any differently in his mouth? Probably not, but he would be home. In his own way he would join the underground again; a dozen years' inconvenience, a few years at hard labor, but he would have tools to work with, would live in intimacy with the weather, his hands would become old friends once more, not a stranger's. Better that than his most recent illness — and it was definitely an illness, Comrades of the Military Tribunal, a pen-and-ink delirium in which I had no existence at all, just as you don't. I admit we Russians are disposed to the fantastic, Comrades, as Dostoyevsky tells us, but even so, tell me truthfully, do you believe this seventy years of nonsense? As far as the fantastic is concerned, Comrades of the Military Tribunal, I've been to America and so am probably a little mad. America affects many that way. What else is there to say?

In his long solitude after sentencing he would think from time to time of his friends, of Eva and Gretchen — well, not Eva so much: the Holy Father would think about her, keep her immaculate in his immaculate dreams. He would think of Gretchen, her future unborn, think of her wet hair against his cheek, the smell of shampoo in his nose, Gretchen moving through the crowds at the Vienna zoo, in Piccadilly or along the Seine some day, her smiling green eyes saying hello to everyone who passed. If you couldn't understand that these days, Comrades of the Military Tribunal, what could you understand?

Weary of the delay, he leaned over to raise the window shade. Fifteen feet away an emaciated East German railway worker in green coveralls leaned against a long iron pole wedged into a switch of track. At his feet two other German railway workers were repairing a faulty switch in the light of a battery lantern. Dimly illuminated in the rectangle of light from the coach window, the German looked up at him. An old man, Andreyev decided. Maybe a war veteran. A Russian at the far end of the coach came quickly down the aisle, leaned over, and closed the shade. After his footsteps died away, Andreyev again raised the shade. The Russian reappeared and closed it. "Who is this man?" he called to someone down the aisle.

"My name is Rudyev," Andreyev said, "a commercial traveler." His hand moved to his pocket and he held out a royal blue Danish cigarette box embossed in gold. "Please, Comrade."

The Russian hesitated suspiciously, thought better of it, and turned away without closing the shade. A moment later he returned to correct the error. Andreyev searched his overcoat for his notebook and instead discovered the Simenon paperback novel he'd bought in Frankfurt. The novel began on a train. Simenon's train was passing through the Belgian countryside; Andreyev's train was stationary in East Berlin's Schlesischer station. He had read the first six pages but began again. After a few minutes, the coaches jolted forward with the clanking of iron couplings. Reassured and then lulled along by the fifteen pages of narrative, he felt the illusion of motion, saw winter fields and woods passing outside, and reached forward to lift the shade and explore the winter landscape, find the moon if there was one, see the distant lights of passing collective farms, the dim lights of trucks and automobiles passing along the roads, homeward bound at that hour, just as he was. Outside the window stood the same emaciated German railway worker he'd seen fifteen minutes earlier, leaning wearily against his iron pole. The same two workers crouched at his feet in the light of a battery lantern. He looked up, saw Andreyev, recognized both were prisoners of a common dilemma, and smiled stupidly. Andreyev nodded in return and closed the shade. Heroic enterprises were always betrayed by trivial ones; such was life, such was love, such was the revolution.

He read his detective novel awhile longer, although it didn't interest him. When the train finally creaked forward, moving out of the yards, he closed the book, opened the shade, put his head back, and watched the passing buildings. After the Russian again came to close the shade, he closed his eyes, forced by circumstance to count the currency in his head. As a younger man during his train journeys across Russia to pass the time he often composed verses in his head. During a sixteen-hour train journey he'd once composed five stanzas of philosophical verse. He was twenty-four at the time and in love. She was very beautiful, very passionate, but not very clever; she imagined herself fond of philosophical verse. He had forgotten the verses but he remembered her. For a young man alone and in love, as he was, a swaying railway coach was very much like the arms of his beloved:

> *The truths we know are not*
> *Self-evident nor sure*
> *And loss of honor can*
> *Reeducate the poor*
> *And crush the common man*
> *Like pestilence or war.*

Honor? He wasn't sure *honor* was the right word. Virtue? Had he ever claimed to be virtuous? No. Perhaps he'd find the right word during the next twenty-four hours, passing across a countryside that, like his own boyish anticipation these last days, was too vast to yet know itself. He was going home and was grateful he hadn't thrown his notebook away. It would be a very long trip indeed, a journey in self-discovery. One had to be prepared.

In the high country of southwestern Pennsylvania foreign news was difficult to come by. The weekly newspaper itemized the foreign news in a five-paragraph box on the last page of the first section above the real estate transfers. Hobgood's Pharmacy on the main square next to the Dollar Store once received a bundle of Sunday *New York Times*es delivered late Sunday afternoon by Greyhound bus during Corkery's undergraduate years but no longer. Hobgood's daughter-in-law told him they now received only four copies of the Sunday *Times*, all for regular customers. One was for Baylor Ogden, the town dilettante and drunk, one for the former publisher of the weekly paper, one for Dr. Wilder, and one for Miss Agnes Hetherton, the retired librarian and county poet.

The afternoon of his arrival the brick house three blocks from the town square in southwestern Pennsylvania was fragrant with the spice of fruitcake and baking cookies. His mother, a secretary with the local Farm Credit Administration, had taken leave, as she always did over the holidays. On the sideboard nearby next to the Florentine bowl of waxed fruit was the box of Vienna chocolates, passed around after dinner each night. "They were so elegant I couldn't bring myself to touch them," she said that first evening. The Bavarian mug was on the knickknack shelf in the parlor along with the Indian arrowheads, the Civil War dumdums, and the oxidizing iron bayonet found by a State Highway Department surveyor in an old roadbed. His father had brought it home. Young Corkery, the naïf, persuaded himself the roadbed might be the wilderness road hacked out by Braddock's troops marching to Fort Duquesne in 1753. His eighth-grade history teacher told him it was a Civil War bayonet.

He'd taken leave abruptly, much to Shaw's disappointment. He didn't tell Elinor, didn't see Louise, Jessica, or Phil Chambers, and didn't say when he'd be back. It was a problem he had to solve alone.

Two days before Christmas he and his father drove to the yellow brick offices of the Pennsylvania Department of Highways on the edge of town for the annual Christmas party. Until his retirement his father had worked as a senior district civil engineer in the construction division. The party was held in the first-floor cafeteria. Food and drink were waiting on the decorated tables — sandwiches, cookies, eggnog, bourbon, wine coolers, and beer. After the speech by the regional director, the celebration spilled out of the crowded cafeteria, up the stairs to the executive suites, down the corridors to the clerical offices, and out the rear double doors and across the windswept lot to the maintenance sheds where the drivers, mechanics, and laborers had carried their beer cans and plastic cups of bourbon and eggnog to stand around under the warm-air blowers or the fire-blackened fifty-gallon drum outside where scantlings and crate lumber burned brightly. Abe Runyon and Charley Fargo were standing there.

"Goddamn, lookit who's here," Charley said. "Where the hell you been, Kip?"

"Your daddy told me you was coming," Abe Runyon said. "When you coming out, cut the firewood I laid up for him?"

"Pretty soon. Maybe next week."

"What's doing in Washington, Kip?" Charley said. "You got them Republicans straightened out yet?"

"Hell, no, he hasn't," Abe said. "He din't lick 'em, he joined 'em, din't you, Kip?"

"Not yet." He didn't know the other two men standing there, both younger, both his age. Charley Fargo told him Orville Crawford was in the VA hospital in Pittsburgh. His wife had left him. His trailer down by the river was still there but another family was living in it, a West Virginia family, dirt poor and living on food stamps, come from Cumberland, Maryland, after the tire factory had shut down. They talked about hunting, the Steelers, Penn State and the Sugar Bowl, engineering division incompetence, poor supervision and rotten maintenance. A cold afternoon under the December clouds off the mountain, Corkery remembered as he listened: snow weather, deer weather, holiday weather, wasn't it? He looked skyward, a world once so familiar but now less so.

Susan Fern had telephoned while he was out. Someone else had called, a girl or a woman, his mother said, but she hadn't left her name; long distance, she thought. He returned Susan's call, thinking something had happened. Jay Fellows was anxious to talk to him; he had something for him, something he was sure would interest him. When would he be returning? Corkery said he wasn't sure but would let her know.

A bundled Sunday *New York Times* and a Sunday *Washington Post* were waiting for him on the dining-room table, sent from Hobgood's Pharmacy by Lucy Hobgood with a note attached. Miss Hetherton was spending Christmas with her sister in Winchester, Virginia. The dispatches under the Paris, Vienna, and Berlin datelines told him nothing. In the foreign affairs weekly review was an article on the coming crisis in Soviet leadership: Andropov was dying.

Out for some last-minute shopping at the shopping plaza east of town on Christmas Eve, he ran into Margaret Noble outside the liquor store. Her blond hair was frosted silver and she was wearing a long camel's-hair coat. They walked through the winter twilight toward her car. Her father was chief surgeon at the hospital; he had operated on Corkery's father.

"What are you doing these days? Someone told me they thought you were working in Pittsburgh now, not Washington."

"No, I'm still in Washington."

"That's what I thought. Lucky you. I guess you know I left Richard." She stopped at a gray BMW and took out her car keys, holding the wrapped vodka bottle under her arm.

"I'm sorry." Dick Noble was senior vice president at the First National Bank.

"Don't be sorry. I got the house and kids, he

got the mortgage, the bills, and his bottles. I'm a survivor." She said this without irony. "I really am, Kip. I've opened a shop at the antique mall." She slipped behind the wheel. "How long will you be around?"

"A week maybe."

"Give me a call. Drop in for a drink. You're not married, are you? You don't look married." She smiled and didn't give him a chance to answer. "Probably not. Richard always said you were so much smarter than the rest of us. Merry Christmas."

The day after Christmas he got a Christmas card from Elinor Wynn with a note attached. She was in Massachusetts but would be back in Washington by the twenty-ninth. She had two tickets to the Kennedy Center for the first weekend in January — Bach, not Bartók — and didn't intend to go alone. "Will you be back by then? Just what are your plans, by the way?"

Wednesday after Christmas he drove out to Abe Runyon's place eight miles from town to cut firewood in the rear pasture. As he left his father's station wagon, Mrs. Runyon called from the back stoop of the old clapboard house, once a log cabin. The siding had been added at the turn of the century and had weathered as dark as creosote. She was a short plump woman with gray hair, wearing a man's brown woolen sweater with a roll collar. The warm air leaking from the open door smelled of paraffin and scorching metal. In the distance he heard the sounds of a television set. A dish antenna was mounted in the side yard.

"Abe said to tell you he can't come, Kip. He's got to carry his Aunt Dora over to the hospital in Jerico. He said he got plenty of firewood, don't you worry none. He said to tell you if you want to hunt some, he had Teddy out Sunday so it's Buster could do with some right smart working."

"Maybe I'll wait until Abe can come too."

"You do whatever you want, hon. Ain't bird season neither, it's done passed, so don't get caught. I'll be inside you be a-needing me."

The two coon dogs in the trot next to the barn were standing against the wire, whining and barking. He stopped to quiet them and hitched the rubber-tired wagon to Abe's 8N Ford tractor and drove out the rear gate and along the creek to the red oak fallen three years ago. He worked at the trunk with the chain saw for almost an hour until the metal chain lost its bite and began to smoke. Without a sharpening file or an extra chain, he split the logs with a sledge-hammer and wedge and stacked them nearby. He drove to the pile of logs he'd cut, split, and stacked the previous summer, loaded them in the wagon, and drove back to the barn. Half the logs he stored in Abe's woodlot and the rest in the rear of his father's station wagon.

He took his Beretta over-and-under and a pouch of shells from the front seat and brought Buster, the pointer, from the kennel behind the machine shed. They crossed the road and went through the gate into the bottomland pasture Abe leased for winter hay. Buster was eager and difficult to control. He overran the first covey in a meadow higher on the mountain; six quail exploded downwind and Buster ran in the other direction, circling aimlessly. As they climbed higher the wind picked up and the cold settled in.

Breathing hard, he moved on. Ten minutes later he flushed a woodcock from a marshy spring but the whistling bird veered off before he squeezed off a shot, disappearing down the slope he had just climbed. In a clearing logged three or four years earlier Buster pointed a covey in a blackberry thicket and held it as he walked closer. He didn't fire as the birds erupted. His mind elsewhere, thinking of George Tobey and Phil Chambers in retirement, of what Eric Prosser had said about envying them the quiet life, he didn't move his Beretta at all as the birds scattered to the surrounding trees. Dusk was falling as he turned along the washed-out logging road that led down the mountain. Eroded to shale and rock on the turns by the spring rains, the logging track ended on a gravel state-maintained road a mile north of Abe Runyon's. The sagging metal gate was overgrown with vines and creepers and closed by a corroded logging chain. A polished maroon Mercedes was parked on the other side of the gate. No one was in the car. He stood at the gate for a minute, listening. He climbed the gate, retrieved his shotgun, and walked to the side window. It was a maroon Mercedes with D.C. license plates. A Pennsylvania road map lay on the front passenger seat.

He called Buster, leashed him, and walked back the gravel road through the dusk to Abe Runyon's. The back porch was in full shadow as he knocked at the door. Mrs. Runyon was puzzled at first but then remembered. She knew the car, a maroon foreign car. It belonged to a lawyer from Washington who had built an A-frame cabin on the next mountain over and leased hunting rights to the old Hurley farm.

Vanity again.

"You're just so terribly restless, I know something's wrong," his mother said that evening when he wandered into the kitchen. Her back was to him. "Your father asked me last night if I knew what it was. I'm not asking you to talk about it, mind you."

"I'm fine."

"No, you're not." He shouldn't be so restless, she told him. He should look up some of his old friends. The Bairds had asked about him and so had the Turners; they always asked about him. He should call them up. Margaret Noble had asked about him too, but she was divorced now and you had to be careful about divorced women.

He went to the Turners' annual New Year's Eve party. The circular drive and the road in front of the red brick colonial in the new subdivision out beyond the country club were lined with cars. He said hello to Ed Turner and his wife in the crowded living room. Ed had his own insurance agency. Some of the guests had come from or were going on to other parties; some were dressed up,

539

some down. In the study a dozen men were watching a college football bowl game. He stood in the door looking in and moved to the dining-room table. Turkey and country ham were set out. The husbands drank beer or bourbon; their wives preferred their bourbon sweet and their wine bubbly. Margaret Noble, sipping vodka plain, was an exception. Baylor Ogden, educated in Philadelphia, like Margaret, was drinking Scotch and wearing a tuxedo and a winged collar, as he did every New Year's Eve. The tradition was begun by his grandfather at the New Year's Eve dinners in the four-story stone house overlooking the public park across from the railroad station, built for his great-grandfather's railroad. The old train station, visible down the long maple- and oak-lined carriage lane from the front portico, was now an antique mall. The stone gates entered a public park. The Ogden mansion was owned by the municipality. Baylor Ogden's tuxedo and winged collar were a relic from the late nineteenth century. He was a local eccentric, a dozen years older, a bachelor, and something of an antiquarian. In his idleness he collected books and memorabilia of early Pennsylvania and was regarded as an expert on the early history of the state.

Ogden was discussing an early settler's diary recently bought by the local historical society with Dr. Fingerhut, a dentist and the society's president. Ogden denied its authenticity with the passion of a man who regarded the past as his personal possession. A few of Corkery's history professors were infected by the same possessiveness, but it had never occurred to him eccentric men of wealth might believe they might own a piece of history as if it were a piece of personal property. He wondered why it hadn't. Washington shared the same delusion.

He saw a few high school classmates, now married and with families, and drifted on to the family room at the rear. A wood fire was burning in the elevated brick fireplace; the rug at the far end had been removed for dancing and the stereo was playing. He heard Emmylou Harris's guitar-string voice and remembered when he had last heard the song.

He talked with Carolyn Quinn, a young blond woman he hadn't seen since high school. She once wrote poetry for his high school paper. Now she was married and divorced, had two small children, drove a school bus, and worked at the farmers' co-op. She didn't write poetry anymore. After a while her boyfriend left the TV football game and came to find her. Carolyn flushed as she introduced him. They didn't shake hands. His name was Rudy and he drove a propane truck. His two thumbs were tucked in his cowboy belt, one hand held a beer bottle. "Been real nice talking to you," Rudy said as he led her away. Twenty minutes later Corkery left.

Two days later, sleepless in the dawn darkness, he got up, dressed, and made coffee. He sat at the kitchen table, reading the weekly paper, put it aside, and pulled on his leather jacket. The moon was still out, cold and pale through the trees. He walked past the old houses whose lawns he had once cut, past the Presbyterian church and on to the main square, standing near the courthouse steps as Mr. Armistead, the courthouse custodian, arrived to unlock the front door as he had for as long as Corkery could remember. He stood watching him, wondering what still moved him after all these years. He continued on to the railroad station, walked along the brick platform, looking in the windows of the new shops, thinking about small-town life. He turned up the hill past the park and the old federal houses. The stores were opening on the main square. A farm truck carrying steers rumbled along the main street toward the livestock exchange as he crossed the main street toward the Rexall drugstore for a cup of coffee.

His parents weren't surprised. "I knew you made up your mind a week ago," his father said.

"I knew you'd get restless, just like you always do," his mother said. "I just hope and pray someday you'll finally settle down, find what it is you're looking for."

He packed the Alfa and by eleven was on his way, around the main square, past the shopping mall and the old garage a mile beyond with the hand-painted sign still in the window after all those summers: BUGS BLOWED OUT OF YR RADIATOR, 50 CENTS. He drove down through the long snow-patched valleys and up again, past the frozen hillside settlements where threads of lonely gray smoke lifted against the dark hillsides, following the blue bus from the Mount Zion Church for four miles along a winding, switchback state road, trying to read the sign three teenage girls were holding up in the back window, a sign they'd amended with a Magic Marker when they'd seen the sharklike Alfa trailing behind them, a sign he was finally able to decipher as he broke free on a stretch of roadway along the Albion River and flashed past:

> *God is Older,*
> *Jesus, too,*
> *We love Elvis,*
> *Who are You?*

He was on the Pennsylvania Turnpike, slipping down through the curves, soaring up the long grades, past the winded trailer trucks trailing diesel smoke like flags of surrender, past the tired Chevys, the custom vans, past the Ford Thunderbirds and powder blue Cadillacs with Florida license plates, past the muddy pickups with their 30.30 deer rifles racked in the back windows and their truck beds piled with cordwood, the new wood-stove homesteaders along the collapsing coal-and-iron frontier.

He stopped for thirty minutes for lunch and for coffee twice, once at a rest area restaurant filled with truckers, hunters, and white-haired retirees, the final time at a McDonald's at Breezeway just off the turnpike. At the mirror in the restroom he might have detected the shadow of the dead

543

king's pox on his cheeks, but he was impatient to get back and find out what Jay Fellows had in mind. He wanted to talk to Elinor and he owed Phil Chambers a visit.

Five minutes later he was on the road again, beginning the long swift descent out of the mountains, feeling neither sadness nor elation but only a certain inevitability to his life, a young man still imaginative enough, restless enough, and active enough to find other careers if it came to that, or so he told himself, a young man who could still believe the world a mystery, waiting to be discovered. He listened to the CBS and ABC afternoon news breaks as he drove, listened to dispatches from Washington and overseas mixing fact, fantasy, and farce, whether the sound bites from the White House press room or the thirty-second world news summaries, as stupidly simplistic as the artifice of Andreyev's Russian mapmakers, carting off villages, rivers, and mountains with the stroke of a pen. The moon came out, a luminous disc in the dusk-entangled eastern sky. Seeing it motionless through his windshield, he remembered the NASA photograph above the desk in Vienna, the planet as fragile as a turtle egg swimming in an infinite ocean of blue. He recalled Elinor's description of Andreyev's new unitary planetary consciousness, far transcending those corrupt old political frontiers that so narrowly defined Washington's world these days. True, he supposed, but how did you convince others? Was she convinced? He didn't know. The radio signals grew stronger with each passing mile as the moon dimmed. He rode them like a beacon all the way to Langley and the massive white building hidden among the trees, the imperial flagship of the old imperial fleet, anchored in concrete in the Virginia hills overlooking the Potomac. He had to smile a little when he thought about that too, remembering the uncertainty and awe of his early apprenticeship. But then truth wasn't what you begin with but what you discover.